WORRY STONES

OTHER BOOKS BY
JOANNA LILLEY

If There Were Roads (2017)

The Birthday Books (2015)

The Fleece Era (2014)

Worry
Stones

JOANNA LILLEY

RONSDALE PRESS

WORRY STONES
Copyright © 2018 Joanna Lilley

RONSDALE PRESS
3350 West 21st Avenue, Vancouver, B.C. Canada V6S 1G7
www.ronsdalepress.com

Typesetting: Julie Cochrane, in Granjon 11.5 pt on 15
Cover Design: Marijke Friesen
Paper: Ancient Forest Friendly 55 lb. Enviro Book Antique Natural (FSC),
    100% post-consumer waste, totally chlorine-free and·acid-free.

Ronsdale Press wishes to thank the following for their support of its publishing program: the Canada Council for the Arts, the Government of Canada, the British Columbia Arts Council, and the Province of British Columbia through the British Columbia Book Publishing Tax Credit program.

Library and Archives Canada Cataloguing in Publication

Lilley, Joanna, author
   Worry stones / Joanna Lilley.

Issued in print and electronic formats.
ISBN 978-1-55380-541-0 (softcover)
ISBN 978-1-55380-542-7 (ebook) / ISBN 978-1-55380-543-4 (pdf)

   I. Title.

PS8623.I43W67 2018   C813'.6   C2018-904135-8   C2018-904136-6

At Ronsdale Press we are committed to protecting the environment. To this end we are working with Canopy and printers to phase out our use of paper produced from ancient forests. This book is one step towards that goal.

Printed in Canada by Marquis Book Printing, Quebec

for my family,
who used to fill up a camper van
and who will always
fill up my heart

STONE WRITTEN

Not a calm or a cool stone
It still carries the charge of its birth
the fracture of every wave smash
the bruise of every pebble smash,
every power hammer of the sea
the jarring fall of every tide
the percussive battery of stone slides
as each pebble rubs its partner up the wrong way.

It carries the record of every knockout blow
etched in white hot lightning stripes.

— ANGELA STONER

One

IQALUIT, 2000

AT MINUS EIGHTEEN, chocolate didn't taste of much. Jenny Ross pressed the hardness with her tongue and tried to extract a flavour. She was standing on a white ocean of tundra. It was her seventh week in Nunavut and she never wanted to leave. The land was treeless, bright, enormous. There were no mountains, only low, rocky hills, and yet the whole landscape felt lifted up, closer to the sun than on any summit she had ever stood.

She broke off another chunk of chocolate. Even though it didn't have any taste, the sugar still did its work; the theobromine still kicked in. She'd hoped she wouldn't need it here in this immense, other country where no member of her family had ever stepped. But she'd interviewed Kavavaow Ishulutak this morning, the Matisse of the circumpolar world, and she had not got what she needed. Eating chocolate softened the memory, turning it from a sharply rendered oil painting into a blurry pastel.

Jenny looked at the long horizon and breathed. This was exactly where she wanted to be at the start of the new millennium. She might not be an artist herself, but at least she was in the art world; she was an art historian. Although, here in this wide, white world, she almost wished she'd become a geographer, geologist, something *geo*, to do with the Earth itself. A *rock guy* like Dominic. That was how he'd described himself when she first met him at the research centre.

She turned to look at his familiar shape across the broad snow, solid in his red down jacket and the black snow trousers she was learning to call pants. She still didn't know how it was possible they were in a relationship, how come this beautiful *rock guy* with curly brown hair wanted to be with her.

He saw her looking his way. "Shall we head back to town, Jenny?" Dominic's voice fractured a quietness that wasn't so much silence as a sound she'd never heard before.

"Coming!" She shoved the chocolate wrapper deep into her pocket and started walking, her heavy boots crushing ice crystals and making the snow squeak. She pulled up her scarf so it covered her mouth as she finished swallowing.

She hadn't left Dominic on his own on the tundra when she'd wandered off. There were two other researchers with them, Kay and Ryan, and they were all drifting back towards the squat snowmobiles. Three slender verticals against horizontals of white and blue snow: a polar Mondrian.

"Remind me again why I'm not home in Virginia?" said Kay, skinny and blonde, as Jenny approached. She was doing jumping jacks to keep warm.

"Uh, something to do with helping people? Um, people who don't have anywhere to live, maybe?" Dominic screwed up his face, pretending to try to remember what Kay's research was. "Or is that you, Jenny?"

Jenny laughed and shook her head. She couldn't think of anything funny to say.

"You mean, there are people here? This isn't Antarctica?" Kay angled a scrawny leg behind Ryan, who was already sitting on one of the snowmobiles with the engine running. "Shoot. I got the wrong pole," she shouted over the noise.

Laughing, Dominic pulled the cord to start the other snowmobile's engine. He and Ryan were in Iqaluit to set up a government geosciences office *to support the responsible development of resources*. The four of them had engaged in quite a few discussions about what *responsible* actually meant.

Sitting on the snowmobile, Dominic gave Jenny a grin and a head tilt as if to remind her to climb on behind him. Although it gave her a reason to hold his waist, she'd rather have been in front steering, negotiating crests and troughs of snow. Not that she'd ever driven a snowmobile. Not yet anyway; she was doing a course next week. But, if Dominic were behind her, holding on, he'd be reminded how much of her there was. She couldn't suck her stomach in all the way back to Iqaluit. She'd suffocate.

Dominic wasn't skinny and she was glad. He was solid and muscular, and she could imagine that in a decade's time — if the miracle of their relationship lasted — he'd have a bit of a belly, the way some men did, and together they'd try to eat less, drink less, exercise more.

Back in town, Dominic bumped them over the grubby snow ruts and parked in front of the research centre where they lived and worked, a giant red Portakabin on stilts. He took off his hat and shook his head, his brown hair recurling. His jaw was a little fleshy and his top lip was a little long, as if he were always on the verge of saying something serious.

"How about thawing out at the coffee shop?" Dominic looked at Jenny as he said it. "Just got to make a quick call first."

Kay tugged at a sleeve with her American white teeth to check her watch. "Udloriak wanted to see me about something. Won't take a sec, then I'll join you guys."

"I need a word with the head honcho too." Ryan grinned. "I'll accompany you."

Jenny and Dominic smiled as their eyes met. They were thinking the same thing: Kay and Ryan were a matching pair — blond, blue-eyed, American — and something was happening between them. Sharing the thought felt almost as intimate as a kiss.

Walking, Jenny felt her kneecaps prickle as her blood remembered its task. She didn't think she'd ever tire of walking through Iqaluit — *ik-ah-loo-eet* — not even in heavy-soled snow boots. The grey, red and yellow wooden buildings weren't picturesque, and she knew from photographs that when the snow melted, the town would look even scruffier and more makeshift than it did now: stilts hammered into iced earth, sewage and water pipes above-ground because of the permafrost below, the grass withered as if there had been a drought. She'd love the flimsiness of this town just as much as the enduring land.

If the other two didn't show up at the café, she would tell Dominic about the Kavavaow Ishulutak interview and ask him what he thought. She was still learning to confide in him; she was too used to keeping her own counsel, replaying events inside her mind as if she were in her own private cinema. It was easier with Helen and Karen, her closest friends. She'd known them so much longer. Helen had been there for the final crumbling of Jenny's family. Karen was part of the rebuilding of Jenny's life afterwards.

Jenny had been seeing Dominic for just over three weeks and she hadn't told him yet that he was only the fourth man — or boy — she'd ever kissed. When he occasionally made a reference to her surely having left a trail of broken hearts behind in Edinburgh, she laughed and changed the subject.

She was grateful they both had rooms at the research centre, along with Kay and Ryan, where living and office space were communal. It made getting to know each other easier, more casual and incremental. Sitting around the kitchen table, sharing the couch, seeing each other go in and out of the washrooms and showers. It had made getting together possible.

Mr. Ishulutak — she couldn't call him Kavavaow — hadn't been the one with a voice recorder and notebook this morning. He hadn't asked her any questions, yet she'd still felt he was interviewing her. His round, black eyes had seemed to watch her, even when he'd had his head down carving.

She'd started by asking him what tools he used and he had carried on chiselling. He couldn't have heard her. He was sitting astride a wooden bench with a chunk of green speckled serpentine cradled in his left arm and wedged between his legs. The grey flecks in his black shaggy hair could have been stone dust. Serpentine was more difficult to carve than soapstone. It had to be treated carefully. A ring on a finger could scratch it. Kavavaow's fingers were bare. Jenny watched him ease the chisel against the hunk of stone. A silicate mineral rich in magnesium and water.

"Is that a four-tooth fine chisel you have there?" Jenny asked. "Is it carbon steel?"

Kavavaow shook his head without looking at her. He was concentrating on chiselling, obviously. He'd suggested the time for the interview, but she was clearly in the way. Artists couldn't schedule inspiration, she knew that. She didn't want to interrupt the work of the most famous artist in the Arctic.

The other interviews she'd done here so far had been with the arts and crafts association administrators, the coordinators of the arts festival coming up in July, and lesser-known artists who carved, sewed, stitched and printed and who gave her tea and chatted easily.

She started again. "Mr. Ishulutak."

"Call me Kavavaow."

At last. Jenny shifted on the dusty plastic chair and crossed her legs so it was easier to write. She glanced at the voice recorder she had placed nearby on a crate. The red light was still on; it was recording. Kavavaow nodded at her, as if he were giving permission for her to speak.

"You use hand tools as well as power tools. Does it depend on the material or the subject, or both?" She was behaving like an amateur, asking closed questions. "What I mean is, can you tell me how you decide which tools to use, what determines that?"

The skin around his black eyes creased. Was this a good sign? It was hard to tell how old he was from looking. She knew, however, that he'd been born in 1949 in Cape Dorset, on an island about two hundred and fifty miles west. His father had been one of the original Inuit artists nurtured by James and Alma Houston, who were credited with launching Inuit sculpture into the world and then — after a trip to Japan — printmaking. Questions about that would be asked later.

"It depends," Kavavaow said unhurriedly, "what the stone asks for. I don't plan it. I pick it up and see what is inside. Like a present."

"Like Michelangelo. He said he saw the angel in the marble and carved until he set it free."

Kavavaow shook his head. Was he humbled by comparisons with the archetypal Renaissance man or insulted by being compared to a symbol of a colonizing continent?

She waited. He evidently wasn't going to say any more.

"So," she prompted, "you see an all-terrain vehicle — a four-wheeler — or a snowmobile or gun inside a piece of stone?"

She waited again, pen in hand. Some artists were feelers rather than thinkers and it was the feelers she was really interested in. Those whose hands chiselled and moulded instinctively.

"I walk down Sinaa," Kavavaow said at last. "Four-wheelers on the beach. The sealift comes in. This is our culture now. Machines. Oil. Rock oil, not seal oil. It's seeped into everyone's culture. All over the world."

Jenny wrote as quickly as she could, not daring to rely on the voice recorder.

"Everyone's culture is changed by machines, not just ours," he continued when she rested her hand. He'd been waiting for her to catch up. "Everyone's tools have changed. The harpoon, the arrow, the gun. The dogsled, the horse and cart, the automobile." He laughed. It was the loudest noise he'd made. His eyes softened. "Down south, people worship the machine. Here, people worship the machine."

Their first session and he was already touching on her Big Questions. To what extent was animism — the attribution of spirit to inanimate objects — still part of Inuit culture? The biggest question would come later, when she knew how to phrase it without offending his people. Was carving the true Inuit art form? What exactly had the Houstons done to Inuit culture back in the fifties when they brought in printmaking, created Western markets?

"So, do you think machines have spirits?" It sounded so crass, the way she said it. Patronizing. She'd reduced her big question to another yes or no answer. He didn't seem to realize it was a question. It was just as well.

He picked up his chisel.

"I can see you're busy," Jenny said. "How about I come back another time?"

Kavavaow nodded a little. She could see relief in his face, surely.

She grabbed the voice recorder to turn it off, her notebook slapping to the floor as she reached. She bent to pick it up. It was covered in stone dust. She didn't stop to brush it off; she slid it straight into her bag.

Kavavaow was hunched over the serpentine, the chisel making tiny scrapes against the stone. Jenny watched him as she put on her coat. She couldn't get used to the idea she was actually witnessing Kavavaow work. She didn't zip her coat up in case it disturbed him. She could do that outside.

"Thank you for your time," she said quietly as she twisted the handle to open the door. She couldn't simply leave without saying anything. "Thank you so much."

The cold outside rasped against Jenny's bare face and hands. She pulled her scarf up over her nose and rushed along the road in the direction of the research centre. All the snow that had been scraped from the street was piled up into high, grubby heaps. She stopped at the next mound and took off a glove. She crouched and eased a small, oval stone from the muck. It was pale orange, under the dirt, and rough. It looked like granite. Dominic would know.

She never knew when the urge to collect a stone would come. This would be her Iqaluit stone. She would take it back to the research centre and rinse the dirt off under a tap. When it was time to leave in August, she would slip it into a sock and pack it in her luggage to take home to Edinburgh. Not that she wanted to think about going home or leaving Dominic.

She still had all her original worry stones, as she called them, collected from childhood places: Birling Gap, Brighton, Dinard, the South Downs. She had all her stones from Scotland too. From Willowbrae, of course, and her summit stones: Tinto, Ben Nevis, Ben Lomond, Ben Ledi, other Bens. She'd even kept the dark pebble from the beach at North Berwick.

At the counter of the steaming café, she bought a hot chocolate with a quiff of cream. She sat at one of the computers along the back wall and eased her snow boots half off so she could wriggle her burning toes. There weren't many other people in the café, just a woman and two men, each sitting separately, each wearing a baseball cap. One of the men was smoking, even though there was a no smoking sign. No one was stopping him. Jenny wondered if they had jobs. She hadn't worked out how this sparse town functioned yet.

Jenny's email slowly opened on the screen. She took a sip of hot chocolate. She was hoping for an email from Agatha Aglak to confirm her interview. Not many people in the art world knew about Aglak yet. She worked in a hangar with the doors open to the cold and a helicopter at one end. She wore a hoodie and a face mask and, when Jenny had called by to introduce herself, she was cutting through a door-sized piece of plywood with a circular saw. An assistant was dipping another strip of plywood into a drum of what smelt like wax. It was pale blue and it looked like ice.

Nope. No email from Agatha Aglak.

Nothing from her friend Karen back home in Edinburgh either.

Unusual. An email from Maddie, Jenny's eldest sister.

Apparently not one of Maddie's sporadic litanies of how many paintings she'd sold; the subject header was "bad news." Jenny didn't want *bad news*. She took another sip of hot chocolate. Still, Maddie's bad news wasn't necessarily Jenny's bad news. She clicked "open."

jenny
It's our mother. Can u beleive it? She's in hopital in Inverness. She's had a stroke. In a comma, the dotors say. Will you go and see her.Ring me
Maddie
x
Ps happy belated easter

Jenny read the message twice.

She pictured her mother lying in the curve of a comma. The woman in the moon. Perhaps Maddie was trying to paint a picture with letters; she was an artist, after all.

She read the email again.

Her mother was fifty-two now. Young for a stroke.

Easy enough for Maddie to ask in an email: would she go and see her. It wasn't even a proper question, having no question mark. Jenny could see Maddie saying it, her dark eyes huge, her black curly hair scribbled over her pale face. Will *you* go and see her.

Would she? Even though she was three thousand miles away from Scotland. Even though she hadn't seen her mother — or father — for eight years?

Jenny felt as if she were looking through ice; everything was blurred, distorted, out of reach. She'd wondered if something like this might happen eventually. In thirty years' time or so, though, not now.

First, extract the truth from the Maddiefied melodrama. When Maddie said their mother was in a coma, was it true? And if she was in a coma, did that mean she was dying?

"'Scuse me?" A teenaged boy was standing beside her, holding out a tray for Jenny to look at. There were tiny soapstone carvings of polar bears and seals, and a row of wooden-handled, broad-bladed knives that she knew were called ulus.

Jenny took a breath and told him she didn't need anything. The boy's shoulders hunched.

"Okay then." She gave him a ten-dollar bill and picked up a polar bear the size of her thumb. It wasn't his fault his timing was terrible.

The boy's smile was broad and sudden.

"Did you make them?" Jenny asked.

He pushed his hat back over his thick black hair. "Yeah." His voice was soft.

"They're lovely," Jenny told him.

His smile broadened even more. He moved on and she looked back at the computer screen. They weren't lovely. They were crudely carved, but she didn't want to be rude. People had to make a living somehow.

She scanned Maddie's email again, briefly closed and opened her eyes, then typed:

Maddie
How bad is she? Have you seen her? I'll ring you as soon as I can.
Is our father with her? Does Sophie know?
Jenny
x

Sophie: their neat-nosed, fair-haired middle sister, who behaved as if she were the eldest. Jenny pressed "send." Once she'd logged off, she tugged her snow boots back on and stood.

Next, ring Maddie. Get more information. What had the hospital actually said? Remind Maddie that she was in Canada. In the Arctic. Why couldn't this have happened when she was at home in Edinburgh? Had they tried to ring Jenny at her flat there? Maddie was the eldest, but Jenny, the baby, was the one they — whoever *they* were — should have rung.

As she walked to the door, pressing her heels into her boots, Dominic, Kay and Ryan entered the café, their laughter curlicuing into shivers of pleasure at the warmth.

She didn't have to say anything; Dominic already had a dimple of concern in his brow, like a dent in a favourite toy. He must have seen something in her expression.

"I've got a wee problem to sort out," she told him. "Back home."

Dominic put a hand on her elbow. She appreciated it; she was feeling unsteady. "What kind of problem?"

"My mother's had a stroke. She's in hospital in Inverness."

The word *mother* tasted rusty in her mouth, metallic, as if she'd bitten her lip.

"Jesus," Dominic said.

"Oh, poor you." Kay clutched Jenny's hand, oozing sympathy as sweetly as jam in a doughnut.

"What can we do to help?" Ryan said. "Just name it."

"Thank you," Jenny said. "I'll be all right. I've just got to find out a bit more. Ring my sister."

"I'll come with you," said Dominic.

"No, it's okay." She'd evidently trained herself too well to deal with family problems on her own.

"You look kind of pale, Jen." Kay's head was slanted like a Bellini Madonna. "Let Dom take care of you."

Jenny's feet wouldn't move. She was plinthed. She didn't want to leave Dominic, her new friends, this low white world. Dominic slid his arm around her shoulders, and this was the lever that released her. Her feet unlocked. Dominic opened the café door and followed her out into the frigid air.

"My sister, who emailed me about our mother," said Jenny as their boots hacksawed across the snow, "she's prone to exaggeration."

"Let's hope she *is* exaggerating."

"My mother's only fifty-two. That's young for a stroke, surely."

"You just never know."

The words weren't reassuring, yet his tone was, as if no one had any control over what happened to them, as if the only responsibility in life was to continue breathing, continue walking across the tundra towards the horizon. Jenny's hands were cold. Her gloves weren't in her pockets where she usually put them; she must have left them at the café. She fisted her fingers inside her pockets until the bones hurt.

"You've never said much about your mom." Dominic said it gently, as if he didn't want to pry. She'd been vague with him whenever the subject of her parents had come up, telling him something about having a different outlook on life from them, that they weren't close. She'd redirected the conversation each time to talk about her sisters instead. That was much easier. She understood their lives. She was proud of them. One day she should probably tell them that.

She knew Dominic's mother had had breast cancer and had been clear for six years, and that his father had died of a heart attack when Dominic was nine. He had no siblings. Their relationships with their mothers were the exact opposite. He had helped his mother through her mastectomy, radiotherapy, chemotherapy and reconstruction. He had told Jenny all about it.

"Look, my family's a mess," she blurted now. "You don't even want to know. I haven't seen my mother since I was seventeen. Not for eight years."

"Holy crap." Dominic put his arm around her. "I'm sorry."

The unsteadiness she'd felt in the café had come back. She was grateful for his arm and conscious of the shiny, slippery fabric of their jackets, how his arm was sliding from her waist to her hip. She anchored them together by sliding her cold hand into his coat pocket.

"What about Maddie and Sophie?" Dominic asked.

He'd been paying attention; he knew her sisters' names. "We're all in touch with each other. But none of us are in contact with our parents. Maddie, who emailed me, she's the eldest. Sophie's the middle one. They're both trapped inside the M25. Or at least I assume they're trapped, because they've never once visited me in Edinburgh."

Jenny didn't know where that had come from; she hadn't realized those feelings were as close to the surface as blood. "Sorry. I'm all over the place." Even though it was cold, she felt a flare of heat, sweat under her arms and at her waistband. The dizziness was getting worse.

"Hey, no worries." Dominic tightened his arm around her. "So, is your dad there with your mom?"

"Maddie didn't say. I suppose so."

"They're still together?"

She'd never even thought about that, the possibility of her parents not being a couple anymore. They existed in her mind as a single entity. "I assume."

Her foot caught a chunk of ice and she stumbled.

Dominic gripped her waist more firmly. "I'm supposed to be helping, not adding to your worries. My parents, I don't know, there was some kind of tension there when I was a kid. I used to worry they were gonna get a divorce. Which is sad, you know, considering how it turned out."

Jenny wanted to say something sympathetic, but the ground was shifting. A gulp of nausea turned the sky black, as if she were looking down a telescope with the lens cap on. Chocolate heaved in her throat. She rushed to a heap of snow and vomited.

Dominic followed and put his hand between her shoulder blades. "Maybe it's the shock."

Jenny searched in her pockets for a tissue. "Or too much cream in the hot chocolate."

"You need to sit down," he said. "Come on."

Dominic kept his arm around her until they reached the research centre. Walking into the thick warm air of the common room gave Jenny goosebumps.

"I'd better have a wash," she said.

"What can I do? Make tea? Isn't that what you Brits do in a crisis?"

He'd spent a year at a London university. How had he survived there, where you had to travel for miles to find the edge of the concrete, where any snow that fell was dirty before it hit the ground?

It was a question as well as a joke, Jenny realized. She shook her head. She wasn't sure she'd be able to keep tea down.

"How about I check out flights online?" Dominic suggested.

He was assuming she was going back.

"I need to phone my sister."

"We've got two outside lines. Modem socket."

"Of course. I must have left my brain out in the snow."

"It's the shock," repeated Dominic, smiling. Perhaps it would become their catchphrase.

When she returned from the bathroom, Dominic held up a yellow legal pad in one hand and a mug of tea in the other. "Looks like there's a pretty good deal here, leaving tomorrow, though it's a red-eye. London Heathrow okay? Or does it need to be Edinburgh?"

She loved how he said *Edinbro*. She realized she was still shivering and looked around to see where she'd left her coat. She couldn't remember taking it off.

"Hey, sit down. You're shaking." Dominic put a hand on her shoulder as she sat.

"I just feel a bit cold."

"Drink the tea."

He held the cup for her as if she were a child. She took a sip. His eyes were heating her more effectively than the liquid could. "You've sussed it, thanks." She took the mug from him.

Dominic chuckled, presumably at the English word *sussed*. "Milk, not black. Milk, not cream. No sugar." His English accent was pretty good. And he'd already told her how he'd nearly been deported from England for putting cream in tea.

She put the mug down. She had to ring Maddie. Had to get this done, decided. She went to the phone and dialled standing up. Somehow she always remembered Maddie's number.

Dominic brought the mug over to her and put it on the table close by. Then he brought over a chair and hung her jacket on it. She smiled to say thank you.

Good. Maddie was in.

"It's Jenny."

"You got my email."

"Any more news?"

"No time for small talk, eh? Is that what the ruthless world of academia is like nowadays?"

"Phoning from here's expensive, you know." Jenny tried to yank out the ruck of irritation in her voice. She breathed, picturing Maddie's large, dark eyes and long, black, curly hair. Their mother's frizziness without the copper colour. None of them had inherited that.

"So how's life in the fast lane?" Jenny said.

"Probably a lot noisier and smellier than life in the Arctic wastes. Have you seen a polar bear yet?"

"I saw paw prints. In a place called Pangnirtung."

"Crikey. Be careful, won't you. I have a feeling they're not as cuddly as they look."

"So speaks Maddie the biologist."

Maddie laughed.

Jenny sat down in the chair Dominic had brought as Maddie told her how the hospital had telephoned her. "God knows how they tracked me down. They said she's had a stroke. Does that mean she'll be paralyzed? Might she not make it?"

"I don't know." Jenny managed to avoid adding something sarcastic about not being a doctor. "Are you going up to see her?"

"I don't know what to do."

Jenny waited for her sister to continue; she could tell she was going to.

"I've got this really big dealer interested —"

"So, it's not our mother you're worried about, it's your work," Jenny snapped. She got up from the chair and sat on the table, turning away so Dominic wouldn't be able to hear as clearly. She was being a hypocrite; Jenny didn't want to leave her work either.

"It's a big one, Jen. It's important. Biggest ever. Anyway, if anyone goes, it should be you. You had a much better relationship with them than Sophie and me. This deal really isn't one I can jeopardize. And I'm sure Sophie is in a play soon."

"I'm not here on bloody holiday, you know." Jenny turned around to raise her eyebrows at Dominic, show him she recognized she wasn't being her professional art historian self. He wasn't there. She hadn't even noticed. She hadn't sensed his body moving away.

"Yeah, I know." Maddie's tone shifted. "This whole thing's a mess."

"Did the hospital mention our father?"

"No. And I didn't ask."

"I don't see how they knew where you were. You've changed addresses dozens of times since we lived at Willowbrae." Saying *Willowbrae* pulled at something in Jenny's abdomen.

"I never lived at Willowbrae."

Jenny heard Maddie take a slurp of something. Perhaps there was a man in Maddie's flat making tea for her too. Or pouring her wine.

She asked Maddie if she'd spoken to Sophie yet and if Sophie was going to Inverness.

Maddie guffawed down the phone.

Jenny held the receiver, wondering if wine had been spilt. She still couldn't see Dominic. Had he gone back to the café?

"Oh, did you know she's moved to Bath?" Maddie said.

"She's left her beloved London?" Jenny hadn't spoken to Sophie for months, and emails never told the whole story.

"Some bloke, I gather."

"I'm shocked and stunned. He must be pretty amazing to get her to leave London. So, what's this play she's in then?"

"I forget the title. It's at the Royal Court, I think. Lead role."

Jenny wouldn't have expected anything less.

"We should go," said Maddie, "when you come back."

"I didn't say I was coming back."

Maddie paused. "But you might?"

"I'll ring the hospital, then decide." Jenny drained emotion from her voice as deftly as she bled the radiators in her Edinburgh flat. "I'll let you know."

Her mother had had a stroke in the middle of Marks & Spencer in Inverness. Jenny tried to picture it, her mother falling to the floor, knees folding. She couldn't, not without knowing which part of the shop her mother was in, whether she fell on carpet or the hard surface of the main track that led you through a department store, whether she was surrounded by tops or trousers or skirts or bras. Jenny had been to Inverness a few times on trips with the university's outdoor club. She'd bought a pair of socks in that Marks & Spencer branch once. They were blue and she still had them.

The nurse on the phone told Jenny her mother was stable and beginning to come out of the coma. As Jenny listened, Dominic put a plate of Oreos next to her mug. He obviously wasn't worried she might throw up again.

"The thing is," Jenny told the nurse, "I'm in Arctic Canada. I'm thousands of miles away. At least three flights."

She shouldn't have said that in front of Dominic. It sounded callous. He had his yellow pad and was writing something. Or doodling. She should tell him to go back to the café. "I mean, is she going to be okay?"

The nurse sighed. "A stroke is an unknown quantity. A strange creature. It takes people in different ways."

A strange creature. A dragon holding her mother in its mouth.

"We can never," the nurse said, "gauge how a stroke sufferer will respond, but your mother is young, in terms of having a stroke. There was a weakness in an artery and it burst, which means blood leaked out into the brain. It's called an aneurysm."

A bicycle inner tube bulging. The quick rhythmic thud as you cycled along Nicolson Street. The bang of the explosion, startling a woman who had just come out of the James Thin bookshop so that she drops the book she has just bought. Putting a foot down on the curb and realizing you'd be late for your lecture now.

"It's really for the consultant to talk to you about this, not me." The nurse seemed to sense Jenny's confusion. "She's your mum's doctor. They're called consultants. She'll explain much better than I can. Just remember that for a lot of stroke sufferers, it's like waking up in another country. One where you can't understand a word of the language."

The signs around Iqaluit were all in Inuktitut. To Jenny, the lines and shapes of the letters were only patterns. If they didn't have English translations underneath, she would never know where she was.

Jenny told the nurse she was grateful for what they were doing to look after her mother and put the phone down.

Dominic was looking at her. Her decision was on his face. Of course she was going.

She tried to smile at him. He shook his head a little as if to say she didn't have to try to be all right.

"They can't really say much. It's too early." Jenny could hear the split in her voice. "The nurse said she's coming out of her coma. I don't know how they can tell."

"She'll be much better once you're there. Once she sees you," Dominic said. "I get that there's stuff between you, but you're her daughter, right?"

He pulled her into a hug. Jenny pressed her face into the shoulder of his fleece. She tried to ignore the dark band on the horizon that was the approaching tsunami of her family.

"I don't want to go," she told him. "What if I don't come back?"

"Of course you'll come back." Dominic tightened his hug. He was laughing at her; she could hear it in his voice.

Jenny opened her mouth then closed it again. She had no idea how to explain to him what her parents were like, how they had a knack of changing the tracks underneath her so she arrived where she hadn't intended to go.

Two

JENNY AND DOMINIC WERE lying on her narrow bed with the light off. Her curtains were open and they were watching pale lights flaring in the sky like threads of sunset snagged on clouds. This was the first time Jenny hadn't gone outside to watch the northern lights when she'd seen them. She'd read about what caused the aurora borealis more than once. The sun was a fire. The northern lights were the embers. That was never what it said.

Jenny had her head on Dominic's shoulder and her arm across his stomach. The fabric of his grey T-shirt was thin as if he'd worn and washed it many times. It was the most comfortable she'd ever been in her life.

"Is anyone gonna meet you at the airport?"

"Maddie said she'd be there, though that's no guarantee."

"Let me know if I can do anything. You might remember something you should have done here, if you're anything like me, anyways. You don't have a cellphone back in Scotland?"

"No, I'm a bit of a Luddite. I'll give you the number for my flat in Edinburgh. I'll hopefully be there at some point." The truth was she didn't like phones; you couldn't see the face of the person you were talking to, and you had to remember everything you wanted to say before you put the receiver down.

"I've written down my email and cell on a piece of paper," Dominic told her.

"Thanks."

Living and working in the same building, all their communication had been face-to-face. Now they would have to introduce phones and email into their relationship. She'd always known her relationship with Dominic was too easy. Whenever you thought something was too good to be true, it usually was.

"I've put it on top of your backpack," he added.

Jenny's backpack was leaning against the wall under the window. She had packed everything she needed, including the new Iqaluit stone. She wasn't taking everything. She wouldn't, for instance, need her bulky snow boots or snow pants six degrees farther south in Scotland. She'd left a fleece jacket in the wardrobe, T-shirts folded in the chest of drawers, research notes in the desk and a towel hanging on the back of the door. Individually these objects were still lifes, details of an existence in progress. Collectively, the composition would be understood easily enough by anyone entering her room while she was away: the occupant of this room was returning.

"You have an awesome backpack," Dominic said. "Those badges. You went to Greenland?"

"Yeah, in my second year at university."

The incredible trip Rob had treated her to. Rob: talkative and tubby and always funny. Until she'd made him sad.

"Wow. It's on my bucket list. What was it like?"

"Fantastic. We went on this boat trip and saw this amazing thing. It's like a mirage. An Arctic mirage. We could see Canada when really we shouldn't have been able to because it was actually too far away, beyond the curve of the Earth's surface."

"The *hillingar* effect."

"Yes!" Jenny shifted to look at him. "You're the only person I've met who's ever heard of it. The funny thing is, unless you know you're seeing it, you don't realize. You need someone to tell you."

"I hadn't thought of that. Sure. How would you know? Apparently it's why some explorers discovered the lands they did. Had a kind of sneak preview of what was ahead. Screwed up some of the Northwest Passage searches too. I love all that stuff. I can't believe you've actually seen it. That's mind-blowing."

Dominic tilted his head and kissed her. They took off each other's T-shirts and Dominic reached to undo Jenny's bra. Feeling her bare skin against his turned her into water. They had done this before, a few times. They hadn't gone any further, not yet. A hand gently on his wrist, a slight shift of her hips away from him. Dominic, she had realized with relief, was good at picking up signals. He was gorgeous and considerate and he had probably slept with many women and learnt from them.

He was pulling down her trousers.

Jenny wasn't going to stop him this time. She didn't want to think about her mother or father or sisters, or analyze the Kavavaow Ishulutak interview anymore, or worry about what would happen to her research because she was leaving Baffin Island. She certainly didn't want to think how long it would be before she saw Dominic again.

She wanted him to press down on top of her and be inside her.

As he moved himself on top of her, Jenny felt her legs becoming rigid. Tears were burning in her eyes. She pushed at Dominic as she sat up. Her throat was tightening. She couldn't speak.

"It's okay, it's okay," Dominic was saying when it so clearly wasn't. He kissed her forehead.

Jenny breathed through her nose. She knew how to do this, how to get the words flowing again.

Dominic was holding both her hands. "I'm sorry. It's still too soon."

Jenny shook her head. "I'm sorry," she managed to whisper. What had happened on North Berwick beach was seven years ago. Was she going to be wedged against that cold sand forever?

"There's nothing to be sorry for. It's okay." Dominic stroked her back.

"It's not okay," Jenny whispered again. "I want to. I really do."

"There's plenty of time. We don't have to do this now. We'll have all the time in the world when you get back."

Dominic lifted the duvet so Jenny could get into bed and then got in beside her, manoeuvring himself into the position he had been in before so she could put her arm across his stomach. She slid her hand across his chest, feeling the dip in his sternum, the soft dark hairs, the stub of a nipple. She kissed his ribs and he kissed the top of her head. She raised her face to his and he kissed her lips.

Dominic seemed so certain she would come back, and of course she would. Her return flight was booked in just under a fortnight. She would come back to this island. She'd finish her interviews. She'd travel north to cross the Arctic Circle. The lands on which the hoop of the Arctic Circle rested — Nunavut, Chukotka Peninsula, Svalbard, Murmansk, Prudhoe Bay — were all members of the tundra club. Before she died, she was going to every one of them. She craved their calm horizons that were like flanges of ice, north and south, connecting to a rod of ice shearing right through the Earth's core, fixing one pole to the other.

Jenny waited until Dominic was asleep and then got out of bed. As quietly as she could, she pulled open a drawer in her desk and took out a small bundle wrapped in a white cloth. She unfurled the cloth to reveal a pale block of ash and a stout chip knife. She was whittling a figure. There were no spaces between the arms, legs and torso. She was aiming for compactness, calm. It might not work. She had brought the wood with her, knowing that trees here were only centimetres high, that there would not be woodlands to walk in and collect from. She had never carved stone, or bone, or antler or ivory, which were the naturally available materials here. Her wood carvings were just whittlings really; she wasn't presumptuous enough to think she could ever be an artist. Maddie was the real artist in the family.

Jenny wrapped the figure up again and put it in the bag she was taking as hand luggage. The knife had better go in her backpack, though she didn't want to separate the tool from the form it was shaping. To separate them was to indicate the figure was no longer a work in progress. She hoped her luggage wouldn't be searched tomorrow. She'd hate for anyone to think the figure was finished. Once she had done as much work on it as she could, she would add it to the carvings on the shelf at home in her flat. She wouldn't look at it directly; it would hover in the corner of her eye. The shape of it would reassemble itself inside her subconscious. Eventually, she would know what she had to do to finish it.

☙

She had a window seat on the plane. Once Iqaluit was out of sight, there were no signs of the human race. You could walk for miles over the rocks and see no one for weeks, perhaps never. You'd become obsessed with food and shelter. Jenny knew she would die quickly; she had no survival skills and she was vegetarian. To live, she'd have to eat fish. She might, somehow, be able to catch a fish, but she wouldn't be able to bash it on the head; she'd let it flap and suffocate to death. Cowardice would make her cruel.

She picked up the fat, dog-eared novel she'd found in the research centre, James Michener's *Alaska*. Hopefully it would be easy to read, like watching a film, and stop her thinking. She turned to the first page then put the book down. Her eyes wouldn't follow the words. She looked out the window again.

She loved how flying turned a map into three dimensions. She wished the plane would rise higher so she could see the whole of Nunavut, the land that just last year the Inuit were finally able to have for their own. Baffin Island was still below her, the land mass that Iqaluit rested on. The island was nearly split in two below its kneecaps, or around its ribs if you looked at it sideways and imagined it was a kind of dog with a long neck. A creature that had been garrotted around its abdomen, wire easing into flesh. This was a land of traps, after all. The worst trap she had read about was used to kill wolves. A strip of baleen was bent over, tied with thread made of sinew, covered in blubber or meat. As the wolf ate the sinew, the baleen strip sprang back and ruptured its stomach.

Dominic had come with her to the airport to see her off. They hadn't talked any more about what had happened the night before. He had kissed her goodbye softly at first and, when she pressed harder, he pressed harder too. She would tell him what had happened at North Berwick when she got back. Or perhaps she would tell him in an email. She could hear her best friend Karen saying that was a dreadful idea; you should never mistake email for genuine communication. Jenny liked email. You could decide exactly what you wanted to say, and if people asked questions in their reply, you could choose to ignore them.

"You need an 'I have seen the *hillingar* effect' badge on your back-pack," Dominic said at the airport. "I'll make you one in exchange for a Picnic."

"A picnic?"

"The chocolate bar. I'm putting in a special order so don't forget. British chocolate is way better."

"Ah, so you only want me for my chocolate."

"Oh, a whole lot more than that." Dominic leant forward to kiss her again.

Three

"WHERE THE FUCK DID YOU GO?" said Maddie when Jenny rang from her hotel room in Inverness. "I waited for ages at the airport and you didn't come through Arrivals, and then I went to some sort of information desk with a man in a ridiculous waistcoat and he told me your plane had landed hours ago."

"I'm sorry." Jenny wasn't certain that she in fact was sorry. "But you were late, and I couldn't wait. I had to get the train to Inverness."

"Why didn't you ring from King's Cross?"

"You wouldn't have been at home by then. You don't have a mobile. I waited as long as I could before I got on the train in case you came to the station."

"You booked the train too soon after your flight got in."

"I've dropped everything. I've just flown three thousand miles. You can't even be bothered to travel four hundred miles."

"Nobody forced you to come."

This was pointless. Jenny let the ball drop to break the childish volley. "Look, I'll ring you in the morning from the hospital, okay? I'm so tired from the flight, I can't think straight."

Jenny changed the topic to Sophie. Maddie still hadn't heard from her. Jenny said she'd try her in the morning.

"I *am* grateful that you've come," Maddie said in a conciliatory tone just before they said goodnight.

Although all she wanted to do was have a shower and burrow into bed, Jenny went downstairs to the hotel lobby and emailed Dominic the name and number of the hotel. She also emailed her friends Karen and Helen to let them know what had happened, that she was back in Scotland. She told them she would ring them tomorrow.

She shouldn't really be staying in a hotel; she should be staying at the hostel down the road to save money. She just couldn't face sharing a room or having anyone ask her what she was doing in Inverness. The only questions hotel staff asked was how long you were staying and whether you needed help getting your luggage to your room. And if you ate breakfast alone in the dining room, with *The Guardian* folded up beside your plate of toast, you should be able to get through the whole meal without saying anything to anyone except please and thank you.

There was someone sitting by her mother's hospital bed. The figure was too small to be her father and it certainly wouldn't be Maddie or Sophie. It was a woman, judging by the sage green shawl over her head and shoulders. Seeing that colour made Jenny want to turn around and walk out again.

She would look only at her mother, lying flat as the Lincolnshire fields Jenny had gazed at from the train as she travelled north. If this even was her mother? The nurse had said the fourth bed on the right. Where was her mother's big curly, coppery hair? Her hair was short and grey now. Her eyes were closed and there was a tube in her wrist and another one up her nose. Her mother's long face had lengthened even more; her cheekbones had become more prominent.

The visitor turned. It was a girl with pale skin and round, blue eyes.

"Maddie, Sophie or Jenny?" the girl said, smiling. She had the names in the right order.

"You are?" Jenny went around to the other side of the bed.

"Piyali. Are you Maddie?" It would be a nice smile if it wasn't so smug. "They said they'd spoken to you."

She looked about fifteen. Light brown hair, from what Jenny could see under the shawl. And short, like her mother's. Her mother could never have talked about her daughters then, never described them, if this *Piyali* thought Jenny was Maddie.

There was a movement and both of them looked at Jenny's mother. Her eyes were still closed, but she had lifted her right hand and was floating it back down to the sheet as if to calm them.

Piyali slipped the shawl off her head so it scooped around her shoulders. Her haircut looked homemade. "Moksha'll be fine again soon. She's moving all the time now. She hasn't said much but she doesn't need to. I know what she means."

Moksha? Was that a pet name? A Gallachist name?

"Is my father, Alasdair, here?" Jenny asked.

At last the eyes became guarded. "No, he's not here." Piyali's accent was English, not Scottish, Jenny noted.

"Not in the hospital? Not in Inverness?"

"He's in India, I think."

Jenny hadn't expected that. "You don't know?"

"He could be —" Piyali started and stopped. "He might be back here. Looking for Moksha."

Jenny tried to keep any emotion out of her voice; she didn't want to give this girl a thing, not even her curiosity. "How come?" Jenny glanced at her mother; her eyes were still closed. She was listening, though, Jenny was sure of it.

"We left," Piyali said.

Jenny tried not to show her surprise. "Do you mean *left* as in came to Inverness for a shopping trip? Or *left* as in not going back?"

Piyali's eyes widened. "Not going back."

Jenny pulled a chair towards her but didn't sit down. "Does anyone know she's here? Anyone from there, I mean."

"Just me," Piyali whispered. She put the shawl back over her head.

Jenny's mother was as still as an astronaut floating outside a spaceship. The safety line had been severed and here was Piyali gripping the loose end as they drifted farther away together in space.

"Why did you leave?" Jenny sat down so she'd be at eye level with Piyali.

"Moksha decided to."

"I thought Gallachism, or Viparanda, rather, had the answer to everything." Jenny couldn't help herself. Her sarcasm silenced Piyali. Perhaps it wasn't the best approach. "Why did you leave?" Jenny repeated gently. "You must have had a reason."

"She was ill." Piyali hunched her shoulders. "She had these headaches and you shouldn't be ill. I mean," Piyali corrected herself, "you should be able to get yourself better. And if you can't get yourself better, then there's a reason for it, and you have to find out what that reason is and self-elucidate."

This girl was from a different dimension. And her clothes were grubby. She needed to find somewhere to wash them. Hadn't they brought any spare clothes with them? Is that why they'd been in Marks & Spencer?

"Where are your parents?" Jenny said.

Piyali sat back up, apparently surprised by the question.

"My birth mother's in San Francisco, I think, and my birth father's in Cape Town."

"You're not close to them?"

"They're callers."

"Meaning?"

"They call in new members. They hardly ever come to Ben."

"Recruiters," said Jenny, understanding. "You don't miss them? You don't miss your parents?"

"I don't need them specifically. Everyone at Ben is my parent."

Jenny sighed. "So why did you leave with Margaret?" It was easier to name her that. Not mother. Certainly not Moksha.

Piyali flushed.

"Weren't you happy there?"

"I was worried about her. She wasn't well."

Jenny had read online in Iqaluit that small strokes often preceded large ones. "Did she have a stroke there?"

Piyali looked confused. "I don't know. I didn't know what a stroke was until I came here. I mean, she wasn't like —" She looked at Jenny's mother. "She wasn't like this."

"Headaches?"

Piyali nodded. "Bad ones. She couldn't work."

"And you have to work."

"Of course." Piyali looked at Jenny as if she were stupid. "Even the pyramids didn't make any difference. She went in for days."

Jenny didn't want to know about pyramids. "What work did she do?"

"She managed the retreats. You know, took the bookings, welcomed the guests, made sure their rooms were cleaned. I helped her."

Jenny laughed. How ironic. The same work her mother had done at their guest house, Willowbrae. The most beautiful home in the world that they had lost because of the Gallachists.

Piyali looked puzzled by the laugh. Jenny didn't explain.

"And what's my father doing in India?" Jenny said.

"He's a caller, too, like my birth parents."

Jenny nodded. "Of course." So he'd got what he wanted. He travelled to India and who knew where else while her mother stayed at home changing bedding.

"And they work on their own practice as well," Piyali added. "Everyone does. Moksha has to do it in the evenings. She's too busy working in the daytime."

Piyali might not think she needed parents, but it was obvious she'd adopted Jenny's mother as her own. Jenny didn't feel jealous, only sad. A daughter needing a mother and a mother who couldn't keep hold of her own daughters finding a new one. As Jenny stood to go and find a doctor, Piyali said, "You've got your mother's eyes, you know."

The doctor led her into a small office along the corridor from the ward. Following behind, Jenny wanted to take a photograph of her so she could carve her oblong, white-coated form. In beech, to match her blonde hair.

As they sat, Jenny asked if Piyali had been at the hospital the whole time.

"She's certainly here every time I am. When someone's admitted in your mother's condition, we tend to relax the rules." The doctor's soft Scottish accent reminded Jenny of the view from her Willowbrae lookout on a clear day, how from the top of the hill, sitting on her stone, the fields and forests were a gentle, green sea.

"It's important to have someone with them, talking to them, touching them," the doctor continued. "And your mum's doing really well. She's getting stronger. At first we let Piyali sleep in a chair beside the bed like a bairn. She didn't say much. Just kept holding your mum's hand. All the time." The doctor chuckled. "She kept shushing us, telling us to watch what we say around her, be positive. She's quite the wee character. I don't necessarily disagree, it's just the way she says it. She was getting quite worked up, but she's calmed down now that she can see your mum's coming to. Is she some kind of nun?"

"It's a religious group. Gallachism. There's a community on Knoydart. I'm not one."

The doctor relaxed, unless Jenny was imagining it. "They've got a thing about electromagnetic fields, haven't they?"

"I didn't know that." Why hadn't she known that?

The doctor crossed her two index fingers and held them up as if she were warding off the devil. "Piyali put something she called a polarizer on the cabinet. A funny pyramid thingy."

Jenny hadn't noticed it. "What's going to happen?" That was enough about Gallachism for now. "My mother, I mean."

"Her young age is a great help. Not drinking or smoking helps too. The stroke took place more on the left side of the brain, so that means her right side is affected. She may have some paralysis. She may struggle with speech. It's difficult to assess the damage straight away. There's always some. It's a matter of where it is and how well the rest of the brain and body can repair or compensate."

"She didn't open her eyes just now."

"She's sleeping a lot. It's partly the medication. We have to be patient. She's doing really well. There are some wonderful people here to help her. Physiotherapists, occupational therapists, speech therapists —"

"Could she make a full recovery?" Jenny interrupted.

"It's possible, yes, but, as I say, it's a matter of how well her body is able to repair the damage." She explained that stroke patients get something called aphasia, sometimes permanently, sometimes temporarily. Their words can come out slurred. They might sound a bit drunk, and they often have blank spaces where words used to be. The doctor gestured at the screen. "They might forget the word for computer, say, or desk. Or even your name. That can be hard. You know what it makes me think of? Censored letters in the war, you know, with words blacked out. And I must warn you. Some stroke patients get very frustrated and they swear, a lot of them. It can be a shock to hear your mum swearing." The doctor gave Jenny a wry smile. "I reckon a bit of role reversal does us all good."

"Thank you," Jenny said, "for explaining."

"Are you here long? You've come from Canada? Whereabouts? I've got relatives in Calgary."

Calgary. Where Dominic grew up. He'd told Jenny he used to make sure he stood somewhere at least once a day where he could see the distant Rockies due west across the prairies.

"I was in Nunavut." Jenny was conscious of the unfamiliar sound of it, how she was trying to pronounce it the Inuktitut way, more *oo* than *uh*. "A town called Iqaluit on Baffin Island, two hundred miles south of the Arctic Circle."

"My goodness. I'm sure your mum will appreciate how far you've come."

Jenny crossed her legs. "There's something I wanted to ask."

"Fire away."

"I was wondering how you found us, well, my sister. The thing is," Jenny paused, "we haven't been in touch with our mother for quite a while."

The doctor frowned slightly. "I gather Emma, one of the nurses, had a chat with Piyali to find the next of kin once we realized she wasn't actually related to your mum. It was a bit touch and go, you see, when your mum first came in. It took a bit of time, but Emma tracked your sister down. She's an artist?"

Jenny nodded.

"Emma told me Piyali didn't even know your mum's proper name," said the doctor, "but luckily her driving licence was in her bag. What did you say they were, Gallachists?"

"Yep." Jenny sighed without meaning to. "Well, thank you for looking after her. And for finding us."

"You're welcome. It's what we're here for."

Piyali was still sitting by Jenny's mother's bedside, her hands together in her lap and her eyes closed. She didn't have a book or magazine or Walkman to entertain her. Jenny took the opportunity to look at the girl. She wasn't beautiful or pretty, those words wouldn't do, yet there was something in her face, partly the easy smoothness of youth, partly the absence of makeup. Mostly, though, her blue eyes that protruded just a little as if there was nothing in the world she wasn't eager to see. Her hands: long fingers, broad palms. Dexterous hands; she could be a sculptor. Piyali's eyelids flickered and Jenny darted her gaze away. Jenny cleared her throat and Piyali opened her eyes.

"I'd like to be on my own with my mother," Jenny said.

"Sure," Piyali said easily. "I knew you were there. I was finishing off my perceptions." Piyali placed the ends of her thumbs briefly against her breastbone and stood up. "I'll come back later," she said, walking away.

"Hang on a minute. Where are you staying?"

"Here."

"The hospital won't let you sleep here forever, you know. Have you got enough money to pay for somewhere to stay?"

"I've got some of Moksha's money," Piyali said. "She won't mind, I know she won't." She looked defensive, even nervous.

"I'm sure she doesn't mind."

Piyali looked relieved.

"You don't have any money of your own, though?" Jenny asked.

"No. Money isn't —" Piyali hesitated. "It's not necessary at Ben."

"It's pretty handy here in the real world. So, do you have enough to pay to stay somewhere?" Jenny repeated. She tutted. "You wouldn't even know, would you? You don't have a clue what that would cost. How much have you got?"

"Nearly two hundred pounds." Piyali said it proudly, as if she'd just learnt to count.

"Cash or a debit card?"

Piyali looked confused.

"Coins? Notes?"

Piyali reached into her pocket.

"It's okay. I don't need to see it. Look, when you can't stay here anymore, go and stay at a youth hostel," Jenny said. "There's one on Culduthel Road. Will you remember that? And don't wait until the hospital asks you to leave." Jenny started thinking about social services and school authorities and whether Piyali existed on anyone's files. "How old are you?"

"Sixteen in human years."

Jenny laughed. She couldn't help it. "You mean as opposed to dog years?"

Piyali looked confused again.

"It's okay," Jenny said. "I know. Age is just an illusion humans have imposed on themselves as a way to cope with the eternity of their existence."

Piyali looked surprised now, as if Jenny had got it right.

Jenny felt suddenly sorry for Piyali. "How long have you been at Ben Gallachie?"

"I was born there."

That explained a few things. So, she was sixteen. Not officially a child. Or was she? Child benefit stopped at sixteen. You could get married at sixteen. Yet you had to wait until you were eighteen to vote. And drink, at least legally.

"If you don't want to go back there when your money runs out, you'll have to get a job or claim benefits. Do you realize that?"

What on earth would this child do without Jenny's mother to help her?

Piyali seemed to sense the questions were over and wordlessly walked away. Jenny sat down and the padded seat exhaled. After a moment, she stood up again and went to her mother's bedside cabinet. On top of it was the pyramid-shaped polarizer that the doctor had mentioned. There was also a box of tissues and a jug of water. No flowers. Nothing of Piyali's. Jenny shoved the pyramid abruptly with the back of her hand; it didn't fall over. Then she pushed it in the other direction, closer to her mother.

She bent and opened the bedside cabinet doors. Her mother's handbag was in there. The same brown leather bag. And a sage-coloured cotton jacket that Jenny unfolded to see if it had pockets with anything in them. No pockets. No other belongings.

Jenny glanced at her mother to check her eyes were still closed. She unzipped the handbag and, crouching beside the cabinet, laid the contents on the seat of the chair. A red and orange scarf Jenny remembered her mother wrapping her hair in. Her mother's leather purse, warm as if it had been in a pocket. Inside the purse, some coins and a bank card. No credit card. No notes. Not stuffed with receipts like it used to be. Jenny unzipped the pocket inside the handbag. There was an envelope containing three creased and dog-eared photographs and a couple of newspaper cuttings. One of the pictures was of the three sisters on the beach in Dinard, sitting on their towels eating baguettes. At least Jenny and Sophie were eating. Maddie as usual was refraining. There was a photograph of Jenny in the garden at Willowbrae, sitting in a deck chair and revising for her Higher exams by the looks of things. The third photograph was just of Willowbrae — the warm sandstone facade, the nine friendly windows — taken from the driveway. That photograph surprised Jenny the most. Tears heated her eyes. There wasn't a photograph of her father.

Jenny flipped the pictures over. There was nothing written on the backs of any of them. She unfolded the yellowing cuttings, although she already knew what they were. She remembered reluctantly handing them over to her parents years ago in the sitting room at Willowbrae.

One had a photograph of Sophie acting in *Speed-the-Plow* and one was about Maddie being in the Royal Academy summer show.

What else was in the bag? A hairbrush, a pen and a nail file. Some headache pills from Boots, nothing herbal or New Age about them. And a CD: Vivaldi's *Stabat Mater*, her mother's favourite piece of music. The case was cracked and the cover was faded. It was the same one that used to lie on the kitchen windowsill at Willowbrae, next to the CD player.

Jenny put everything back where she'd found it and sat down again. Glancing to check no one was watching, she reached to touch her mother's hand. It felt cool. Cold. She covered her mother's fingers with her own and watched her mother's face. There seemed to be movement, a crinkling of the eyelids, a razor line of white eyeball. Her eyes didn't open.

"I need to talk to you," Jenny whispered. "I need to find out what's going on."

There. She had spoken. Lying still and silent in a hospital bed, her mother had won.

Four

BRIGHTON, 1987

JENNY IS SITTING IN the kitchen at Brighton, reading while her mother cooks. Radio 4 is on, the oven door squeaks open and clanks shut. Her mother enjoys Jenny's company in the kitchen; she likes an audience. However, Jenny is mostly here because she's sure her parents are hatching a plan and she wants to know what it is. She can tell because they look the way Sophie looks all the time. Their eyes gleam and it's hard to get their attention.

Sometimes their plans happen. Sometimes not.

Moving to France didn't happen. Building an extension onto the house and running a bed and breakfast didn't happen. But the art materials shop did. Turning the flat above the shop into a gallery did too. Jenny likes to find out about the plans as early as possible so she has time to decide whether they're good plans or bad plans and then tell her parents. She also likes to find out so she can make sure everyone gets a say. By everyone she means Maddie and Sophie.

Jenny always knows how her sisters will react. She knew when she told them about their parents' plan to move to France that they'd hate the idea — because it would be too far away from their precious London, the only place to be when you want to be an artist or an actor. She also knew they wouldn't like the bed and breakfast idea — they wouldn't want strangers in their house. Nor would she.

Jenny had interrupted a plan the other day, at Beachy Head, just along the coast from where they lived in Brighton. They'd gone there for a walk and ice cream to celebrate the start of the school holidays. Jenny ignored Sophie, who was daring her and Maddie to creep as close as they could to the edge of the cliff, calling it her new "suicide" game. Jenny crept up instead on her parents, who were sitting on a bench. It wasn't difficult. They were often engrossed in talking to each other and not really noticing what was going on around them, although her father did keep looking across the cliff to the glittering sea. Jenny ran in a semicircle across the grass so she could come up behind them.

"Look at that," she heard her father say. "Doesn't it make you want to sell up and sail around the world?"

When Jenny's mother laughed, he added, "I'm serious, Margaret."

"That's why I'm laughing, *Alasdair*." She stressed his name because he'd used hers.

"We've got to do something worthwhile with our lives."

"Yes, but if it's sailing around the world or any of the other things we want to do, it's going to have to wait until the girls are a bit older."

"People do it all the time, pack up and take their children with them. Or pack them off to a boarding school."

Jenny had to stop herself from gasping out loud. Her father was surely joking. Her parents didn't believe in boarding schools.

"We're socialists, darling, remember?" her mother said.

Her parents weren't arguing exactly, they just weren't happy with each other. It was easy to imagine their faces. When her father was grumpy, his face still looked neat and tidy and mild, yet it became smaller and his eyes shrank. When Jenny's mother was grumpy, her long nose and her dark eyebrows went askew and it made you want to reach out and put everything back where it should be.

"Needs must," Jenny's father said.

"We can't afford it."

"Boarding school or sailing around the world?"

"Both! Either!"

"Your parents could lend us a few bob," said Jenny's father.

Grandma and Grandad, who tell people they live in Sutton Coldfield because, Jenny's mother says, they're too snobbish to admit they really live in Birmingham.

"On that note," Jenny's mother said, "your father must be close to kicking the bucket."

Jenny knew her mother was only teasing about Grandfather dying. Her mother often said things that made you wince.

"We're going to have to do something, I tell you." Her father sounded more serious. "I can't —" He stopped.

"Alasdair, we've just spent all that money on opening the gallery. That's going to have to be our adventure for now, paying off the loan." It was Jenny's mother who looked after the money; when she paid a bill, she put it in the filing cabinet at one end of the dining room next to the oak desk. "You wanted the gallery as much as I did."

"I know." Jenny's father sounded so sad, as if he'd realized he'd made a terrible mistake. Jenny wanted to climb over the back of the bench and give him a hug. She also wanted to carry on listening.

Jenny's mother sighed. "The girls, well, Maddie and Sophie, we couldn't whisk them off into the great blue yonder." She gestured at the sea. "They're too talented. If they're going to make a go of things, they can't afford to waste any time."

"Boarding school it is then." Her father was still joking. Surely.

Her mother's tone of voice altered. She sounded more serious. "I do think Jenny needs to go to a different school, though. One that pushes her harder. Naomi isn't exactly our sort either."

Jenny had heard her mother make such comments about her best friend Naomi before. Because Naomi didn't do anything extra like piano or ballet lessons and had parents who watched too much television. She hadn't heard her mother talk about going to another school before, however. Not in this more definite tone. It was time to stop the conversation.

"Not all your children have to be prodigies," her father was saying. "Jenny's not twelve yet. Give her a chance."

Jenny clambered over the back of the seat and pushed her bottom in between them. Her parents both laughed and her father slung his arm around her.

"I don't want to go to a different school," Jenny said. "And you don't believe in boarding schools. And Maddie and Sophie need to finish school so they can go to London. So, I'm afraid sailing around the world isn't an option, not until you've got shot of us all."

She was mimicking their adult language but she meant it too.

"Okay, Jenny Wren. We'll do as we're told." Her father was smiling. Neither of her parents seemed to care that she'd been eavesdropping.

"We'll invite Naomi to our house more often," her mother said. "Show her there are other ways to live."

As she sits in the kitchen reading, Jenny hears the glug of wine being poured, which means supper is almost ready. She doesn't believe her parents are thinking about sailing around the world anymore, but she's not making any progress on finding out what they're plotting instead.

"*The Pale Horse*." Her mother is bending to look at what Jenny's reading. "You should be reading Thomas Hardy or D.H. Lawrence by now at your age. Or at least Daphne du Maurier."

"I've got to finish all the Agatha Christies first."

Jenny loves reading, but if she could have her way, she wouldn't be reading anything right now. She'd be sitting at the table drawing with her coloured pencils. She used to do that every evening while her mother cooked, until her mother told her to stop making a mess on the table just before supper. It's true there had been a pile of red, yellow and orange pencil shavings beside scattered pencils when she said it. Jenny draws in her bedroom now.

"I haven't heard you practise the piano today," says her mother. "Or yesterday, come to think of it." Her mother pokes a knife into a bubbling lasagne and pulls back from the heat. "You'll never be a pianist if you don't practise."

"I don't want to be a pianist." Jenny hasn't said this to her mother before, not directly. She's been hoping her mother would get the message via the lack of practising. She resists the urge to look down at her book. It's not easy seeing disappointment dulling her mother's eyes.

"No," Jenny's mother says at last, looking away first. "I don't think the piano is your forte."

Jenny winces at the pun and her mother smirks. "I don't think it's worth trying another instrument. No, you're going to have to concentrate on school work, I think." Jenny's mother pushes back the head scarf she wraps around her coppery hair when she's cooking. "You could be a university lecturer. You'd be good at that." She gave a quick laugh. "You could teach at Sussex. God forbid."

The University of Sussex is here in Brighton, just a couple of miles away. It's where Jenny's parents met.

"Does that mean I don't have to practise anymore?" Jenny says.

Her mother shakes her head in mock despair.

"You can't get a piano on a sailing boat anyway," Jenny adds, watching her mother's reaction.

Her mother tuts. "Your father gets restless."

"So what's the new plan?" She says it lightly, in the same spirit as the piano on a boat comment.

"There's no plan," her mother says. "But there is something."

Jenny closes her book. She knew it. "Tell me."

"Go and round up the troops. We'll tell you all together. Don't look so worried. It's good news."

Jenny lays her book down open-winged on the Guatemalan rug they bought in the Lanes. She calls Maddie and Sophie from halfway up the first flight of stairs and then goes out to the garage, where her father is making rectangular plinths for an upcoming sculpture exhibition in the gallery.

Back in the kitchen, Jenny puts one hand on the door jamb and stretches out one of her legs behind her to ease her midriff; she can feel a stomach ache coming on. She gets it when she's worrying about something. It must be because she doesn't know what her parents' news is.

If she were in bed now, she'd put a stone from her collection on her stomach. She's discovered that if she puts one on her tummy when it starts to ache, the pain goes away, mostly. The stone from Birling Gap Beach is her favourite at the moment. She picked it up when they went for a swim after Beachy Head. It's white and it has a dip in it for her thumb. Her mother hasn't yet noticed the chalk dust on her nightie. It just looks as if she got carried away with talcum powder.

Her mother is watching her stretch out her leg. "You want to be a gymnast now, do you?"

"Of course not. I'm just stretching."

"Just as well. You're such a clodhopper. And I didn't mean yell up the stairs, Jenny. I meant go and get everyone. Why does everyone have to be so loud? I can't hear myself think."

Jenny is suddenly sick of her mother's comments. "You always tell me what I can't be. You never actually ask me what I want to be."

Her mother, slipping her hands into oven gloves, looks startled. She laughs. "I assume if you knew what you wanted to be you'd tell me. Well?"

Jenny stares. She wants her mother to work it out. What does her mother think her youngest daughter most loves doing, that she's stopped her from doing anymore at the kitchen table?

Does she really have to say it? "I like drawing," she says quietly.

Her mother looks serious for a moment and then laughs again. "God, no thanks. Two artists in the family is quite enough. Look, darling, I know you love playing with your coloured pencils, but being an artist isn't quite the same as that. You have to have a lot of talent. You know, like Maddie. It's a very tough world. Daddy's learnt that the hard way, and we see it all the time at the gallery."

The backs of Jenny's eyes are burning. She can't speak.

"I honestly think you'll make a great teacher. You're so kind and understanding. You can draw in your spare time. Do it as a hobby."

"You think hobbies are stupid!" Jenny shouts. "And you always say those who can, do, and those who can't, teach."

Jenny strides over to the sink and stands with her back to her mother. She wants to run upstairs to her room and pick up her Birling Gap stone, but she also wants to know, needs to know, what this news is. She turns on the hot tap fully so the water splashes up. Drops of water burn her forearms as she pushes up her sleeves to wash up a saucepan.

Sophie glides into the kitchen. She glides everywhere, her hair a smooth, flat sheet of gold behind her. "Mummy's girl," she says to Jenny as she passes.

When they're all sitting at last, except Grandfather, who lives with them and for whom they never wait, Jenny sits too.

"Well." Their mother is smiling, standing at the table. A strand of her hair has come adrift from her scarf. "Things are going well at the gallery." She clasps her hands in front of her. "So we've decided to send Sophie up to London every Saturday morning for NAPA drama classes."

A grin slides onto Sophie's face. "Really? Up on the train? On my own?" This is news to her. Big news.

"I'm certainly not driving you up and down to London every week-end," their father says.

And Jenny knows it has to be London. Drama classes in Brighton just won't do.

"Blimey." Maddie's dark eyes are large. She didn't know this was coming either.

Sophie and their mother are hugging. "Just for the summer," their mother is saying. "We'll have to see after that."

Sophie is definitely going to become an actor now, a famous one.

Jenny catches Maddie's eye and Maddie raises her eyebrows.

Their mother plonks a steaming lasagne on the table. "Dig in. Maddie, have a proper amount please. And everyone have salad."

Grandfather is standing in the doorway.

Even though he's lived here for four years, he behaves like a guest. As ever, he's wearing his brown suit as if he's still the head teacher at Tillicoultry school. Jenny's father tells him to come in.

"Don't want to get in the way."

"You could at least pretend you want to be part of this family," Jenny's mother mumbles, too quietly for Grandfather to hear.

"Come and eat something," Jenny's father says, more loudly. "You've got to keep your strength up."

"I'm not hungry, son. I'll just have a cuppa." He comes cautiously into the kitchen as if he's worried the floor might give way at any minute.

Jenny, who is still vibrating from shouting at her mother, gets up to check the kettle has enough water in it and pushes the switch down.

"Don't encourage him, Jenny," her mother says, her voice low. "He should wait and have a cup of tea with the rest of us later." More loudly, she adds, "You've got to have supper. A cup of tea's not enough."

"I don't do anything, don't use up any energy." Grandfather moves past Jenny towards the draining board. He's looking for his cup and saucer. He's said many times he doesn't see why people bother putting washing up away when it's only going to be used again. He finds the cup and saucer in the cupboard with a grunt, then sits in Jenny's reading chair while the kettle boils, pushing her book out of the way with the toe of his polished shoe until the cover is bent against the skirting board. "I'll just get my cuppa then I'll be off."

Jenny reaches down to rescue her book.

"You should have some of this lasagne. It's delicious," their father says.

Maddie groans. "D'you think Italians ever eat whole wheat pasta? I think not."

"Don't be so narrow-minded." Their father makes a face at Maddie, who screws up her face at him. They grin at each other.

"Sophie's going to go to NAPA, to drama college, every Saturday," says their mother at Grandfather volume. "In London. The National Academy for the Performing Arts," she stretches the words out dramatically. "She's already so talented, think what this will do for her."

"Thought you already did acting at school." The chair is too small for Grandfather; his knees are too high. Sophie calls him Granddaddy Long Legs. "Hope you don't end up on the telly," he continues. "It's all rubbish except the sport and even that's going downhill. And I don't mean just the skiing." His cheeks lift and his eyes crinkle and he chuckles. Jenny likes it when he laughs; he looks so much nicer.

"I'm going to do theatre," Sophie says.

"No one goes to the theatre these days. It's too dear," he tells her.

Sophie opens her mouth and leaves it open to signal her speechlessness.

Grandfather gives Jenny a head tilt. He wants her to make his tea for him. Her mother frowns but doesn't stop Jenny from getting up. He likes his tea as orange as rust and will watch Jenny to make sure she remembers sugar. "Prescription day tomorrow, Margaret," he says.

"I hadn't forgotten." Jenny's mother takes a sip of wine. "We'll sort it out in the morning. I'll go into the gallery a bit later." Her parents call it the gallery, as if the shop below it had come second, was the afterthought. Yet they had bought the shop first and then a couple of years later converted the flat upstairs into a gallery.

Grandfather takes the tea Jenny is handing him, the tremor in his wrist rattling the cup in the saucer. It's because of the war. The shock waves from all the bomb blasts are still ricocheting through him. He lifts the cup awkwardly at an angle. The tea almost slides over the rim as he takes a gulp with his large lips, not bothering to check if it's too hot first. He puts the cup back in the saucer. "Is anyone else being visited by poltergeists?"

"What do you mean, Dad?" Grandfather isn't known for his belief in anything beyond the chairs-and-tables physical world.

Jenny's mother rolls her eyes.

Jenny hopes Grandfather hasn't noticed.

"I put my pills on my bedside table when I go to bed," Grandfather says, his cup rattling, "and then when I need them in the night, there they are over by the sink. It's either a poltergeist or I'm losing my marbles."

"You probably move them when you get up in the night to go to the loo," says Jenny's mother. "You're probably half-asleep and don't realize." She glares at Sophie then scoops a spoonful of lasagne onto Maddie's plate.

Jenny isn't sure what the glare is for.

Grandfather grunts. It isn't his agreement grunt; he doesn't have one of those. After another loud sip and the clatter of the cup landing back in the saucer, he says without looking at Sophie, "What about the fiddle? I haven't heard any practising lately."

"Here we go," Jenny's mother says.

Sophie isn't meeting anyone's eye. Jenny hasn't heard her practising either, not for ages. She wonders if there are any other neglected musical instruments in the house. Her recorder. The triangle and maracas that gather dust on top of the piano. She helps herself to more lasagne.

"That's enough, Jenny," says her mother. "You're already bigger than your sisters."

Jenny drops the spoon back in the dish. "I'm still hungry." Although, abruptly, she isn't.

"I didn't give you my fiddle, Sophie, for it to just stay in its case," Grandfather says. "If that was what I wanted, I'd have kept it in my wardrobe. You wait until you're my age and riddled with arthritis and then you'll regret not using your fingers while you can."

"Yes, Sophie is a very good violinist," Jenny's mother tells Grandfather. She disapproves of calling a violin a fiddle. "But she's an even better actor. It's important to concentrate on what you're best at. I'm sure," she adds drily, "you've heard the expression jack of all trades."

Jenny isn't sure if Grandfather is even listening.

It's funny when she thinks about it. Sophie has two talents and she has none. You'd have thought their parents could have planned that better. There's no doubt her mother is right about Jenny's lack of talent. But that isn't going to stop her drawing. She loves doing it too much. She loves how she loses track of time and how she always knows which coloured pencil to pick up without having to think about it. She's drawing a picture of Brighton beach at the moment, with the orange, white and grey stones of the shingle beach enormous in the foreground. She's looking forward to getting on with it after supper.

Grandfather puts his large hands on the arms of the little chair and stands up. "Maybe I'd better have a wee bit of that. Keep my strength up."

He comes over to the table and sits in his usual place next to Sophie, where he ends up every mealtime after pretending he isn't hungry. Perhaps Sophie gets her acting talent from him as well as her violin talent. Sophie shifts her chair to put more space between them. Jenny gets up and fetches his tea from where he's left it on the floor and puts it in front of him on the table. He doesn't say thank you. He never does and no one ever tells him off for it. That's the war, too, probably. It excuses you from having to be grateful for anything.

"I've heard a few with the bow and there's a knack to it you can't learn." Grandfather spoons a generous helping of lasagne onto his plate. He doesn't take any salad. "You're born with it, like it or not, but if you don't use it, you'll lose it. Talent doesn't hang around forever. It goes off and finds someone who'll appreciate it."

Jenny watches Sophie's face. She sees no evidence that Grandfather's words are having any effect.

He gave her the violin months ago, after he heard her play solo in the Christmas concert. It's the only family event he's been to since he moved in with them. As soon as they'd got home he told them all to wait in the kitchen. It was so rare that he behaved as if he were part of the family that they'd all done as they were told. He took ages coming back downstairs. Jenny thought he was carrying a briefcase at first. He laid it on the kitchen table and opened the catches with his long fingers as cautiously as if he were opening a bird cage. He told Sophie it was hers and she stepped towards it looking scared and excited all at once, like when they were queuing up for the fair ride last summer where you were in a spinning drum and the floor dropped away.

Their mother tried to stop Sophie taking it. She told Sophie she had to concentrate on acting if she was serious about it. She didn't have time to mess about with a violin.

Sophie had looked at their mother with her empty vessel expression. That was how Jenny had heard Sophie describe it. She'd been taught it at an acting class. How to make her face blank.

Everyone watched Sophie pick up the violin, even their mother. Once it was resting under her chin, it didn't look as if the violin had ever been Grandfather's at all.

When Jenny comes out of the bathroom in her dressing gown and slippers ready for bed, Maddie is sitting on the top bunk, cross-legged. She looks like a pixie, up there in the middle of the room. Jenny doesn't laugh though. Maddie is like a cat; she doesn't like being laughed at. Jenny climbs up to join her sister.

"Guess what Sophie said to me?" Maddie's dark eyes are large in her thin face. Jenny resists the urge to reach out and touch her cheekbones. "She said one summer of classes was all very well, but what she really needed was permanent classes, as otherwise in London they don't take you seriously." She flings out her arms. "I mean, don't you get sick of her always being the favourite? It's going to cost a bomb and Mummy and Daddy can't even afford it. It's not as if the business is doing very well. That's why we only went on holiday to Brittany. That's why you're not doing anything big for your birthday."

"Oh." Jenny hasn't thought about her birthday yet. It's a whole month away. "Mummy said the gallery's going well."

"Mummy says a lot of things."

Maddie picks something up from the bed. It's Jenny's Brighton stone; she'd fetched it on the day after they got back from France because it didn't seem right that she didn't have one from her own beach. She'd cycled down to the sea, walked eleven paces across the shingle — one for each year she'd been alive — and there it was, orange and speckled and smooth like a slightly squashed egg.

"Your extra lessons with your art teacher are free, aren't they?" Jenny scoots back so she can push her bare feet under the duvet.

"They're not lessons," Maddie snaps. "Matt, Mr. Sanderson, and I are equals. We discuss techniques. Ideas. He's so articulate visually. His stuff is amazing."

"Better than Daddy's?"

Maddie leans forward to look at the unframed canvas on the wall. Trees, rocks, waves are painted in yellows, purples, blues, different colours than they are in real life yet everything looks just right. You either see the shapes or you see the colours, never both together. It's like the duck and rabbit optical illusion; you can't see them both at the same time. Whether it's a good thing or a bad thing, Jenny likes it. Maddie's looking as if the question interests her and she hasn't considered it before, which Jenny doesn't believe is true.

"Daddy's problem," says Maddie, flipping the Brighton stone from one palm to the other, "is that he didn't persevere. He never developed a truly original style. His own vision."

"He had to feed us."

"You sound older than me sometimes," Maddie says. "There was only me at first. That was when he should have stuck to it instead of working all the time. And I didn't eat much."

Jenny resists saying she still doesn't. "I bet," she says, "they make more money with the shop and gallery than he would have painting."

"You don't get it." Maddie pinches the top of her nose with her thumb and forefinger. "It's a calling, it's not about money. And actually I don't even know if what you say is true, the way things are going." The tiny coloured beads around her thin wrist tap together as she pushes her fingers through her hair. "Matt was telling me about foundation courses the other night."

Jenny knows Maddie has to get A levels before she can do a foundation course. She's seventeen. One more year to go. "In London?"

"Where else? The only other place you can decently go if you're serious about being an artist would be New York. Or Paris, perhaps." Maddie yawns. "I'm too lazy to learn French. Or American."

They both laugh.

"Mummy thinks I should be a teacher."

Maddie makes a face, pressing her chin down onto her neck. "Do you want to be a teacher?"

Jenny shrugs. She isn't going to tell Maddie what she said to their mother about wanting to be an artist. It's nice, having Maddie sitting on her bunk. Telling her could either send her off in a huff or she'll laugh at her like their mother had.

"Actually, you'd be a good teacher," Maddie says. "You're patient. You're nice to people. And you're the cleverest of all of us. I mean, you came top in something, didn't you?"

Jenny shrugs again.

Maddie narrows her eyes. "Which subject?"

"English. And science. And history."

"First in three subjects?" Maddie clarifies. "Bloody hell, Jenny Wren. You're a boffin."

"Don't call me a boffin." She doesn't mention she came second in maths and geography.

Maddie looks at her. Jenny wishes she knows what she's thinking. "Okay, but you are one."

They both flinch. They've heard a thump.

"Christ, Grandfather again," Maddie says. "I bet he's having one of his funny moments. I'm not going. Last time I went, his tea was all over the carpet. It made a bloody awful mess, especially with all that sugar in it and globs of dunked custard creams. Sophie says he pushes things off on purpose."

Jenny hangs her feet over the edge of the bunk. "What if nobody else heard him?"

"He's getting worse," says Maddie as Jenny thuds to the floor. "I can't believe he didn't even buy Mummy a card for her birthday, let alone a present. She does so much for him. You know what he said to Sophie when she asked? He said he doesn't buy cards for people he sees on their birthday. That's so weird." She lands lightly on the floor after Jenny as if she's made of sticks and paper.

"Daddy says it's because of the war," says Jenny, at her bedroom door. She hopes Maddie isn't going to take the Brighton stone with her. It's best not to say anything, best that Maddie doesn't know it's special.

Maddie mutters something. Jenny doesn't hear what. She crosses the landing and knocks on Grandfather's door. It's ajar by a few centimetres. "You all right, Grandfather?"

He doesn't reply, so she knocks again and goes in. He isn't in his armchair as he usually is; he's standing by the sink, leaning on it, hard. Jenny hopes it isn't going to break.

"I tripped over my book, coming to get my pills."

"Did you hurt yourself?"

"Only my pride." He picks up one of the containers of pills and tries to twist off the lid. Jenny wants to help but he doesn't look as if he'll appreciate it. "These things are supposed to be childproof, not pensioner proof. I'm sure I had them over by my chair, but then here they were on the sink. I must be going doolally. Or it's my pet poltergeist again." He flips the lid off and rattles two blue pills onto his crinkled palm. Slapping his palm against his mouth, he picks up a glass of water with the other hand.

Jenny watches his thick lips as he swigs the pills down. She bends to the floor and picks up the book Grandfather must have tripped over. It's his Bible. It's heavy and has a black cover with a raised pattern on it. He tells her to put it back by his chair.

"Why are you reading the Bible?"

"Maybe I'll answer that question by reading it." He's leaning on the sink again as if taking his pills has exhausted him.

"Mummy and Daddy don't believe in God."

"They don't need to," Grandfather says. "They believe in themselves instead, like everyone else these days."

Jenny doesn't understand how it would be possible for anyone not to believe in themselves when they obviously existed. "The Bible's just a story, isn't it?"

"Depends who you ask."

Jenny waits until Grandfather is making his way back to his chair. She asks him if he's all right, and when he doesn't answer, she leaves the room.

Jenny pads downstairs to the sitting room. The news is on television, but neither of her parents are watching. As she stands in the doorway, her father puts his magazine down and her mother raises her head from the novel she's reading. She looks how Jenny feels when she's absorbed in a book and someone has interrupted her. She tells them Grandfather fell over but he's okay.

She's about to follow her father out of the room when her mother puts out her hand. "Thank you, Jenny, for going to him," she says. "I know he's a gruff old man and I lose my patience with him. Come here."

Jenny takes her mother's hand and is pulled into a hug.

"You know I want the best for you, don't you?" Her mother's voice is close to Jenny's ear.

Jenny shrugs inside the hug. If she tries to speak, she'll cry. It isn't fair that Maddie and Sophie have talents and she doesn't.

"We'll keep focused on your school work. You'll be picking your options next year. It'll be fun deciding. You can choose whatever you like, you can drop music and art. Actors and artists always need audiences. Not everyone can be up on the stage."

As usual, her mother doesn't seem to need Jenny to say anything. Jenny stays inside the hug for another few moments, then kisses her mother on the cheek and goes upstairs.

When she climbs the ladder up to her bunk, she sees that Maddie has left the Brighton stone on top of the duvet. She wriggles under the covers and rests it on her stomach, right where her belly button is.

Five

JENNY RAN ALL THE way back from Inverness hospital. Jogging along the quiet pavements as shiny cars whooshed past, she observed the damp grey of the road after a rain shower, the pink and yellow of old stone walls that paled when the sun came out. As she neared the city centre, the houses became older — Victorian, Edwardian, she assumed — and more beautiful than the plainer, newer houses of the outskirts where the hospital was.

Of course the older, detached houses all reminded her of Willowbrae — a gable, a slipped slate, a line of moss on steps — but really this whole country was home. The broadleaf trees she ran underneath were so verdant and flourishing and extravagant after her weeks in broad, white, bare Nunavut. Yet she missed Nunavut too. How could she simultaneously love such different lands?

Had her mother loved Willowbrae as much as Jenny had, after all? Was that why she'd broken the rules and kept that photograph? Gallachists weren't allowed to keep anything from their old lives: not photographs, not clothes, not money and certainly not daughters.

"I've got all these appointments set up with potential buyers and I haven't produced enough for my next show yet," said Maddie when Jenny rang her from her hotel room. "I don't see how I can get up there."

Jenny sat down on the bed. "I believe there are trains to Scotland nowadays and even planes."

"Ha ha."

Jenny had taken the Iqaluit stone out of her backpack and was holding it now in her hand, rubbing her thumb gently over the roughness. She hadn't shown Dominic the stone after all to ask him what it was made of. She would have felt silly, explaining about her stones. Now she wished she had, so that he would have touched it, felt the weight of it in his hand. "There's a girl with her," she told Maddie.

"What girl?" That got her sister's attention.

"She's sixteen and she's called Piyali and apparently they left Ben Gallachie together. She told me they'd left for good and nobody from there knows where they are. Including our father."

"Bloody hell."

"Quite. Our mother's been looking after this girl for years, I reckon. She doesn't have a clue about anything in the real world. They're letting her sleep at the hospital, but she won't be able to keep doing that. She'll have to go back. Or I could ring social services."

"Would you do that?" Maddie sounded uneasy.

"It's not like calling the police. I don't think she'd have to go into care or anything at her age. Someone's going to have to look after her. Show her how things work. But it's our mother we have to worry about first."

Jenny explained how she hadn't seen their mother open her eyes yet, how her long, frizzy, coppery hair was now short and grey and all the rest of their mother's colour had gone with it. "You should come. It's different, you know, when you see her."

Maddie paused. "I'll try. I really will." She sounded as if she meant it. "I can't believe this is happening."

Jenny put the phone down and lay back on the bed. The mattress was quicksand and she let herself sink into it. Why was she the only one here? How did her sisters manage to resist the tug of her parents' fish-ing line that was so painfully hooked into Jenny's flesh? She'd left the hotel phone number on Sophie's answering machine in Bath three times.

She sat up and dialled Karen's number.

"Do you want me to come?" Karen said when Jenny had updated her. "I can take a couple of days off work. Nae bother."

Jenny laughed. "I hereby appoint you my honorary sister. Thank you, but I'm going to work on them first. It's weird, isn't it, that you've never met my mother?"

"Even weirder that you've met mine and we're still friends."

Karen's mother lived on her own in a flat in Wester Hailes, just inside the Edinburgh bypass. Karen was the only one of her four siblings who had anything to do with their mother, and she was always saying she didn't know why she bothered.

"Just say the word and I'll hop on a train," Karen said. "And your flat's all yours if you need a bolt-hole. I haven't needed it, but I might hang on to the key, if that's okay with you."

Karen was in the process of ending a three-year relationship with a man who had abandonment issues.

"Absolutely," Jenny said. "If he gets too much, just pretend you're going to a conference and stay in my flat instead."

"I'm here for you, you know that. I'm your defence against regression and depression."

"Thanks, Karen. That means a lot."

"Any time, okay? Just get the train to Edinburgh and we'll go for toasted tea cakes."

Jenny had been planning to leave the best until last, her reward for making so many calls in one evening when she usually took more of a nineteenth-century approach to using the telephone. No. Dominic had to be her next call, not her last. She couldn't wait. He might not even be there; it was still morning in Iqaluit and he might have found another excuse to be outside rather than indoors in front of a computer.

"Hi, Dominic Allen here."

"It's Jenny. In Scotland."

"As opposed to the Jennys I know in Romania, Ghana and Tasmania?"

Jenny felt suddenly jealous of these imaginary Jennys all around the world who knew Dominic and might see him again before she did.

"Oh, right," he continued as she laughed. "You're the Jenny that took off on me two days ago, right?"

"I really miss you," she told him.

"Not as much as I miss you." He was sounding serious now. She knew exactly what his face would look like at that moment, the slight lengthening of the skin between his nose and lip.

She made a sound that wasn't a word as she tried to speak. Her throat had sealed over.

"Hey, you okay?"

Jenny breathed as deeply as she could. "Yes," she managed to say. "Everything's okay. I mean, my mother's doing well in the circumstances." She breathed again and gave him an overview of what the doctor had said.

"You've got to get your sisters up there," he told her. "Share the load. They should be taking equal responsibility, not leaving you to do all the heavy lifting. They're being selfish."

She'd heard him use this uncompromising tone before when he'd talked about the geosciences office he was setting up, complaining about the federal government's part in it, stifling what the new Nunavut government wanted to do. He'd used a similar tone, too, when she'd told him about the Kavavaow Ishulutak interview, making it clear he thought the sculptor should have had more respect for Jenny and if he'd committed to an interview at a particular time, then he should have followed through.

And now he was using this tone for her own family, and she had to admit she didn't like it. She acknowledged the cliché that it was okay for you to criticize your own family but not okay when your partner did it. And yet, there was a sweetness to Dominic's defence of her and she appreciated that.

"I'm working on it," she told him. "They're both really busy people."

"So are you." Dominic's tone was a little more mollified. And now she felt cross with herself for making excuses for her sisters.

"Tell me what's going on there," she said to change the subject. "What's the temperature?"

"A balmy minus six."

"It's plus twelve here. T-shirt weather."

"Yeah, right. That's what I thought when I was first there. It's so goddam damp I wore thermal underwear all summer."

Talking to Dominic gave Jenny the energy to make the last phone call. That, and a mini bottle of red wine from the fridge. This was the call that meant she had to accept her research was postponed.

She pictured Aynslie, her PhD supervisor, as they talked, sitting in her lime-green chair in her office at the University of Edinburgh, blonde and hearty and from Toronto. Always happy to debate whether Canada or Britain was the better country to live in. Aynslie herself arrived at a different conclusion every time.

She told Jenny not to worry about her research, that it would all get worked out as her mother's situation became clearer. She also told Jenny that a *guy* had come looking for her, just the day before. He'd said it was personal, nothing to do with Jenny's research. When Jenny asked, Aynslie described him as early fifties, slim. Fair, silvery hair. Nice blue eyes. Mild Scottish accent. He had declined to leave his name.

"You know who it was?"

"I've a feeling it was my father." Jenny's chest felt tight. "I haven't seen him for eight years."

"Holy shit. What do you want me to do if he comes back? Give him your phone number? Have him arrested?"

As usual Aynslie's laughter was infectious and Jenny laughed too. "Yeah, the latter," she said. "Dereliction of parental duty must surely be an arrestable offence."

All her calls now made, Jenny lay back on her pillows and sipped at her glass of wine, absorbing what Aynslie had told her. Her father — surely that was who the visitor had been — wasn't in India. He was right here in Scotland, after all.

All these years, Jenny had blamed her parents equally for destroying the family. Her mother and father had such different personalities — her mother outspoken yet pragmatic, her father diplomatic yet impulsive. When it came to life-changing decisions, though, they acted in unison; they became a single person. Jenny didn't want to untangle nerves and sinews, intentions and influences. She didn't want to think about which of them had done what, separate leader from follower.

She refilled her glass. Was her father looking for her only because he thought her mother might be with her? Jenny's name would be on the university website somewhere, no doubt, listing Aynslie as her supervisor. She had students. She worked in the office at the Centre of Canadian Studies. *Professor Ross*. Not yet. Never, at this rate.

Would he think of checking the hospitals? Were hospitals allowed to disclose the names of their patients? If only her mother would wake up and tell Jenny what had happened, how it was possible that her father didn't know where her mother was. Assuming Piyali was telling the truth.

She should tell her sisters what she'd found out about their father, but she couldn't face any more telephone calls. And, anyway, if they were here, they'd know. Why weren't they here?

Jenny put her glass down and picked up the book on her bedside table. She was using the receipt Dominic had written his contact details as a bookmark. He'd used a blue pen. The D of Dominic was large and generous and the dots of the i's haphazard. The receipt made her smile. It was for Reese's Peanut Butter Cups. They made a perfect couple, compatible down to their chocolate preferences.

She got up from the bed and started going through the pockets of her rucksack. There might be some chocolate stashed somewhere. There wasn't, she knew; she never lost track of her chocolate supplies.

She stopped looking. She was so tired. Perhaps she could get through this evening without a sugar fix to smother what she was feeling. She would lie down, just for a few minutes, and then she would go out looking for food. Proper food. She would be sensible and get a takeaway. Indian. Her favourite. *Carry-out*, in Scottish.

Lying on the bed, she closed her eyes and interlaced her fingers over her rib cage so she didn't have to put her hands on her fleshy stomach.

She was so weary, yet her brain wouldn't stop chugging like a broken cistern trying to refill itself. She'd spent years training herself not to think about Brighton, about Willowbrae, shoving her memories into a suitcase and sticking it in the attic. Yet now she could feel every strap and clasp sliding and snapping open.

She opened her eyes. No. There was no point thinking about it; the past couldn't be changed. She got up from the bed, put her jacket on and left the room.

Forty minutes later, Jenny was back in her hotel room leaning on a stack of pillows and flicking through television channels as she ate vegetable korma, palak paneer, pilau rice, four onion bhajis and garlic naan bread.

She should be doing something productive while she ate, not watching television. Looking through the research notes she'd brought with her or, once she'd stopped using her hands to shovel in food, working on the block of ash that was still in her rucksack. But why? It was ridiculous to think of herself as a carver or sculptor. She was barely even a whittler. She was a watcher, not a doer. A researcher, not an artist. Her mother had made that clear to her years ago.

When all the cartons were empty, Jenny tore open the wrapper of one of the Picnic bars she'd put on the bedside cabinet. The chocolate and crisped rice and raisins were dense and chewy and delicious. For the moments it took to eat the bar, her mind was as blank as snow.

She could soon feel all the food heating the soft fat on her stomach and hips, a familiar burn. She felt relaxed now. That was how it worked; it was better than Valium. She closed her eyes. Surely she would sleep. She wouldn't think about the Brighton or the Willowbrae days. She could still see the lines she had drawn in ballpoint pen on scraps of paper compulsively during her first few weeks at university, the flow charts of her parents' decisions, of all her "shoulds" and "shouldn't haves" written down and bounded by boxes.

She turned off the lamp and made herself think of the white horizon outside Iqaluit, holding on to Dominic's solid waist through his red down jacket as they rode the snowmobile back to the research centre. That was where she should have been; she had to think of the future. She willed herself to sleep deeply as her body worked hard to digest all the food. She would skip the REM stage; she wouldn't have any dreams.

Six

ACCORDING TO THE red geometric lines on the clock radio in her bedroom at Brighton, Jenny has eleven minutes before she has to unsnuggle from her duvet and get to the bathroom if she wants to beat her sisters. It's February and fog has been sticking to the south coast of England for days. If you go to the beach, the sea sounds the same, but you can see only a few metres of grey waves before water and sky merge. Her sisters find it dreary and depressing; Jenny finds it mysterious.

Ten minutes. A double-decker bus goes past the house, droning as it struggles uphill. She knows it's a double-decker because the single deckers don't rattle her bedroom windows.

The Brighton house is cold, what with its Regency drafts and insufficient radiators. Moving through the house is like swimming in the sea; every now and then you find a warm spot. Jenny swims from warm patch to warm patch every morning as she gets ready for school, from her bed to the bathroom, from the bathroom back to her bedroom and then down to the kitchen. Grandfather is allowed an electric heater, but his room doesn't count as one of the warm patches.

At first, Jenny thinks her radio has come on early. No, the murmuring, if that's what it is, is coming from the direction of the landing. There are only two other bedrooms on her floor: Grandfather's and her parents'. The sound is more of a groan now. More like a tree creaking than a human sound. Perhaps it's the poltergeist Grandfather has been saying for months moves his things about.

Jenny listens for the noise again. This time it's very small, as if the poltergeist is at the bottom of the garden. She'd better investigate; it's impossible to doze now. She rolls over onto her stomach and slides down from the bunk to the carpet. A rush of worry stops her putting on her dressing gown or slippers. It's too quiet. She wants to hear the noise again.

Across the landing, Grandfather's door is ajar as usual. Perhaps the poltergeist is in there now, sitting at the foot of the bed or having a bath in the hand basin. Poltergeists are small, Jenny is sure.

She knocks quietly on the door and asks Grandfather if he's all right. Her voice is crackly like a sweet wrapper. She knocks again, more loudly, and pushes the door open.

Grandfather is sitting propped up in bed against his usual four pillows with his eyes closed. There's no sign of the poltergeist.

She goes closer. With his eyes closed, Grandfather looks so peaceful. He never looks like that when he's awake.

"I just wanted to check you were all right." Jenny says it loudly, in case he wakes up and is startled to see her there.

He doesn't move. His eyelids don't even flicker. He looks so still. Too still. His chest isn't moving. Jenny is aware of the slow rise and fall of her own chest, how she's pulling air into her body without even thinking about it.

She goes even closer. "Grandfather." She speaks as loudly as she can without shouting.

He must be pretending. She puts her hand on his shoulder — the nylon fabric of his pyjamas is slippery — and gently squeezes. He's warm. He must be all right. She squeezes harder.

"Daddy!"

She runs to her parents' room. Her father is up on one elbow in bed, looking confused.

"You've got to come and see Grandfather." She says it quickly, before her throat closes over. "Please, Daddy."

He tells her to wait on the landing while he goes into Grandfather's room. He comes out less than a minute later and stands in his blue-and-white-striped pyjamas, looking at Jenny and her mother, his hands on his hips. At first, he doesn't seem able to speak. "I'm afraid he's gone," he says softly after a moment. "Poor Jenny Wren. What a shock."

The three of them hug, her mother in her long burgundy dressing gown that makes her look like a queen.

Jenny tries to imagine that Grandfather really has *gone*, as her father put it. That he got up early and went up the hill to Five Ways to catch a bus, in his brown three-piece suit with ironed sleeves and trouser legs and polished shoes. Or perhaps if they look out Jenny's bedroom window right now, they'll see him slowly bending to fit inside a taxi.

Her dressing gown cord trailing three steps behind her, Sophie taps barefoot downstairs from her room on the top floor. She wants to know what all the whispering is about.

Maddie comes downstairs next in her short red nightie, her thighs as skinny as Jenny's arms.

Their parents are discussing whether to call 999 or the doctor. Their mother decides they should call 999 and their father goes downstairs.

Sophie goes towards Grandfather's door.

"What are you doing?" their mother asks.

It's obvious. She's going into Grandfather's room. "I'm going to see."

"Wait."

Sophie tuts and stares at her mother. "I just want to have a look." She moves closer to the door.

"Don't be so disrespectful." Their mother's voice is like a drawer being slammed shut.

"You said once we're dead, we're dead. End of story. Oh, he's looking down on us, is he? On his way to Heaven?" Sophie sneers. "You don't believe in Heaven."

"I don't know. Nobody does," their mother says. "Do we have to have this conversation now?"

Sophie laughs but it isn't a real laugh or even her acting laugh. "When exactly should we have it, if not now?"

Their father has come back upstairs. He goes into Grandfather's room and Sophie follows. Maddie goes in next. Jenny's mother holds out her hand and they go in together.

Grandfather is still sitting up. His eyes are still closed. The room still smells like Grandfather, of pink custard and mops and clothes that are only ever dry-cleaned.

"How do you know he's really dead?" Sophie says. "Did you hold a mirror up to his mouth? Did you feel his pulse?"

"Good grief," their mother says. "You don't know when to stop, do you?"

"I'm just asking."

Their father lays his hand on Grandfather's shoulder where Jenny had touched him too. Jenny looks at Grandfather's polished shoes beside his armchair. The shoes look so alive. In the Christmas holidays, Jenny had found a grasshopper sitting on a dock leaf in the garden. She'd crouched down expecting it to hop away, but it never moved. When she snapped off a stem of grass and gently tapped the leaf, the grasshopper fell noiselessly to the ground, lying on its side. She thought she'd killed it, scared it to death, but now she sees it had already been dead. She buried it by the back wall, hoping the weight of soil wouldn't crush its fragile, airy carcass. She made it a tiny cross out of oak twigs.

As soon as you're fully grown, you start dying. There is no in between. Now their mother has one fewer body to feed and take to the doctor and change the bedding for. Their mother lifts the net curtain she hates because it's working class yet had hung because Grandfather had wanted it. She looks out the window, or perhaps at her own reflection as it's still dark outside. Jenny doesn't think her mother isn't sad that Grandfather is dead, yet there's a calmness in her long, strong face.

Now her mother is picking up a container of Grandfather's pills from the sink. Jenny remembers what he'd said about the poltergeist moving them around. Perhaps the poltergeist will live in her room

now; they probably get lonely. Moving things around is just them trying to play and make friends. Perhaps it will move her stones. She won't
mind, as long as the stones stay in her room.

Sophie turns and catches their mother's eye as she stands holding the
pills. A colour comes into Sophie's face as they look at each other, a
blush, even though Sophie never blushes. As Sophie's face darkens,
their mother's face pales, as if there has been a transfer of some kind
from one to the other, of coolness or of blood.

Their mother is probably still cross with Sophie for being insensitive
and perhaps Sophie feels guilty now she realizes that Grandfather
really is dead.

Yet her mother doesn't look cross, exactly. She looks afraid.

Jenny's father puts his arm around her shoulders. "Come on," he
says and leads her out of the room.

Her mother, Maddie and Sophie all follow.

Seven

JENNY DOESN'T KNOW what to do about all the arguing. It's her mother and Sophie; they're furious with each other. Jenny can't work out why. When she asks Sophie, her sister says it's because their mother hates her. When she asks their mother, she says it's between her and Sophie.

They seem to know when Jenny is close by. A door closes, a voice lowers or the argument stops altogether and Sophie thunders upstairs to her bedroom. They must hear her coming. Jenny's mother is right; she's a clodhopper. She's heavier on her feet and has fatter thighs than either of her sisters, even though she's the youngest and not even a teen-ager yet.

When their mother tells Jenny and her sisters they must be at Sunday lunch the next day because there's going to be a family announcement, Jenny wonders if it's connected to all the arguments. She hopes it is, so she can find out what's going on. She's been going to sleep with her Ditchling stone a lot lately, the gentle weight of it easing the ache in her stomach. She found the stone after the arguing started, when she cycled all the way up Ditchling Road, under the A27 bridge, out of the city, up the long hill as far as the South Downs Way, the long-distance path she wants to walk one day. She turned into the empty carpark and stood astride the crossbar. Brighton was out of sight, below the broad rise of the hill. There was no glimmer of sea. Everything was green, yellow, brown or grey.

The stone was lying on the ground where chalky soil met grass, an irregular shape with one edge that was almost sharp. She picked it up without thinking and put it in her saddlebag. It's the largest stone in her collection.

Today, the day of the announcement, it's not one o'clock yet and Jenny's sisters are in her room, one sitting on each bunk bed so she can see both of them but they can't see each other. Jenny is in the chair at her desk where she's been drawing, though she hid her paper and pencils in her drawer when Maddie and Sophie came in, along with the wrapper from the Twix bar she'd just eaten.

Sophie wants to know, not for the first time, if Jenny has found out what the announcement is. Jenny tells her she still has no idea and is Sophie sure it's nothing to do with the arguments she's been having with their mother? Sophie says that's got nothing to do with anything.

All them already know that Grandfather has left three-quarters of his estate to Jenny's father and only a quarter to his other son, Fraser, in Australia. They don't know, however, how much money Grandfather actually left in his will. When Jenny asks, her parents are vague, talking of inheritance tax and capital gains tax and other matters she doesn't understand.

Jenny has heard her parents talk about whether to give another quarter of the money, or at least something extra, to Fraser. She doesn't know what they have decided to do. Perhaps that's the announcement. She suggests this now.

Sophie and Maddie both say they hope not.

Sophie thinks their parents are having a mid-life crisis because they were forty this year and they wish they'd done more with their lives. She reckons they're going travelling, leaving the three of them to fend for themselves. Jenny's stomach shifts when Sophie says this. She hasn't forgotten the boarding school conversation she overheard at Beachy Head the summer before.

Maddie wonders if they're buying a bigger gallery with Grandfather's money.

Or a trust fund, Sophie adds, for her and Maddie's careers. Perhaps even for Jenny to go to university, because what else is there for Jenny to do but that?

Jenny tells Sophie that going to university isn't actually a bad thing and that some people in fact want to go, if they're lucky enough to get in. Sophie just laughs.

Downstairs in the kitchen at one o'clock, Sophie sighs melodramatically and rests her head on her arms. After Grandfather died, Sophie shifted along the table, filling his space so she's nearer Jenny. She mimics him sometimes, hovering in the kitchen doorway saying she isn't hungry then harrumphing down on Jenny's wooden reading chair. She does a good Scottish accent.

Their father comes into the kitchen holding a blue folder Jenny hasn't seen before. He sits at the table with both hands flat on top of the folder as if he's trying to stop it from springing open. He's definitely trying not to smile.

Their mother ladles carrot soup into bowls. It smells like cauliflower cheese for the main course, one of Jenny's favourites. "I can't believe you're all actually here," their mother says.

"It wasn't apparent we had a choice." Maddie is filling up a glass of water at the sink.

Jenny sits down next to Sophie and tears off a chunk of French bread, easing out the soft middle to eat first. She knows why Maddie drinks water before every meal; it's so she won't eat as much. She's read about it in one of her friend Naomi's magazines.

Their mother sits and doesn't pick up her soup spoon. She looks at their father and they smile at each other. "We have some very exciting news," she says. "We've been thinking about something like this for a long time. It's been a pipe dream really, but Grandfather's money has made it possible."

Jenny can feel her heartbeat in her arms and legs.

"We're moving," says their mother, "to Scotland."

"To the Borders," says their father.

"All of us?" Jenny says.

"Of course all of us!" their mother says.

Jenny is aware that neither Maddie nor Sophie has said anything yet.

"It's going to be our new home and our new business," says their mother. "It's a guest house, a bed and breakfast. It's beautiful. It's on three acres. It's in the country. It's called Willowbrae. Daddy's going up to see it tomorrow."

Sophie grunts. Jenny thinks she knows why. Their parents haven't even viewed the property yet and they've made their decision. Her sister looks calm. Her hands are clasped in front of her and she's looking down at the table. Surely this proves she's known all along what the announcement was going to be.

"You can't run the gallery from Scotland," Maddie says.

Their mother tells them they're selling everything — the gallery, the shop and the house. "We know you'll miss your friends and it's a big upheaval, but it's such a beautiful area and to be honest we're sick of England and the attitude here and we're tired of living in a city surrounded by concrete. It's going to be such an adventure."

Sophie clears her throat. Everyone looks at her. "Correct me if I'm wrong, but you're saying we're going to leave Brighton and move hundreds of miles to the middle of nowhere just as I'm taking my GCSEs and Maddie's taking her A levels? And I'll be able to get a helicopter to my drama class in London every Saturday, will I?"

"Of course we're not going right now, darling," says their mother, ignoring the helicopter comment. "We'll wait until your exams are over. We'll move in the summer holidays. We'll find you some drama lessons in Edinburgh or Glasgow. And we'd like Maddie to do her foundation there as well, instead of London, so she's closer to home."

There's a gasp from Maddie.

"It's not as if moving away from London is going to wreck our lives or anything." Sophie stands up. "You're completely mad and completely selfish." She runs out of the kitchen.

Everyone else stays where they were, listening as she thuds up the stairs two at a time. Jenny had got it wrong. Sophie is a good actor, but surely she had no idea this was coming.

"Sophie! Your soup!" shouts their mother.

Jenny waits for the ache in her stomach to come yet it doesn't. She feels oddly still and calm. They're all moving to Scotland together. When Sophie's footsteps are more a vibration than a sound, she leaves the kitchen. When she comes back a few moments later, the others are still there, Maddie resting her chin in her hands, the sleeves of her sweater pulled over her hands like mittens. Their mother is saying something quietly about the Glasgow School of Art. Their father has a grin on his face. Jenny heaves up the atlas she's fetched from the sitting room and lays it open on the table.

"Where's the Borders?" she says. "Where exactly are we moving to?"

At school, Jenny experiments on her friends. She plonks an atlas in front of them in the school library, open on a page showing the whole of the United Kingdom, and asks them where the Scottish Borders are. The clue, she says, is in the words, but they don't even know where England ends and Scotland begins. Naomi traces her finger all over Wales before the others' giggles make her fold up her finger and give in. Vicky and Yumimi know that Scotland is generally in the north but they aren't very quick to find even Edinburgh, although it's written in capitals. At this point, they are told to leave the library, because they're making too much noise.

Then Miss Harkins spoils it all in geography by showing everyone where Jenny is moving on an overhead projector. She shows them where the Scottish Borders are first, then uses Edinburgh and Glasgow as two reference points, placing the Borders at the inverted apex of a triangle. Jenny doesn't see why places must always be seen in relation to where the nearest cities are. Willowbrae, the house they're moving to, is in the country. The nearest town is Peebles, which is not much more than a mile away and is just a small country town. Jenny's father brought back some leaflets from the tourist office after he went up to view the property. There are hills, forests, a river.

Jenny's friends have started to treat her differently now; they're still as friendly, it's just that they sometimes talk as if she isn't there. Jenny feels as if she's already starting to disappear. She doesn't mind. She should probably feel sad, yet instead she feels excited.

She can't wait to live in a big house in the country and go exploring. Her only worry, she tells Naomi, is that Maddie and Sophie are so angry about it. She wishes she knew how to make them happy about moving. She hates all the arguments. Sophie is barely talking to their parents now. Naomi asks Jenny more than once if she's scared about moving and Jenny says no, which is true. Naomi tells Jenny she's brave; Naomi can't imagine ever living anywhere except Brighton.

Grandma and Grandad — Jenny's mother's parents — think the move is foolish rather than brave. They drive down from Sutton Coldfield in their Vauxhall. They stay in Grandfather's old room and don't seem to mind that they're sleeping in a room where someone has died, perhaps because when you're old, you think you should get used to the idea that you will die yourself one day.

Grandma says she doesn't know how often they'll be able to drive all the way to Scotland to visit. It's a terribly long way away. Jenny's mother says that's a shame as she doesn't know how often they'll be able to drive south, as they'll be so terribly busy getting the new business up and running.

Grandma is wearing a pale pink trouser suit that, if you catch sight of her in your peripheral vision, Sophie says, makes you think she's naked. Grandad as usual is wearing fawn trousers with ironed creases down the front. Grandma always calls Jenny by her full name, Jennifer, and Grandad winks at Jenny every time she says it. Grinning, Grandad asks Jenny if she knows what the word *Sassenach* means and, if she doesn't, she should look it up.

Eight

THEY DRIVE ALL THE way to Scotland, four hundred miles, in one day. Their mother drives most of it, apart from when she turns into a service station and says to their father: "Your go. I'm falling asleep. I don't want to kill everyone."

The second service station they stop at, where her mother takes over the driving again, is small, really just a café. There's a pond by the carpark with neat and tidy ducks on it. Scotland feels very close now. Jenny's father has written out the route in large letters on the back of an envelope and closed the ashtray lid on it so it will stay there for the whole journey. Jenny is the backup navigator and holds the map on her knees the entire way. Even without seeing it on the map, she would have been able to tell the Scottish border is close by the way the grass is paler and longer, the hills are lumpier and the sheep are more yellow.

Sitting on Jenny's left and right, Maddie and Sophie listen to music on their Sony Walkpersons, as Sophie calls them. Because the tinny noises are on both sides and somehow balanced like stereo speakers, it isn't as annoying as Jenny thought it was going to be. Anyway, she's reading the best book she's ever read, resting on top of the atlas: *All the Day Long* by Howard Spring. She'd found it in a second-hand bookshop in North Street in Brighton and will keep it forever. She's hoping Peebles has a second-hand bookshop, a library and an art gallery.

Her father, in the front passenger seat, mostly sleeps, even in stop-and-start traffic jams, and even though her mother has the radio on, tuned as always to Radio 4. Jenny likes being in the middle of them all, knowing exactly where each of them is.

Peebles is a street, a bridge, a church tower, a river. In Brighton, you have to go to the hills. In Peebles, the hills come to you. You can probably see the hills and the woods from wherever you stand. You can from inside the car anyway. Jenny watches the side of her mother's face from the back seat; she isn't quite smiling, but there's something relaxed about her cheek, her mouth, even after such a long drive.

"It's so incredibly green," Maddie says.

Jenny asks her what type of green it is and Maddie tells her it's Prussian green.

Their father has been awake ever since they crossed the border into Scotland. He's giving more detailed directions now.

"Bloody hell," says Sophie, when they take a left turn into a leafy lane with no road markings. She brushes off her headphones. "Welcome to the sticks."

"Bicycles," says their father, matter-of-factly, "if you can't cope with walking a mile. And the bus goes along the main road."

The trees are tall and almost meet overhead. The sunlight on the lane is dappled as if they're in a boat on a canal.

"This is it, slow down. This is it." Their father sounds excited, as he had when they'd first decided to open the gallery.

The name of the house is carved into the stone wall by the gates: *Willowbrae*. Their mother indicates right but instead of going through the gateposts, she brakes.

"What on earth are you doing?" Their father looks up and down the lane. There's nothing coming.

"Savouring," says their mother, both hands on the steering wheel. "You can't even see the house. I'm about to move into a house I've never seen except in photographs. It feels very, hmm," she pauses to identify the right word, "decadent."

"I think the word you're looking for, Mother, is insane," Sophie says.

Their mother is right. You can't see even a single roof tile through the thick trees. The gravel driveway is curved, sealed by leaves. There are oaks and a copper beech like the one in the school field at Brighton as well as lots of other trees Jenny doesn't know the names of. She soon will. You can't live in the country and not know the names of trees. "Can we go?" she says.

Her mother laughs. "The suspense." She rolls the car along the drive. One, two, three, four. Jenny counts the seconds until they can see the house. Nine seconds. A nine-second driveway.

They've seen photographs, of course, but the warmth of the yellow-ish stone, bright in the sunlight, is unexpected. Five windows on the first floor, four windows on the ground floor, each with twelve panes. A glimpse of basement windows through bushes. A red front door. There's a triangle above the front door and columns on either side, with a crinkly pattern at the top. Jenny has never seen a such a friendly-looking house.

Nobody's moving. Nobody's saying anything.

As soon as her mother stops the car, Jenny stretches across Maddie and pulls the handle to pop open the door.

"Ow," says Maddie as Jenny wriggles across her sister's lap. She slides out of the car headfirst. Her palm is the first part of her to touch Scotland.

She is soon upright, running up the eight steps to the front door, deliberately putting a foot on each one even though they're so shallow she could easily leap up them three at a time.

At the top of the steps, she stops. Who has the key?

Jenny's mother hugs her from behind. "Daddy's got the key. Have you seen the windows, how the glass is all watery because it's old? That doesn't show up on the photos."

Jenny has read that the house is Georgian. Built about 1800. There's a Victorian part as well, out of sight.

Jenny twists in her mother's hug to look back at the car. Her father is holding the door to the back seat open like a chauffeur. Neither Maddie nor Sophie is getting out.

Jenny runs back down the steps and veers left across the bright green lawn, soft as if it has rained recently, then left again along the side of the house. She keeps running, up four stone steps past a bay window and a patio with tubs of flowers, to another lawn.

Is it still part of Willowbrae? Is this someone else's house? She stops running. She wants to go right around the building. She's a wolf, sniffing the perimeter, making sure it's safe to go inside. But she can't trespass on someone else's property.

"I can't believe it!" Her mother is crossing the lawn, her copper hair red in the sunshine.

"Is this still it?" Jenny says.

"Yes, this is still it. It's all ours."

It's a U-shape, sort of, or an E without the middle stem. When they go all the way around the back to the other side, there's a courtyard with buildings on three sides, all connected. They stand on the gravel and remember how the particulars said a newer section was added in the 1870s to link the original house to the coach house and stables.

The grey slate roof is shining in the sun and the courtyard is in the shadows. The gravel here is mossy and the bottoms of the walls have a greenish tinge to them.

Jenny and her mother keep going until they're back where they started.

The car is empty. The front door of the house is open and a set of keys is dangling from the keyhole. Inside, the hallway floor is covered with geometric tiles, red, blue and yellow, with a red border. Jenny and her mother can hear voices, loud, on the verge of shouting. They wince at each other.

They find the others downstairs in the basement where the kitchen is.

"Aga, butler sink," Sophie is saying, "island, or whatever this thing is called." She thumps the free-standing counter in the middle of the room. "Very *Country Life*. Although the industrial dishwasher spoils things somewhat."

"More *Cold Comfort Farm*, perhaps," Maddie says.

Sophie laughs. "I'm surprised you weren't able to find something a bit more remote, you know, like the Outer Hebrides. I mean, this is virtually civilization. London's only four hundred miles away."

"For Christ's sake, Sophie," their father says. "How many times? London is not the centre of the universe." He crouches down by the Aga, one of his knees cracking.

Sophie kicks a kitchen cabinet.

"Hey!" their mother shouts. "Don't be such a vandal."

"I feel sick." Maddie droops onto a stool. Her face is even paler than usual, her eyes blacker. "Why isn't our furniture here yet? I want to go to bed. My body isn't designed to get up at four a.m."

"Don't worry, Maddie," says Sophie, "we'll look after you. Father will go and get a doctor. It will only take him about five hours there and back."

Their mother manages to get Sophie and Maddie out of the kitchen by suggesting they go with her to make sure they like the rooms they chose from the particulars. When they're the only ones remaining, Jenny asks her father, who is opening and closing the Aga oven doors, if being here makes him feel more Scottish.

Her father tilts his head to think about it. "Yes. I think it does. I always felt a bit of an outsider in England, to be honest, but here, even just being across the border for, what, a couple of hours, I feel much more myself." He stands up and looks around. "I hope they've left instructions somewhere."

Jenny slides open a couple of drawers to help him look.

"Don't you want to go and make sure no one else gets your room?" her father says.

"No point. If I go with them, they'll want the room I want just because it's the room I want. If they don't think I care, then they'll pick the ones they really want, which they've already chosen anyway."

Her father laughs. "Very strategic." He opens his arms and Jenny walks into his hug. "Thank you, by the way."

"What for?"

"For being normal, Jenny Wren, for being normal."

They're allowed to sleep in the guest rooms that night, seeing as the beds there are already set up, but Jenny heaves a mattress into her new little L-shaped bedroom to sleep there. She's going to have a single bed, as there isn't room for the bunks; they'll be put in one of the guest rooms to make it a family room.

There are no streetlights here, and if Peebles gives off an orange glow, Jenny can't see it. She loves her room. It's in the Victorian section at the back, rather than in the Georgian part. Her room isn't large but it has a window seat and a view of trees and hills. Today, she went in every room and looked out every window at the sharp, dark forest and the rounded, pale hills. She can't wait to explore. There might be streams. Burns, they're called here. She might see a fox or even a badger. There's a stile over the drystone wall behind the house she climbed quickly over and back again earlier this evening. She picked up a stick there because its shape reminded her of a running deer. She's put it on her windowsill.

She's more tired than she'd realized when she goes to bed. She switches the main light off, as they haven't unpacked their bedside lamps yet, and finds her mattress in the soft darkness. She lies looking at the sky through the uncurtained window, waiting for her eyes to adjust in case there are stars. There are no buses passing by to rattle the windows as there were in Brighton, only the wind.

Nine

EARLY ON THE SECOND morning at Willowbrae, Jenny is in the coach house looking for traces of blood on the flagstones. The coach house dates from the eighteenth century and she's searching for evidence that it was built on top of the ruins of an older building. She's sure it was. Her family has moved to a violent land, or at least it used to be, where gangs of raiders called reivers roamed as the wars between England and Scotland raged on. The reivers stole livestock, burnt down houses and murdered people. And they did it right here; she can feel it.

Yesterday afternoon, she'd bought a local history book with her pocket money in Arthur's, the second-hand bookshop in Peebles. Last night, reading it as she went to sleep, she dreamt she was living in the coach house and the reivers came. They held her head up by her hair and cut her throat. Blood, sticky as tar, soaked the flagstones and her corpse was left for the wolves to finish off.

"Jenny!" It's her father calling. His voice sounds worn as if he's been shouting for ages. "Jenny!"

Is she supposed to have done something? Are they going out? She runs out of the coach house. "Here, Daddy."

Her father is standing on the back lawn in his slippers, the hems of his jeans wet from the dew.

"Thank God. Come here." He holds her for a few moments, until his sweater makes her nose itch and she pulls away. "Let's go in." He keeps hold of her hand.

He won't tell her what's the matter. They go along the side of the coach house and across the gravel to the back door. Downstairs in the kitchen, Jenny's mother is standing with one hand starfished on the table.

"Jenny, thank God." Her mother holds out her arms. Jenny can't return this hug because her mother is pinning her arms to her sides. "I knew you hadn't gone," says her mother into her hair. "I knew she hadn't," she says to Jenny's father.

"What's happened?" Jenny says. "Tell me."

Her mother lets her go. "They've run away." She sits, as if saying it makes her feel weak. "We thought they'd taken you with them."

Maddie and Sophie gone? It's a joke, bound to be. They'd be back as soon as Sophie got hungry. Maddie didn't get hungry.

Her father grabs an envelope and a set of keys from the sideboard. The keys are for the new second-hand car they collected yesterday. Now that they live in the country, they're a two-car family.

Jenny wants to know where he's going.

"Police station with some photos," her father says. "Then driving around looking for them. Maybe they haven't gone very far."

"They'll be back later," Jenny says.

Her father stops with the keys in his grip.

"What do you mean?" Her mother's voice is sharp. "You know where they are?"

"They're just trying to worry you," Jenny says. "They've probably gone to Glasgow for the day or something."

Her parents look at each other. They don't believe her.

Her father leaves and her mother hands her a piece of paper. "This was in Sophie's room, on her dressing table. They've taken clothes. I can't find their building society passbooks."

The note is in Sophie's small, neat handwriting that always reminds Jenny of Sophie's small, neat nose.

Dear Mother and Father

We must go where we need to be. We have things we must do, just as you do. We'd hoped you'd support us but we can see you have other priorities, that our futures aren't important to you. We don't feel we know you anymore and you've already made it clear you don't know us, particularly your middle child.

Don't try to find us.

Sophie and Maddie

They have both signed it but the words are Sophie's. Ever the drama queen. That reference to the middle child. What does she even mean? It could still be a joke. They could have taken their clothes and passbooks to make it look more real. If they've really gone, wouldn't they have given Jenny a hint? Don't they trust her?

Jenny's legs feel suddenly empty, as if all the bones have been taken out. For a moment, she can't tell if she's standing up or sitting down. She puts a hand on the table as she'd seen her mother doing. Touching her fingers to the wood makes her able to feel her toes again. They haven't even mentioned her in the letter. Because they hadn't wanted to lump her in with their parents?

She's an idiot. She's always thought it was her parents who were going to run away, sail around the world. She thought Maddie and Sophie would get used to Scotland, would grow to love it as much as she already does. They'd find the courses they wanted to do in Glasgow. Glasgow was arty, that's what their mother said.

Her mother is on the telephone, explaining to the police that only two of her daughters are missing now.

"No," her mother is saying, "just because one daughter has turned up, it doesn't mean the others will. Jenny wasn't missing, we just couldn't find her." She tuts. "No, you don't understand. The other two are different."

Jenny runs up the two flights of stairs to her room. She gets down on her knees and looks under her bed, bedside table, chest of drawers and wardrobe in case the note has floated like a feather to the floor. She tugs her furniture away from the walls in case the note has fallen behind them, perhaps lodging on the skirting board. She lifts up the rug in case the note had tickled its way underneath, the way foxtail grass travels up towards your armpit if you put it inside your cuff. The gaps between the floorboards are too small, surely, even for a sliver of paper. There's nothing under her pillow or inside her bed or in her drawers or inside her shoes. There's no note for her anywhere.

She goes back downstairs to the kitchen. Her mother is looking through her leather handbag, most likely for her keys. "We don't even know what time they went. The police are making me feel like some stupid Englishwoman who can't keep track of her children. They say they'll do what they can but they say they're sixteen and eighteen and they left a note so it's not as though they were abducted, God forbid."

Her mother sinks into Jenny's reading chair. "I can't believe they've been so foolish. This is all Sophie. I know it is. Maddie wouldn't sneak off like this. Sophie thinks she can do whatever she likes. She's got no moral compass, absolutely no sense of right and wrong."

Jenny puffs out her cheeks. Her mother is being melodramatic. That's where Sophie gets it from. "It's just, I think, that she wants things her own way."

"Yes and woe betide anyone who gets in her way." Her mother is suddenly furious. Her face darkens as if she's been yanked upside down and the blood has gone to her head. "She'll end up in Holloway prison if she's not careful. I still can't believe she —" She stops as if she's about to say something she shouldn't.

"What can't you believe?" Has Sophie done something Jenny doesn't know about?

Her mother shakes her head and takes a deep, noisy breath. "Never mind. Come on, let's go and look for them." She slaps her hands on her knees and stands. "I can't stay here not doing anything. Take something you can eat for breakfast on the way."

As her mother drives slowly along High Street, looking right while Jenny looks left, Jenny asks her to drop her off because she has an idea.

She has to do it on her own, she tells her mother. Her mother looks suspicious and fearful all at once.

"I'm not running away or anything," Jenny reassures her. "I'll meet you at the tourist information office. You could ask them the best ways to get to London."

"You think that's where they're going?"

"There or New York," says Jenny, making her mother smile then grimace. "I'll see you there in a few minutes."

Her mother gives her a mock salute.

Jenny runs down the street and then slows to a walk as she nears the bridge over the River Tweed. Running will draw too much attention to herself.

They're on the bridge again, a cluster of crows, as she'd hoped. The Goths who Jenny had seen Maddie and Sophie chatting to yesterday when they all went into town. Black eyeliner, black spiked hair, black sweaters and leggings. Silver studded straps around their ankles and wrists. More Maddie's style than Sophie's.

Jenny puts her bag over one shoulder instead of across her chest to make her look older. Or perhaps it makes her look younger. In jeans and a blue-checked shirt, she looks, probably, twelve. Not the nearly thirteen that she is.

This had seemed such a good idea. Now, she isn't so sure.

She aims for the boy sitting on the bridge wall, his back to the river. He has a Mohican haircut, black with green tips, and his cheeks have smiling potential. He has one skinny black leg up on the wall and shiny silver buckles on his boots. Jenny leaves it until she's a few steps away before she tries to make eye contact.

When she says hi he lifts his chin in response. He looks amused rather than threatening.

"I'm Jenny," she says. "I've just moved here from Brighton with my sisters Maddie and Sophie. They were, um, chatting with you yesterday. I think it was you?"

"Might have been," he says. "We're a friendly bunch."

She'd said please and thank you to the man in the bookshop yesterday, but this boy is the first proper Scottish person she's had a conversation with. His accent is different from Grandfather's. Jenny hears rhythms, the tumble of tune, before the sounds become words. She wishes he'd talk and talk.

"The thing is," she says, "we can't find them. We think they've run away. To London."

Now came a smile. "They're not daft then."

"But I love Peebles," Jenny can't help saying. "I wish I'd always lived here."

"You say that now," says the boy. "You've only just arrived. It's pretty enough, but the highlight of the year is when someone dares to cross the road without looking both ways."

A girl with bright blue eyes and thick black eyeliner comes over and sits beside him. There's the chin jerk again. "She likes it here," the boy says to the girl.

She rolls her eyes but grins at Jenny. "Where do you stay?"

"Oh, no, we're not just staying," says Jenny. "We've moved here permanently."

"Right," says the girl. "Stay means live around here. I have to translate for my English cousins too."

"Oh," says Jenny, catching on. "So, then we stay at Willowbrae. It's a guest house up —"

"I know it. Big house. Nice."

She pronounces house *hoose* and there are so many ups and downs in her words, it's as if she's singing.

Jenny looks back at the boy. "Did they talk to you about going?"

"They wanted to know how to get to London." He laughs. "Actually, they said, which way is London?"

"They're not really map people," says Jenny.

"I told them to go the tourist information office," says the boy.

"But then Clara offered them a lift," the girl said quickly.

"To London?"

She laughs. "No, just to Motherwell station. It's on the way to Glasgow, kind of. You can pick up the train to London there."

"Is Clara here?" asks Jenny. "What time did she take them?"

"There was a party last night, so it would have been after that. Pretty late. And, no, Clara's not here. Give her Clara's number, Jem."

The boy takes a black notebook out of his pocket. He writes down a telephone number and tears out the page for Jenny.

The boy and the girl both say "See ya" as Jenny says thank you and walks away. In England, they would have said *wotcha*. The river below the bridge is ruffled. There must be stones near the surface.

They had got on a train. Not in a strange man's car. Jenny curls her fingers tightly around the piece of paper and runs as fast as she can to the tourist information office.

The Godsend arrives the next morning. Jean, a woman who worked for the previous owners, who is very Scottish and has a rough, scratchy voice from smoking too many cigarettes. Jean is going to prepare the house for the guests who are arriving in two days' time, while Jenny's parents drive down to London to find Maddie and Sophie.

Jean is also going to look after Jenny. Who doesn't need to be looked after and who should really be going to London too.

Jenny's mother sits on Jenny's bed to try to explain.

"We're going to be driving around, finding people to talk to, in boring police stations and hostels and offices and colleges. We'll be doing a lot of waiting. You'll be terribly bored. You'll be much better off here. You can help Jean. It will be fun and she'll need your help. And you're starting your new school soon. You don't need the disruption."

Jenny closes the book she's reading and puts it on the bedside table. She reaches to switch the lamp off, leaving her mother sitting on her bed in the dark.

Ten

JENNY WANTED TO KEEP walking east past the hospital where her mother lay to Culloden battlefield and the moor, even though it was raining. She'd never been to Culloden. She could learn about the short, bloody battle that routed the Jacobites. She needed to walk; the flesh on her stomach and hips was pushing against her jeans. She wanted to walk until she couldn't feel her body anymore. She wished she didn't have to go through the glass doors of the hospital and down the glossy corridor that led to her mother's ward.

Piyali was sitting by her mother's bedside and her mother's eyes were still closed. She looked less pale than yesterday.

"You came back." Piyali looked pleased.

"Well spotted." Jenny reached in her bag and held her hand out to Piyali. "Here."

"What is it?" Piyali said.

"Have a look."

Piyali took the little red purse Jenny handed her. "It's lovely. Thank you so much."

"Look inside," Jenny said patiently.

Piyali struggled with the clasp and Jenny resisted helping her. Piyali opened it at last and took out some folded money and a piece of paper.

"There's a hundred and fifty pounds there," Jenny told her. "That will help you keep going for a bit longer. And I've written down the numbers and addresses for a couple of hostels. Remember what I said about going there before they chuck you out of here? I'd go to the Youth Hostel Association hostel rather than the independent one. It might be more expensive, but it's likely to be safer. They have more rules. Oh, and this." Jenny handed her a map of Inverness that she'd found in her hotel room. "I've marked where the hospital and the hostel are. You know how to read maps?"

Piyali nodded unconvincingly. Jenny unfolded the map and laid it at the end of her mother's bed. She pointed to the hospital which she'd circled with a pen.

There was no comprehension in Piyali's face. It might as well have been a map of the moon.

"Never mind." Jenny folded up the map again. "I'll take you to the hostel later on. We'll walk there using the map and then you'll understand how it works."

Piyali was staring at Jenny.

"What?"

"You're being so kind. I'm very grateful."

"The outside world isn't evil, you know. Whatever you've been told. Everyone does their best."

Jenny sat by her mother's bed. Piyali took the cue and, clutching the purse, left the ward.

Looking at her mother's face used to be like looking at surface of the sea: it was always moving, changing. Now, her face was motionless, an empty swimming pool. Jenny sat holding her mother's cool, flat hand. Gradually, it warmed.

For a time, Jenny watched the other patients or the nurses. Other times, she watched nothing at all. Piyali was keeping away a long while. Perhaps she was spending all the money Jenny had given her in the shop at the hospital entrance, unable to resist the boxes of chocolates and magazines.

Jenny felt her mother's hand move. She was certain of it. A tiny jerk, then nothing. She gently squeezed her mother's fingers.

"Mmmmm," her mother murmured, her eyes still shut. "Maddie."

Jenny took her hand away.

Her mother opened her eyes and slowly focused on Jenny. "Maddie," she repeated. The word sounded collapsed; the vowels had fallen out.

"She's not here. Not yet." Jenny resisted adding anything sarcastic.

Her mother looked cross.

It was possible, Jenny realized, that Piyali still thought Jenny was Maddie; Jenny hadn't contradicted her. Piyali may perhaps have told her mother that Maddie had been here.

"I think your *friend*," said Jenny, stressing the word, "may have got us mixed up."

Her mother stretched her mouth into a lopsided smile. "Maddie," she said again.

"No, I'm Jenny." Did her mother really not recognize her?

"Sophie."

Jenny understood now. "You want to see them?"

Her mother moved her head. More of a nod than a shake.

"I'm sure they're coming." Jenny hoped she wasn't lying. It was time to change the subject. "You left that place?" Her mother's eyes weren't comprehending. Jenny would have to say it. "Ben Gallachie."

Her mother made a sound; it wasn't a word.

"You chose to? Because you were ill?"

Her mother shrugged with one shoulder and turned her head to one side.

"It's important that I know," Jenny said. Her mother wouldn't look at her. "Da —," Jenny said, then stopped. "Our father has been looking for me. I think because he's looking for you."

Her mother turned her head back to Jenny, her eyes large. She looked afraid.

"You don't want to see him?" Jenny said.

A head shake this time, surely.

"Why not? What's happened?"

The question seemed too much for her mother. Tears filled her eyes.

"He doesn't know you're here," said Jenny gently.

Her mother shut her eyes. She sighed. It sounded like relief.

Jenny reached into her pocket and gripped the Iqaluit stone. How did you do that, exactly — stop your father from seeing your mother? Post a guard at the hospital entrance like they did in *The Godfather*? She didn't know where her father was now or even if her mother was thinking straight. Her mother's eyes were still closed. What a convenient way of shutting down communication. I have had enough; I will close my face now.

Jenny let go of the stone and gripped her hands together, digging her nails into her skin so she wouldn't cry. She couldn't do this. Not on her own. Phone calls to sisters wouldn't do. Responsibilities were too easily shirked by telephone. She would go in person. She would book Piyali into the youth hostel and first thing tomorrow she would catch a train to London and drag Maddie back with her and Sophie too. Her sisters were coming to Inverness whether they wanted to or not.

"I'm going to get them." She didn't need to say who she was talking about.

Her mother smiled lopsidedly and closed her eyes again.

After she had phoned to book a train ticket, Jenny stayed with her mother for several more hours, sitting by the hospital bed while Piyali came and went, as if mindful that Jenny and her mother might want to be alone with each other. From time to time, Jenny's mother opened her eyes, on each occasion smiling at Jenny, then falling asleep again.

At about five in the afternoon, Jenny told Piyali she was taking her to the youth hostel. They walked together along the streets, mostly in silence but with Jenny occasionally pointing out a landmark to help Piyali find her way back to the hospital.

"I'll be back in a day or so," said Jenny when she'd helped Piyali check in. "They'll have a kitchen here you can use. Do you know how to cook?"

Piyali looked indignant. "Of course. I've taken my kitchen rotations just like everyone else."

"What about shopping? Do you know about supermarkets? How to buy food?"

Piyali didn't look so confident now.

"Come on, then," Jenny told her. "I think I saw a Morrisons around here somewhere."

Eleven

JENNY WAS DOZING off to sleep when the telephone rang. At first she assumed it was the hotel wake-up call she'd booked so she wouldn't miss the train to London.

"Did I wake you?"

Jenny's body softened to cotton wool at the sound of Dominic's voice. "No, well, yes, but that's fine by me." She switched on the light and stuffed an extra pillow behind her back.

Dominic asked her how her *mom* was and she gave him an update. She hesitated, then asked if she could tell him something. Perhaps it was because she was tired, or because she was weary of keeping it all to herself, as if she were the only person in the world who had a difficult family. Dominic was her boyfriend. They were supposed to trust each other. They were supposed to share things.

She took a breath. "The reason I hadn't seen my parents for so long is because they joined a cult, well, a commune. I don't know. It's called Ben Gallachie. I was sixteen and they sold our house and I was so angry with them. They'd already ruined things with my sisters and then they ruined things with me." She stopped and winced while she waited for Dominic's response.

"Wow," he said. "I guessed it was something big, you know, in your family."

"Sorry, though."

"What for?"

"For dumping it all on you. For having a crazy family."

Dominic laughed, then apologized for laughing. "You mean, there's someone out there I could be dating who doesn't have a crazy family?"

"Point taken." Jenny was glad she'd told him, more than glad. She felt hopeful, a flash of belief that she'd be able to help her mother, that she and Dominic would always be together. "There's more."

"Go for it."

Jenny told Dominic her mother had run away and that it looked as if her father was trying to find her.

"Jesus. I only called to hear your voice." Dominic was smiling, she could tell.

"Well, you've certainly heard it."

"I wish I was there. I wish I could help out."

"You are helping, believe me. Thank you for making me laugh."

"Go get your sisters. They should be with you on this."

When they had said goodbye, Jenny hung up and switched off the light. She hated conducting her life by telephone. She hated how phones reduced people to a thin line like dental floss that could so easily snap. And she hated always being the dinghy tied to the back of her parents' yacht, trailing along behind them. Here she was now, lying in a hotel room that smelt faintly of stale smoke, dragged all the way across the frigid, wide Atlantic.

She wished her body hadn't prevented them from making love time and time again at the research centre. She reminded herself that Dominic had said it was okay, even though it so clearly wasn't.

Christopher had happened early on in the second year at university, just as she had been beginning to feel like a normal person again. He started sitting next to her in the lecture theatre. He was English and spoke with a bit of an American accent because he'd spent a couple of years in Washington while his father worked there. He had fair hair and a shapely nose and cheekbones and blue eyes that made him look as if he never had a mean thought. Christopher Williamson. The most ordinary of names.

It had been after a neoclassicism lecture that Christopher had asked Jenny if she wanted to go to the seabird centre in North Berwick with him. She liked that he was interested in birds. They went by train that Saturday and he was so easy to talk to. They took the boat trip to Bass Rock to see the gannets. They saw puffins, guillemots, shags, cormorants and fulmars, even seals. It was June and the sky was clear and sunlight sparkled on the rolling water. Afterwards, they sat for hours in a café drinking milky tea from big white mugs and eating chips covered in salt, vinegar and ketchup from the same plate. They went for a long walk along the beach. Jenny took her sandals off and teased Christopher until he took off his shoes as well, and Jenny saw that his toes were as shapely as his face and she wanted to carve his feet out of marble.

They walked until they were hungry again and turned around to go back to a pub they'd seen with chairs and tables overlooking the sea. Jenny drank wine and Christopher drank beer and Jenny started wondering what time the last train went back to Edinburgh. They watched the sun set and the moon rise and Jenny stopped worrying about the time and they walked down to the edge of the water again. They sat on the dry sand and Christopher put his arm around her and they kissed. It was dark and they were away from the pub so no one could see them. Christopher reached both hands around her and unclasped her bra, and Jenny shivered as she felt his hands on her bare skin. They lay down on the sand together. He slid his hands all over her and she felt smooth and beautiful and she kissed him and pressed her fingers into his shoulder blades and down his spine.

When his fingers reached between her legs, she tensed and started to feel each of his fingertips in a different way. Her skirt was up and he was tugging at her underwear and she said, "No, Chris."

She didn't mean no, never, just not at this moment, perhaps not for many moments. She didn't want this right now, tonight, on the cooling sand. She wanted them to lie together, her head on his chest, kissing now and then, listening to the waves breaking, wondering how high the tide would rise and should they move farther back up the beach. Sleeping, eventually, until the sound of gulls woke them and they could sit up sleepily and watch the dawn and not think of Turner or Impressionists because they had the real thing in front of them.

Her underwear was around her thighs now and Christopher was undoing his trousers. She tried to say slow down with her hands. He was kissing her and she didn't want to hurt his feelings by breaking the kiss so she could speak. She tried to push his pelvis away, burrow away from him into the cold sand. He was strong and it was too late and he was inside her and it hurt because it was the first time and Jenny wondered if she would leave blood on the sand and someone would see it and know what had happened. She shoved at his hips again and tried to push him out of her.

Christopher rolled off and lay flat on his back beside her. "What's going on?"

Jenny squeezed her eyes shut to force the words out. "It just feels, you know, too rushed."

"We were getting on, weren't we?"

"Yes." She mustn't say sorry, she mustn't.

"Shit, Jenny, you can't do this to people. It's humiliating." He was doing up his trousers while he was lying down, sliding the tongue of his belt through the buckle. "This has never happened to me before." He stood up, his silhouette black against the starry night sky. Jenny eased herself up.

He walked away. Jenny stayed sitting on the sand and watched his form wane into the darkness. She moved to another piece of sand and pulled up her underwear, wishing she had some tissues to wipe the stickiness between her legs. She lifted her hips to pull her skirt down, then slipped her arms out of her sleeves to do up her bra. She didn't understand how they had both ended up offended. She pulled her knees up to her chest and hugged them while listening to the waves. She stayed there until she fell asleep and woke to the sunrise and

Christopher was still nowhere to be seen. She watched the sunrise on her own, making herself think of her favourite Turner painting, *Sunrise with Sea Monsters*, which she loved because of its title and because it was painted in Margate, of all places, and there weren't any sea monsters in it, not that she could see.

She stood up, shivering, and brushed the sand off her clothes. She walked briskly back towards the town, and as she left the beach to cross over some grass she stooped to pick up a small, dark pebble. She pushed it into her pocket and kept walking. She had slept all night outside at the edge of the sea and that was remarkable and wonderful. That was what the stone would mark, not what had occurred earlier in the evening.

She walked quickly to get warm, up through the town to the railway station, expecting to find Christopher there. He wasn't. No one was. It was Sunday. Four hours until the first train left for Edinburgh. She went back into the town and walked around until she found a café that was open. She ordered tea and toast and went to the ladies' toilet to wash her face and wipe between her legs with some paper towels. There was blood on her underwear. She would throw them away when she got home, but for now she put a pad of toilet paper in them so the wetness wasn't as unpleasant.

Christopher wasn't on the train. She hid around the corner of the station building watching to see who else boarded before she did. Two couples. One woman on her own. Jenny got into the same carriage as her.

When she got back to her room in the university halls of residence, Jenny had a long shower then sat at her desk and started her neoclassicism essay on Winckelmann's belief that art should aim at noble simplicity and calm grandeur, which she thought was an interesting idea but not right at all. She placed the dark pebble from North Berwick next to the other stones on the narrow ledge along the wall by her bed.

At the art history lecture on Tuesday, Christopher sat in the back row while she sat three rows, as usual, from the front. She didn't try to talk to him and he didn't try to talk to her. She had no idea how he'd got home. It was surprising how easy it was not to cross paths or even make eye contact.

Jenny didn't have any friends at university she knew well enough to tell what had happened. She wrote a letter to her school friend Helen in London and Helen rang as soon as she got the letter and told Jenny to go to the police. Jenny said, no, it hadn't been like that. She and Christopher had misunderstood each other and Jenny had learnt she'd have to be more careful in future. Talking of being careful, said Helen, was he wearing a condom? No, she told Helen, he hadn't worn a condom. Yes, she would let her know as soon as her period started and, yes, she would go to the doctor to get tested for sexually transmitted diseases, including HIV. Yes, she would ring in future, not write a bloody letter. Thankfully, twelve days later, Jenny's period started and she rang Helen to let her know. She never did go to the doctor.

Twelve

JENNY IS BEHIND in maths — though catching up — and ahead in English and history. Of her three new friends at the school in Peebles, she likes Helen best. She loves how Helen's long brown hair curves around her oval face like water around a rock in a stream, how her freckles are blurred, as if they're floating under her skin. She likes going to Helen's after school and eating — if Helen's mother isn't home yet — cheese and crisp sandwiches that you crunch up with the flat of your hand before you take a bite.

She likes Wendy and Mhairi too, very much. Wendy is short and blonde and Mhairi is gingery and tall and they're both pretty and giggle a lot, which means they're different from Jenny. Helen is more similar to Jenny: quieter and brown-haired.

"So your father's Scottish and your mother's English." Helen is clarifying. Her accent, like the rest of her, has no hard edges. They're sitting on their own in the living room with plates on their knees and the television on. It isn't that this isn't allowed at Jenny's house, it just isn't something they do.

Jenny nods and takes a bite of sandwich, trying not to get crumbs on the carpet. "He was grown-up before he moved to England, I think. In Brighton he didn't sound Scottish, but now we live here he does."

"That's weird."

"I know. I didn't think accents changed."

"Perhaps you'll start sounding Scottish," Helen says.

"I'd like to."

"I'll give you lessons." Helen laughs. They're quiet while they both take another mouthful. On the television, a black-and-white cat with an English accent is standing upright in a garden while a multi-coloured butterfly flies past. At least it's supposed to be a cat; it looks more like a squirrel. Jenny doesn't know if this is deliberate or because the artist can't draw very well.

On the wall above the television there's a small, dark wooden cross with a bronze Jesus attached to it, glowing in the soft light coming through the net curtains. Helen has told Jenny she goes to church with her parents every Sunday, and Jenny has pictured yellow and red stained glass outlined thickly with lead. She wants now to tell Helen she's never been to church. In a church, but never *to* church.

Helen has questions about Jenny's sisters next. It's a conversation that started a couple of weeks ago and continues, sometimes, when Mhairi and Wendy aren't around. Jenny tells Helen that her sisters are at college in London now, that they ran away. She has to stop mid-sentence to seal her lips together, as if that will stop the tears seeping out of her eyes.

"I'm sorry." Helen puts her plate on the floor. "I didn't mean to upset you."

Jenny shakes her head and wipes her eyes on the back of her hand. A shred of cheese falls to the floor and she bends to pick it up. Bending over must squeeze the air out of her lungs because she lets out a sob.

Helen tucks her hair behind her ears. It's what she does when she is concentrating. She does it a lot in maths. Neither of them are saying anything; it doesn't seem to matter.

After a while, Jenny is able to start talking again. She tells Helen that her parents found her sisters staying in a hostel near the art college that

Maddie was planning to go to. The college helped look for them. "I was really annoyed. My parents left me here with Jean, you know, who works at Willowbrae. My parents call her the Godsend. Actually it was fun in the end. She showed me how to use the dumb waiter. Our very first guests came before my parents got back."

"So your parents let your sisters stay in London?"

"They're sixteen and eighteen. There's not a lot they could do." Jenny isn't sure if she believes this but it's what she's heard her parents say. "I talk to Maddie on the phone. There's a phone box near their flat."

"What about your other sister?"

"Sophie. She won't talk to us. Not to me or my parents. She won't even write. I write to her every week. She never answers. She didn't even sign my birthday card. Maddie signed it for both of them. She tried to make it look like Sophie's writing but I knew it wasn't. Maddie sent me an Everything but the Girl album and said it was from both of them. I can't ask Maddie about Sophie because she gets cross. She's sick of everyone asking about Sophie all the time."

Jenny feels like a bath when you pull the plug out. Everything is emptying, sucking out of her. She hasn't told anyone else about the letters. Not even Jean, who knows a great deal about Jenny's family by now. It's too embarrassing; to write and have nothing come back, week after week. A broken boomerang.

The cat on the television is talking to a rabbit.

Helen wants to know where Jenny is posting the letters. Jenny tells her she's checked with the post office that the post box she uses is emptied regularly and it is.

"Have you asked Maddie if the letters are definitely arriving?"

Jenny shakes her head. Helen looks at her questioningly. "I don't want to hear that Sophie burns them or throws them straight in the bin."

"Plus Maddie might get cross that you're asking about Sophie again."

"And ask why I don't write letters to her." It's difficult talking about it. Yet easier than not talking about it.

"There's no way Maddie would be doing anything?" asks Helen. "You know, hiding your letters or intercepting Sophie's?"

"She's not scheming like Sophie."

Helen puts her plate back on her knees and eats more of her sandwich. "I don't get why Sophie won't answer your letters," she says after a while.

A cloud must have covered the sun because the Jesus on the wall isn't gleaming anymore.

"Because she didn't want to move to Scotland and I did. That puts me on Mummy and Daddy's side." Jenny feels herself blush. "I mean, Mum and Dad." She isn't supposed to say Mummy and Daddy; she knows that from Brighton. It makes her sound posh. And childish.

Helen doesn't seem to notice the correction. She shakes her head with frustration, her hair sliding around her shoulders. "You weren't the one who moved. It was your parents. Are you sure there's not more to it? There must be."

"I haven't done anything. Not that I'm aware of."

"Why does she hate Scotland so much, anyway?" Helen sounds curious, rather than insulted.

"She doesn't, really, I don't think," Jenny says carefully. She doesn't want to offend or lie. "It's just that we moved too far away from London. The centre of the universe. Brighton was only sixty-five miles away. An hour on the train."

"But she's in London now." Helen presses her finger on the crumbs on her plate and lifts them to her mouth.

"Exactly. She's got what she wanted. She's doing the course she wants. She got good GCSE results. You know, like Standards."

"I know what GCSEs are. We're not like English people. We actually know about places that exist outwith Scotland." Helen isn't being mean, just matter-of-fact.

Jenny likes the word *outwith*, which means outside of something. She has learnt it since moving to Scotland. She hasn't used it herself yet, although she intends to.

Helen looks at the television, but she doesn't really seem to be watching. "I reckon she's having a bairn."

"No, she can't be pregnant. It would mess up her career plans. And I can't be an aunt, thank you very much. I'm only thirteen."

"Then she's in jail." Helen giggles. "For drug dealing. Caught by the polis," she adds, putting on a Glaswegian accent.

"Mibbe." Jenny tries out her Scottish accent, then laughs. She has no idea why they are both finding all of this funny.

"Give her my address," Helen says, suddenly serious. "Tell her I'm your friend and she can write to you here. I bet it's only because of your parents that she doesn't write back. She's afraid they'll read her letters. My mum's always trying to read my diary. Give her this address and she'll write to you here. I know she will."

Thirteen

IT'S FOUR DAYS until Christmas and two days until school breaks up. The Christmas tree Jenny and her mother have got from High Street — even though her father kept saying they could go into the forest and get their own — is decorated and up in the living room in front of the window. You can smell the pine needles. The car still smells of pine needles too. Jenny likes having a part of the forest indoors. She has her legs hooked over the arm of the sofa and is reading an Agatha Christie. Her mother is reading the paper and her father is watching television, channel hopping. It's becoming annoying; she's read the same sentence at least three times. It's nice, though, that they're all together in the same room and don't have any guests for a change. The previous owners of Willowbrae had closed at Christmas and opened up for New Year and her parents have decided to follow the same tradition.

"Christ," Jenny's father says. Jenny looks up from her book and her mother looks up from *The Guardian*. On the screen, a fire is burning in darkness. People in fluorescent jackets are moving about, glowing as though they're on fire too.

"It's Lockerbie," Jenny's father says. "That's, what, thirty miles from here."

Jenny swings her legs back to the seat.

"Oh, no." Her mother puts her hand up to her mouth.

The reporter is saying a plane has fallen out of the sky. Houses are on fire.

A Pan American Airways jumbo jet has crashed. There were two hundred and forty-four people on board and so far, the man on the television is saying, there are no reports of survivors. They'd been going to America. They'd left Heathrow expecting to land in New York five hours later. If the plane hadn't crashed, they still wouldn't be there yet.

People are being interviewed. They saw a huge fireball. Someone says they were driving on the motorway when their car was hit by something that came from above. Another reporter is saying there's a crater in the middle of Lockerbie that's twenty feet deep and a hundred feet long. The prime minister is shocked. The Queen is shocked. When the reporter says that, Jenny's parents don't even snigger or get cross as they normally do whenever the Queen or Maggie Thatcher are mentioned.

The news ends and Jenny's father reaches for the remote control. He turns the volume right down but leaves the picture on. Jenny's mother's face is scrunched up and her father is gently shaking his head.

Jenny realizes she's closed her book on her thumb and is pressing down on it with her other hand. It hurts.

"I mean, we're not on the flight path but bloody hell," says her father.

"Those poor people, all expecting to be home for Christmas," says her mother. "Can you imagine?"

Jenny has never been on a plane, though she's seen enough of them in films. She imagines falling through the air still strapped to the seat, the seat belt breaking, falling headfirst out of the chair into darkness as thick as mud. Or towards the lights of a town, like upside down stars.

They all sit talking and not talking for some time, watching the silent television screen, looking out for the next news flash.

Jenny has an urge to ring Helen. She wonders if Naomi in Brighton is watching. She hasn't thought about Naomi for ages. It's sad how you forget people. Perhaps Maddie will go to the telephone box to ring to check the plane hasn't fallen anywhere near them, if she even realizes

Lockerbie is in Scotland. Jenny knows Sophie won't ring.

Upstairs in her room, she doesn't draw the curtains; she doesn't want to block out the sky. At first she thinks she'll lie awake all night, the window making night-squares that float sometimes miles away, other times within reach. Yet she does fall asleep and she doesn't dream about falling planes. She dreams that her parents decide to invite guests for Christmas after all and all the guests sit around the kitchen table in front of the Aga opening Jenny's presents.

Of course it's all everyone is talking about at school. Even the teachers don't seem able to concentrate.

"Was it a bomb, do you think, Miss?" says Nicholas after Miss McInnes has taken the daily register. "Or a mid-air crash?"

Jenny likes it when Nicholas speaks in class; she's had a crush on him since she joined the school and it gives her an excuse to look at him. Not that it's right to think about him in that way in a situation like this.

Miss McInnes is pale. What if she knows someone in Lockerbie? What if her parents live there and were in one of the houses? You can't tell by looking at someone what they have inside them.

Miss McInnes says she doesn't know and that probably nobody knows yet. She doesn't say anything sarcastic as she usually does, something like not being an aeronautics expert. She suggests they have a minute's silence for everyone who has died in the plane and down on the ground. Jenny tries to send comforting thoughts to all the families who will be missing someone this Christmas. She has to stop, though, after a few moments; she's starting to cry.

It takes all that day and evening before she realizes. It isn't even a realization exactly; her mind works it out while she's asleep. She's only been in bed for an hour when she wakes up. The Willowbrae stone on her stomach — she found it in the woods while her parents were in London looking for her sisters — hasn't worked; she can feel an ache.

She knows why Sophie hasn't been replying to her letters. Her sleeping mind is cleverer than her waking mind.

She can feel the knowing in her fingers and wrists and armpits. It creeps into her stomach and churns up the pain there and saliva gushes; she's going to be sick.

Standing up, her stomach is calmer. She goes downstairs. She can hear voices in the living room. Of course, it's the woman who runs the gallery and whose husband is a doctor. Moira and Tom.

They each have a glass of red wine in one hand and they're laughing. Her father is saying something about an unmade bed.

"What's the matter, Jenny Wren?" Her father is sitting back in his armchair, legs crossed, his smile left over from making everyone laugh.

Jenny stays by the door. "She's dead, isn't she? Why didn't you tell me?" She feels calm. Her voice isn't shouting. "She's dead and you didn't tell me."

"Is she sleepwalking?" says Moira.

"I'm not sleepwalking. I'm asking a question."

Her mother rushes over and Jenny raises her arms to stop the hug. "Have you had a nightmare?" Her mother turns to Moira. "Hardly surprising with that awful, awful crash."

"I think we're all having nightmares." Moira takes a sip of wine.

"They didn't have a chance in that plane," Jenny's father says. "It was a flying coffin."

"I've been writing to her every week and she's never replied," Jenny says. "She's dead, isn't she, and nobody's told me."

"Oh, darling."

Moira looks confused. "Who's died?"

"No one." Jenny's mother puts a palm on Jenny's forehead. "You've got a temperature."

Jenny lets herself be hugged. The tears are coming now. Her blood is bubbling and spitting like when they leave the kettle on the Aga too long.

"Oh, for God's sake." Jenny's father stands. He's got his foot on one of his art magazines. "That stupid girl has got you all worked up." He goes to Jenny, puts his palms gently either side of her face and kisses her forehead. "She's so bloody self-centred."

Jenny's mother guides her out of the room. "Sophie's fine, darling," she says as they go upstairs. "She's just being Sophie, the drama queen. She's just horribly cross with me and Daddy. Not with you."

Jenny doesn't go to school in the morning, even though it's the last day of term. She hasn't slept all night and her face is swollen and her head is burning from so much crying. When her mother brings her an Aspirin fizzing in a glass of water, Jenny tells her she doesn't want to have Christmas. She wants them all to go to London to see Sophie. She has absolutely no proof that Sophie is all right. Not one letter or telephone call. Not even a signature on a birthday card.

Jenny tells her mother that if they don't all go together, she'll go on her own. Her mother opens her mouth to say something then just nods at Jenny instead.

☞

At five o'clock in the morning on Christmas Eve, Jenny is sitting in the back seat of the car wrapped in a sleeping bag. There's still a scent of pine needles in the car, as if they've brought the Christmas tree with them. They haven't brought the tree but they have brought other pieces of Christmas. A cooked turkey and Christmas pudding that they can heat up in the oven. Mince pies. Packets for making bread sauce and chestnut sauce even though they aren't packet people. A hexagonal tin of Quality Streets and string bags of walnuts, Brazil nuts and hazelnuts still in their shells. They've even remembered the nutcracker. And there are other bags too that only the person who had packed them is allowed to open.

Jenny looks back as her mother drives them away, just in time before the driveway curves and they lose sight of Willowbrae. They've deliberately left a light on in the kitchen, although their staff member, Jean, says she'll check the house every day. The low glow from the basement level makes it look as if the house is floating up to the sky. Or as if the kitchen is on fire. What if there really is a fire? No one will be there to call the fire brigade. Willowbrae will burn to the ground. It will be like

Manderley in *Rebecca*. People will see a glow and think the sun is rising.

This is how it feels to get your way. This is how Sophie must always feel. It isn't what Jenny expects; it makes her feel old. Actually, she feels young and old at the same time. This journey is her responsibility; it's up to her to make it go right. That's why she feels old. She only really feels young because she's wrapped in a sleeping bag like a baby. If she takes the sleeping bag away, she won't feel young at all.

It's still dark when they drive past Lockerbie on the M74. They can't see anything except street lights to the east where the town is and a few lit-up windows. There are no fires, no flashing lights. It looks like anywhere else. Jenny's mother switches the radio off when they see the Lockerbie turn-off sign and doesn't put it back on again until they are in England.

A third of the way down a long road of red-brick terraced Victorian houses with white-painted windows, Jenny's mother slows the car and points up at a first-floor bay window. "That's the sitting room."

Jenny's parents had found the flat for Maddie and Sophie after they'd tracked them down in London. They'd paid the deposit and the first three months' rent and crossed their fingers that both Maddie and Sophie would be eligible for housing benefit as well as college grants. They were.

Her mother has to drive for another hundred yards or so before they find room to park. Jenny suggests she goes to the flat first, on her own, and her parents agree. At least her father does. Her mother doesn't say anything. She yanks the handbrake until it creaks and keeps her hand on it as if she might change her mind and drive off again.

Jenny takes a bag with her from the back seat — it's Maddie's, really, the bag she used for hockey — and walks closely along the garden walls, rather than on the road edge of the pavement, in case Sophie comes out of the house and sees her. There are soggy cigarette ends here and there on the pavement, flattened by feet and rain, and a trail of Kentucky Fried Chicken packaging in the gutter.

Jenny presses the latch of the gate and goes through. It's only three steps to the front door which has two doorbells. There are no names beside the doorbells but Jenny knows from writing letters they are in flat A. Top button. She pictures the postperson sliding her letters to Sophie through the silver letter box, week after week. Perhaps an old lady lives in the downstairs flat who is so lonely she steals other people's post.

Jenny pushes the bell. The vibration flashes down to her toes, flipping her stomach over on the way down. It will be better if Maddie answers the door. If Sophie answers, she might slam the door in Jenny's face and they'll be back to square one. Just four hundred miles closer, plus the thickness of one door.

They're in the middle of London and yet it's quiet; there's just a distant roar that, if you close your eyes, you can imagine is a stream. A burn. A bird is calling. A robin. The Christmas bird. Jenny painted a robin, sitting on the handle of a garden fork, on the card she made for Jean. For Maddie's card, she painted a snowman holding an artist's palette. For Sophie, a snowman wearing a theatre mask. For her parents, she painted a scene of Willowbrae in the snow. She's nervous about everyone's reactions to her childish paintings, but she's had such a lovely time creating them she's decided — courageously — that it will be worth it.

Someone is thudding down the stairs. Jenny steps back as the door opens. It's Maddie.

"I'm not on my own. Mummy and Daddy are out in the car," Jenny whispers as she rushes into the shared hallway. "Happy Christmas."

Maddie looks scared then giggles. "Bloody hell. Bloody, bloody hell."

"You haven't said Happy Christmas."

"Happy Christmas," Maddie says.

"Or hugged me."

Maddie's thin shoulders fold up like a fan inside Jenny's arms. Maddie's black hair still smells of sandalwood.

"I can't believe you're here," Maddie says. "Blimey, you've grown. You're going to be taller than me, damn it."

They stand looking at each other. Jenny doesn't have a plan for this next bit, how to get from here to upstairs.

Jenny can tell from Maddie's face that Sophie is in.

"Let's you and I go up first," Maddie suggests. "We'll get the parents in a bit."

So Sophie isn't in prison. She hasn't been sold into the white slave trade. She hasn't gone on a worldwide theatre tour or moved to Hollywood.

Maddie opens one of the two doors in the hallway and Jenny follows her upstairs, careful not to knock the bag against the wall. The stair carpet is worn and there's beige, flowery wallpaper on the walls. It isn't how she's imagined a London flat would be.

On the landing, Maddie tips her head towards a door at the front of the flat.

"Sophie," calls Maddie. "Guess who was at the door?" Maddie takes Jenny's arm. "You go in first," she whispers, nodding encouragement. Her eyes are bright.

Sophie is sitting on a red sofa scattered with blue cushions reading sheets of paper. She looks up and, when she registers who it is, stands.

Jenny tries to smile but her face won't cooperate. Sophie is supposed to be opening her arms for a hug, yet she's just standing there with her fingers in the front pockets of her jeans.

"And there was I thinking it was Father Christmas at the door." Sophie looks the same. She doesn't look as if she's had a baby or caught AIDS. Her fair hair is longer, past her shoulder blades now. That's all that's different. She's even wearing the same jeans.

"Where are they?" Sophie takes her hands out of her pockets and crosses her arms.

"Out in the car," Jenny says.

"Sent you as the advance guard, did they?"

"Actually, it was my idea to come. To London, I mean. I've got something for you." Jenny puts the bag on the floor. "You left it at . . . You left it behind."

Jenny slides a violin case out of the bag. She holds it out towards Sophie, whose face is as blank as the new eraser in Jenny's pencil case, still wrapped in its cellophane. Surely this will get a reaction.

Sophie doesn't take the violin case, so Jenny lays it on the carpet and opens the clasps. She loves the clunk they make as they pop apart. "It's yours. You should have it with you. Don't you miss it? I mean, you could play it just for fun. You're so good at it. I don't know if it's true what Mummy says about people only being able to be good at one thing, do you?"

"You bitch," Sophie says. "I didn't think you had it in you."

A hot shiver of anger shakes Jenny. "What's that supposed to mean?" she shouts. "What have I done?"

"You know exactly what it means."

"I don't think she knows, Sophie," Maddie says.

Sophie rolls her eyes. "Of course she knows. Why would she give me this, otherwise?" She flicks her hand at the violin.

"What don't I know?" Jenny says.

Sophie tightens her folded arms.

"Tell me!" Jenny is shouting again. "No one ever tells me what's going on. I'm not a baby. Why haven't you phoned, not once? Why have you ignored all my letters? How could you!"

Sophie is calm when she speaks. Jenny hates how she's able to make her face so blank. "You can't sit on the fence, Jenny. You can't be everyone's friend."

What does Jenny have to do to get through to her? "How am I sitting on the fence? You ran away without even telling me. You just disappeared."

"You would have come with us, would you?" Sophie says.

Jenny hesitates. "It's not my fault if I like Scotland."

"This has nothing to do with Scotland," says Sophie, "not specifically. If our dear parents want to hide away in the wilds of God-knows-where, that's their lookout."

Nothing to do with Scotland? Jenny looks at Maddie, who scrunches up her face. "I don't get it. Just tell me."

"Our parents," sighs Maddie, "haven't been very nice to Sophie."

Sophie sits back down on the sofa with a harrumphing sound.

"What have they done?" Jenny says. "Apart from move."

"They think," says Sophie, placing both hands neatly on her thighs, "I'm a murderer."

"Mummy accused Sophie," says Maddie slowly, as if to give Sophie plenty of time to stop her, "of killing Grandfather."

Jenny feels stupid, as if she's come last in an exam. All her exams ever since she'd started school. "How . . ." she starts to say but gives up. "But no one killed Grandfather," she says at last. "He died in his sleep."

Propped up on four pillows in his nylon pyjamas.

"Not according to the parents," Sophie says.

"It doesn't make any sense," Jenny says. "Even if someone had killed him, *you* wouldn't do something like that."

"Of course she wouldn't," Maddie agrees.

No one has killed Grandfather. That sort of thing happens only in films and Agatha Christie novels. How can their mother even think such a thing? What does their father think? Something must have sparked the idea. She daren't ask. If she questions Sophie to gather more information, then Sophie will think she agrees with their mother.

Jenny scans the weeks and months since Grandfather died. She's missed something in the family as huge as the Lockerbie crash; she hasn't been paying attention. "Hang on, when did she say this to you?" Jenny is remembering the arguments at their Brighton house. After Grandfather died. Before the Willowbrae announcement.

"You might be clever at school, Jenny," says Sophie, "but you're a dullard when it comes to real life."

The doorbell rings.

"Shit." Maddie looks out the window. "It's them."

"They're not coming in," Sophie says.

"If they come in, they can apologize," Jenny says. "I'm sure they will. I know they will."

"You're going to have to make a choice, Jenny," says Sophie. "Them or us."

"Give her a break, Sophie," Maddie says. "She's only thirteen. What do you want her to do, move in with us?"

Sophie shrugs.

"No, really," Maddie continues. "This has nothing to do with Jenny. And we did abandon her. We should have told you we were going," she says to Jenny.

The doorbell rings again.

Jenny wants to go and answer it and Sophie can tell. "That's right. Run along to Mummy and Daddy."

Obviously nothing she or Maddie has said has sunk in.

Jenny goes downstairs to the front door. She doesn't rush. She's trying to think. Someone has taken a pair of scissors and cut her brain into tiny pieces. The violin. What an idiot, bringing it for Sophie.

By the time she opens the door, Maddie is right behind her. There are smiles and hugs. Before they go upstairs, Jenny tells her parents what Sophie has told her. "You can't really think that."

Her father puffs out his cheeks and sighs. Her mother raises her eyebrows, then suggests they go upstairs and put the kettle on. She's got the mince pies.

Sophie is standing at the top of the stairs looking down. She's carrying her coat. "If you're coming up, then I'm going out."

Her mother tells her it's time to grow up.

"Please don't go, Sophie," says Jenny quickly. She doesn't care if she's begging. She wants to sort this mess out and they can only do that if they're all in the same place. "I haven't seen you for five months."

Sophie hesitates, then drapes her coat over the banisters. "For you," she says to Jenny. "Not for them."

Jenny and Sophie stay on the landing while the others go into the kitchen. They can hear their mother filling the kettle. She's talking too loudly about not bothering to heat up the mince pies. Their father is asking Maddie, also too loudly as if they're in a bad play, where he can find the plates.

"I'm sorry I brought the violin," Jenny tells Sophie. "I didn't realize. Though I still think you should have it because you're so brilliant at it. Anyway, I'm sorry."

"Stop saying sorry. They're the ones who should apologize." Sophie's fingers are back in her jean pockets, pushing her elbows out at odd angles.

"Yes, they should." Jenny turns and goes into the kitchen. It's small and painted bright yellow and someone — Maddie, surely — has painted blue owls on the cabinets.

Her father is getting mugs and plates out of cupboards and her mother is taking the lid off a tub of mince pies. Maddie is sitting at the little table doing nothing, the sleeves of her black sweater pulled over her hands. It's like walking into the kitchen at Brighton, although not really.

"Could you say sorry to Sophie?" Jenny whispers to her mother. "She's ever so upset. I'm sure everything would be fine if you apologized."

"Oh, Jenny," her mother says at normal volume. "I know you want everyone to get on all the time and for there to be blissful harmony, but Sophie did something very wrong and it's not that simple."

Jenny's father says he'll go and talk to Sophie. Jenny and Maddie follow him into the living room where Sophie is back on the sofa, pretending to read what Jenny can now see is a script.

"I'm sorry, Sophie," their father says. "We should have done this a lot sooner, come to see you. We've been so busy setting up Willowbrae, getting settled in. And we thought a cooling-off period would do us all good. But that's no excuse."

Sophie doesn't say anything.

Their father crouches down. "The thing is, as you know, Mummy's got it into her head that all your, you know, shenanigans meant that Grandfather couldn't get to his pills in time and that, unfortunately, precipitated his death. Now I don't know, nobody knows, exactly what happened. We know his angina got worse. We know he had a heart attack. Maybe that would have happened anyway. Maybe his time had come."

He stands up again, wincing as if his knees hurt, and sits at the other end of the sofa. He runs his hand through his hair. His hair is fair so the grey in it looks silvery, Christmassy really. There aren't any Christmas decorations in the flat, Jenny realizes. Not one.

"You do see, don't you," says their father, "that hiding his pills was a dangerous thing to do?"

The poltergeist. Grandfather said he had a poltergeist who kept moving his pills. That or he was going senile, that was what he said. Once, Jenny found some of his pills in the downstairs loo. She took them back to Grandfather's room and he'd grunted at her. Perhaps he'd thought she was the one hiding them.

"I didn't *hide* them," Sophie says. "I just moved them a couple of times. Just for a joke. I thought it would help keep his faculties sharp. It was just a game. He liked games."

Jenny couldn't remember Grandfather ever playing games.

"Everyone likes games when they know they're playing one," says their father, "but not when someone's playing tricks on them. That's one-sided, that's not a game. And you did do it quite a few times, didn't you, not just a couple." He pauses. Jenny knows what he's doing. He's pretending he's calm, that there's all the time in the world, that he's thinking off the top of his head and hasn't been planning this conversation throughout the whole car journey.

"I just want to suggest —" he pauses again "— that moving or hiding his pills, whatever we want to call it, was an irresponsible thing to do. Can you see that? Even doing it once, let alone doing it over and over, and after Grandfather started having his falls." He doesn't wait for Sophie to respond. He flicks up his eyes as if he's still thinking on the spot. "So it's actually just a short leap, mentally, from that possibility of something bad happening, to your mother thinking you may have done something deliberately. You see what I mean?"

Jenny hears her mother coming along the landing. She turns to try and stop her coming in by holding up both hands. She's going to ruin it all. Her mother ignores her. She's in the room and she's standing in front of Sophie with her hands on her hips. Maddie, by the radiator, closes her eyes.

"I know you're young," says their mother, "and perhaps you didn't realize the full implication of what you were doing, but, no, I'm not going to apologize. I warned you. I caught you at it and I warned you, but you didn't stop. You never do. If it wasn't for you, Grandfather would still be with us."

"And you'd still be in Brighton running a nice, clean art gallery instead of standing up to your elbows in a sink of bacon grease every morning. You didn't even like him." Sophie says it with a laugh. "None of us liked him."

"That," says their mother, leaning forward into Sophie's face, "has nothing to do with anything. He was your grandfather and he deserved to be treated with respect."

"He wasn't even your father. Why do you care so much?"

Their mother is shaking. She clenches her hands into fists and walks over to the window. Jenny has never seen her so angry.

Sophie gets up quickly from the sofa and runs out of the room. They listen, not for the first time, to the sound of her feet hammering on each step. Nobody moves, not until they hear the front door slam.

"She's feeling guilty," their mother says. "That's why she can't stay and talk about it."

"I was dealing with it, Margaret," their father says. "I was getting somewhere."

"Stop being so soft." Their mother sits down heavily on the sofa. "She's got a good point, though. He was your bloody father. Why am I always the one doing this? Why don't you ever get angry?"

"Anger doesn't get you anywhere," their father says.

"I don't think," says Maddie slowly, "Sophie ever meant to hurt Grandfather. She was just playing games."

"Oh for heaven's sake," their mother says. "You're as bad as your father."

Jenny keeps quiet. She doesn't know how many times Sophie hid the pills. She doesn't know how reliant on them Grandfather was. Why didn't anyone tell her about any of this?

The violin. She looks around for it. It isn't on the floor anymore. She goes out of the living room and opens the door to the next room along the landing. It's Sophie's room, obviously. Jenny can tell because it's neat and tidy and there's a Royal Court Theatre poster on the wall. The belongings in the room — books, a jewellery box, a makeup bag — are all unfamiliar, bought since Sophie ran away.

The violin case is on the bed. Jenny presses open the clasps. The violin is inside. Jenny touches the strings gently, then closes the lid and fastens the clasps again.

They stay for another hour or so, eating mince pies and drinking tea, even though Jenny doesn't know how they can digest anything and even though they know Sophie won't come back until they've gone.

They go out to the car to fetch the Christmas presents they'd brought and Maddie gives them some small packages she says she hasn't got round to posting yet. The packages are paintings, about nine inches square. You can feel the wooden frame and the tautness of the canvas through the grey sugar paper and masking tape that Maddie has used for wrapping paper. Maddie has drawn spindly Christmas tree shapes on the paper with her graphic pen. And rabbits with spiky ears and round tummies. Jenny doesn't point out that rabbits are more of an Easter thing.

"We'll leave you Christmas, as it were," says their mother, coming back from the car with carrier bags of food, including the Quality Streets.

Maddie uses her nails to slice open the seal there and then, even though it isn't Christmas Day yet. She eases the lid off and holds the tin out to Jenny. "Take some for the journey," she says. "Take lots."

Fourteen

THE TRAIN WAS scheduled to stand at Edinburgh station for seventeen minutes before it continued to London. Where Maddie would meet Jenny at King's Cross and list all her excuses for why she couldn't come back to Inverness to see their mother in hospital. Jenny resisted the urge to get off the train and go home to her little top-floor flat with her view of Arthur's Seat. Instead, she sat listening as a small boy checked with his parents once again that they were going to visit the Tower of London.

"Yes, Callum," his mother said patiently. "We'll stay there as long as you like."

"You can stay there a very, very long time if you want," the boy's father added, making Jenny smile.

Jenny had bought her flat a year ago, at last spending the eight thousand pounds her mother had sent her after Willowbrae was sold. The envelope containing the cheque had lain unopened in her halls of residence mailbox for several days after it arrived halfway through Jenny's first term at university. She was learning to wait until she was in between essay deadlines before she read her mother's correspondence. Each envelope was a potential wrecking ball; she could not risk it smashing into her. The envelope with the cheque in it contained only a short note, in her mother's usual handwriting that was as flamboyant as her hair used to be. *Darling Jenny. This is for you. Use it for you. I miss you and I love you. Mummy.*

There were many ways Jenny could have used the money over the years; she had been waiting to know the right way, or if she should spend it at all. It was Willowbrae money; it could not be used carelessly. When she saw the cheque, Jenny felt as if hot coals had dropped into her stomach. She almost tore it up; she had it in her fingers ready to rip. Yet eight thousand pounds was a lot of money.

She never replied to her mother's letters or cards. She told herself she would talk to her parents only if they came to her and told her they had left Ben Gallachie. Whenever she spoke on the phone to Sophie, Sophie would ask her if she'd heard from their parents and then she'd remind Jenny she must never give in. It was the only way to make their parents realize they were wasting their lives, that they had run away from reality. If Jenny communicated with them even once, their parents would think they could live in both worlds, but they couldn't. They had to choose.

It was a plan, a strategy of sorts, and that was what Jenny needed in order to deal with each day and the next. Jenny knew Sophie was right. The sisters' reaction had to be drastic in order for their parents to realize they'd made a deeply foolish decision. Yet sometimes, usually late at night when the halls of residence quietened, the strategy didn't make sense to Jenny after all. More than once, sitting at her desk, she started a letter to her mother on the lined, hole-punched paper she took lectures notes on. And, then, in the morning, she would read what she had written and she would tear it up.

Jenny relied entirely on her degree timetable for instructions. Attend this lecture. Write this essay. Give this presentation to your seminar group. Travel to Italy with your class to sketch and take notes about the paintings and sculptures you see. She didn't miss a single lecture, seminar, tutorial or deadline; she was never late for anything.

Jenny's parents never came, not even to visit. Eventually, during the first term of the third year at university, her mother's letters stopped, although a Christmas card came and a birthday card the following summer and then another Christmas card, though only with a brief, perfunctory message each time.

Jenny assumed her mother had given up, until a letter arrived early the next summer. Jenny was about to open it when she realized the significance of the timing; she had just finished her final exams. She knew what the letter would say. *It will be hard to find a job, even harder to find work that's worthwhile. Come and live with us. Come and help us save the human race from themselves. We love you. We miss you.*

Jenny never opened the letter. She ripped it up and put it in a bin.

She'd never received anything from her father, not once.

Jenny kept the cheque her mother had sent her for several months before she worked out what to do with it. By then, she had moved out of the halls of residence — she felt vulnerable there after the North Berwick incident — and was sharing a flat in Stockbridge with some other students, which was fine except she got less work done and grew tired of drawing up cleaning rotas that everyone ignored. She took the cheque to the bank on George Street, wondering if cheques had expiry dates.

The woman at the bank asked Jenny why she hadn't deposited the cheque for so many months. Jenny told her, concisely, that there had been a split in the family and she'd had difficulty deciding whether to accept the money. The cashier was kind and told Jenny that accepting cheques with older dates was at the bank's discretion but she didn't see any problems.

Seven years later, at the age of twenty-four, doing two part-time jobs as well as the part-time PhD, Jenny was able to take on mortgage payments: a home for a home. It was the only thing she could ever rightfully do with Willowbrae money. The flat she bought was small and she was glad; it couldn't be shared. A bedroom, bathroom, kitchen, living room. The kitchen was really part of the living room. The bedroom was L-shaped; it had an extra nook you didn't expect and that was where she put her desk and worked and worked. She loved being on the fourth storey, climbing up four flights of wide steps that still smelt of the quarry the stone came from. Her street was a sandstone canyon. The living room window looked out the back, onto the grass and rocks and gorse and volcanic upheavals of Holyrood Park. It was the view she had dreamt of while she had lived in halls.

Even though she had planned to be in Nunavut for five months, she had saved up enough money so she wouldn't have to rent her flat out to anyone else. She could go home right now if she wanted and sit in the green armchair in front of the window. Unless Karen was staying there after all. Karen didn't count as anyone else; she was Jenny's closest friend.

"Take this key," she'd said to Karen when she'd left for Baffin Island.

"To your flat? The holy bastion?"

"Just in case you need to get away from the ex. You might need some window therapy."

Karen knew about Jenny's window, how it could get a person through just about anything. Karen knew about Jenny's family, how Jenny had spent hours in the university library looking up Gallachism in books, journals and on microfiche. That was how they had met, while Jenny was trying to find out why her parents thought Gallachism was the answer to life, the universe and everything. Initially, she had found very little. An entry in a dictionary of faiths that noted it was considered a cult. An article in a journal of religious studies about the rise of cults in contemporary Britain.

In her fourth year, when more information was appearing on the internet on the university computers, Jenny started looking again, typing Gallachism, Ben Gallachie and different spellings of the name of the leader, Viparanda, into different search engines. At last, she found a photograph of Viparanda standing on a little boat moored at Mallaig Harbour, across from the peninsula where the commune was situated, grey mountains rising in the far distance behind him. Jenny stared at the photograph. Viparanda was white. English. His real name was Colin Smith, born in Woking, Surrey. She almost laughed out loud, there in the university library.

She'd been taken in by his Gallachist name, assumed he was from India. Colin Smith was looking calmly at the camera while his followers were loading supplies onto the boat and busying themselves with ropes. He was in his fifties, tall and lean with short white hair and a white-trimmed beard. He was wearing a green kurta and loose pyjama-like trousers, stylishly ascetic. He had dark, deep eyes and was almost good-looking. There, standing on the boat while activity went on all around him, he had the look of a prophet.

The article was about a man from Kent who had given everything to the Gallachists and was taking Viparanda to court to get it back. His wife had died; he'd been vulnerable in his grief. That was the argument.

According to the article, Viparanda had split up from his wife when his architecture business failed and, estranged from his two children, he'd gone travelling in India. When his parents both died and left him four hundred thousand pounds, he used it to buy the Knoydart land. He'd started the commune in 1982 with a small group of followers, an assortment of middle-aged British and Australian couples whom he had apparently persuaded to leave their white-collar jobs, sell up their houses and cash in their investments to join him.

Karen caught Jenny at it. Karen with her dyed-black hair and an indoor pallor who was studying for a history of art degree like Jenny. They sat in the same lectures but they'd never talked much before.

"*Guru for the middle ages*," Karen read on Jenny's screen. "He looks creepy. Knoydart? That's in the west coast boonies, isn't it? Jenny?"

Jenny looked up from the monitor. "Sorry, I got a bit engrossed."

"I'll say," Karen agreed. "That was my third attempt at breaking the Ross barrier."

"I don't have a barrier," Jenny said in a small voice. She really didn't want to be that sort of person.

"I'm kidding, I'm kidding," Karen said. "It's just that you're very good at being, let's say, focused. Everyone's very envious of your ability to concentrate and ignore all the distractions going on around you."

That sounded better, or at least less bad.

"Hey," Karen said. "You okay?"

Jenny nodded. She didn't seem able to say anything. Her jaw was aching as if she'd been clenching it. She wanted to run outside and hit something and she never hit things.

Karen put her head on one side. "How about a hot chocolate down-stairs?"

Jenny hesitated. She'd just wasted loads of time, yet there was no way she could sit here any longer.

She hadn't gone to the university library café with Karen intending to tell her about her family, yet that was what happened. It was the way nothing seemed to faze Karen.

"There's nothing you could have done to stop them," Karen told Jenny. "You do know that, don't you? We can't take responsibility for what our folks do. I mean, Christ."

They'd become friends after that and had started a master's degree in art history together the following autumn, although Karen had dropped out a few months later. These days, she worked at a social inclusion partnership in Edinburgh helping people from poor backgrounds train for jobs in the arts. Karen loved it. It was a real job, useful.

Fifteen

JENNY AND HER parents have been living at Willowbrae for three and a half years now and Maddie and Sophie have still never been back. Her parents have become used to it and Jenny, who is sixteen, supposes so has she.

At first, after the Christmas fiasco, she tried to find out the facts of what had happened to Grandfather. It was clear that their mother would need proof to be convinced that Sophie hadn't meant to cause Grandfather any harm.

When Jenny asked her mother if they still had any of Grandfather's old prescriptions — the plan being to find out what he'd been taking and what the effect would have been if he didn't take it — her mother closed down like a shop shutter crashing to the pavement. More attempts only led to her mother telling Jenny she had too much time on her hands and she should take up piano lessons again or try another instrument, seeing as she was never going to become the next Rachmaninoff. Or she should join some teams. Hockey. Netball. Swimming.

She couldn't spend her life reading books and wandering in the forest.

Probing Sophie for information had been even more hazardous. When, a couple of weeks after the Christmas visit, Jenny asked Sophie on the phone if she minded if they talked about Grandfather, Sophie accused her of not being on her side and almost hung up.

In the interests of maintaining relations with both *sides*, as Sophie put it, Jenny stopped her investigations and tried to accept that her family was no longer one thing. It was like in biology. Her family had started off as a single-celled organism, a protozoan. But a nucleus always divided sooner or later. It was called binary fission and you couldn't stop it happening. What was funny — though she certainly didn't feel like laughing — was that when a nucleus split into two, the two new cells were called daughters. The thing was, binary fission was a one-way process. Once a cell had divided into two, it couldn't become one again.

Jenny has, thankfully, been able to ring Sophie and Maddie ever since that Christmas visit; their parents paid for a phone to be installed in the London flat.

Jenny has been to London to see her sisters three times, always during the summer holidays, travelling south on the train on her own. Maddie takes her to art galleries and Sophie takes her to plays. Their mother sends Jenny off with sandwiches for the five-hour journey and instructions to find out as much as she can about her sisters' lives, or at least to check they're eating properly and don't have any of the wrong friends. Once Jenny is in London, her sisters say they aren't interested in hearing about their parents, yet nevertheless manage to bring them up in conversation surprisingly often.

Jenny loves seeing her sisters — trying to keep up with their squabbles and banter — and she loves the plays and galleries and cafés and shops and streets full of people from every country in the world. But always when she sits on the train going home, looking out at the backs of terraced brick houses with their stubby gardens littered with brightly coloured children's toys or rusting bicycles and fridges, she can't help feeling that London is a hard, grey vast machine and she is lucky, once again, to have escaped.

Last winter, Jenny's parents had the idea to convert the coach house into studios for workshops. The first courses started the following spring. Painting, sculpture, yoga, even shiatsu and primal scream therapy. "We're not just a boring B&B anymore," her mother likes to say. "We're a holistic, self-development centre."

Jenny's parents are developing themselves too. Her father has been using Maddie's old bedroom as a studio and he now has enough paintings for his very first show. The light is on late in his studio each night, and he's always on the phone to Moira at the gallery talking about frame sizes and mounts and angles of lighting. Jenny's mother makes jokes about being an artist's widow, although really she and Jenny are enjoying him being so happy, so entirely in his element.

The exhibition at Moira's gallery on Peebles High Street will comprise a dozen large canvasses that are abstract and a series of smaller paintings in which you can decipher elements from a world populated by humans: figures and hills and buildings and water.

Displaced, an Alasdair Ross Exhibition. That is what the leaflet says and the large serifed lettering stencilled carefully in grey on the white wall as you enter the gallery. Places with which her father has a connection. Or a disconnection. A relationship, anyway. *Tillicoultry. Brighton. Delhi. Shimla. Shepherd's Bush. Peebles.* The topography of a life so far. The geography of middle age. The globe according to Alasdair Ross. It's simple and it's engaging. You could argue that the paintings themselves are likewise simple and engaging. Jenny is hoping to do a degree in art history; she likes to put forward arguments about paintings. The non-figurative paintings, the six-footers — *Newhaven, Seaford, Eastbourne* — are especially appealing. Easy on the eye. Pretty, even. Harmonious colours, Kandinsky-esque forms. Jenny is proud of her father. She's also glad that Maddie and Sophie won't see this exhibition, will not slash the canvasses with their word-swords.

Now, helping to hang the paintings one by one on the walls of this large white room, Jenny sees that *Agra* is missing. Agra is where the Taj Mahal is. Her father, Alasdair Ross, loves the Taj Mahal. He told Jenny about it many times when she was little, how when they were still students he and her mother had queued before dawn to see the marble lit by the sunrise and how it had been worth it. Did it mean too much to him and therefore his attempts to paint it have failed? No. Jenny knows without asking why it isn't there. It would present her father as a tourist rather than a traveller. You can be ironic about Seaford, Eastbourne, Shepherd's Bush. You can't be ironic about Agra or the Taj Mahal, the most beautiful human-made structure in the world. A building that floats, dissolves, where mist and flocks of birds swirl, conceal, reveal. The Taj Mahal is too beautiful. It is too hackneyed.

Lockerbie is here, though. A town that Alasdair Ross has never actually visited, as far as Jenny knows, only driven past on the motorway. They were glued to the television like everyone else when the Pan Am plane fell from the sky thirty miles from Willowbrae. Debris was found as far away as the east coast of England.

Everyone, Jenny supposes, has their Lockerbie and this is her father's. Jenny's would be painted in soft bands of grey in the style of Rothko. It would be one of her ceiling paintings. She has a whole collection. She paints them at night in her mind when she lies with her eyes open and the ceiling seems to hover and float and not be solid at all.

Lockerbie is on the floor leaning against the white wall of the gallery. It's the smallest painting in the exhibition and it will be the centrepiece. It will have a wall to itself.

"Dead centre?" says Moira as the three of them stand on the wooden floorboards looking down at *Lockerbie*.

Jenny flinches but neither Moira nor her father notice the insensitive phrasing.

Her father puts his arm around Jenny and gives her a sideways hug. "Exciting, eh, Jenny Wren? My own show."

"It's brilliant." Jenny hugs him back. "There'll be queues all down High Street. We'll need crowd control."

Her father laughs and kisses the top of her head.

The three of them are quiet for a moment, looking at the *Lockerbie* painting.

"I'm not sure I should include it," Jenny's father says. "Or give it so much prominence."

"It's very powerful." Moira clasps her hands. "It's going to resonate with everyone. It needs breathing space."

It's the only painting with close-up figures in it: two people hugging and behind them two others in a hug. The image looks familiar, as if Jenny has seen it on television or in a newspaper, as if her father might have cut it out and copied it. It proves he can paint people, in his own abstracted way. Jenny has never doubted his ability; it's more the sort of thing Maddie or Sophie would question. Jenny's worry is that the people look as if they're identifiable Lockerbie residents who lost their families, their homes, when the plane fell.

She feels the urge to step back and she does; she doesn't want to intrude. The woman facing the viewer has her eyes tightly closed and the hair of the person she's clasping is dishevelled. The strongest pictorial element, the cleverest element, is the repetition of the hand on the back of each of the two people being hugged. Hands, laid flat, each wearing a wedding ring.

Once the painting is hung and the label is in place, Jenny stands in front of it on her own and puts her palm over the title. That's better. She wonders if her mother knows about this painting. She wants to hear her opinion; she'll definitely have one. Her mother isn't here, though.

"They don't need me," she said that morning in the Willowbrae kitchen. "I'm too busy anyway."

It's true; her mother is busy with rehearsals. Last autumn, she joined the PADS, the Peebles Amateur Dramatic Society — or the humdrum "am drams," as Jenny's father calls them — and is playing Ruth Condomine in *Blithe Spirit*, the character who finds herself competing with the ghost of a dead wife.

"Noël Coward wouldn't be my first choice," Jenny's mother says, rather a lot, on the telephone, in shops when she bumps into friends and acquaintances, to guests. "But fun all the same and a good way to exercise my acting legs again."

Jenny wasn't aware her mother ever had particularly muscular acting legs, although it's true she was in a couple of plays at the University of Sussex and received excellent reviews in the student newspaper. Her mother still has the twenty-three-year-old cuttings in a folder in a drawer in her bedroom.

Jenny hasn't seen her parents this happy since the day they moved into Willowbrae. Her father's private view takes place three nights before the opening of her mother's play, and her parents are drifting around the gallery with a glass of champagne in one hand, using the other to touch an arm or shake a hand or, in Jenny's mother's case, occasionally interlace fingers with a female friend, lipstick smiles glistening. Her parents have accumulated a lot of friends since they moved to Scotland, Jenny realizes, looking around the gallery. More, probably, than they had in Brighton.

Perhaps she's the only one thinking her sisters should be here too; not her real sisters who still won't set foot in Scotland, who if they were here would be getting tipsy on champagne and making sarcastic comments about their father's paintings that Jenny would be praying he wouldn't overhear. Not her real sisters, but the Maddie and Sophie of her imagination, who did not run away from Willowbrae and who are at college in Glasgow, sharing a flat there, where Jenny and her mother often drop in for a cup of tea when they go shopping on Sauchiehall Street before the drive home.

The next evening, while her mother is putting on her coat ready to go to the community hall for the dress rehearsal, Jenny asks if she can go with her. Her mother says no. She wants Jenny to see the play as the audience will see it, even though she concedes that Jenny already knows the entire play from helping her learn her lines.

Her mother is delving in her leather handbag now for the car keys. When she looks up, the skin around her eyes is taut.

"You're nervous?" Jenny laughs. She can't help it. Her mother is never nervous.

"People will be judging me."

"You'll be fantastic." Jenny gives her mother a kiss and a hug. They are the same height now; she doesn't have to reach up. "You'll be the star of the show."

She watches her mother as she goes down the hall. She can't remember ever having to give her a pep talk before.

She learnt after the Christmas trip, of course, when she was thirteen that her parents are far from perfect, that they make mistakes and are capable of doing things she disagrees with deeply. Yet this is the first time she's realized that her mother has any self-doubt, that launching your amateur dramatics career at the age of forty-three is nerve-wracking and that her mother has nerves to be wracked.

One of the benefits of her parents being so engrossed in their own artistic pursuits is that, for some time, they've been paying less attention to whether or not Jenny has any of her own. Jenny did start piano lessons again, at her mother's insistence. However, shortly before her fourteenth birthday, she told her mother she was giving them up once and for all; she loved listening to other people playing the piano but had no desire to play herself. She would devote the time to school work instead, which was the only area where her mother seemed to think she had any talents anyway, so why not put all of her energy there?

Her mother has apparently accepted Jenny's decision. More than once, Jenny has overheard her mother telling someone, "Oh, Jenny's the clever one in the family. All the brains went to her. Heaven knows where she got it, although Alasdair's father was a head teacher and I come, bizarrely, from hordes of engineers. It's Maddie and Sophie who are the artists like me and Alasdair."

Jenny is fully aware she doesn't have what it takes to become an artist, but that doesn't mean she can't still enjoy doing some drawing and whittling. It isn't exactly a secret, it's just easier not to make a thing of it and therefore avoid being reminded of what she already knows.

She loves the soft rattle of a set of coloured pencils in their tin. She has the ordinary kind and the watercolour kind, and charcoal sticks and a set of pastels too, bought with the money she earns from helping out at Willowbrae on Saturdays. She can't remember a time when she hasn't loved drawing. The whittling — she worries it's pretentious to call it carving — is a newer discovery. The sticks themselves aren't new; she's been picking up sticks like a dog ever since her first day at Willowbrae, adding them to her stone collection.

The whittling started because she happened to be coming home from a walk with a small beech branch in her hand when she met Brian in what she calls the donkey field by the stile to the woods. She calls it the donkey field because it looks as if it should have a donkey in it.

Brian, an older man with white hair and bright blue eyes, was teaching a sculpture workshop at Willowbrae that week. He admired the wood she was carrying and asked Jenny if she was going to carve it. She felt herself blush and said something about being more of a collector than a shaper. The moment she said it, she was embarrassed. There was an affectation to her vocabulary that she would have mocked in anyone else.

Yet Brian hadn't mocked her. He'd smiled and invited her to his sculpture workshop that evening. He'd dismissed her concerns that the paying guests would object if she joined his class for free and so, without telling her parents, she'd gone along. She hadn't taken any of her sticks with her because she hadn't intended to do anything, just watch. That was until Brian plonked a block of clay the size of a loaf of bread in front of her, along with a smaller oblong of wood that had three sticks of metal stuck into it, which he told her was an armature.

"Everyone's having a go at sculpting someone's head," Brian said. "Why not have a try? Sandra over there needs a partner. I was going to pair up with her, but I'm sure she'd much rather sculpt your head than my ugly mug."

After Jenny had had a go for a couple of hours — and loved every minute — and Brian and Sandra and quite a few others in the workshop had said kind things, Brian showed her a box of wood-carving tools. "This is what you need for that piece of beech. It's a nice, hard wood which means you can really add some detail." He closed the lid and handed the box to her. "Borrow it. I won't be using this all week. Have a go and see what you think."

And now she loves whittling even more than drawing. She sits in her window seat with an old tea towel across her lap to catch the shavings from her chip knife and sees what emerges from a stick. She calls them wood spirits. A crow had emerged at one end of the beech. Other sticks have revealed a fox, peregrine, rabbit, even a snail.

Occasionally nothing identifiable emerges and the stick remains abstract; they're the ones where the tree's own spirit manifests.

Jenny has a wooden box under her desk that she uses as a footrest when she's doing her homework. She found it in a charity shop in Peebles and tied it to her bicycle rack with a bungee cord to bring it home. She keeps her art materials in it. If her parents assume she only uses it as a footrest, then that's fine by her.

Sixteen

JENNY AND HER father are sitting in the front row at the Peebles community hall and *Blithe Spirit* is due to begin in fourteen minutes. The seats are uncomfortable and they've kept their coats on because of the draft. They've heard about a fundraising campaign to build a proper arts centre in Peebles and they joke about making a major donation.

While they're waiting, Jenny asks her father if he's got any red dots on his paintings yet. He hasn't, unfortunately. She reminds him the show is open for another two weeks yet. There's plenty of time.

All the seats are filling up, they're relieved to see. Her father tells Jenny, not for the first time, that he thinks am drams should steer clear of comedy. "No doubt your mother's going to have to carry the whole cast. What if no one laughs?"

When the play starts, they realize laughter isn't going to be a problem. As soon as the maid comes running on stage, the audience laughs. Not that it's *that* funny. Jenny's mother's line about the maid who has left to get married — *the reason was becoming increasingly obvious, dear* — gets another big laugh and Jenny begins to relax. Her mother's stage husband, Charles Condomine, is being played by a good-looking, dark-haired man who in real life works, appropriately, for Scottish Widows in Edinburgh. He is very good. Understated yet confident.

Jenny's mother is confident too, yet something is beginning to happen to her. She isn't having any trouble remembering her lines or where she's supposed to be on the stage. That isn't the problem. It's when she says her line about Julius Caesar being *neither here nor there*. She hammers a pause in between each word as if she expects every syllable to get a laugh. Yet it's Charles who has the punchline. And when she turns to the audience to deliver the line, *If I died, I wonder how long it would be before you married again*, Jenny clenches her hands, she's so worried her mother is actually going to wink. Jenny knows nothing about acting, nothing at all. She can't even articulate what it is, except her mother seems to be — surely not — overacting.

How many times has Jenny sat in front of the television or gone to the theatre and heard her mother criticize someone for overdoing it. Her mother's body language is as exaggerated as the way she's saying her lines. When she first encounters the peculiar Madame Arcati, she widens her eyes and arches her back like an actor in a silent film. Jenny is supposed to be coming here again with Helen on Saturday. She's going to have to be ill.

Jenny glances at her father; he's staring forward. He isn't moving. He doesn't even seem to be blinking. Jenny follows her father's cue. She keeps her eyes strictly on the stage and lets the audience guide her laughter until the interval.

At the trestle table that serves as a bar, waiting for their drinks, Jenny's father says, "This play was written in six days at Portmeirion in Wales in 1941."

"I can see how it would have been a bit of light relief in the middle of the war."

They take their drinks over to an empty space in front of a window.

"It's only the first night," her father says. "I'm sure she'll, you know, relax."

"And can we tell her," says Jenny carefully, "that she ought to relax?"

"I think we'd better, yes."

Of course they don't. At the end of the evening, they tell her she was wonderful and the moment has gone.

At lunchtime on Saturday, Jenny goes down to the kitchen to get herself something to eat. She has a hankering for a ploughman's lunch: a chunk of mature cheese, a dollop of dark pickled chutney, a tearing of fresh French bread. She hopes someone has been to the bakery. Saturday is always changeover day. Her parents and Sam, one of their three part-time staff members, are getting the coach house ready for the next workshop, while Jenny is changing bedding in the guest rooms upstairs with the other staff members, Christine and Jean.

In the kitchen, there's a note on the table in her father's handwriting. *We've popped out for lunch*, it says. *See you later. M and D xxx*. This is odd. They can't have finished at the coach house yet. Jenny checks the bread bin. French bread. Perfect. And cheddar and a jar of chutney in the fridge. Her stomach gurgles as the fridge door swings shut. She tears off a few inches of bread and thumbs it open to butter it. She slides the kettle onto the Aga plate for a cup of tea and flicks through the pages of the *Borders Gazette* lying on the kitchen counter while she waits for it to boil.

A gang of boys caught breaking into a house. A fire in the White Feather pub. An article about riverbank erosion. Now the arts pages. Jenny stops flicking. There's a photograph of her mother and the actor playing Charles Condomine. The heading: *Blithe Spirit: unhappy medium*. Underneath, a review.

Margaret Ross looks the part, the review starts. *She knows how to hold the stage and at first gives the impression of embodying the spirit of Ruth very comfortably. However, it's as if there's a ghostly voice whispering in her ear, telling her to turn it up, turn it up until the audience wants to start shouting, turn it down, turn it down. If only the ghostly voice would tell her it's not panto season anymore.*

Jenny stops reading. Very droll. Those references to spirits and what not. Nice to know the reviewer is having fun as she rips Jenny's mother to pieces. The reviewer must have been at the first night for it to be in the paper today. That's unfair. She could at least have gone to the second or third night once the cast got into their stride. She scans the rest of the review. The reviewer has it in for a few other cast members too, especially the poor woman playing the medium. These were the am drams for heaven's sake, not the Royal Shakespeare Company.

Jenny grabs the paper, dropping half of it on the floor. She bends to pick it up. She'll hide it. She'll twist up each sheet to set the sitting room fire until her hands are black with newsprint ink.

Of course. It's too late; her mother has read it. Hence the note from her father about taking her out for lunch. *The reviewer just picked up on the fact you were a bit nervous*, her father would be saying over arrabbiata and a glass of red wine. There's a restaurant in Galashiels they like; that's where they'll be. *All you need to do is relax and stop thinking about the acting so much. You know the role inside out.*

No, if he says that, her mother will know the reviewer was telling the truth. Jenny's father will have to come up with something else. *It's only a local rag. Some young upstart who knows nothing about acting. No one will read it.* Only everyone in the entire Scottish Borders. *You are Ruth when you're on that stage. You know what, though, I know I've been rude about am drams, but I don't think you need to worry about the rest of the cast. I think you can relax more when you're on that stage. They're doing fine.*

Jenny puts a chunk of cheese in her mouth. The kettle boils and she puts the paper back together again and returns it to the counter. She pours water onto the tea bag, quickly stirs it and chucks it in the bin. A splash of milk. She'll take her lunch to the dining room where Jean and Christine are probably eating their sandwiches. She'll pretend she hasn't seen the review.

On Saturday night, Jenny's mother does much better. Her father's pep talk, assuming there's been one, must have worked. Her mother is no longer the worst member of the cast; she's as mediocre as the rest of them. Jenny doesn't have to feel embarrassed in front of Helen or her parents, who are here too. If only the reviewer had come tonight instead.

"Look who's here," Helen says to Jenny during the interval, indicating the direction with her eyes.

Jenny looks and blushes. It's Nicholas from school. Helen is well aware that Jenny has had a crush on him for years.

"Shall we go and say hi?" Helen says.

"No!"

Helen also knows that Jenny and Nicholas once kissed, a long time ago at their friend Wendy's fourteenth birthday party. It was dark and Jenny was sitting cross-legged by a fish pond because she was feeling rather queasy after drinking too much cider. Nicholas had sat down next to her and asked her how come she was always so calm and Jenny said she wasn't calm at all and then Nicholas kissed her. It was lovely until he pulled away and told her he'd better not because he was going out with Angela.

Jenny didn't think that, two and a half years later, Nicholas was still going out with Angela. She never saw them together at school. He'd never told her that, though, and she'd never asked. He probably didn't even remember the kiss.

Jenny doesn't know how other girls do it, get boys to ask them out. No doubt it would help if she was pretty or thin. On the one hand, she doesn't care what anyone thinks of her, which is why she wears long, baggy tops with leggings and big boots. On the other hand, she desperately wants to find her soulmate and be with him for the rest of her life. She wishes it could be Nicholas and yet she doesn't see how. She doesn't even have the courage to catch his eye. Anyway, it wouldn't work; she's into Erasure and the Pet Shop Boys. He's into heavy metal. He's letting his dark hair grow longer and it suits him, with his blue eyes, although he could do with washing it a bit more often.

The following weekend, there's another newspaper review to contend with. It isn't in the *Borders Gazette*. If only it had been. It's in the Sunday edition of the *Saltire Times*, the national paper. Unlikely to be read by a great deal of people, or particular daughters in England, but it's hard to pretend it won't be seen by thousands of people all over Scotland. Sunday papers hang around in people's houses longer than dailies.

Borders painter accused of exploiting Lockerbie. That's the headline in the arts section, although it's a small headline, only a couple of columns wide. There are no quotes from any of the Lockerbie victims' families. No evidence of any such interviews. The comment has come, apparently, from a gallery visitor. Jenny can imagine it. You'd be standing in a gallery in front of a painting and some friendly chap close by, wearing a creased linen jacket and concealing a notebook and pen in his pocket, says something like, "It's very moving, but I do wonder how the families of the Lockerbie victims might feel about it, whether they might feel a bit exploited."

And you'd murmur, "Yes, I wonder" or, simply, a musing "Hmm." And, hey presto, the reviewer has his headline.

Jenny doesn't know much about newspapers, but she does know that journalists aren't exactly known for their scruples.

She finds her father tightening handles on a chest of drawers in one of the guests' bedrooms. She describes the scene she's imagined. He looks up from where he's kneeling and moves the screwdriver from one hand to the other.

"It's okay, Jenny. I know it's just one perspective."

"It's not a perspective," Jenny says. "It's a load of rubbish."

He switches the screwdriver back to his right hand and carries on twisting. Jenny waits for him to look up again. He doesn't, so she leaves the room.

The trouble is, the reviewer wasn't very kind about the other paintings either. He said that, without the meaning their geographical titles imparted, they're just nice colours you might find down at B&Q.

Two mornings later, they're all in the kitchen when Moira rings Jenny's father to tell him she's sold two of his paintings. One person has bought *Tillicoultry* and someone different has bought *Lockerbie*. And at the asking price; no one haggled.

Jenny tells her father that the *Saltire Times* review did the trick after all.

"I'm just glad to get rid of it," her father says, taking a sip of coffee. He means the *Lockerbie* painting, she knows. At least he seems a little pleased.

There's better news later in the week for her mother too. The review of the play in the *Borders Reporter* is positive. Margaret Ross even gets a special mention.

Margaret Ross held my attention most. She manages to convey Ruth Condomine's vulnerability at key moments in the love triangle even though the character is domineering and frequently furious. I'll be looking out for her next production.

When Jenny suggests they all go out for a meal to celebrate, her father tells her not to get carried away and her mother changes the subject by saying she's waiting for a frozen food delivery.

Her parents are too quiet. They're too polite. Jenny isn't used to it. They have always been attentive to their guests' needs and done whatever they can to make people comfortable, but not in this smiling yet humourless way. They will recoup, both of them. They just need time to put things in perspective and realize there will always be bad reviews as well as good reviews. There will always be paintings that sell and paintings that don't. Success is never absolute and mediocrity isn't failure. There's always a risk when you do things that are public.

Jenny wants to say all this. She doesn't, because it's hard to give your parents the wisdom of your experience when you are still only sixteen. She wants to tell them that if you're courageous and put yourself on stage or hang your paintings in a gallery, you're inviting comment and judgement. You are entering the world of analysis and opinion. You can't expect everyone to love what you do. Her parents surely know all this; there is no point saying it. So Jenny is quiet and polite too and concentrates on revising for her Highers and trying not to think about blue-eyed, dark-haired Nicholas at school.

She decides not to tell her parents when Maddie informs her on the telephone that one of her paintings has been selected for the Royal Academy Summer Exhibition, which is about as prestigious as you can get when you still haven't even finished your degree.

Nor, a week or so after that, does Jenny mention *Backstage* magazine's review of Sophie's performance in *Speed-the-Plow*, a play put on by her drama school in which the director reverses all the gender roles and casts Sophie as Bobbie rather than Bobby Gould. Sophie sends Jenny a cutting. It's a very good review, excellent, and there's a black-and-white photograph of Sophie on stage, looking attractively mannish, her usually shoulder-length fair hair neatly cropped.

Jenny folds the glossy page back into the same creases and returns it to the envelope. She puts on her coat, slips the envelope into her pocket and goes out for a walk. She crosses the donkey field to the stile and walks up through the woods to the look-out stone. It's large enough to sit on and she does so often, staring out over the soft, pale hills and dark forests. She likes to think the stone is a meteorite, but it's granite, heaved up from earth.

When she gets home, she takes the cutting up to her room and puts it in a drawer.

They will bounce back, both of them, Jenny is certain. They just need time to recover.

"Have you seen this, Margaret?" Jenny's father comes into the living room holding a magazine open. Jenny's mother has Radio 4 on and is sewing buttons back on a couple of shirts. Jenny is going over her notes for her history exam. The voices on the radio are comforting rather than distracting.

"Look." He holds the magazine in front of Jenny's mother's face. "Maddie, as in our Maddie, is going to be in the Royal Academy summer show."

Her father definitely looks pleased, yet there's something else in his expression, something he's trying to conceal, as if the ochre ground is showing through in a Dutch painting.

Jenny's mother takes the magazine, her face shining. "Look, Jenny."

Jenny puts her notes down and goes over to her mother's chair. "That's great."

"It's more than great, it's fabulous." There's a constriction to her father's smile. "I'm going to ring her. Why on earth didn't she tell us?"

He leaves the room and Jenny bends her head back over her history. After several minutes, her father comes back, looking confused.

"Maddie says she told you on the phone a while ago," he says to Jenny. "She'd expected you to tell us."

Jenny feels as if an ice cube has been dropped down her back.

Her mother puts down her sewing. "Is that true, Jenny? You knew about this?"

Jenny glances at her father. "I just didn't think, you know, it was a good time —"

Her father is too agitated to sit down. "I'm not that small-minded, am I? Is that what you really think of me? God, I hope not. I mean, this is wonderful news. We have to share the good news in this family. You mustn't keep this sort of thing to yourself. It's selfish." He flicks through the magazine. "This is it. She's off. She's away. She's going to be a household name."

Jenny's mother is watching her. "Why are you squirming?"

"I'm not." The ice cube is in the small of Jenny's back now.

"I know that look. You're keeping something else from us, aren't you?"

Despite the ice cube, Jenny's face flushes.

"Out with it." Her mother reaches to turn the radio volume down. "You're too young for hot flushes."

"Sophie's had some good news too."

"Oh?" Her mother glances down at her sewing then looks back at Jenny.

"She had a good review. She sent me the cutting. You mean, Maddie didn't share that good news with you, Daddy?"

Her father looks puzzled again and she feels mean.

"She was in *Speed-the-Plow*," Jenny says. "They swapped roles, you know, genders. She played Bobbie Gould."

"Go and get the cutting then." Her father flaps his magazine at her as if he's talking to a simpleton.

Jenny gets up. "It's just a review."

"Well," says her mother. "I for one would like to see it, if it's not too much trouble."

As Jenny leaves, she hears her father say, "You know she's told them about our disasters, don't you?"

"No, I haven't!" Jenny shouts to them from the hallway. "And they're not disasters!" She runs up the stairs two at a time. She most definitely hasn't; she's not going to give her sisters ammunition.

When Jenny returns, she hands the cutting to her mother, who unfolds it and reads it before passing it to her father. Jenny sits and tries to concentrate on the causes of the Spanish Civil War.

She hears her father whistle. "This is it for both of them. Look how all your efforts have paid off, Margaret. I hope they appreciate just how much you did to get them there. It's not just talent that's got them there, you know, it was a lot of determination and sacrifice on your part. All those extra classes for Sophie. We could have dragged them back here from London kicking and screaming, but we didn't. I just hope those little minxes realize that and are grateful one of these days."

Seventeen

THE WOMAN TEACHING the Introduction to Gallachism course at Willowbrae, Deepali, is alone in the guests' sitting room when Jenny takes in a scuttle of coal to stoke the fire. None of the students is there, nor Pranay, the other teacher. Deepali gives Jenny a generous Julia Roberts smile. Jenny returns it, feeling she should unpick some stitching so her mouth will widen further. Deepali's glossy hair is so black it's almost blue and her amber eyes are liquid. Jenny tries to imagine what it would feel like to be beautiful. Deepali is sitting cross-legged in an armchair. The television isn't on, even though the election results will be coming in by now. Nor does she have a book or a magazine in her lap or earphones on.

"Where is everyone?" Jenny digs the shovel into the scuttle and heaps some coals onto the fire.

"Exploring Peebles' nightlife, I believe."

"They'll be back any minute then."

Deepali laughs politely. Fair enough. It isn't the most original of jokes.

"Your course is popular," Jenny says as she stands watching the fire. Each lump of coal is glowing like a planet with its own sunrise. "We ended up with a waiting list."

"There are many people looking for fulfillment in life," Deepali says, refreshing her smile.

"I'd never heard of Gallachism, to be honest."

Deepali is wearing the sage kurta she's worn since she arrived. As the floaty fabric isn't quite designed for Willowbrae drafts, she's also wearing a blue cardigan. "Why don't you sit down?"

Jenny doesn't want a long conversation. Nor does she want to be rude to a guest. She hangs up the shovel and sits on the arm of the chair nearest the fire.

"Gallachism," Deepali says slowly as if she's explaining something very complicated, "is about seeing yourself as a spiritual being, not just a body." Deepali smooths her fingers along one arm. "It's about living in the here and now, being in the present, so you really experience life and see how everything is connected to everything else."

It seems obvious so far. "Do you have a god, like an Allah or a Buddha or, well, God?"

"We have Viparanda. But he's a spiritual leader rather than a divinity."

"I see," says Jenny, though she doesn't quite.

The cardigan Deepali is wearing: Jenny recognizes it. It's one of Jenny's mother's, one she hasn't worn for years. She doesn't say anything.

"You're very welcome to come to one of our meditations," Deepali says. "The evening sessions are open to anyone, each night at nine in the coach house."

"Thank you." Jenny stands up. "The thing is, I've got quite a lot of work to do, you know, for my Higher exams."

"Of course." Deepali is glowing like the coal, gazing up at Jenny from the armchair. "The offer's open. Come tonight. Any night, just drop in. Then you can see for yourself."

"Maybe." Jenny tries to look as if she has lots of essays to write. "Thank you." She smiles as widely as she can and leaves the room. She's crossing the hall to go downstairs to the kitchen when Jean comes out of the dining room.

"Hiya," Jenny says. "I thought you'd gone." The smile she gives Jean fits her mouth much better.

"Almost. Tables are set for breakfast. One more load of laundry to hang and then that's me. What are you up to?"

"It was chilly in the sitting room, poor Deepali, so I topped up the coal."

Jean scowls. "What did she say to you?"

"She was telling me about Gallachism. She invited me to one of their meditations."

"You stay away from that lot." Jean lowers her voice and crosses her arms. "They give me the creeps."

"She's very friendly. She never stops smiling."

"It's all a front. They're just trying to suck you in. They're not living in the real world. Whatever you do, don't go to any of their," she pauses, "things."

"What do you mean, not living in the real world?"

"They're off in some commune in the middle of nowhere. Up near Mallaig. They don't know what real life is like. They've given up and run away. Tell me you won't go to any of their meditations or whatever they call them?"

"Of course not." Jenny has no intention of going; she's got too much work to do for her Highers.

"Thanks, hen." Jean looks relieved. She smiles a little. "I'll see you tomorrow."

"Did you vote?"

"Nothing could have stopped me," says Jean. "Labour will sort things out. No one's going to vote for the grey numpty."

"It's throttling us," Jenny hears her father say as she reaches the threshold of the office.

Jenny's mother is sitting at the desk looking at bank statements and her father is standing beside her.

"Let's talk about this tomorrow," Jenny's mother says. "I'm so tired I can't think straight."

Her father rolls his eyes.

"Talk about what?" Jenny says.

Her mother tuts. "The loan for the conversion is harder to pay off than we anticipated."

"Than *you* anticipated." Jenny's father gestures at the desk. "*This* is what I anticipated."

"But we've got plenty of bookings," Jenny says. "We're full up, aren't we? And local people doing courses too?" How long have they been worrying about this? Would they have told her if she hadn't walked in on the conversation?

"We need to charge more," her father says, "but that risks not getting as many bookings. Bloody recession. We picked the worst time to expand the business. All our money's well and truly sunk into the property."

"We'd be in a worse position if we still only had the guest house," Jenny's mother says.

"Would we?" says her father. "At least then there would be time in the day for one of us to get a job."

Jenny's mother scoops up her hair and drops it again. "No, it's a lot cheaper for us to work at Willowbrae than for us to pay someone else. And it's not possible to run the guest house with just one of us."

"I completely disagree." Jenny's father's voice rises. "One of us could absolutely run the guest house while the other got a job. And that's exactly what we should have done when we got here. I can't believe you made us expand. Finding people to teach workshops, organizing all the advertising, printing brochures. It's so much work. And cost. Christ, we didn't even have a mortgage and now we've got this monstrosity of a debt."

Jenny doesn't know if her father is overreacting or not. She stays at the threshold.

"It's perfectly manageable," says her mother. "As Jenny says, we're always booked up. We just have to ride through this storm."

"Stop talking in clichés. You sound like a politician."

They glower at each other.

"I just got invited," Jenny says to unlock their glares, "to a Gallachist meditation. They have one every evening at nine in the top studio. Anyone can go."

"Oh?" Her mother looks at the clock on the wall. "You'd better get cracking. That's in ten minutes."

"I'm not going," Jenny says.

"What does it entail?" her mother says.

"Not sure, really. Something about living in the here and now and everything being connected to everything else."

Jenny's mother stretches. "I could do with a distraction."

Jenny's father shakes his head and leaves the office. "I'm going to watch the election," he says gloomily. "That'll cheer me up."

"Jean doesn't trust the Gallachists," Jenny says to her mother.

Her mother takes a band from her wrist and twists her hair through it twice. "Jean doesn't trust anyone. She's scared of having her mind opened. People like her always are."

"I don't think —"

"It sounds interesting." Her mother interrupts her. "I thought so when they got in touch about holding their course here. Though I imagine all that would happen if I tried to meditate right now is that I'd fall asleep."

"I'm going up to draw an isovel diagram showing river velocity." Jenny kisses her mother and says goodnight. She calls into their sitting room to say goodnight to her father too. He's grimacing at the television now. He's probably blowing the money situation out of proportion because he's so annoyed about the election. The map on the screen is turning Tory blue.

"I fell asleep." Jenny's mother tips the cutlery onto a tea towel with a crash. She laughs. "I knew I would. They shouldn't have got us to lie down."

They're emptying the last load from the dishwasher. Christine is drying the fruit juice glasses and Jenny is stacking plates.

"I might book myself a place on the next course," Christine says. "I could do with a week's sleep."

"What did you have to do?" asks Jenny.

"Keep awake I think was part of it." Her mother picks out a handful of forks and starts drying them. "All you had to do was lie there and concentrate on your breathing. Harder than it sounds. It was actually incredibly relaxing. I might go again."

It's nice to hear her mother laughing. She hasn't laughed since that stupid review, not properly, not with that layer of carbon paper in her voice as if she's keeping a record of all human foolishness.

"Right," says Christine, when everything had been put away. "That's me offski." She takes off her apron and goes to fetch her bag and coat from her usual hook in the hallway. Jenny and her mother call goodbye and sit down to have some breakfast.

"Did you go to the meditation too, Daddy?" Jenny asks when her father comes into the kitchen.

"Certainly not. If I want to fall asleep, I go to bed, except I can't sleep anymore because we're in such a financial mess." He starts spreading margarine onto a piece of toast left over from upstairs. "Oh no, of course it's fine now, isn't it? John Major is going to lead the country out of recession. How could I forget." He plops a dollop of marmalade onto his toast.

"Don't be such a drama queen," Jenny's mother says.

Her father takes a mouthful of toast and bends to kiss Jenny's mother on the top of her head.

"Hey!" Jenny's mother flaps up her hand as he leaves the kitchen. "Don't get marmalade in my hair."

Jenny is going to bed a couple of nights later when she sees a light on in her father's studio. It's the first time she's seen him in there since the *Saltire Times* review.

"Just thought I'd have a go," he says when she pushes the door open. He's sitting on a stool in front of a large canvas on which he has sketched a few marks in charcoal.

"You mustn't stop," says Jenny. "I love your paintings. You sold two!" Her father only grunts at this. "If I wasn't saving up for Australia, I'd buy one myself."

"You're really going to go and see my brother, eh?"

The annual card at Christmas from Uncle Fraser and Auntie Sue in Melbourne had got her thinking she might have a gap year and go there before university. "Who knows. I'd better write to him first. Remind him I exist." She laughs. "What does he do for a living?"

"Good question. Property, I think." Her father twists the stick of charcoal in his hand. It's good to see his fingers black again. "He's done it, hasn't he."

"What do you mean?" Jenny leans against the door frame.

"Well, he's seen the world and still managed to have a family and a home. It doesn't have to be either or."

"Travelling isn't everything," Jenny says.

"I suppose not."

"And we love Scotland. Imagine if we still lived in Brighton. So smelly and all that traffic."

Jenny stays for another few moments. Her father marks the paper with lines that look as if they're going to form themselves into a tree, or perhaps a bird. He's holding the charcoal loosely and he's watching his fingers rather than the shapes they're forming, as though he has no idea what his hand is going to draw next.

Eighteen

THE TRAIN FROM Scotland to London arrived on time and Jenny saw Maddie waiting for her by WHSmith as she crossed the King's Cross concourse. They hadn't seen each other since the previous summer when Jenny had gone to London to see the exhibition of Rembrandt self-portraits. Their hugs were usually quick hands-to-elbows clutches, but this time they hugged properly and Maddie even kissed Jenny on the cheek. Maddie was as thin as ever. She didn't smell of smoke, though. Jenny would ask the smoking question later.

"You really think it was him looking for you?" Maddie said as they followed the signs for the Tube. Maddie's knee-high boots clicked along the concourse while Jenny's soft-soled boots hardly made a sound.

"I can't be sure, but yes."

"Shit, what if he tracks *me* down?"

"It wouldn't be difficult," Jenny said. "You're all over the internet. Ah, maybe not."

Maddie was about to protest.

"They don't like electromagnetic fields," Jenny explained. "That must include computers. But he probably wears special gloves or some protective outfit like a radiation suit. Or wraps himself in tinfoil."

Maddie laughed. "I don't know if you're joking or not."

"Nor do I."

Neither of them had managed to talk to Sophie yet, though they'd both left several messages. Jenny had made sure she'd told her that their father might track her down.

"What are we so afraid of?" Maddie said. They had reached the entrance to the Tube and joined the queue at the machines so Jenny could buy a ticket. "He's only our bloody father."

"It's not us." Jenny took out her money. "It's her."

Jenny's stomach contracted as she thought of her mother lying in the hospital bed. What if their father was there right now, enticing her back to Ben Gallachie? Jenny was mad to have left her unguarded. She had given Maddie and Sophie's phone numbers to Piyali, but Piyali possibly didn't even know how to use a telephone. Jenny couldn't tell what was going on behind Piyali's blue gaze.

"You have to come to Inverness, Maddie. You have to help me. Sophie too."

"I know, but it's so weird. Does she even want us there?"

"She asked for you and Sophie specifically so, yes, she does." While Maddie was taking this in, Jenny continued. "The thing is, if he finds her, I'm sure he'll take her back there, and she really doesn't want to go."

"How can you know that? You said she was still groggy." Was Maddie still looking for excuses not to come back with her?

"You should have seen her face," Jenny told her. "Then you'd know."

Over dinner that evening in an Italian restaurant near Maddie's flat, Jenny tried to persuade her sister once again to return to Inverness with her the next day. Maddie had an interview with *Canvas* magazine booked, however, and Jenny couldn't convince her to ask them to postpone it or see if she could do it by telephone from Scotland or en route. Maddie told her it had taken too long to set up.

It was a bit much, Jenny pointed out, asking for an interview on a bank holiday, but Maddie said it was an American magazine — the illustrious *Canvas* — so they didn't know or care about that. When Maddie told Jenny it might be her only chance for an interview in such a prestigious magazine, Jenny could see Maddie really believed it.

It was endearing that Maddie still seemed to think her success was formed of clay, that it hadn't yet been hardened into the certainty of ceramic by the heat of a kiln. She accepted Maddie's proposal that they simply travel north to Inverness the day after instead.

Hi Jenny

It was good to get your email. That's good you caught up on sleep at your sister's flat. Hang in there, OK? I'm thinking of you all the time. You'll be back soon and then we can really talk. Hey, Kay and Ryan say hi and get back as soon as you can (and, no, they're still "just good friends"). They say it's not the same here without your British humor. Humour, I should say, am I American? We went out to the glacial valley again. Beautiful. Sunset is getting later and later each day (if it wasn't, I'd be worried). The solstice festival sounds awesome. How about we make some snow sculptures? They're stashing blocks of snow specially for it.

I miss you. Come back quick.

Dominic
xxx

"Anything interesting?" Maddie placed a red coffee mug beside Jenny. It was the day after the *Canvas* interview and Maddie was still in her nightie and dressing gown. There was a lot of red in Maddie's flat, Jenny had noticed. She could feel Maddie looking over her shoulder at the computer screen. Thank God Dominic hadn't said anything about her sisters, or anything intimate. She closed his email and stayed facing the computer so Maddie wouldn't see her blushing. She started to look up train times.

Maddie wanted to know if Dominic was Canadian and what his job was. "Are Canadians like Americans when it comes to English accents?" Maddie asked next. "Americans can't get enough of it. I had a dealer from Pittsburgh after me once. Pittsburgh! I don't even know where that is. Hey, the Arctic would be the ultimate wedding destination."

Jenny took a sip of coffee, even though it was too hot and didn't have any sugar in it.

"You know your geologist wrote that email very carefully, don't you? There's nothing slapdash about it. Got the spelling and punctuation right. Most people don't bother. I don't. And he deleted and re-typed those kisses at least six times while he decided how many to put. I can tell. It leaves a trace like rubbed-out pencil."

Jenny rolled her eyes at Maddie.

"Don't worry," Maddie added. "You'll be back on Boffin Island before you know it."

"It's Baffin Island, not Boffin."

"You don't say. Right, I'd better get dressed. By the way," she said from the doorway. "Does he know you could have been a scientist? You were good at everything at school."

"Shall I book our train tickets for tonight?" said Jenny, ignoring her. "We could get the night train."

"Don't change the subject. You've got to stop being so modest, Jenny. Honestly, you have to blow your own trumpet if you're going to get anywhere in this world."

"Have you rung your gallery yet to tell them you've got to go away for a couple of days?"

"Don't be so bossy." Maddie came back into the room and went over to the phone.

Maddie said she hadn't known until after the *Canvas* interview yesterday that she had two meetings today, organized by her gallery. One was with a potential client she said was on the level of Saatchi and there was no way she could miss it. As far as Jenny was concerned, that didn't mean they couldn't leave this evening, though. It was hard to be sure whether Maddie really didn't know what was in her diary one day to the next — which wouldn't actually surprise Jenny — or if she was deliberately coming up with reasons to avoid going to Scotland.

Maddie took the phone over to the sitting room window and looked down onto the street. "Andrew, hi. I've got Francis wotsit at the studio at eleven, right, on my own? But this afternoon you're going to join me for the big one? I hope so."

Jenny looked at her watch. It was twenty to eleven. Maddie's studio was close, but surely she couldn't get there that quickly. She wasn't even dressed.

"And then," Maddie was saying, "I might have to go away for a day or two. Family stuff. Skeletons in the cupboard and all that." She paused, listening. "Yeah, yeah, I'll be back for the Tate Modern preview," she said, laughing. She listened again. "Shit," she said. "Shit. Hold on a sec." Maddie put her palm over the receiver. "A man saying he was my father went to the gallery yesterday afternoon asking to meet me," she told Jenny. "They thought he was a client until he said who he was. He wanted my number and address, but they didn't give it to him. He said he'd ring them at midday today in case they'd had a chance to talk to me. What shall I say?"

They stared at each other.

"He's changed tactics," Jenny said. "He didn't tell my PhD supervisor who he was."

"I don't want him pestering Andrew or the others there. Or suddenly turning up on my doorstep, here or my studio."

"Better to do it on our own terms? That's if we think we should meet him."

"If we met him, we could try to suss him out."

"Let's say we'll meet him somewhere neutral," Jenny suggested. "If Andrew's okay being our go-between?"

"That man loves a bit of intrigue. I don't want to meet him anywhere public. We're bound to argue. A client might see me."

"Or the media." That was what Maddie really meant. "Not here in your flat, surely."

Maddie shook her head. "What about my studio? If we're both there?"

Jenny would have thought that Maddie's studio was even more private than her flat. "If you're okay with that. What time shall we say? One o'clock? Between your appointments?"

"Yeah, let's get it over with."

Jenny had been thinking more about the urgency of getting back to their mother.

"Oh my God," Maddie said when she'd put down the phone, half-laughing, her lips in a wide smile. "I really, really don't want to do this."

She was flattered. Flattered their father had found her through the web, had found her gallery, because it meant she was well-known.

"Weren't you seeing Andrew? Or am I getting mixed up?"

"No, I was seeing him, but it was getting a bit too intense for my liking."

"You don't want intense?"

"God, no. That's what art's for. I just want to have fun when I'm not working."

Jenny didn't see the point of a relationship unless it was intense. Not that Maddie was asking.

"I'll get dressed," said Maddie, leaving the living room, "or I'll be late."

"I think you already are," said Jenny, out of Maddie's earshot.

After Maddie had left the flat, Jenny carried a plate with two slices of toast to the kitchen table. She had plenty of time for breakfast; the studio was within walking distance. Through the window she could see the backs of houses, brick walls and gardens crammed with bushes and trees and sheds and greenhouses in a delightful, urban miscellany of straight lines, oblongs and foliage. The next-door neighbour's cherry tree was in bloom. If you had a bird feeder out there, you'd attract all sorts of species.

She mustn't forget to ask if Maddie had their grandparents' telephone number in Sutton Coldfield. Jenny had the number in her old address book at her flat, so she could always get it if she needed to. At some point they'd have to ring their mother's parents, Grandma and Grandad, to let them know what had happened. Jenny wanted to know what was going on between her parents before they did that, though.

She'd rung the hospital yesterday, between long naps, and the nurse had said her mother was doing well. It was hard to know exactly what that meant without seeing her. While Jenny of course wanted to get back to her mother, at the same time, there was a comfort to being in

Maddie's bright flat, sleeping, drinking tea, looking through Maddie's art books, pretending it was a normal visit and their parents hadn't really cut through the membrane that, for eight years, had separated their lives as definitively as if they existed in parallel universes.

When Jenny had finished her toast, she picked up the phone, licking margarine grease off her fingers. She dialled Sophie's number, waiting for the click of the answering machine.

"Hello?"

Sophie was actually there.

"It's Jenny."

"I was wondering when I'd hear from you again." Sophie's voice was gluey, as if she'd been rehearsing a crying scene. "So you came all the way back from the Arctic wastes to rush to the mother's bedside like a lapdog."

"I'm in London now." Jenny ignored the bait. "At Maddie's."

Sophie grunted. Jenny didn't know how to interpret that. She told Sophie she needed to ask her something. "Has our father tried to get in touch with you? He went to the university to look for me and now he's rung Maddie's gallery."

"Don't think so, unless he was the heavy breather I got the other night." Sophie didn't sound perturbed.

"The thing is, if he contacts the gallery again, we've asked them to let him know we've agreed to meet him. At Maddie's studio at one o'clock. Today. We need to find out what he's after."

"When will you learn to stop playing into their hands?"

"That's not fair. Our mother could have died. It was touch and go, the hospital said. You haven't seen her. She's scared. We need to find out what she wants. If she wants to leave, then I think we should help her do that."

"I don't see why we need to get involved." Sophie said. "I can't forget everything that's happened, just like that. I know I was an idiot in Brighton, but they accused me of murder and then they gave up on me. They came to see me and Maddie in London once and that was only because you made them. I haven't laid eyes on them for nearly twelve years, Jenny. I honestly don't think I owe them anything."

After the call, Jenny went to the kitchen. No one in her family was doing what she wanted them to. Why wasn't she used to that? She filled the kettle then rinsed out Maddie's red cafetière. Coffee was probably banned at Ben Gallachie. Her mother used to love it. Coffee until lunchtime then tea in the afternoon, as otherwise she wouldn't sleep. Jenny remembered Grandfather coming into the kitchen every morning in Brighton and complaining about the smell of her mother's coffee. Boot scrapings, he used to call it. Grandfather had hated so many things. Everyone in her family had so many opinions, it was a miracle there were any left over for her.

⌒

"Don't listen to your mother," Grandfather says to Jenny one Saturday in his room at the house in Brighton. She's brought him his afternoon cup of tea and a custard cream because he only ever comes downstairs at mealtimes. Which is entirely his choice. Jenny remembers looking around to see if he's talking to someone who has come in behind her. She doesn't know what he's talking about.

"Her bum's oot the windae — all that rubbish about only being one thing in life."

Ah, so Grandfather is still cross about Sophie not playing his violin.

He's sitting in his armchair in the brown suit and waistcoat he always wears. It wasn't until he died that Jenny found out he has three brown suits; she'd thought he'd worn the same one every day.

"You do whatever you want," he tells her. "Just make sure you get your qualifications. You're cleverer than the lot of them, those glaikit sisters of yours. The world's your oyster if you've got qualifications. They're yours, no one else's. Once you've got them, no one can take them away from you. Then you can do whatever you like."

He says it crossly, as if she really should know this by now.

Jenny puts his cup of tea down on the little table by his armchair. She has no clue what to say. It's because he used to be a head teacher, she assumes. He'd say the same to anyone. "I won't forget," she says.

Grandfather grunts as if he doesn't believe her.

He doesn't say anything else so she leaves the room. She glances back before she pulls the door shut. He's dunking his custard cream in his tea and he doesn't look up.

⁓

It came back to her, his advice, every now and then. After a while, after he'd died and they'd moved to Willowbrae, she began to wonder if it hadn't been very particular advice aimed specifically at her after all.

Nineteen

JEAN STANDS IN front of Jenny on the landing at Willowbrae, holding a can of polish and a yellow duster. "Do you have a minute?"

"Of course. Though you know polishing isn't exactly my forte."

Jean doesn't smile.

Jenny follows her into the guest bedroom that has the same view as her own room.

"Your mum and dad." Jean is clutching the polish and cloth with both hands. "I wanted to check if you'd noticed. You're in your room so much, revising."

"They're better, you mean. Back to themselves?"

Jean shakes her head. "They're going to an awful lot of those Gallachist meditations."

"It's just a way to relax. All they do is lie on the floor and fall asleep." Jenny's father has started going to the meditations as well. If that's why they both seem more like themselves again, then she's glad.

"There are Gallachist courses here all the time now." Jean's brown eyes are round and serious. "Pretty much every week."

"Well, they're good business."

"It's a dangerous organization. It's a cult."

Jenny laughs. "They're just meditating."

"I never told you, did I?" Jean sits down on the bed. "About Paul."

Paul, Jean's son, who Jean and her husband haven't seen for a long time. He's in New Zealand and they've fallen out, that's all Jenny knows.

"What's happened?" Jenny sits down beside Jean.

"Nothing new. He's in New Zealand like I told you, but the reason he's there and won't have anything to do with us is that he joined —" she pauses. "A cult. New Nazareth. He got involved with them in Glasgow. We tried to stop him, but he joined anyway, and then they were looking for people to start things up in New Zealand, so off he went." Jean pulls the edges of her cardigan together and holds them with fisted hands. "He thinks Jesus has been reincarnated. There's this woman they worship."

"They think Jesus has come back as a woman? So I suppose it's a religion. Is that such a bad thing? I know we're not religious, but lots of people are."

"It's a cult, not a religion. What if I never see Paul again?"

Jenny reaches for one of Jean's hands and holds it. Jean's hands always look tanned. Not from holidays — from years of sitting and standing outside so she can smoke. She doesn't smoke anymore, although the tan remains like a tobacco stain. Not after she'd had cancer years ago, before Jenny met her.

"Why didn't you tell me all this before?"

"It's hard to talk about it. We've failed at our job. Parents are supposed to keep their bairns safe. I keep praying he leaves one day."

Jenny scans her mind as if somewhere among all the useless studying she will find a solution. "Can't the police do something?"

"There's no crime. Not if Paul's there willingly." She takes a deep breath, her chest juddering as she lets it out again. "These sorts of folk are very persuasive. That's why I'm worried about your mum and dad."

"But this is nothing like that. I mean, it's not, is it?" She thinks of Deepali's liquid eyes, her fingers stroking her own arm. "This is a completely different group."

"It's not normal to shut yourself away from the rest of life. That's when things happen."

"But they're not shut away. They're here at Willowbrae."

"They have a place. I told you, up near Mallaig. A commune. They're only here to recruit folk. It's the only reason they have any connection with normal life."

"I'll talk to them," Jenny says. "My parents. I'm sure there's nothing to worry about. They're too cynical to believe in anything. But I'll talk to them."

Jean takes her hand away from Jenny's. "I see them floating around in those eejit clothes and it makes me feel sick. Alan doesn't like seeing me like this. He's worried the cancer will come back. They're on the list, that's the thing."

"What list?"

"Alan and me. We're in touch with this organization in Glasgow, Free Minds, that helps parents. Have been for a long time. They have a list of groups they've identified as cults. The Gallachists are one of them. That's why I know about them." Jean takes another juddering breath. "The Free Minds folk even sent someone out from their Wellington office, years ago. They tried. They're trying all the time with the Nazareths, apparently. He's been in so long. They say the longer it is, the harder."

"I'm so sorry." Jenny doesn't know what else to say.

"I want you to promise me you won't let anyone recruit you."

Jenny laughs. It just comes out. The idea is ridiculous.

"These people are powerful." Jean isn't laughing. "They blether on and wear you down. What I want you to promise me is that if you're ever thinking of getting involved with them, you'll come and talk to me. You won't do anything without talking to me."

Jenny stands up. She shrugs. "Okay." It's an easy promise to make.

Jenny flicks through the bookings diary. Jean is right. There are Gallachist workshops almost every week right through the summer. Jenny slaps the diary shut. Her mother is in her bedroom. The wardrobe door is open and she's throwing clothes onto the bed. She's donating them to a jumble sale to help raise funds for the new arts centre. Jenny yanks off a bin liner bag from the roll and starts folding up skirts, shirts and jackets and putting them inside. She puts a couple of sweaters aside to try on for herself.

"So, tonight," Jenny says. "Are you going to the meditation session again?"

"Yep." Her mother throws a mustard-coloured shirt onto the bed. Jenny doesn't mind that one going. "You should come, darling. Relax you for your exams."

"I don't need relaxing."

"I'm not so sure." A skirt is flung next. Royal blue corduroy. Knee-length. Jenny remembers her mother wearing it at the gallery in Brighton with woolly tights. "You're looking pale. All the exam stress. You're losing weight too."

"I'm fine." Jenny means it; she's terrified, of course, but she's filling each day with as much revision as possible. If she fails, at least she'll know she's done her best. That won't make her feel any better, but it will be the truth. She should write that down somewhere so she doesn't forget when the exam results come out.

"Why do you have to go to the session?" Jenny says. "Can't you just lie on the floor somewhere on your own and meditate?"

"Oh, we're sitting up now," says her mother with mock pride. "And it's not meditation as such. Well it is, but it's more guided. Visualization. You know, you picture things. Things you want to deal with." Jenny's mother puts her hands on her hips and looks at all the clothes on the bed as if someone else has put them there.

"You know they're on a list, don't you?" Jenny says. "The Gallachists."

"What do you mean, a list?"

"It's a cult, Mummy. They're on a list of cults."

Her mother turns to Jenny, laughing. "Oh, this is Jean, isn't it, I can tell."

"Well, yes, she told me, but that's not the point."

"It's not her fault, darling, but Jean isn't educated." Her mother pushes the remaining hangers along the rail, lifting clothes to look at them as if she's in a shop. "You shouldn't just believe everything she says."

"Her son, Paul. He's in a cult in New Zealand. She just told me."

"I'm very sad to hear that, but it has nothing to do with Gallachism. Honestly Jenny, I wish you wouldn't go off half-cocked. Jean doesn't know what she's talking about half the time. She reads the *Mirror*, for heaven's sake."

"She hasn't seen her son for over thirteen years. He doesn't have any contact with her or Alan. He's brainwashed."

"Now *you're* sounding like a tabloid."

Jenny drops the jacket she's been folding; she's out of words.

"Look," says her mother more softly. "There are plenty of reasons for children not to have anything to do with their parents. And vice versa. As we know in this family only too well. It's very sad that Jean is estranged from her son, but perhaps the cult, if that's what it is, is just a convenient target to blame."

Jenny pushes her knees against the bed to keep herself steady. She wants to ask her mother what it feels like not to have seen your daughter for over three years. Is that something she's working on, trying to *deal with*, when she meditates?

"I do feel sorry for Jean, of course I do," her mother says, "but she's got no right to tar Gallachism with the same brush. All we do is sit around and try to let some space and light into our lives. Peace, you know? She should try it instead of ripping it apart."

Space and light. Jenny tries to imagine a clear blue sky. Instead, she pictures the ocean, water that is never still. When she first saw buoys bobbing on the sea as a child, Jenny didn't realize they were attached to underwater ropes. She thought they were floating freely. She used to worry about them, lying in bed in her room in Brighton, imagining them drifting farther and farther out to sea.

"To be honest," her mother says, "that woman needs to watch what she says. She's our employee and the Gallachists are our clients. Very good ones. I've already had to have words with her about how rude she is to them. Sam and Christine don't have any complaints."

Sam and Christine, their other staff, wouldn't dare. Jenny puts a burgundy skirt on top of the pile inside the bin liner. It's nearly full now.

"You should give it a go, Jenny. Then it won't be such a mystery for you and you won't fill your head with all this rubbish. I really do think it will help you with your exams. I'm sleeping so much better these days. It helps put everything into perspective."

"Maybe." She won't, though. All she has to do to find peace and light is go for one of her rambles in the woods.

They have five bin liners full of clothes by the time they finish. Jenny helps her mother take them out to the car then goes up to her room. She has to read over her notes about the Cold War. What she really wants to do is whittle the latest stick she's found in which she can see the form of a frog emerging. She believes, when she works on her wood spirits, she's discovering shapes that exist already, not creating them. She wants to sit in her window seat easing off parings of wood with her chip knife and not think about anything else. If her mother wants to give all her nice clothes away and waste her time sitting in a trance every night then let her.

Her mother has sacked Jean. Or Jean has left. It's hard to tell which. Her mother is vague. She says they had a bit of a row and ended up coming to a mutual agreement. Jenny feels guilty because she told her mother what Jean had said about Gallachism being a cult. Her mother says it didn't make any difference. It was a storm that had been brewing for some time.

It's the afternoon before her first exam — history — and Jenny cycles into Peebles to Jean's house, the air flowing over her knuckles as she pedals into the wind. She should be revising Mussolini's rise to power in 1925. Cycling so quickly along the lane might even be more useful at this late stage. More blood is getting pumped to her brain, more oxygen, than when she sits at her desk.

Jenny knows where Jean lives; she used to visit Jean and her husband Alan on her cycle ride home from her piano lesson. That was a long time ago, when Jenny was thirteen. Jean would always give her a glass of blackcurrant squash and a Tunnock's Snowball, sticky and gooey and delicious.

Jean is in and they sit in her kitchen, but she doesn't offer Jenny anything to eat or drink. She says she didn't realize Jenny's mother had
such a low opinion of her and, no, she didn't resign. She was definitely
sacked.

Jenny apologizes for telling her mother what Jean said about Gallachism being a cult and then she apologizes for her mother. For saying
whatever she said. "She doesn't think before she speaks," Jenny says.
"She doesn't think about things from other people's point of view."

Jean doesn't seem to want to talk about it, so Jenny gets up to leave.
She turns as she opens the back door to say goodbye and sees Jean take
a packet of cigarettes out of her handbag. Jenny opens her mouth to say
something, but the hostile, unfamiliar look Jean gives her stops her. She
hears the click of Jean's lighter just before she closes the door.

She will visit Jean again when she has time to think, when she's finished her exams. She will tell Jean she has to stop smoking. Why would
she do something so self-destructive? How could she risk getting cancer again?

Jenny's exams are spread over three weeks. All she does is revise, sit
exams, eat and walk briskly up to her lookout stone and back, using the
time away from her desk to test herself on whichever subject is coming
up next. It's not possible to think about anything else. She ignores her
mother's recurring advice to take a break and meditate with her. Taking a break is too stressful, Jenny tries to explain. She notices her parents aren't watching as much television and wonders if that's because
they're trying not to distract her. She eats supper with them as usual,
but mostly with her handwritten notes beside her plate. Sometimes
she'll persuade her father to test her on river basin management or the
advantages and disadvantages of trade alliances.

She's counting the days until the exams are over and she can get on
the train with her friend Helen to go and see Maddie and Sophie in
London. She's never gone with a friend before. Helen keeps joking that
she doesn't believe Jenny's sisters really exist.

Twenty

SOMETHING IS GOING ON. Jenny's mother has that shine in her eyes she had when they moved to Scotland and again when they decided to convert the coach house. Even though Jenny's father doesn't seem to be spending any time in his studio, something is energizing him as he chats with the guests, phones through the orders to the bulk food company and sings through the steam as he unloads the dishwasher.

Jenny and Helen are back from London, where they had a brilliant time celebrating the end of their exams: galleries, a play, shopping, watching buskers and two parties. They slept on inflatable beds on the floor of the sitting room in Maddie and Sophie's flat — the same flat Jenny had made her parents drive to for Christmas — talking until the early hours about the future and how they would remain friends wherever their lives took them. They went to Stanfords travel bookshop in Covent Garden so Jenny could buy a guidebook for Australia. They took the train to New Cross so Helen could stand outside Goldsmiths University where she hoped to do her teacher training.

There is more work for Jenny at Willowbrae now that Jean has left. She plans to work as much as she can over the summer to save up to go travelling, and perhaps find a part-time job in Peebles as well. Now that exams are behind her — and even though she won't get the results for weeks — she can at last think about the rest of her life.

A week or so after the London trip, Jenny's mother tells her she and Jenny's father would like a little talk with her. "Nine-ish tonight in the living room," her mother says. "After Sam and Christine have gone home."

Jenny is looking forward to finding out what her parents are up to. Maybe her father is going to have another exhibition or her mother is in a play. Or directing a play. That could be something her mother would be very good at. Jenny might even suggest it. Such things wouldn't require *a little talk*, though, surely.

It has to be something to do with the business. She hasn't asked them lately how things are going financially. She was so caught up in exams, then visiting Maddie and Sophie and, now, working at Willowbrae, visiting Edinburgh with Helen and walking in the woods. Perhaps they're building an extension on the coach house so they can run more courses and make more money. Perhaps they're going to requisition Jenny's bedroom while she's travelling in Australia so they can fit in more guests. Yet why the light in her mother's eye and her father's energy?

At nine that evening, Jenny finds her father sitting in his armchair jiggling one knee up and down like some of the boys did at school. He's made them a cup of tea and has brought in the biscuit tin.

"So what's all this about?" Jenny dunks a Bourbon biscuit and lifts the soggy end quickly to her mouth.

"Let's wait for your mother." Her father reaches to take a biscuit too, then changes his mind and sits back in his chair. Now his foot is bobbing. He picks up one of his art magazines and flicks through it.

"You're not meditating tonight?" Jenny says.

"No, no. We wanted to find a quiet time when we could have a chat with you."

Jenny's mother comes into the room. "Marvellous," she says when she sees the tea. "Thanks, Alasdair." She sits down heavily. "That's better." She takes a glug of tea as if it's the first liquid she's had all day.

"So, what's the big news?" says Jenny.

Her parents look at each other and her mother gives a tiny nod.

"We know how much you love Willowbrae." Jenny's father leans forward and rests his forearms on his knees.

"So do you."

"Yes," says her father. "We do. Very much. We've been very happy here."

Her mother catches her father's eye and he winces. "What I mean is," he adds quickly, "we've reached a stage in our lives. And so have you. You're off travelling soon. Then university. It's a very exciting time for you."

"And," says Jenny's mother, cutting in, "it happens to be a very exciting time for us too. We've made a big decision and we want — well, you're an adult now. You're not going to want to hang around us anymore. You've got such an exciting time ahead of you."

That word again. *Exciting.* Jenny isn't sure she wants excitement. She tries to think of the tawny owl emerging from the stick she's been carving in her room upstairs; it's slipping back into the grain of the wood. She can't see it anymore. "You'd better just tell me."

Her mother looks at her tea but doesn't pick it up. "We've decided to sell Willowbrae. We're going to join the Gallachists at their centre near Mallaig. It's called Ben Gallachie."

Jenny can't speak; her throat is being squeezed by a pair of pliers. They have to be joking. She feels a sound scratching in her throat.

"Daddy," she says, looking at him and not her mother. "You can't agree with this?"

"I do, Jenny Wren. This is a joint decision. Very much so." Her father crosses his legs. "We're doers, not facilitators. We don't want to wash sheets and scrub frying pans for the rest of our lives."

"But why join the Gallachists?" Jenny tries to keep control of her voice, to keep it from stretching as thin as thread. "There's so much more you could do here if you wanted to —" She pauses. "You know, if you wanted to be more fulfilled."

Why hasn't she seen this coming? Why don't her parents ever tell her what's going on?

"The courses have been fantastic," her father says, "but we need to be doing something for ourselves now. We need to learn, grow. Those aren't things you do only when you're young. You're going travelling. You're going to experience so much. Learn so much."

"Or," says her mother and stops. She looks at Jenny's father as if they've agreed that the next line is his.

"Or," says her father, "and don't answer straight away. Please think about this very carefully. We want you to come with us."

Jenny stands. She can't possibly sit any longer. "You're joining a cult and you want me to come with you."

"You'd love it, Jenny. On a sea loch at the foot of the mountains. You can walk for miles. You'd have to work for your keep, we all do, but you could be a teacher, you know you'd be great at that. Passing on the learnings of the supremes. Or a gardener, then you'd be outside all the time. You love being outdoors."

Jenny's mother gives her father a nod. She's telling him he's done a good job.

Her father goes over to the sideboard and takes some photographs out of a drawer. He spreads them out. "Come and have a look. Come on."

"I can see them from here." They're pictures of Ben Gallachie, of course. Little white houses with long grey roofs, right on the water. Above, vast green mountains, some with snow on top. It's beautiful.

"They sent us these. That's not Ben Gallachie itself, that's the village," says her father, going closer to Jenny. "It's called Inverie. This," he holds up a photograph towards her as if he's performing a card trick, "is Ben Gallachie."

The picture has been taken from the water. There's a narrow, stony beach and beyond it a terraced row of original stone cottages with a long turf roof. Beside a stand of tall Scots pines, there's a large, wooden structure farther into the trees; it's unfinished, two pyramid shapes are emerging. Again, hills and mountains rise up gloriously behind the buildings. There are so many greens and blues and yellows. No orange;

the bracken hasn't turned colour yet. There would be red squirrels and red deer and pine martens and mountain hares. Perhaps even a wildcat.

"You can only get there by boat," her father says. "Isn't that fantastic?"

Her parents are both watching her as she looks at the photograph. Her father is right. It's the most perfect place to live that Jenny could ever imagine, apart from Willowbrae. She will never see it, though. She will never go there.

"So, let me get this right." Jenny rests her hands on the back of an armchair. "You don't want me to do a degree. You don't want me to go travelling. You want me to join a cult." She doesn't know how she's managing to talk so calmly. She doesn't know how she's managing to talk at all. Her parents have gone mad and she's talking to them as if they're still rational human beings.

"Please stop calling it a cult, Jenny," says her mother. "We're a group of people trying to be spiritually connected. We're trying to make the world a better place."

"This would give you so much more than a degree ever could," her father says. "So much more. You've no idea."

Jenny clutches the back of the chair. "You've gone insane."

"Quite the opposite." Her father is using his patient voice. What used to be his Sophie voice. "They've worked it out, you know? The meditation, the self-awareness, the consciousness. You must have noticed how peaceful it's been here since the Gallachists started coming." Her father looks at her without blinking. "We're going to help save the world, Jenny."

He really believes what he's saying. An idea lights up her mind like lightning. "You can do that here," she says. "Solar panels. Wind turbines. Recycling. Grow vegetables. Make Willowbrae sustainable, an example of alternative energy. People would come to see it. We could have courses on alternative energy, sustainability. There's a place like that in Wales I've heard about."

"It's not just about the environment," her father says, as if he's explaining something that she should have worked out for herself. "We're talking about the human race's spiritual survival."

"How do you know they're not the same thing?" Her blood doesn't know which way to flow. Her fingers are hot and her toes are cold.

Her father smiles. "That's why you should come with us, Jenny Wren. You have these wonderful thoughts. If you come with us you'll be able to explore ideas like that."

"Why are you doing this?" She mustn't cry. She has to reason with them. Get them to see what a terrible mistake they're making, how they're wasting their lives.

"You're an adult now. We've made our decision." Her mother is ending the conversation; Jenny knows the signs, how she closes her face by narrowing her lips. "We're selling Willowbrae. The first viewer's coming on Saturday."

Jenny's father frowns; he doesn't think Jenny's mother should have mentioned that.

"It's already for sale?" Jenny can feel her lower lip quivering. She realizes, then, that the estate agent came while she was in London. Her parents had planned it all. The quivering stops. For all she knows, her heart has stopped too.

"We waited until your exams were over," her mother says. "We didn't want to interfere with that."

She feels cold, empty. The shock of it all has gouged her out. "That's very considerate of you. Thank you for informing me. I'd appreciate it if you could let me know what date I need to be out of the house by." She rushes out of the room.

She doesn't go upstairs or out into the woods; she goes to the reception desk and picks up the telephone receiver.

"Hello?" she hears Sophie say after a few rings. Pliers are gripping Jenny's throat again. She manages to squeeze out a noise but it isn't a word.

"Jenny? Is that you?"

Jenny tries to dislodge the pliers gripping her throat. "It's Mummy and Daddy," she whispers. "They're joining the Gallachists."

"Who the fuck are the Gallachists? A pop group?"

"I told you. The people they've been meditating with for the last few months, the group who keep running courses here."

"Oh, those weirdos. So, what's new?"

Jenny breathes to open her throat. "They're selling Willowbrae. They're going to live with the Gallachists. Somewhere near Mallaig."

"I've no idea where that is, but I imagine it's beyond the back of beyond. They're bonkers. I thought they were bored and unfulfilled, not actually insane."

Jenny makes a noise that comes from all the hollow places inside her.

"Get out of there," Sophie says. "Come and live with us. Go to college in London. Get away from them as soon as you can."

Thoughts arrive like barbed arrows. They fire at Jenny at any moment from any direction, whatever she might be doing. Brushing her teeth, hanging out washing, reading a novel. They enter her easily and are impossible to yank out. Her parents would rather join a cult than be with her, their daughter. Her parents have chosen a group of people they barely know over her, Maddie and Sophie. They're running away from life. It's not a holiday or a gap year. It's forever.

And Willowbrae. She's losing her home. What will she do without her lookout stone? Her window seat. Going down the steps to the basement and the warm, noisy kitchen. The curve of the banister up to the first floor. The skirting board by the bathroom door that's coming loose.

Sitting on the loo, a spear pierces her navel: she won't be going travelling. She will have to work during her gap year. She has to fend for herself now. She has to burn all her plans and start again.

Jenny finds her mother straightening chairs and tables in the upstairs studio after she's vacuumed the carpet, her hair tied back with a drab green headscarf.

"What if I ran Willowbrae?" says Jenny. "I could be your manager. You wouldn't have to pay me much. Then you needn't sell it. I don't have to go to university."

Her mother pushes a chair under a table. "That's sweet of you, but we need the money from the sale. We need to pay off the loan and then the rest will be invested to cover our keep at Ben Gallachie."

"Willowbrae's a business. It makes money. You'll pay off the loan eventually and I can send you money to live on."

Her mother shifts one end of a table. Jenny doesn't get hold of the other end to help her. "The thing is," her mother says, "we can't join Ben Gallachie if we have any debts or assets. It's one of the practices. You have to be unburdened. Nor are you supposed to have any ties to the non-Gallachist life, such as businesses or properties."

"Or daughters?"

"Don't be like that, Jenny. You're not Sophie. Come with us. We don't want to leave you behind. We want you with us."

"No, you don't. You just don't want the bother of daughters who have different opinions from you. Well, don't worry, I'll be out of your way soon."

Her mother closes her eyes as if words can never express how much pain Jenny is causing her. Her mother, ever the drama queen. Jenny leaves the studio and shuts the door behind her.

Jenny begins to hear a gentle voice in her head, a feathery voice, perhaps an owl's, telling her to sleep as much as she likes, to stop and look out the window for long moments as she makes the beds, to take a stack of chocolate biscuits from the pantry and go up to her room and sit in the window seat to eat them. She doesn't need to have meals with her parents anymore if she doesn't want to, however often they come to her room to get her.

It's a kind voice. It's also practical. Late one night as Jenny sits in her window seat, the voice tells her to ring UCCA, less feathery. Tell them you need to start university next term after all. Explain that you have to because you no longer have parental support. Get on with your career. Don't have a gap year to save up money. Work while you're at university. Ring the grant office too. They'll know what to do. They'll help you.

Sometimes the kind voice is silent. Another voice takes over then. This other voice is as loud as a pneumatic drill when you walk too closely to roadworks. It has nothing of owl or bird, only machine. This voice tells her she's stupid to have imagined she could ever have gone to Australia to travel and meet Uncle Fraser and his family. This voice tells her there's no point seeing much of Helen anymore as they're bound to drift apart once Helen is at university in London and Jenny is in Edinburgh.

This voice instructs Jenny to gather her wood spirits from around her bedroom and the sticks drying in the storeroom and take all of them to the edge of the vegetable patch where they have bonfires. Go to the kitchen, the voice tells her, and find a box of matches. Next, collect some old newspapers from the pile in the utility room.

The sticks burn quickly; they are dry after all and the linseed oil makes the flames a nice bright orange that shows up well even though it's daylight. Jenny is good at following instructions. She obeys both voices.

She carries on working her shifts at Willowbrae. She doesn't talk much to the staff, Sam and Christine, who are whispering together a lot, now they've been given their notice. Christine smiles at Jenny with sad eyes, and Jenny smiles back quickly and leaves the kitchen or carries on down the hallway, even if it means pretending she's going somewhere other than she intended. Sam has been much quieter anyway since Jean left. She hardly says anything to Jenny. She looks at her as if she thinks Jenny should be able to stop her parents selling up.

Jenny tries to pay as much attention to Willowbrae as she can. She lifts warm piles of clean sheets from the utility room and feels the soles of her feet on each stair as she goes up the two flights to the guests' bedrooms. She feels the smooth coolness of each brass door handle she turns, not bothering to tell her father when a rose — if that's what they're called — is loose because it doesn't matter anymore, and anyway she likes the little jangle it makes. She polishes chests of drawers and bedside tables and even runs a cloth along skirting boards and flicks the duster along picture rails. She will not be angry with this house; she will honour it, wash its basins, its showers, its hair, its feet.

She starts taking a small sketch pad and a 4B pencil up to the lookout stone. She sketches the view from every angle, twisting herself around on the stone, the soft Tweed Valley, the distant bare hills, the thick forest behind her. Back at Willowbrae, she enters each room and chooses something to draw. An egg and dart moulding. A twelve-paned window. The bevel of a skirting board. A view of the corridor leading to her room. The sitting room mantelpiece. The Aga. The eight mossy steps leading up to the front door where horizontal meets vertical. She takes photographs. Many. She will get them developed in Edinburgh when she's ready to look at them.

Jenny isn't rude to the people who come to view Willowbrae twice. She tells them it's a wonderful house and she's sure they'll love it as much as she does, even though she knows that isn't possible. When she isn't working, she walks. She can't read books or watch television. She can only eat standing at the counter when the kitchen is empty or alone in her bedroom, and she can only eat bread and cheese and chocolate biscuits: nothing cooked. She can't drink tea or coffee. Heat makes her nauseous. There's already too much heat in her. It burns in her lungs and stomach and scorches her throat. Only by moving can she keep the fire under control. The one place she can sit is the lookout stone, and only if she speeds up the hill so quickly she can hardly breathe by the time she reaches the top. Even then, she has to rise from the stone to walk again after a few minutes; the fire is flickering at the backs of her eyeballs by then.

Twenty-one

THE FREE MINDS office is on West George Street near the junction with Hope Street, which is either apt or unkind, Jenny can't decide. West George Street is Jenny's favourite road in Glasgow. The buildings are the colour of sand when the tide has been in and is on its way out again. She's found the phone number and address with the help of a nice lady at directory enquiries and here she is now, walking up the wide stone steps that make her feel homesick for Willowbrae even though she hasn't left yet, not quite.

According to the doorbells beside the black door, the Free Minds office is two flights up, above an architect and a solicitor. Jenny doesn't ring the bell. She turns the polished silver knob and opens the door onto a large hall. Although there's a lift, an old-fashioned one with a metal door you draw closed yourself, Jenny crosses the black-and-white diamond tiles to the staircase. She needs to keep moving.

On the second-floor landing, the sign on the door says Free Minds in pretend handwriting below a white triangle of a yacht on a blue dash of sea with a curve of gull above. The door says please come in, so she does. A largish woman sitting at a reception desk looks up and smiles kindly. She's wearing loose clothes in autumnal colours that suit her chestnut hair. She takes Jenny's first name and asks if she'd like to see someone, then tells her to have a seat. That's all Jenny has to do: nod and sit on the sofa. She closes her eyes for a moment. The sound of the traffic outside is reassuring; lives are carrying on as normal.

This woman probably thinks Jenny has escaped from a cult. The sympathy in her eyes, the gentleness, as if Jenny is a horse she's trying not to scare. Jenny opens her mouth to explain it isn't herself she's come about and then shuts it again.

A door opens and a tall man with glasses and brown hair comes over to Jenny and introduces himself as Phil. When they shake hands, his hand is warm.

They sit by the window in Phil's office, in curved blue chairs with chrome legs. "You found us okay?"

Phil's Scottish accent is mild. Jenny wonders where he's from.

"Yes, thanks. It's not too far from the station. The journey went really quickly. I was reading about Tsar Nicholas the Second and Alexandra in the paper." She's talking too much, revealing her nervousness.

"Ah, the skeletons. And where did you get the train from?"

"Edinburgh, but I got the bus first from Peebles. I live near Peebles. For now, anyway." She looks down to avoid Phil's face. His knees are broad and square.

"And," says Phil, "was it your choice to come and see us today?"

"Oh, yes." Jenny looks at him now. He seems to like starting sentences with *and*. Perhaps it's a strategy for cult escapees.

"Would you like to tell me why you wanted to come?"

There's a knock on the door. The receptionist comes in and sets two mugs of strong tea down on the table, smiling at Jenny when she says thank you. Jenny picks up the mug nearest her and takes a sip. It's the first hot drink she's had for ages. She can feel the heat of it on the insides of her elbows.

The only person she's told about her parents, other than Maddie and Sophie, of course, is Helen, and even that was difficult. It doesn't make sense for her to be embarrassed about telling people what her parents are doing, yet she is. Embarrassed and ashamed. She made Helen promise she wouldn't tell anyone else. Not that Helen would; she isn't like that. Jenny wants to be the girl who lives at Willowbrae, not the girl whose parents are running away to join a cult. She hates that she even cares what people think.

"Whatever you tell me is entirely confidential," Phil says. "I won't write anything down."

"A friend of mine said you know about Gallachism," Jenny says.

"Yes, we do." When Jenny didn't say anything else, he continued. "A commune on the Knoydart Peninsula. The leader is Viparanda, self-styled guru. An eclectic set of beliefs drawing heavily on Buddhism — meditation, reincarnation and so on — but very much westernized. They target middle-aged people with significant savings and assets who are from English-speaking countries and have become disillusioned with life. Said to be broadening their targeting to the young, in order, presumably, to sustain the community. We're starting to see babies born into Gallachism now." He pauses.

Jenny takes a sip of tea while she takes all of this in.

"Have you been approached?" Phil says gently.

Jenny keeps both hands around the mug. "It's my parents."

Phil sits back in his chair and sighs. "Right."

"They're moving to the commune as soon as they sell our house. I can't get through to them." She tells Phil how it started with the workshops, how it was her fault her mother went to a meditation session in the first place.

Phil shakes his head and tells her that the Gallachists would have been working on her parents already. It wouldn't have made any difference if Jenny hadn't told them about the meditation sessions. The workshops are simply recruitment drives. He says it is likely the Gallachists researched the property and business specifically with recruitment of the owners in mind.

He asks Jenny how old she is and what other family she has and is relieved to hear she's going to university in the autumn. "My advice is to get on with your life but don't shut down communications. Try your best to keep the channels open, whatever happens. I know it's hard. What they're doing to you is incredibly hurtful. Try not to let that turn into anger against them. Feel sorry for them. They're vulnerable and they've been brainwashed. They're your parents. They're supposed to know what to do but now the roles are reversed."

He asks her if she's considered going to university in London so she's close to her sisters, but Jenny tells him she doesn't think she can face it; she's not a big city person. She's losing her home as it is; she doesn't want to lose Scotland altogether.

She realizes, as they're talking, that he's not going to call the police or a psychiatrist. Soldiers aren't going to storm Willowbrae and rescue her parents.

"Will you come and talk to them? Get them to see sense?"

"I can only do that if they're willing to meet me," Phil tells her. "I can phone them and see if they'd agree to a chat."

"There's no point. They won't."

"Take my card and I'll give you some leaflets as well. If you see any chinks, any sign they're open to changing their mind, ring me and I'll ring them and try. Don't give up. Never give up."

As Jenny walks down the stairs, it occurs to her that neither Phil nor the receptionist asked her full name. They have no record of who she is or who her parents are, no way to trace her or check how things are going. It's true that Phil told her to keep in touch, call him anytime. One of the leaflets he's given her is about counselling. He encouraged her to meet someone once a week. There's a counsellor in Edinburgh, he told her. It's free.

Sitting on the train back to Edinburgh, Jenny places the Free Minds leaflets in front of *The Guardian* so no one can see what she's reading. As well as the leaflet about counselling, Phil gave her one written for students. *You are a particular target of cults in the first term of your first year. They like to recruit young, intelligent and capable people who are interested in exploring different ideas and who may be feeling unsure of themselves.*

And a leaflet for parents. *However intelligent and capable your children are, they are at risk because they are questioning what life is all about and your answers to these questions might not be sufficient for them anymore.*

Jenny had looked at all the leaflets in the rack before she left; there was no leaflet for children whose parents had joined a cult, not even one parent, let alone two. She could write the leaflet herself and send it to the Free Minds office. *As your parents get older, you may find they ask questions you cannot give them the answers to: Why is my work so unfulfilling? How did I get to be this age and achieve so little? What happened to my dreams?*

Twenty-two

ALMOST EVERY EVENING, her mother finds Jenny in her room or in front of the television and presents her with an object. Her parents aren't allowed to take anything to Ben Gallachie that isn't essential. Jenny isn't sure what essential means exactly; presumably it extends to underwear and a toothbrush. She does know — because her parents have told her — that anything they do take will become the property of Ben Gallachie.

"If you still insist on not coming with us, this might come in useful," her mother says one evening while Jenny is watching *Dances with Wolves* on video, even though she's seen it before. Jenny presses pause on the remote control. Scratchy white lines score across Kevin Costner's pretty face.

Her mother is holding out a butter dish.

"I never eat butter," Jenny says. "Margarine comes in tubs."

"But we got it in Brighton from that lovely kitchen shop in Gardner Street, remember?"

"I won't use it." Jenny points the remote control at the television.

"Do you think Maddie or Sophie would want it?"

"Doubt it."

"I'll put it with the other stuff we're sending them, just in case."

Jenny presses play and keeps her eyes on the television screen until her mother has gone.

The next evening, it's the set of six blue Denby mugs. Jenny agrees to take two. She bought them for her parents three Christmases ago and she likes them. She also accepts a kettle and the big red bath towel. She says no to a spatula, a set of kitchen knives, a mixing bowl, a teapot and cozy and an electric blanket.

Sometimes, when everyone's in bed, Jenny goes to Sophie's old room, where her parents are putting everything. There's one pile for Maddie and Sophie. One pile for charity shops. She takes a tea towel from the charity shop pile; it was given to them by a grateful guest and it has some of Jenny's favourite plants on it — ling, spear thistle and mountain avens — all conveniently in flower at the same time.

Another night, she finds a couple of empty boxes and fills them with books from her room. She carries the boxes to the charity shop pile. They are her children's books — Anne Fine, Joyce Stranger, Laura Ingalls Wilder — and her Agatha Christies. She keeps Grandfather's Bible. It was Grandfather who gave them Willowbrae, even if her parents don't want to keep it.

On another nocturnal visit to Sophie's room, Jenny notices a piece of wood on the Maddie and Sophie pile. It's the stick that looks like a running deer that Jenny found by the stile on the day they arrived at Willowbrae, the very first stick she collected. She doesn't know how it got here, how it survived the burning. Perhaps she dropped it when she gathered up the sticks from her room. Perhaps Grandfather's poltergeist was real after all and had come quietly with them to Willowbrae.

She picks up the stick and takes it to her room.

The day before Jenny is leaving Willowbrae, her mother comes to her room and gives her a cheque for seven hundred pounds.

"Don't tell Daddy. It's all supposed to go to Ben."

Jenny is on the window seat, hugging her knees. Ben again, not Ben

Gallachie. There should be guidance in the Free Minds leaflets for dealing with the steady strike of words you do not want to hear, the repetitions that create deep and lasting bruising.

"It's from my building society account." Her mother fiddles with the knot in her head scarf, tightening it as if her hair is trying to spring out. "I haven't closed it. It hasn't even occurred to Daddy. You know what he's like about details. I'm going to give you more money when the sale goes through. All of you. Don't tell him."

Jenny hesitates, then takes the cheque.

Her mother presses her hands to her cheeks. "If you come with us, you won't have to worry about any of this. Money, I mean. You can focus on what really matters in life."

Jenny considers handing the cheque back to her mother. Her mother seems to sense this and quickly leaves the room.

Jenny looks at the cheque. She should tear it up. Just as she should have left days ago, weeks ago. Taken charge. Except she's been hoping her parents will change their minds. It's that these are her last ever days with them and her last ever days at Willowbrae and she will not deprive herself.

She will keep the cheque. She'll use the money for something significant, not just baked beans and washing powder.

The car is loaded up with Jenny's belongings, her bicycle is on the roof rack and she's leaving. The fire she's carried inside her has burnt out at last, and now she feels as if she's full of cold ashes like the grate on winter mornings. She sits in the back seat, an elbow on one of the soft holdall bags full of clothes. Her parents are in the front. She looks back as her mother drives them away. The last part of Willowbrae she sees is the right-hand corner of the front of the house, the crenellated stonework, stained by lichen. She wants to do the journey twice. Once looking backward. Once looking forward. She wants two selves.

Her mother turns right onto Edinburgh Road at the Peebles roundabout. Past the garage on the left. A glimpse of Eddleston Water as it runs close to the road. The sheep on the slope. The Hobbit pub. The ramshackle drystone walls that she loves and wants to become part of when she dies, when her soul ossifies. The land flattening as they go north, the distant hills as golden as sand dunes. Joining, at last, Biggar Road and over the curving bypass into the city. No roadkill, unusually, the whole way. She is spared that.

Jenny and her father wordlessly lift her bicycle down from the roof rack and Jenny locks it up in a bicycle rack. They carry the rest of her possessions up the three flights of stairs to her room. Her mother has given her two boxes of food, as if she doesn't know what a supermarket looks like. There are no other university students here yet. There are older people staying in the rooms instead who are attending conferences and people from other countries who are learning English. She's lucky the university people have taken pity on her and found her a room she could move into early. The halls of residence, thank goodness, is right next to Holyrood Park and the little mountain in the middle of it, Arthur's Seat.

When she reaches her new room, her parents lagging behind her in the corridor, Jenny goes first to the window. The view is not of the park; it's of the inside quadrangle. All she can see are other people's rooms and one evergreen tree. There's nothing to tell her what season it is. She'll have to draw the ugly, red and yellow spotted curtains so she can't see the view. She hasn't used curtains since Brighton. She'll buy new ones. Something plain that doesn't make her go cross-eyed. She'll use her mother's money for that. She scans the rest of the room. Pale pine everything: bed, desk, shelves, bedside table and doors to a built-in wardrobe. Space under the bed to store things. An ensuite shower room. An emerald green carpet. It will be okay. She'll be all right; she'll walk in the park every day.

"It's nice." Her mother, behind her, sounds surprised. "Apart from those curtains."

Her father opens the wardrobe door and runs his fingers over the hinges. "Not too badly made."

Jenny throws her window seat cushions on the bed. They match the carpet.

Her mother is looking in the ensuite bathroom. "Remember our grotty first flat, Alasdair?" She laughs, the small room deadening the sound.

"This is luxury in comparison," Jenny's father says.

They seem reluctant to leave. They make her find the communal kitchen with them, down on the next floor, and the shared lounge and washing machines and dryers.

"There's nowhere to hang out washing," says Jenny's mother, just as Jenny is thinking the same thing. "I hope those dryers aren't too expensive."

"Radiator," says Jenny, matter-of-factly.

"Don't wear damp clothes," her mother says.

Jenny leaves the laundry room and hears her parents following her.

"So," says her father when they get back to her room.

"So." Her mother adjusts the strap of her leather shoulder bag, standing just inside the doorway. "We'd better get going."

"You'll come and see us off the premises?" says her father.

Jenny follows them out of the room.

"We're all off on our adventures now, Jenny Wren," says her father as they reach the car, jiggling the keys in his hand. He can't wait to go.

"It's not long until half-term," says her mother. "Not long until we see you."

Jenny shakes her head. There weren't many words left in her and now she's running out.

"What does that mean?" her mother says.

Jenny has to suck air through her nose to open her throat up again; if she opens her mouth, the tears will come out. After a few seconds she manages to say, "You know what it means. I'm not coming at half-term."

"You don't know that yet." Her mother smiles with her mouth if not her eyes. "You can't work all the time. You must have a break."

"If not half-term, then at Christmas," her father says.

"I'm not coming at Christmas," Jenny says. "I'm not coming at all. I'm not setting foot in that place."

"You don't mean that," says her mother. "You know we can't visit you. Not until we've transferred. We've told you that. The process can take months. So you'll have to come to us." Her mother stretches her arms towards Jenny. Jenny steps back out of reach. Her mother wraps her arms around herself. "Don't make us have to choose. Please."

They stand looking at each other; neither seems able to move.

"I'm not making you do anything. You've made your choice."

Her mother opens her mouth. Instead of words, a shriek comes out, a split sound, like the fox Jenny sometimes heard on her evening walks at Willowbrae. For a moment she even thinks it was a fox, yet how can it be, here in a city carpark.

"She doesn't mean it." Jenny's father puts his arm around her mother. "She's just cross. By the time half-term comes round, she'll feel differently. She'll have had enough of the city. She'll want to come and explore our mountains. I'll take some photographs and send them to you," he says to Jenny. "Give you some ideas. We can walk up Knoydart together."

"I do mean it."

Her father is glaring at Jenny as if she's a two-year-old having a tantrum.

"I'm not coming." Jenny's words flow easily now, steady as the waters of Glensax Burn. "I never will. You've made your choice and it's obviously not us, your daughters. Let me know when you've left that place and are back into the real world again. Then I'll see you."

She walks back towards the halls of residence. She has gone against the advice Phil gave her at Free Minds. She has torn up the imaginary leaflet they should have written and she doesn't care. Parents aren't supposed to abandon their children. Parents aren't supposed to wreck their family once, let alone twice. She's not going to try to keep hold of everyone's hands anymore, attempting to force them together. She's letting go. She hasn't the strength.

Jenny keeps walking. She doesn't turn around and her parents don't come after her. She counts as she walks. She's reached sixteen by the time she gets to the door to the building. Still counting, more slowly now, she opens the door, walks through it and lets it swing shut behind her. She still hasn't heard the sound of the car engine being turned on.

In her new room, Jenny closes her door and draws the spotted curtains. She kneels on the floor and opens the flaps of each of the cardboard boxes. She knows she won't hear footsteps on the stairs, although she listens anyway. The running deer stick is easy to find; it's in the same box as the iron her mother made her bring. She puts the stick on her bed and looks around. She'll need all of the shelf space for her books. There's no picture rail to hang anything from. No coving, no Georgian features. There's a narrow ledge above the panelling around the bed. She places the stick there. Tomorrow, she'll buy a hook and some nylon thread. She'll hang it from the ceiling.

Later, when she's finished unpacking and has pushed the empty bags and flattened boxes under her bed, she goes out into the city. The air is different from Willowbrae's. More sea than earth. More traffic pollution than forest. She walks towards the rise of Arthur's Seat where the sky soaks straight into the earth. She walks to Samson's Ribs, the six-sided columns of basalt that she last touched on a geography field trip three years ago.

She lays her palms on the rock to feel the vibration of the eruption that took place three, four hundred million years ago. She's just a small stone that once spilt from a much larger batholith and the batholith looks no different for it.

After a while, she goes back to the halls and gets her map. She unlocks her bicycle and cycles in the direction of Portobello. When she gets to the seafront, she leans her bicycle against the railings and stands on the beach facing out to sea. She bends to lay her hand flat on the cool sand. She notices a smooth white pebble a few feet away and picks it up.

It's dark by the time she cycles back. She doesn't have any lights but the police don't stop her. She passes a newsagent and puts on her brakes. She locks her bicycle up and goes inside. She buys two bars of Dairy Milk chocolate and two bags of Maltesers. She cycles back to her room with the carrier bag swinging from her handlebars.

Back in her room, she takes the pebble from Portobello Beach and puts it on the ledge above her bed, beside the deer stick and the other stones in her collection. She pushes the bag of chocolate under her bed; there's a comfort in having it there. Next, she goes downstairs to the pay phone she's seen in a recess in the corridor by the shared lounge. It's after eleven and there's no one about. When the timer light snaps off, she slides down to the floor and sits with her back against the wall in the dark.

Maddie answers and Jenny tells her she's in Edinburgh, in the halls of residence. All moved in.

"Well done," Maddie says. "Was it awful?"

Before Jenny can answer, Maddie starts talking to someone else. "Sophie wants to talk to you. I'll hand you over."

"You made it," says Sophie. "You're shot of them now." Sophie's voice sounds much farther away than it does on the Willowbrae phone. "Will you be okay until term starts?"

"I'm right by Holyrood Park, it's so beautiful, and there's loads of reading to do. And the national gallery and the portrait gallery." She pauses. "They want me to visit at half-term."

"Of course they do. They want you to become a proper little Gallachist. No one here's heard of them, you know. I've been asking. It's just some obscure little cult. But remember what we agreed. No contact."

Jenny sighs. Every time Jenny speaks to Sophie on the phone, her sister tells her it's the only way.

"Don't set foot in that place," Sophie says. "Don't visit them. Don't communicate with them. Ignore them until the day they leave and tell you they're not brainwashed anymore. It's the only way to make them see sense. Do you promise?"

Jenny hesitates.

"They've got to realize they can't just opt out of life. Look what they've done to you — they've abandoned you. You can't be wishy-washy. Being nice to them isn't going to work."

"I wasn't nice to them. I was horrible." Jenny clenches her fingers and toes so she won't cry.

"No contact, okay?"

Jenny shuts her eyes and nods even though Sophie can't see her. "Okay."

"Good," Sophie says. "You're coming to stay with us at half-term?"

"Thank you. I'll see how things go. I'll have lots of essays to write."

"Oh, Professor Ross. You're such a boffin. You're definitely coming here for Christmas, though. That's non-negotiable."

Christmas. Jenny hasn't thought as far ahead as that.

"Trafalgar Square for New Year. You've never seen anything like it."

Back in her room, Jenny takes her diary down from its new place on the shelf above her desk and finds the page for the twenty-fifth of December. It's a Friday. She picks up a pen.

Maddie and Sophie's, she writes. *London*. As if she might otherwise forget.

Twenty-three

Maddie's studio was on the third floor of a giant stack of freight containers welded, bolted and cut to form a series of honeycomb spaces for artists to work in. Maddie had a whole container to herself while some of the others were divided in half. With the size of some of her canvasses, she needed a whole one.

"I read an article about these studios a while ago in one of the Sunday magazines," said Jenny when she arrived. "You must have seen it? They mentioned you. They're obviously all the rage. They're building them in the East End as well now."

"I don't know who'd want to be stuck out there."

"So I rang your gallery before I left," Jenny said. She knew Maddie didn't have a phone in her studio. "He phoned them like he said he would so they told him we'd be here."

"This is it, then," Maddie said.

"And I rang Sophie. Let's just say I don't think she's going to be joining us."

"Excellent."

Maddie looked around as if to decide whether it was worth tidying up. Jenny looked around too. Large holes had been cut into two sides of the metal walls for windows and the door. If Jenny were an artist, this was just the sort of place she'd love to work in.

"So what are you painting at the moment?" Jenny asked. There were many canvasses of different sizes leaning against the walls and piled on shelves. One or two she had seen before but most were new. The new ones that she could see she decided she would call abstract urbanscapes. The distant purple of a mountain range became the purple of a glassy office block, the orange of autumn bracken became a sunlit red-brick facade. That was how Jenny saw it.

Jenny said, "So many people live in cities and love it, but they don't realize it's not just because of all the people-stuff, the buzz. These paintings help you see that."

Maddie pushed her fingers through her short curls and smiled without making eye contact. Jenny wasn't sure whether the smile meant she was right or if it meant she was over-analyzing as usual.

"I really like them, Maddie."

"Oh, they're all rubbish." Maddie took her cigarettes out of her back pocket and lit one.

"The people buying your work obviously don't think so. I think they're brilliant. You're selling lots, aren't you?"

"A fair amount, thanks to my gallery, thank God. I hate that side of things. Pricing and haggling. To be honest, I think most people only buy my stuff to match their decor."

"Philistines," said Jenny, in mock condemnation. She walked over to a large, paint-splattered easel. The canvas on it was covered in a drop cloth. Jenny plucked at it then looked at her sister for permission to remove it.

Maddie frowned. "I don't want any bloody art historian comments."

Jenny sighed. "I only want to see what you're working on."

"I'm not showing him anything. He should have come to my exhibitions if he wanted to know what I was doing."

"True enough." Jenny gently slid the sheet off the canvas. She stepped back. "It's gorgeous." It was another abstract urbanscape. Jenny's brain formed blue, green and grey curves and planes into the reflection of a park in an office building. "It looks finished?"

"I suppose," said Maddie, nodding. "I never really finish anything, just give up."

Jenny glanced at her watch.

"Sorry if this is boring you." Maddie picked up the sheet and wafted it high into the air to cover the painting again.

Jenny tutted. "I'm not bored. Don't be ridiculous. I'm looking to see how long we've got before our father, remember, is going to be here. Why do you always have to take things so personally?"

"You don't have to pretend you like my work if you don't."

"You're not listening." Jenny tried not to raise her voice. "Our father will be here in about nine minutes." Jenny breathed in deeply; it didn't make her feel any calmer.

"I wish we hadn't agreed to this," Maddie said.

"So do I."

"Look." Maddie stretched out a thin, blue-veined hand in front of her. Her fingers were shaking.

"Have another cigarette," Jenny said. "I might join you."

The studio intercom buzzed.

"Not bad." Jenny looked at her watch again. "He'd be early if he wasn't eight years too late."

Maddie went over to the intercom and pressed the button. She didn't say anything.

"Hello? Is that Maddie?" said a man's voice. A light Scottish accent.

"Who am I speaking to?" Maddie said.

There was a pause. "It's me. Your father. You know it is."

Maddie didn't reply. She pressed the buzzer to let him through the main door.

"We'd better go down and meet him," Jenny said. "He'll never find his way up here. This place is a maze and the timers on the light switches only last five seconds."

"You go," said Maddie. "He won't be expecting that. I'll throw up if I move."

"Thanks." Jenny rolled her eyes.

She clunked down the metal stairway to the first landing, where the light from Maddie's studio evaporated. She twisted the light timer as far as it would go and went along the corridor quickly to the next set of stairs. When she reached the ground-floor hallway, she saw her father coming towards her in the dim lighting. It was him; she knew his walk. She twisted the nearest timer switch on.

His fair hair was silver-grey and fashionably short, brushed forward and slightly messy. He was wearing a well-cut black jacket and a pair of tan chinos and was carrying a briefcase. He looked like an affluent Londoner, younger than fifty-two. There was nothing of the ashram about him. As he got closer, she could see he had a tan. More Goa than Knoydart Peninsula.

Jenny kept her face as expressionless as she could as he approached. She knew her eyes would be giving her away. His smile became sheepish as his arms rose. He was expecting a hug. Jenny stepped back. It was as if there were a piece of wood wedged behind her ribs. It hurt her chest each time she took a breath. Why the hell wasn't Maddie here? Jenny kept her arms by her sides and her father dropped his arms too. She turned and walked back up the metal staircase, glad of the noise her footsteps made, glad he was behind her and she didn't have to look at those blue eyes.

"I can't believe you're here, Jen," her father said to her back. He was following her up. "I was looking for you in Edinburgh."

Since when did he call her Jen? The wood in her chest was heavy; it took all her effort to keep walking up the stairs.

"I'm so glad the three of you are still friends," he said.

What did he mean, *still friends*. They were sisters, not friends. Sisters didn't choose whether they were connected, although parents evidently could. Jenny wasn't going to let him know anything about Sophie. If he was expecting her to be upstairs too, he was going to be disappointed.

"Jenny Wren," her father said behind her. "You mustn't keep being angry with me. You can't hold anger inside you for all these years. It's very bad for you."

It wasn't anger, Jenny wanted to tell him. The hardness she was carrying in her chest was all the accumulated love she would have given him and her mother if they hadn't left. It wasn't a piece of wood after all, it was bone. Your sternum did not complete the ossification process until you were in your mid-twenties; that was how this lump had grown inside her.

Jenny reached the door to Maddie's studio. She pushed it open, stepped over the high metal threshold and entered without looking back. She went to stand by Maddie at the far end of the studio and they both watched their father lean his bag against the wall by the door. He looked at ease, as if he were always walking into artists' studios. He appraised the room with his blue eyes. There were no paintings showing, Jenny suddenly realized. Maddie had turned them all to the wall.

Instead of attempting to hug either of them, their father closed his eyes and sniffed. "That's a good smell. Brings back memories."

"Turps and oil paint?" Maddie said sharply. "Gives me headaches."

Their father walked towards the easel Jenny had unveiled earlier. The three of them were forming a scalene triangle, each of the three sides a different length.

"Can I have a look?" Their father indicated the easel with his head.

"It's not finished." Maddie took out another cigarette and lit it.

"I don't mind," their father said.

"I bloody do." Maddie took a long puff.

"Something else then. I'd love to see what you're working on. I loved what I saw at Damage earlier. Fantastic stuff, Maddie."

Watching her sister, Jenny suspected that flattery was getting her father somewhere. Like a skilled acupuncturist, he knew where to pierce a meridian and let the qi of vanity flow. Had he always been able to do that or was it a Gallachist trick he'd learnt?

Maddie stubbed out her cigarette in a plastic cup and walked over to one of the stacks of canvasses leaning against the wall. "You can have a look at these, if you must," she said, snapping off a loose thread from the edge of an unprimed canvas.

Their father was in front of the canvasses within moments. Maddie flipped the first painting over with one hand, and he crouched so he was at eye level with it. After a few seconds, he looked at Maddie as if to ask her to show him the next canvas. She did. He still hadn't said anything. They looked through a stack of about eight paintings and then started on the second stack. Jenny picked up a copy of *Time Out* from a paint-spattered workbench and sat on a stool.

"Maddie, these are fabulous," their father said at the end of the second stack. "You're brilliant."

Of course she was. She was his daughter. And she was falling for it. Maddie was trying to look modest, trying not to smile.

"There's something, I don't know, atonal about them," he said. That sounded like more of a music than an art term to Jenny. "Something discordant, yet still within the range of the palette you're using. You're using colour to define emotional resonances in a completely fresh way." He stepped back. "I'm impressed. I really am. These are gorgeous."

"How's your painting going?" Jenny asked him.

Maddie looked interested in knowing the answer to that question too.

Their father smiled at Jenny as if he pitied her. "Creativity manifests in a different way for me now, Jenny. I create through presence, through being. I don't need the medium of paint to express myself anymore. My breath is colour, my thoughts are form. So are yours, if you so choose."

Maddie looked puzzled, as if she didn't know whether she had just been insulted or not. Jenny checked their father's face. It was absent of irony.

"Don't get me wrong," he said to Maddie. "We need artists in this world. It's just not my time. I've been an artist and I will be again if I want that. Perhaps next lifetime." He laughed.

Jenny could tell he wasn't joking. "Why are you here?" It would take hours to find out at this rate.

"Because I want to see you." Their father turned to Maddie. "Jenny was nearest, so I went to Edinburgh first. Nearest to BG. Ben Gallachie, I mean."

"I know what BG stands for," said Maddie. "Bonkers and Gaga."

The flattery hadn't worked then.

"I know my decisions have been hard for you to understand," he said. "I know some of what I'm saying will sound strange to you. I'm trying to live in a spiritual dimension. That's not as easy as it sounds."

Jenny couldn't listen any longer. "We know you're not here to see us. We know who you're looking for."

She heard Sophie's voice telling her not to play into their parents' hands and stopped talking.

Maddie scooped her packet of cigarettes from the workbench as if she were getting ready to go. As their father moved into the beam of one of the bright studio lights, his tan disappeared. "I am here to see you." He was speaking deliberately, calmly, as though he were the one in control. "And, yes, I also happen to be looking for your mother."

He paused. Jenny stayed silent. She looked at Maddie to try to get her to keep quiet too.

"She's been going through a difficult time," their father continued. "She's very confused. I'm really hoping she's been in touch with you and that you know where she is and that together we can help her. I know how much she's missed you. She needs her daughters."

"Oh, just shut up," Jenny snapped.

Maddie looked as if she were watching a gripping film, and their father just stared as though he didn't know who Jenny was anymore. Well, he didn't.

"We want to know," Jenny said as firmly as she could, "why she ran away."

Her father pressed his lips together as if the situation was worse than he thought. He was such an actor.

"Why?" Jenny felt something in her body give, as though a nut, seized up by rust, had at last been oiled and loosened.

"She wasn't self-elucidating," he explained gently, as if he were telling them their mother was a drug addict.

Maddie caught Jenny's eye and tapped her finger against her temple.

Their father ignored her. "There are certain codes you have to live by out of respect for the rest of the community. She accumulated too many violations. Eventually, in that situation, an entity will attempt to reject its own existence. The first step tends to be self-withdrawal from one's community."

"So it was nothing," Maddie said, "to do with the fact that she was seriously ill and none of you gave a shit?"

Their father blanched. Could he fake that? Did he really not know? "What do you mean?"

"That's all you need to know," Jenny said.

"She's had a stroke," said Maddie at the same time.

Jenny put her hands on her head in frustration. She and Maddie should have agreed beforehand what they'd tell him.

Maddie shrugged at Jenny, wincing. It was her way of saying sorry for letting the cat out of the bag.

Their father leant on a workbench. He seemed to shrink, as if his backbone were retractable. "Where is she?"

"I'd have thought you'd be able to work that out," Jenny said. "Aren't you supposed to have telepathic powers?"

"Spiritual development enhances non-physical communication, yes," said their father, ignoring Jenny's sarcasm, "but when someone is unwell, it clouds perception. Both ways."

"I'd say having a stroke is a bit more than unwell," said Jenny.

"Where is she?" he repeated. "In London?"

Neither Maddie nor Jenny spoke. Jenny shook her head at Maddie. They mustn't tell him anything else.

"Look," said their father. "I imagine she's in hospital if it's as serious as you say. I can ring every hospital in the British Isles if that's what it takes. I can get my staff to help me. So you might as well just tell me. Save a lot of bother."

"Actually, I'm not sure hospitals will disclose information to just anyone, including your *staff*," Jenny said.

"Well, then I'll do it myself. They'll tell me." He stared at them. His blue eyes softened. Jenny tried to work out what he was thinking. What percentage were his thoughts Gallachist and what percentage were original Alasdair Ross, the father, the dreamer?

"I love her and I need to see her," he told them. "We're your parents. We love you and we always will. We never wanted it to be like this. It's the last thing we wanted." He closed his eyes. "Please tell me where she is."

Jenny felt toast and coffee push up from her stomach. He was beginning to sound like their father again. But they mustn't tell him. They mustn't. They had to know what their mother wanted first. They had to make sure she got better.

He looked at her. "Jenny Wren. Please."

"No." The less she said the better.

"Maddie?"

Maddie shook her head.

Their father sighed and ran his fingers through his silver hair. "I'd hoped the two of you would be more mature by now." He waited a few more moments and then walked to the other end of the studio to pick up his bag. "I'll find her myself then. You're wasting a lot of people's time, I hope you know that."

He stepped over the high threshold and left the studio.

Twenty-four

JENNY TUTTED AND moved to one side as a woman stood in front of her and blocked her view of the departure board. There were too many people. Space should be a human right. You couldn't hear the announcements properly either. Peace and quiet should be a human right too.

It was expensive flying to Inverness, especially buying a ticket to travel the same day, although probably not much more than the cost of the night train. It wasn't a difficult decision; the journey was under two hours by air and more than eight hours by train. Although Jenny did opt to save a hundred pounds by choosing a slightly later flight, which then gave her the benefit of having more time to argue with Maddie.

Jenny understood that Maddie was meeting a big client and that, under usual circumstances, such a meeting would extend into drinks and dinner. Yet even international art dealers must have mothers who sometimes needed visiting in hospital. Surely they'd understand if Maddie cut the wining and dining short.

Maddie had assured Jenny, though, that she'd travel up the next day. Not that she'd let Jenny help her book her ticket when Jenny offered. Maddie said it would take ages for their father to find out which hospital she was in so, really, there was no great rush.

Jenny felt the large bar of Dairy Milk chocolate in her pocket. It was comforting to feel the squares through the wrapper. She had a few pages of the James Michener's *Alaska* to finish, plus she'd bought *The Accidental Tourist* from WHSmith, so she wouldn't run out of reading material on the flight. The plane was cramped and hot and, despite having a window seat, there was no view of England or Scotland, except for a few minutes during taking off and landing. All of Britain, it seemed, was completely covered by clouds.

Jenny was relieved to see that Piyali wasn't sitting by her mother's bedside when she entered the ward that evening; it would make it easier for her and her mother to try to communicate. She smiled at an elderly lady she recognized from when she was here three days ago and continued into the ward.

Her mother wasn't in her bed. A much younger woman was there, her long hair dark on the pillow.

Jenny walked to the end of the room, checking each bed. Where was her mother? She went back to the entrance to look at the name of the ward. Yes, she was in the right place. Jenny went to the nurses' office to find out where her mother had been moved.

The nurse looked up from her desk. Her eyes were small under her dark fringe. "I'm afraid you've missed her. She was just picked up, not long ago at all."

"What do you mean? By who?"

"The private hospital people," said the nurse, as if Jenny should know.

"What private hospital?" Jenny was still hoping she was wrong.

"I'm afraid I'm not able to share that information."

"I'm her daughter," Jenny said, trying to sound reasonable, normal.

"I'd like to help, really," said the nurse, softening. "But our policy is to respect the privacy of our patients. I'm sure if your mother wants you to know where she is, she'll ask someone to contact you."

"Surely she wasn't well enough to be moved?"

"Your mother has made very good progress. As long as a patient is in a stable enough condition to be transferred, then this is a normal procedure."

"And she seemed okay about going? She wasn't forced by anyone?"

The nurse looked shocked by the suggestion. She shook her head and her fringe rearranged itself. "Of course not. We would never allow that to happen. Her discharge papers were all in order. I saw your mother leave. They wheeled her out in a wheelchair."

Jenny walked down the corridor, not sure where to go next, what to do. She was too late. The Gallachists had taken her mother. Straight to Ben Gallachie? You had to get on a boat to reach the peninsula. Would they do that at night? How dare her father put her mother in danger like this. How had he found her so quickly? As soon as he'd left Maddie's studio, he must have telephoned the staff he'd boasted about, got them ringing all the hospitals. And made phone calls himself. Husband, next of kin, looking for his wife. Phone calls starting with Scotland because that was home? Because that was where Jenny usually was? Or Piyali. She could have become scared and asked the Gallachists to come and get them. There were so many possibilities.

Jenny felt suddenly light-headed. She sat down on a chair in a waiting area off the corridor. Should she hire a car? Drive along the dark roads and try to catch up with her mother? She wouldn't even know which vehicle she was in.

Despite what the nurse had said, her mother couldn't have wanted to go. That was kidnapping. Should she call the police?

"Jenny!" a voice called behind her.

She turned. It was her father, standing in the corridor. Smiling. "I've been waiting for you. I knew you'd be along sooner or later. I must have got an earlier flight than you. What, no Maddie? Sophie?"

Jenny's peripheral vision went black. "How could you?"

He sat beside her as she stood up.

"She's gone to the right place, Jenny. We'll get her better." He lowered his voice. "Hospitals do their best, but there are principles about the human body that they aren't aware of. We try to tell them, but, frankly, they aren't listening."

Jenny turned away. She couldn't look at him. The polished floor was gleaming. For a few seconds it was hovering; she couldn't tell where the floor started.

"We had to come and get her. Surely you can understand that. We'll get her better. We've been very concerned." He sounded disappointed, as if his wife were a naughty child and had forced him to do something he didn't want to do.

"So concerned that you've taken her out of hospital, away from medical care? That makes perfect sense."

"Come to Ben with me, Jenny Wren," her father said. "Come with me and you can see Mummy and you'll know she's okay. It's wonderful of you to come all the way back here from Canada."

How did he know that? From the nurses?

He was an odourless, poisonous gas; she couldn't stop him seeping into her. "I'm not coming *with* you," she said. "I'm going there myself. Regardless of whether or not you go. I'm going to get her out."

"And take her back with you to Canada?" her father said. "Oh no, of course, Maddie will look after her, won't she. Or Sophie. Yes, Sophie's the ideal person to look after your mother and nurse her back to health. So trustworthy. Especially as those two have always got on like a house of fire."

Jenny stared at her father. She'd never been violent in her life, but right now she wanted to slap him. "All the things you've ever said about Sophie? You're just as bad, do you realize that? Worse, in fact. You think she's a murderer? Well, at this rate, you're going to be a murderer too."

Jenny could see the Gallachist machinery turning inside her father, instructing him not to react to what she had said.

"We're going to get your mother better. Come and see for yourself how well we're looking after her. The car's gone with your mother, of course. I wanted to stay and wait for you. We're too late for the bus to Fort William now, so we'll have to go in the morning. It will do you good to be at Ben. I can see how tense you are, how exhausted. Your energy field is so washed out. Ben Gallachie will give you your colours back."

Jenny walked away from him. She turned once and glared at him. "Do not follow me."

Jenny rang from a pay phone by the hospital café and booked a bed in a backpackers' hostel near the bus station. She couldn't imagine her father staying anywhere but a hotel, plus she needed to start being more careful with money. Even so, she called a taxi next; she didn't feel like walking all the way to the town centre carrying her rucksack in the dark.

She was lucky. The hostel was quiet enough for her to have her own room. She dropped her rucksack onto a bed and stood in the middle of the room, her mind a spinning coin. She could hear a rumble of traffic and another faint drone, perhaps the hostel heating system. She was wasting time staying here; she should have rung around all the garages looking for a car to hire and driven herself to Mallaig tonight. No, the garages would have closed ages ago. This was Inverness, not London. She'd go and check the bus timetable on the hostel computer and see if there was a bus that left before the car hire places opened. With any luck, her father would catch a later bus. And at least if he ended up on her bus, she'd know where he was.

There were a couple of other things she had to do before she could shower and sleep.

First was to call Maddie, but she reached only her answering machine. Probably still out dining with the would-be Saatchis. Jenny left a brief message telling her what was happening.

Next, Sophie. She dialled the number.

"It's me. Jenny."

"I do recognize your voice, you know."

"I want to tell you I'm doing something else you won't approve of." Jenny leant against the wall of the hostel hallway. She could hear a piano being played. She visualized Sophie, small-bottomed in her jeans, standing in a high-ceilinged living room looking out onto a park. Or standing beside whoever was playing the piano, accompanying them on the violin.

Sophie sighed. "Go on then."

"She wasn't there when I got to the hospital. They've taken her back to Ben Gallachie. God knows what happened but I don't think she was well enough to be moved. So," said Jenny, hesitating, "I'm going there. I have to make sure she's all right. It's our fault they found her. We told him she'd had a stroke."

She waited for Sophie to swear and tell her she was an idiot but she didn't. "Be bloody careful," she said instead. "Have you got a mobile?"

"You know I haven't."

"Bloody Luddites. You and Maddie. Get one before you go and give me the number."

"I don't need one. There must be a phone there. Our father must have rung them to tell them where our mother was. Sophie, are you okay? Your voice sounds a bit funny."

"Oh. Just a sniffle. Too many outdoor scenes."

"Is that a piano I can hear?" Jenny asked.

"That's Michael. He's practising. He's always practising. Bloody musicians." Sophie was joking but she meant it too.

"How long have you been together?"

"A few months. We met at New Year. I'm sorry I've been so crap at keeping in touch. It's been busy."

"When did you move to Bath?"

"Pretty much New Year." Sophie laughed. It was the sort of laugh you'd make if you were given a grapefruit on the day you decided to give up sugar.

It took only a few minutes for Jenny to jog along the streets to the Youth Hostel Association hostel she'd booked Piyali into. She looked around the lobby, but she couldn't see anyone wearing a sage shawl or a sage anything else. Jenny had no idea if Piyali had gone with her mother or if she'd even been there when her mother was taken away. Jenny certainly hadn't been about to ask her father if he knew where Piyali was. She wrote a quick note giving Piyali Maddie's and Sophie's numbers again and left it at the reception desk.

As Jenny walked back to her hostel, she felt for the bar of Dairy Milk in her jacket pocket. It was still there. She slid her fingers over the even squares.

Twenty-five

HER FATHER WAS at the Inverness bus station. Jenny leant her rucksack against the wall and adjusted the straps, pretending not to see him for as long as she could. She'd decided against driving. Hopefully she could get a one-way car hire in Mallaig and take her mother to the hospital in Edinburgh.

Her father put his bags down next to her rucksack. "I had a feeling you'd be on the first bus out of town." Jenny carried on tightening straps. "Look," he added when she didn't respond. "I know I steamrollered you and I'm sorry. How about a truce?"

Steamrollered didn't sound like a very Gallachist term.

"My guys were making calls to hospitals and police stations before I even met you yesterday," Jenny's father continued when Jenny didn't respond. "We were going to find her sooner or later." When Jenny still didn't speak, he sighed. "What I'm trying to say is that not knowing where your mother was wasn't the only reason I wanted to see you. I've wanted to see you for a long time. I've really missed you, Jenny. I had this hope, dream, that I'd find you all together — Mummy, you and your sisters. Silly, I know, after all we've been through." He paused. Jenny studied a blob of squashed chewing gum on the pavement and tried to tune him out. "And, of course," he added, "I needed to find out where your mother was. We knew she wouldn't just run away and disappear. We knew she had to be in trouble."

"So much trouble you've taken her away from the only place that could help her." How did he manage to do that? Say things she couldn't help reacting to.

"Hospitals only treat the body. We know how to really get her better. As soon as you see her, you'll understand. We've less than an hour's wait for the train at Fort William and I've already arranged for the boat to be waiting for us when we get to Mallaig."

As the bus carried them through the rumpled hills of the Great Glen, Jenny wished Dominic were there beside her, instead of having to see her father in the seat across the aisle, sleeping with his head resting against the window on his rolled-up jacket. She didn't know how he could sleep so easily. Her body seemed to have forgotten how; she'd woken up every hour in the hostel trying to work out what her mother was really thinking, what she really wanted. At three o'clock in the morning, Jenny decided she'd call the police and tell them her mother had been kidnapped. By four, she'd decided instead that she would call the media. A tabloid that would write headlines about how a cult had forced a middle-aged woman who had suffered a stroke to leave hospital.

Jenny had done neither of those things. Not yet anyway.

First, she wanted to see her mother. Look at her strong face, brown eyes. Talk to her. Then Jenny would know what she needed to do.

Jenny looked out the window and tried to think about something else. The loch was blue under the clear morning sky. She watched the flickering water, searching for the Loch Ness Monster. She wondered what Dominic would say about it. A couple of years ago, when she read an article about it and learnt how many sightings there'd been in the decades since the *Daily Mail*'s famous 1930s photograph, Jenny decided that it did exist, deep in the loch with the white eels and the Arctic char that had been found there, or at least that it had once lived, even if it might now be dead. Had Dominic ever been to the Great Glen, to see where the top of Scotland slid off the rest of Britain and how the rough edges had been sanded down by glaciers ten thousand years ago?

The bus went around a bend and her father woke up. "That's better," he said.

In that moment, he sounded like her father again. Jenny felt a burn at the back of her eyes and turned her head away; she wasn't going to cry in front of him.

"I'm glad I didn't have to stay in London long." Her father shifted to the aisle seat so he was closer to Jenny. "I don't know how your sisters stand it. It's so contaminating."

Jenny wouldn't tell her father that Sophie wasn't living in London anymore. She opened *The Accidental Tourist* and started reading.

"So you were in Canada?" Her father wasn't taking the cue. "That's what the hospital told me. Whereabouts? I was in Canada, what, three years ago. In Ontario. Are you working there? Something to do with your PhD?"

Jenny kept her book open but took her eyes off the page. If only he'd stop talking. It was like travelling with a child.

"I honestly want to know, Jenny Wren. You always did want to travel. I'm so glad you're getting to do it. That woman I saw at the university was very protective of you. Didn't tell me anything. Good for her. I could have been any Tom, Dick or Harry."

Jenny closed her book. She should ignore him. Stick her fingers in her ears. Yet she couldn't help being curious about who he was after eight years of Gallachist indoctrination. Were the glimpses she saw of the man she grew up with really him or just wishful thinking? Was there any of her original father left? A tone of voice, a hand raised to hair, the steadiness of the blue eyes that focused on her. Were these — had they always been — simply biological manifestations that would exist whatever happened to his personality?

"I'm still me, Jenny," her father said, as if he knew what she was thinking. She looked past him and out the window. "I'm still the idiot who wanted to sell up and sail around the world. I'm still your father. We can talk, can't we?"

"I don't see the point." Jenny's eyes were burning again. It wasn't fair. He was her father and he wasn't.

"I'm proud of you, Jenny. You've already done a lot with your life. I'm your father. I just want to know how my beautiful daughter is doing, how your life is going."

Jenny was shaking her head. She didn't know if she wanted to shake the words down her throat so she wouldn't say anything or shake them out of her mouth. "You're an idiot. You've taken her out of hospital, for God's sake. I was going to call the police. I still might. I might go to the media."

Her father was half-smiling, uncertain.

"I'm serious. You've done something really stupid, really harmful."

Her father held up his hand. His tone was conciliatory. "Come and see her first. Then decide what to do. If you want to go to the police or whoever after that, then by all means do. But see for yourself first."

He got her talking eventually. He kept pressing to find out what she'd been doing in Canada. When she explained, as briefly as she could, he knew where Baffin Island was and that surprised her. He wanted to know what had got her into Arctic art and she told him she'd come across a book on Inuit art that had belonged to one of the Willowbrae teachers.

It had been Brian's sculpture class. Brian, who had lent her his wood-carving tools. She'd gone back to his class every day after school, learning how to work with clay. Brian talked to her about the differences between modelling — building up — and carving — taking away. All week he kept a collection of art books out on a table and it was the one on Inuit art that had intrigued Jenny. It had smears of clay between its pages, the way the novels Jenny read always ended up filled with biscuit crumbs.

She'd flicked through the pages and stopped on a spread of figures shaped like larvae, others like miniature totem poles. They had bared teeth, swollen lips. Some were cartoon-like, with simplified bodies and round black spots for eyes and big nostrils. They were made by the Greenlandic Inuit and they were called tupilaks.

While the ones photographed in the book were made out of antler and soapstone, tupilaks, she discovered, were originally made up of bits of animals, birds and even human remains. Sometimes, so it said, parts of children's corpses. The Greenlanders who made tupilaks knew about witchcraft, she read. They went off to a secret, remote place to make them, then enchanted them with magic spells. When the tupilak was ready, you put it into the sea and sent it off to kill your enemy. You had to be careful in case someone with more magical powers used yours against you. She could visualize a tiny tupilak bobbing in the waves, drifting towards you, scarily, against the current.

That was what had got her into Arctic art. That and the once in a lifetime trip to Greenland in the second year of university with Rob — jovial, soft-fleshed, Edinburgh born and bred — who she'd met at a party in the flat she shared with other students and who'd made her laugh. Poor Rob. Nearly thirty years old, working in a travel agency and obsessed with Vikings, hence the trip to Greenland. He'd already been to Scandinavia and Iceland. The flames of any sexual feelings she'd had for Rob had burnt out soon after they'd met, yet the powder-soft ashes of remembered friendship were still warm, even now. He had been fun and he had been kind. She had needed that after Christopher and the beach at North Berwick. She had even kissed him.

Jenny didn't tell her father about Brian's class or the trip to Greenland.

Her father was saying to Jenny now, here on the bus, that she should publish academic papers, of course, but that she should also write a book. A coffee-table book. "You could photograph the Inuit, write about their customs, beliefs. It could be anthropological as well as about art."

"I'm not a photographer. Or an anthropologist."

"Don't limit yourself. You can be anything you want to be."

She ignored the tinpot philosophizing; he'd be quoting *Jonathan Livingston Seagull* next. "I don't think," she added, "the Inuit need people like me coming in and objectifying them."

She wasn't going to tell her father that she'd had a few papers published in noteworthy art journals and that a book on Inuit sculpture was part of her eventual plan, when she had completed her thesis and

was experienced enough as an academic. A bookshelf book, not a coffee-table book.

The bus was going through Fort Augustus now, crossing the river
and then the canal. As her father turned to look at the famous series of
locks, Jenny took the opportunity to pretend to start reading again.
This time, he seemed to take the cue. After a few moments, he slid
along his seat again so he was next to the window.

Although she stared at the words on the page, Jenny was thinking of
Greenland and of Rob and how her time with him had been necessary,
that to use him as a stepping stone to get across the river had been the
only way to continue. Regardless of whether or not that was true, she
should have been kinder to him. He had given Jenny her Arctic Circle
crossing. He was gentle, generous. He had taken her to Tiso's on Rose
Street and bought her a fleece jacket, hat and gloves, thermal long johns
and a down jacket. Then in the Easter holiday, they flew from London
to Copenhagen, then Copenhagen to Kangerlussuaq, a little town at
the end of a stony, snowy fjord where five hundred people lived scattered below a cliff like rockfall. There were no trees. Jenny had picked
up small stones whenever the snow let her find them.

In Sisimiut, they went on a boat trip. They saw icebergs and hump-
back whales as they stood on the deck with mugs of hot chocolate. They
saw the *hillingar* effect, an Arctic mirage: Canada, looming, where it
should not have been. Perhaps it had been Baffin Island, a place she
hadn't yet known she wanted to see.

They flew to Nuuk to see the five-hundred-year-old Qilakitsoq
Mummies where Jenny gazed for ages at the tupilaks carved from
bones and teeth and reindeer antlers. In Greenland, you could buy
them in the souvenir shops. It didn't feel right to transplant a Greenlandic spirit from the Arctic to Edinburgh. It could even have been bad
luck.

It had got down to minus fourteen, the coldest Jenny had ever been,
and she'd loved it.

At Fort William railway station, her father went off to find a pay phone
to let his cronies know he and Jenny were on schedule to catch the train

and to arrange for the boat to be waiting for them. Jenny sat on a bench and gazed at the mountains. She liked Fort William and she felt sorry for it. It was the home of Britain's highest mountain, yet it had none of the prettiness of Pitlochry or Oban.

Her father had left his bags with her, a holdall and the briefcase he'd brought to Maddie's studio. Jenny looked around to check if he was on his way back, then shifted along on the bench so she was right beside the briefcase. She bent over and unzipped it. If her father suddenly appeared, she'd pretend she was doing up her shoelaces. The briefcase was padded and inside was a white, plastic disc the size of a dinner plate and about an inch thick. She quickly slipped it out and had a look at both sides. It was lighter than she expected and it didn't have any writing on it to say what it was.

She wondered if it was something to do with electromagnetic fields, the equivalent of the tinfoil she and Maddie had joked about. Jenny put the disc back into the bag and hurriedly zipped it up again.

Clouds were forming along the broad mountain summits, wisps that looked as if they were going to build up like candy floss. She'd been up Ben Nevis, counting one, two, three, four to keep the rhythm as she stepped steadily up the zigzagging path on shale that skittered under her feet. Occasionally, she'd seen a stub of rusted metal — iron probably — poking from the ground and had to be careful not to trip on it. She'd never found out what those pieces of metal were for, imagining they were glimpses of the vast mountain's secret armature gradually being exposed as the mountain was eroded by people in Ronhill leggings and Gore-Tex walking boots.

When her father returned, he had a newspaper and a bag of food. "Still your favourite?" He threw Jenny a packet of cheese and onion crisps. They were, as it happened. She hesitated, then opened the bag; she hadn't realized she was hungry. Her father had brought them hummus sandwiches as well and bottles of apple juice.

As he munched on a sandwich, Jenny asked him if there was a phone at Ben Gallachie. She knew there was a village, Inverie, about a mile away from the commune, so there was probably a phone box there or, if she had to, she would knock on someone's door.

"There's one landline at Ben. So you don't have a mobile phone?" her father asked.

She shook her head. Perhaps she should have pretended she did. He'd know how vulnerable she was now.

"I'm glad you don't. Electromagnetic fields, EMFs, are a serious danger to people. Hardly anyone realizes that. Non-ionizing radiation interferes with our bodies' bioelectromagnetic processes. The health effects are serious. Leukemia, lymphoma, cancer, Alzheimer's, depression. There's no end to it. We have to protect ourselves."

He reached for a black cord hanging around his neck and showed her the coloured beads hanging from it. "That's why I wear this. Quartz crystal, red jasper, amber. There's a bigger version in my bag, there. It's called a polarizer." He indicated the briefcase. Jenny kept her face neutral. "We're making them at Ben. I'm testing it. We're going to sell them. Polarizers and decent sleep. That's the best protection against EMFs. I'll get you one. Too many risks. Computers, hair dryers. Landlines are okay, but never get a cordless phone. Microwaves. Televisions."

Jenny knew some people believed living near a power line could cause cancer. What she'd heard sounded credible, although she'd never researched it. If only someone else was telling her all this instead of her father; she might be more inclined to believe it.

He offered her a sandwich and she declined. The more they talked, the more she felt as though her father himself had an electromagnetic field and was tampering with her body cells. It was better if they sat in silence. She got her book out of her bag.

"You're probably curious why I wasn't around when your mother was ill. I was in India, working." It was at least consistent with what Piyali had told her. "I help people who are looking for truth, looking for a better way to live."

"Doesn't India have enough religions already?"

Her father laughed. "There are many people there who are searching. People from all over the world who have lost faith in life. We give people back their spirit, their purpose."

"People who are running a guest house but don't find it as fulfilling as they thought it would be?"

"Quite." It was almost fun, provoking him into giving only a one-word answer.

"So do I get to meet the great Viparanda at Ben Gallachie? Is that where he lives?"

"He doesn't believe in rooting yourself in one place. The whole planet is his home. I was just with him in India."

"You go where Viparanda goes, do you?"

Her father hesitated. "One thing I do is arrange the introductions between Viparanda and new Gallachists. He likes to meet everyone."

So her father brought promising recruits to Viparanda and Viparanda closed the deal.

"I've got to know him well," her father was saying. "Not everyone has that honour. I've been very lucky."

Surely he didn't really believe he was lucky, Jenny thought. He probably thought the special relationship he had with the saviour of the world was his due.

Jenny started reading. The April sun was warm on her skin. Although they were sitting several inches apart on the bench, the shadows on the ground made it look as if they were one person. Jenny shifted over. It didn't make any difference.

"You're still a bookworm, I see," her father said after a few minutes. His newspaper was unopened on his lap. As he spoke, a cloud concealed the sun and their shadow disintegrated. "Sometimes, you know, it's good to just sit and be there, be present. Observe, take in what's going on right now. It gives you a break from being a victim of your mind. Ironically, it's a practice called mindfulness."

"Yes, I've heard of Buddhism." Jenny stopped herself from calling him a patronizing git.

"Gallachism has never claimed to be entirely novel," he countered. "Some of it is a distillation, refinement of truths humans have already discovered. Though there are new truths too."

"A one-stop shop."

"Seriously, Jenny. I know how bright you are academically but don't overdo it. Give your inner, intuitive self attention as well. Sometimes you need to put the book down and spend some time with yourself. Get to know yourself, accept yourself as you are. You never know, you might even find yourself good company."

"Maybe you should take your own advice," Jenny heard herself say. "You're always talking. Why don't you practise what you preach and shut up for a minute."

Her father said nothing for several moments. She wasn't going to apologize. "I know this is a difficult time for you, Jenny," her father said in his patient voice. "It's hard for both of us. There is something I think we do need to talk about, though."

Jenny sighed. More talking.

"How's Sophie doing?" her father said.

Jenny knew where this was leading. "She's doing brilliantly. You must have seen that when you looked her up online."

"Do you see much of her?"

"Now and again." That was enough information to be going on with.

"I'm concerned about what you said to me earlier at the hospital. I don't think you fully appreciate what Sophie did."

The sun came out again. Jenny squinted and held her book up to her brow to shade her eyes. "She didn't realize," she said steadily, "what the consequences of her actions would be. She was fifteen. It was a game. Admittedly, it was a mean, stupid thing to do, but that doesn't make her evil."

"Not evil, no. But she still hasn't transferred herself for it. She needs to undergo a major elucidation program."

"You're talking gibberish."

"Until she deals with it, she's at great risk to herself and all those she forms relationships with. She won't find happiness until she comes to terms with what she has done. And, frankly, Jenny, I'm disappointed that you don't see the seriousness of her actions."

"Oh, for God's sake." Jenny got up and walked along the platform, away from him, away from the noise of him.

From time to time in the past eight years, Jenny had seen people wearing floaty, dull green clothes on Princes Street handing out leaflets enticing her to quiet places. The first time, she took the leaflet before realizing what it was. But then she fisted it into a ball and threw it in a bin. It was not worthy of being taken home to be recycled.

She stayed far along the platform looking at the light changing on the Nevis Range. When the train came and she had to put on her ruck-sack, her father opened the carriage door and held it for her without saying anything. She stepped up onto the train. She had promised her-self she would never go to Ben Gallachie, and yet here she was, getting on the train with her father as if they were on a day out. She had to do it. She had to take her mother away from that place.

The journey to Mallaig was beautiful, of course it was. At Loch Eil, she turned to look again at Ben Nevis. She tried to count the set of locks called Neptune's Staircase in the Caledonian Canal and obviously the Glenfinnan Viaduct was glorious. She loved seeing the little white church that had featured — according to an American woman who was sitting behind them — in the film *Local Hero*.

Her father was speaking. It didn't matter; she didn't have to listen. He was talking to the American woman and her husband. He was tell-ing them if they had the time they should go over to Inverie on the Knoydart Peninsula. It was stunning and they wouldn't regret it. Make sure you have your camera, he was saying, and now the American woman was telling him she did watercolours, landscapes, and it sounded like the ideal place for painting. Jenny knew her father wouldn't be able to resist that and he didn't. He told her he was a painter too, and so was his daughter. Not this one, no. She was a clever academic.

Jenny kept her head bent and her eyes on her book and tried to stop listening. Now he was saying something about non-toxic oil paints made with linseed oil and oil of spike lavender and that hardly anyone realized it but actually these things were nothing new. Rembrandt and Rubens had used lavender oil. Her father was right, Jenny knew. She'd learnt about it when she was studying the Baroque.

It had been good-smelling oil paint and turps in Maddie's studio yes-terday. Jenny used to love cycling down to her parents' art shop after school each day when they lived in Brighton. She'd sit by the till serving customers or doing her homework.

"My daughter gets terrible headaches," her father was saying, as if he saw Maddie every day, not every eight years. "I'm trying to get her to switch to non-toxics."

Jenny hadn't had the privilege of hearing that particular conversation even though, strangely, they'd all been together in Maddie's studio the whole time.

Twenty-six

A SMALL BLUE BOAT was waiting for Jenny and her father at Mallaig Harbour. The name *Matilda* was painted on the side in white. There was nothing on the boat to indicate who it belonged to. As Jenny stood on the quay at the top of the steps where the boat was moored, a man in yellow waterproofs stained darkly with oil, or perhaps fish blood, walked past. He glanced down at the boat, then caught Jenny's eye and there was anger in his face, Jenny was sure of it. She quickly smiled at him. The worst he would think of her, perhaps, was that she was another naïve victim.

To the northwest far away, there was a range of mountains, a duvet of clouds pulled over the grey knees of the peaks.

"That's Skye. Cuillin Ridge," said her father, coming up the stone steps and looking where Jenny was gazing. "You don't get to see that every day, even if you're right under them."

Jenny wished he wouldn't keep telling her things she already knew. You'd think it was her who'd been living on a different planet, not him. She carried on looking at the distant mountains.

"Right." Her father picked up his holdall and briefcase. "Cameron's ready for us. Let's get on board."

Jenny trod cautiously down the steps wearing her rucksack and crossed the little gangway onto the boat. A young man, Cameron presumably, reached his hand towards her elbow. He didn't touch her. He had ginger hair and was nice-looking, which made Jenny miss Dominic. He was in his late twenties or so and, wearing jeans and a sweater, he looked as normal as her father. Perhaps he had nothing to do with Ben Gallachie and ran some kind of water taxi service. If that was the case, though, the fisherman wouldn't have given Jenny that look.

"Cameron's been at Ben for, what, five years now?" her father told her after he'd introduced them. No, he was not from the normal world.

Cameron nodded. "You've not been to Ben before?" he said to Jenny, as he guided the boat out of the harbour. He glanced at her, then returned his eyes to the water.

"No." Jenny swept her hair away as the wind blew it across her face.

"It's a beautiful spot." Cameron flashed a sweet smile as if he were a red-headed Keanu Reeves. "I hope you like it."

At least he didn't tell her she'd love it.

After a few minutes, Jenny went to sit at the back of the boat, leaving her father to talk with Cameron in the cabin. She could have stayed there, listening to their conversation, trying to understand their strange language and getting angry. Instead, she leant over the side of the boat and trailed her hand in the water. It was cold and invigorating. She lifted a finger to her mouth to taste the salt. They were heading for a row of white buildings across the water. The village of Inverie, presumably. She suddenly recalled the photographs her father had made her look at in the living room at Willowbrae. One of them had been of that row of white cottages.

The Knoydart hills were still rusty with bracken, although there were large patches of early summer growth as well, bright green. It was difficult to perceive this peninsula as part of the mainland and not an island. The mountains to the east might as well have been an ocean; it would take days probably to walk to the nearest road and that was if you knew where you were going. For the last few minutes of the journey, Jenny watched as grey-blue waves endlessly merged, separated and merged. Looking up, it was the image from another of the photographs her father had spread on the sideboard eight years ago. There was the narrow, stony beach, the boulders defending the land from the erosion of the sea.

They weren't heading for the village anymore, they were going farther along the shore, inland. Jenny felt a queasiness that wasn't seasickness.

Now, terraced cottages with a single turf roof. She remembered those from the photograph too. The next building she could see was constructed from two wooden and glass pyramids, with a stone, rectangular section connecting them. Piyali had said something about pyramids and there had been that contraption on her mother's bedside table at the hospital.

Another structure among the trees looked like a large greenhouse half-buried by a landslide. Along the shore, a dome with hexagonal segments reminded Jenny of plans she'd once seen in a newspaper for the Eden Project being built in Cornwall.

The boat was aiming for a narrow jetty sticking out into the water. Jenny glimpsed a small wooden pyramid in the trees. Now two, now three, now perhaps half a dozen. Maybe her mother was inside one of them. Perhaps that was where she should go first.

Jenny stayed seated as Cameron steered and her father threw a rope towards a woman standing on the jetty. She was dressed like Piyali, a sage dress and a shawl that slipped off her shoulders as she reached to grab the rope. Jenny's breathing felt shallow so she made herself inhale deeply. Mountains and water were her allies. The village was along the coast, no more than a mile away. A normal village, not a Gallachist village. She could get help there surely, to organize a boat back to Mallaig if she needed it. She'd seen a lane that probably connected the village to the commune. Or she could walk along the shore if she had to. Once the *Matilda* was moored, Jenny stood up and hoisted her rucksack onto her back. She should have left most of her things in Mallaig, in a locker or something, and just brought the essentials.

The woman on the jetty put her arm out to help Jenny as she stepped off the boat. Jenny twisted away.

"Welcome to Ben Gallachie." Another big Gallachist smile. "I'm

Neela." Jenny ignored her. The woman was in her forties, perhaps, with shiny brown eyes and short grey hair. When Jenny's father disembarked, Neela reached forward, not to help him off the boat, but to touch her fingertips to his chest above his heart. He nodded at her. The gesture was odd, although it didn't look sexual.

Jenny followed her father, Cameron and the woman as they walked in the direction of the largest, two-pyramid building.

"Jenny." Her father stopped and put his briefcase down. He nodded to Cameron, who was carrying his holdall, and he and the woman continued walking.

"Let's sit here." Her father indicated a bench that looked as if it had been carved out of a fallen beech tree with a chainsaw. It was positioned to face the glorious view of sea and hills.

"There's something I should tell you, just so you know how things are here. Don't worry, it's nothing too dramatic. It's just that I realized you wouldn't know."

Her father sat and put his foot on a rotting log. It collapsed under the weight of his foot and a dozen pale woodlice ran to find something else to hide under.

Jenny stayed standing, watching the woodlice.

"Not long after we came to Ben," said her father, "your mother and I —" He paused. "Let me backtrack a bit. You see, couples often find it difficult when they come to Ben because they're always trying to elucidate each other. It's hard to break that habit. They end up hindering each other's progress. They don't mean to, it just happens because of the nature of the traditional marriage or partnership bond. Partners can't help but have expectations of each other. Gallachism teaches that people are individuals first and foremost. No one has emotional responsibility for anyone else. It's very freeing and it's essential if spiritual progress is to be made. It actually allows for much stronger relationships."

All except one of the woodlice had found a new hiding place. Her father seemed to have come to a stop, unusually. She was tempted to walk away, but she had a feeling she needed to hear this. "So," she said, to prompt him.

"So, couples stay friends, of course, and may continue a relationship, but the marriage commitment doesn't actually exist in Gallachism."

"So, you're telling me you're divorced."

"It's called dissolution. We mutually made the decision to dissolve the marriage relationship." Her father said it precisely, pedantically, as if she'd leapt to a wild and irrational conclusion.

"So you're divorced," repeated Jenny.

"Well, in legal terms, yes. You see, we're one big family here. Support, relationships, they're universal."

She made the next connection. A question formulated. "I assume," she said, "this means you've dissolved — I think that's the term — your relationship with your children too?"

"Jenny. This is pointless."

"I think you need to answer the question." Jenny felt as calm and still as the sea would be if the moon no longer tugged the tides and the wind no longer blew.

"It's different here. Children are loved and nurtured by everyone. They don't need a traditional mother and father support structure."

"That's a yes then."

"You mustn't be so resistant. It's not good for you." He looked past her to the bay. "You're still my biological daughter —"

"That's a relief," Jenny interrupted.

Her father took an irritated breath. "It's more of a spiritual step, a detachment from traditional, restrictive bonds with other beings, to create an equalization. The truly amazing thing is that I can offer you this entire community as a parent."

Jenny laughed. It burst out like a sneeze. It was one of Sophie's grapefruit laughs. She faced the sea. "Presumably you made this decision when you came here?" She'd been an orphan for nearly eight years without knowing it.

"If you knew more about Gallachism, you'd understand," her father said. "I can give you some material to read, to help you."

"No thanks." Jenny set off down the path. "What I want to do now is see my ex-mother."

As they approached the double-pyramid building that Cameron and the woman had disappeared into, the door was opened by a man wearing a tunic. While sage was no doubt supposed to be calming and restful, Jenny was beginning to find it nauseating.

"Yashodhan!" the man called out. He was laughing. He tapped Jenny's father's chest as the woman on the jetty had done. Again, her father nodded. It was, Jenny realized, an act of reverence. She didn't know whether to laugh or throw up. The man was hugging her father now, smiling at Jenny over his shoulder.

"You must be Jenny?" The man held out a hand. "I'm Aarav." He had an American accent.

Jenny ignored the offer of a handshake. "I'm here to see my mother. Do you know where she is?"

Aarav and her father looked at each other.

"It's awesome that you've come to see Moksha," Aarav said. "She's doing great. You can see for yourself later. I guess she's in an elucidation session right now."

Those names, Moksha and Yashodhan. They must have some Gallachist meaning.

"I could do with some of that myself," said Jenny's father. "I don't know what we're doing wrong, but London isn't getting any better."

"I know what you mean," Aarav said. "I'm always like that when I come back in."

"Let's find your room, Jenny," her father said. "I'll catch up with you later, Aarav."

"Sure thing. Acorn five is ready."

Jenny followed her father — Yashodhan — around the side of the main building to the long, low cottages with the turf roof. It was like a motel, except instead of paving in front for parking, there was grass, and instead of a swimming pool, there was the sea.

"This is our visitor accommodation. This one's free." Her father turned the knob of the fifth door and entered. There was a carving of an acorn hanging above the door because, decided Jenny, its occupants, the visitors, were deemed to be in their spiritual infancy.

Her father stood in the middle of the room and looked around admiringly as if he were seeing it for the first time. Jenny had to admit it was a lovely room. Whitewashed walls, honey-coloured wooden furniture and an unbleached cotton quilt on the double bed. The window had a window seat and, when her father twisted the blinds open, blue water sparkled. It was evening now, yet still so light. "There's a shower and loo ensuite. A kettle in that cupboard too and some fennel tea. It's a Ben brew. You must try it."

Jenny lowered her rucksack to the floor. "Where can I find her?"

"As Aarav said — and you shouldn't have been so rude to him, by the way — she's in an elucidation session, so we'll have to wait a little bit. We can't interrupt that. As she comes out, I'll arrange it so she gets a message letting her know you're here. Supper's served soon, so I should think we'll be able to see her after that. You must be hungry. I have some things to do. Why don't I come back and get you in a few minutes? Give you time to freshen up and get settled in."

Jenny looked at her watch. "I don't need to freshen up and I certainly don't need to get settled in."

"We go at a slower pace here, Jenny. Try to embrace that. Okay, I'll be back as soon as I can." He pointed at the inside door knob. "There's the key. Not necessary here, but I know what you townies are like."

Jenny waited for several moments after her father had gone before she locked herself in, trying to let the offensive townie reference go. She didn't need a wash. She wasn't going to unpack. She would stay only as long as she had to in order to get her mother out of here. She didn't want to eat any Gallachist food, but it was true she was hungry. She put her hand into her jacket pocket and took out the bar of Dairy Milk. It was broken in two places now. She broke off a row and ate it, then put the rest of the bar back in her pocket.

She would give her father five minutes, and then she would go and find her mother herself.

There were three books on a bookshelf in the corner of the room. Each of them Gallachist texts, of course. Each written by Viparanda. Where was he now? Still in India without the revered Yashodhan to look after him? She must have read somewhere in an article online that Viparanda liked to arrive unannounced and never said how long he would stay. There was always a room ready for him, just in case. He didn't observe clock-time either. Even ate supper at breakfast time sometimes.

The title of the book she picked up was *What's the Point of Gallachism?*

A clever, clever title. She opened the book. She could see that Gallachists didn't make the mistake that Jehovah's Witnesses made by using
cheesy illustrations of blank-eyed happy people in an interpretation of
Eden. Instead, there was white space and minimalist pen-and-ink illustrations in which pyramid shapes featured rather a lot. She turned to
the back for an index. There wasn't one, so she looked for the table of
contents. There was a chapter on dissolution. Did Gallachists not realize that dissolution meant debauchery as well? She found the page.

> Traditional, folk relationships limit the potential of human spiritism.
> They are as limiting to the spirit as being a conjoined twin is to the body.
> Imagine sharing a heart with your sister, or being fused to your brother
> at the shoulder and rib cage. We're not going to mince words here. Life
> is a serious business. And so is death. We need to be present for every
> moment. Those of you who are too wrapped up emotionally with your
> husband, your wife, your children or even your pets, will not make it.
> That goes for your house, your car, your holidays in the sun too, by the
> way. You'll be too attached to the life you're leaving. Too attached to
> material comforts and too attached to relationships. And that includes
> your relationship to your own body. Think about what this means.
> Imagine not being able to free yourself from the bodies you've roped
> yourself to. Imagine not being able to get out of your own body because
> you've become too attached to it. It's pretty much the same as being bur-
> ied alive. It's true you won't be there forever. We'll come and get you
> eventually, dig you out. But we've got an awful lot of other things to do
> before we'll have time to rescue the dying. We're too busy saving the
> living.

Jenny closed the book. It could do with some editing and should be
less histrionic for readers of any intelligence. Nevertheless, she could
see its attraction. Especially if you were feeling alienated from everyone
else on the planet, which wasn't such a rare state of mind.

So if you didn't dissolve all your family relationships, divorce your
spouse as well as your children, then your soul would be trapped for,
what, decades, millennia, eons? Trapped where, exactly? Just how long
would it take to save the six billion or so non-Gallachists on the planet?

And how exactly were the Gallachists doing this saving anyway? Through meditation? Wasn't that like nuns and monks all over the world praying for the souls of the rest of the human race? Or did everyone in the world have to meditate in order to free themselves?

Jenny stood at the window. Her parents had dropped her and her sisters into a glass of water like vitamin C tablets until they fizzed into nothing. The sea was beginning to look more silver than blue now; the sun was setting. She was terrified of spending a night here; she didn't trust any of them. She must see her mother as soon as possible and leave. She wished she could talk to Dominic. Or Karen. Her father had said there was a telephone here. She would get him to take her to it.

This place had a lot to answer for. This stupid, beautiful place where everyone smiled all the time and didn't know what was going on in the real world. If she had learnt one thing growing up in the Ross family, it was that nothing was permanent, however much you thought or wished it was. Well, that law was universal and it applied to Ben Gallachie too. She hoped these grinning, hemp-wearing people all realized that.

She removed the receipt with Dominic's contact details on it from her book and folded it up and put it in her wallet. Then she slid her wallet and passport into a jacket pocket. She took the Iqaluit stone out of her rucksack and put that in a pocket too. She wanted everything important with her all the time. Just in case.

She'd felt the bar of chocolate when she'd put the stone in her pocket. All she'd eaten today was a muesli bar she'd bought at the hostel that morning and the packet of crisps her father had given her. She wasn't hungry anymore; the row of chocolate she'd eaten just now was still stuck in her throat.

This was ridiculous. She wasn't going to wait any longer. Her mother was here somewhere. She was going to find her right now.

Jenny opened the door and saw her father sauntering along the path towards her, looking around at the sea, the mountains, the buildings, looking as pleased as if he'd created them all himself. He was wearing the Gallachist uniform now — a kurta and loose leggings.

She didn't wait. She walked quickly along the path ahead of him.

"Jenny! Wrong way."

She stopped and turned. "Where is she then?"

"Come with me and I'll take you to her. Come on, this way."

She went towards him. "You said a few minutes." Jenny looked at her watch.

"You really have an obsession with time, don't you? We can help you with that, you know. Why don't you start by giving me your watch?" Her father held his hand out.

Jenny laughed. He meant it. That was what was so funny.

He turned around abruptly. "Come on." He hadn't appreciated her laughter.

She followed him along another charming, winding path towards the back of the large building with two pyramids. Inside, a sunny corridor led to a large dining hall. It was all pine and glass and lightness, even in the evening sun, and the room smelt pleasantly of linseed oil. There was so much wood: the pyramid, the floors, the tables and chairs. And so much dull green. The half a dozen or so long tables had plenty of people at them, all wearing loose trousers and kurtas. Even though there were more than a hundred people in the hall and everyone appeared to be in conversation, the noise level was low. Everyone she could see who wasn't wearing a head covering had short hair. She was glad she had longer hair these days.

Jenny scanned the room for her mother. "She's out? She's here?"

"As I said, supper first and then she'll probably be ready for us."

Jenny was momentarily speechless. "You said you'd take me to her."

"Elucidation isn't something you can schedule. Come on, look. You must be hungry." He pointed to a long counter with many dishes on it. "There's carrot and coriander soup, lentil dahl, homemade bread and salads — rice, potato, couscous, coleslaw. All vegan."

"Hiya." It was Cameron, carrying a plate. Also now wearing sage green. At least it went well with his gingery colouring.

"I don't want anything," Jenny told her father. "I want you to take me to my mother."

Cameron leant towards her and said quietly, "If you've got an eating disorder, we can absolutely help you with that."

Jenny stared at him. "I'm here to see my mother. Nothing else."

Cameron smiled as if he felt sorry for her, then went over to the buffet.

It was as if she were a different species from these green, smiling people all around her. Jenny tried to get her father's attention. People were coming up to greet him, welcome him back, tapping him with their fingertips above his heart or close by, as if touching him would bring them luck. He smiled each time but the smile didn't linger longer than it had to. A couple of women in their forties were talking to him now. "Welcome back." One of them reached her hand towards him.

"It's good to be in an elucidation zone again," Jenny's father said.

"So, how is he?" The other woman tapped Jenny's father. She had clear blue eyes like Piyali, making Jenny wonder where the girl was, if she was even here.

"Is he coming here soon?" said the woman who had spoken first.

"He's well and I don't know." Jenny's father smiled at their eagerness. "We can't know, can we? However, he wants to see you all soon. I'll tell him how keen you all are to see him when I return to him."

The women beamed at each other. They went to sit back down at their table where Jenny could see them updating their cronies.

"Let me guess. Your fearless leader Viparanda?"

"I know you don't mean anything by it, Jenny, but I'd appreciate it if you'd speak of Viparanda in more respectful terms."

"You know what his real name is, don't you? Colin Smith. He's from Woking."

"Everyone has to be from somewhere." A glimpse of her old father, just for a moment. He picked up a plate. "Look, you'll have heard people call me Yash or Yashodhan. When we join Ben, we're given the opportunity to have a new name given to us. It's a way to acknowledge your new existence, your new role in the universe. I was given the name Yashodhan. Come on, grab a plate."

"No," Jenny said. "I'm going to find my mother now."

"You can't interrupt her. I told you. She's in an elucidation session."

"Does Jenny know what all our mumbo-jumbo means?" Cameron said. Jenny hadn't realized he had come back. It was the good cop, bad cop routine. "Your mum has had a very traumatic experience outside without Gallachist support." Cameron's Keanu Reeves smile was back. "Elucidation is about returning yourself to the present. You stay in until you've transferred. All the madness outside? The sadness, depression, frustration, all that unhappiness. It sticks to you."

If Cameron wasn't going to sit down and eat his plateful of food, she'd get some information out of him. "So where do these sessions take place?"

"It doesn't matter. We'll meet her in her room when she's finished," her father said.

"In those little pyramid structures you may have noticed," Cameron said at the same time. "Each one is an oasis. You can hear the stream rushing along underneath — they're built over a burn — and the wind in the trees, but nothing much in the way of human-originated sounds. You should try it while you're here. It's very rejuvenating."

"From what I saw of her in hospital," Jenny said, moving towards the door, "I wouldn't have thought she's quite ready for advanced meditation in a hut hanging over a river."

"She's being taken care of," Cameron said gently as he too moved closer to the door. "Don't worry. We know how ill she's been . . ."

Cameron was still talking but Jenny didn't hear what he said. She was on her way out of the dining hall.

Twenty-seven

JENNY JOGGED ALONG the back of the building, looking beyond the lawn. She spotted one of the small pyramids through the trees and cut across the grass; she could hear the burn. She didn't look back to see if her father or Cameron were following her. She couldn't hear them. She kept moving until she reached the water. Here they were: six cute little pyramids straddling the stream. She headed for the narrow wooden bridge that led to the first pyramid. As she was about to step onto it, she noticed a smaller, rectangular hut like an ordinary garden shed a few metres away. The door was opening and a figure was coming out like a sentry on guard.

"You can't —" the figure said, then stopped. "Oh, hello."

It was Piyali. She had come back after all. Hardly a surprise. She wouldn't have got Jenny's note at the hostel.

"Which one is she in?" Jenny said.

Piyali hesitated.

"If you don't tell me, I'm going to look in each one."

"She's just finishing up a transference. Then she'll be out to see you."

"Jesus, is she on her own in there?"

"She's much stronger now. Her colours are —"

"Which one?" Jenny interrupted. She stepped onto the bridge. It was the width of three planks.

"Have some respect, Jenny." It was her father. He had caught her up. "You can't just barge in."

Jenny crossed the little bridge and opened the door. A man was sitting in a lotus position on a futon in the middle of the floor. He was naked, as if he were posing for an art class. The man opened his eyes and placidly turned his head to look at her.

Jenny quickly shut the door and crossed the bridge back to the bank. One down, five to go.

"Jenny!" Now it was Cameron calling her. "Please don't disturb anyone else."

"Then tell me which one she's in."

Cameron nodded at Piyali.

"The fourth one." Piyali pointed.

Jenny ran along the path.

"Let me go in first." Piyali ran to catch up with her. "She needs to be prepared."

"I have seen my mother naked before," said Jenny, although she wasn't sure whether she in fact had, not completely.

"It's not that," said Cameron, also catching them up. "That's an optional thing. An interruption undoes all the work you've done, sets you back. You have to close it off properly with the steps."

Jenny looked around to see where her father was. He was standing a few feet away. For the first time, he looked as if he didn't know quite what to do. Perhaps he wasn't as *dissolved* from his family as he thought he was.

Jenny let Piyali cross the bridge ahead of her and followed closely behind. Piyali pulled a thin rope at the side of the door — there was a gentle chime — and tapped twice on the door before she turned the handle.

Jenny had been expecting her mother to be sitting or lying on a futon like the man in the other pyramid, but she was in a wheelchair. Couldn't she walk?

Her mother turned to look at Jenny, her slack face tightening into her lopsided smile. She held out her hand.

"She can walk." Piyali was defensive. "She gets tired quickly and everything here's so spread out. But she's much stronger than she was in hospital."

There was definitely a reassuring brightness in her mother's eyes. She was so much more animated than when Jenny had last seen her four days ago. Not that this ridiculous treatment had anything to do with it. Her mother looked so different from the Willowbrae days — the short, grey hair, the unflattering dress. She was at least wearing a chunky blue and red Fair Isle knitted cardigan on top of it, although that was worrying because it was a warm evening.

Jenny took her mother's hand, the long fingers she'd so often watched holding a telephone, folding sheets, stirring porridge. The hand tugged Jenny forward and she bent to kiss her mother's cheek. It was soft and wet, or it may have been Jenny's own cheek that was wet; she couldn't tell.

Jenny straightened, still holding her mother's hand. There was a hole in the floor a few feet from the wheelchair, about a metre square. Through it, you could see the water rushing underneath, shallow and splashing and noisy. The pyramid smelt more like tree than wood, as if it were still growing.

Her mother noticed Jenny sniffing. "Air," she said, and stopped. "Piyali?" She sounded cross, as if whatever it was she'd forgotten was Piyali's fault.

"Oxygen." Piyali indicated a vent in the wooden tented ceiling.

"It's. Very. Healing." Jenny's mother's words lurched out of her mouth.

Jenny knelt beside the wheelchair. Her mother still hadn't let go of her hand. "How are you feeling?" Jenny felt like a well-behaved child, asking the questions her parents had trained her to ask. She should have spent the time on the way here working out a proper plan. She should have brought a doctor with her. How was she supposed to tell how well her mother was? She had to think this through rationally. Yet her mind was frozen, as if she'd left it out on the tundra.

"I'm not. In this. All the time." Her mother laughed abruptly. She looked at Piyali as if she wanted her to say something.

"It doesn't fit on the bridge," Piyali explained. "I help your mother over and then fold up the wheelchair and bring it in for her."

"I'm a baby," her mother said with her half-smile. She was like a baby again. That was what she meant.

"How on earth did you manage on that boat?" Jenny's question was for Piyali.

"We managed," said Piyali simply.

"Down those harbour steps?" The thought horrified Jenny.

Her mother said something sibilant that Jenny didn't quite catch. It sounded like *sick*.

"You were sick? On the boat?"

Her mother moved her head; it was more of a wobble than a nod or shake.

"She felt queasy," Piyali said. "Lots of people do. She wasn't sick."

"Did you tell them where she was?" Jenny asked, although she knew it had been her father.

"No," said Piyali, losing her confidence. "They just arrived."

"You really think sitting over a stream in a pyramid is better than being in hospital?"

Piyali stared at the water through the hole as if Jenny had reminded her where they were.

"Has a doctor been to see her here?"

Piyali shook her head.

"Stupid question," said Jenny to herself. "Can you," she said to her mother, "move your arms, your legs? Everything?"

"This arm's. Weak." Her mother lifted her right arm a few centimetres with her left hand. "My leg too." Her words were coming out in fits and starts.

"I'm getting you out of here," Jenny said.

The door opened and her father came in.

"All right?" he asked. No one responded.

"You came," her mother asked Jenny, "from Canada?"

"Yes. I'm doing some research there. I'm studying sculptors."

"The nurse told us." Piyali was crouching on the floor, her feet flat and without putting her bottom on the ground.

Her mother twisted her hand in a gesture of frustration. "You must. Get back."

"I will. Once I know you're okay."

"I'm fine. You go."

"We should leave Moksha now," Jenny's father said. "She needs rest. Piyali, have you finished the steps?"

Piyali widened her eyes. She'd forgotten.

"I didn't give her a chance to do anything," Jenny said.

"I'm sorry," Piyali told Jenny's mother.

"Do it now then." Jenny's father opened the door to leave.

"Why did you run away?" Jenny said to her mother.

"Look." Her father came back into the pyramid. "We don't have these sorts of conversations in here. These spaces are for transferring, not accumulating."

Jenny felt cold air rising from the stream. "I'm going to take you to your room now," she told her mother. "You'll show me the way, won't you, Piyali?" Piyali nodded.

"Have you had any supper?"

Her mother shook her head.

"Lunch?" Jenny said.

"A little," said Piyali.

"Too much food interferes with the transference process," her father said.

"For God's sake. Okay, so dining room first, then bedroom. Or we can bring you some supper to your room, that's probably a better idea."

She took hold of the wheelchair's handles and started pushing. "Piyali, will you help me? Show me what you do to get across the bridge."

"He was. A little boy," her mother said as Jenny wheeled her along the gravel paths to her room. It was in a row similar to where Jenny's room was, except a new building, not a row of converted cottages. "Your father. When we got here. I hardly saw him." Her words were like the wheelchair; it would roll along until the little wheels at the front hit a larger stone and jolted. "He had new. Toys. Then. Travelling. India."

Piyali was in front of them and Jenny's father was behind. Her father didn't seem to care if he heard what she was saying. Cameron had disappeared. Too many Rosses in one place, probably.

"Mother was left. To clear up the mess," her mother said. Jenny glanced behind. Her father was walking along in the dusk with his hands in his pockets. He did look rather like a little boy.

Her mother's room was similar to Jenny's inside, except with more books, as well as CDs and a CD player on top of a chest of drawers. There was a shawl draped over a chair — a bright, coppery red. Jenny recognized the polarizer on her mother's bedside cabinet that she'd had at the hospital, or one very like it.

Her father tutted as he came in. "Where did all this stuff come from?"

Her mother's grimace was as lopsided as her smile. "Naughty."

Jenny smiled. She stepped forward to help, but her mother grasped Piyali's arm to lift herself out of the wheelchair and into an armchair. Jenny was glad her mother had someone looking after her so attentively in this place, yet it was hard not to feel supplanted. She was also aware that Piyali was the same age that Jenny had been when she'd last seen her mother.

"Shall we get some supper for you?" Jenny suggested. Her mother nodded.

It was a relief when her father said he'd go and left the three of them on their own.

Piyali was helping Jenny's mother take off her cardigan, easing her delicate right arm out of its sleeve.

"Into bed," her mother said.

"What about supper?" Jenny said.

"Too tired."

Jenny looked at Piyali, who gave a small shrug of resignation. Piyali told Jenny there was a nightdress in the chest of drawers and Jenny fetched it; it was white, thank goodness, not green. Piyali was helping Jenny's mother to stand again now. She asked Jenny to pull her mother's dress up to her waist and then together they eased her down again into the chair.

"We'll change your underwear in the morning, all right, after your wash?" Piyali suggested. Jenny's mother nodded a little. She didn't seem to have any words left. Her right eyelid was drooping.

Jenny had been wondering if, after her mother had some supper, she could wheel her into the village and find a boat to Mallaig there and then. Go over there tonight if possible. It was obvious now that her mother needed to rest. Jenny would go to the village alone tonight and find out when the boats ran. They could get the first one in the morning.

Piyali stepped back so that Jenny could carefully pull her mother's dress over her head, stopping to gently unloop it from her mother's right hand where it had caught. She wasn't wearing a bra. Her breasts were narrow and low, the nipples broad and dark. Piyali was ready with the nightdress.

"I want to take you away from here tomorrow," Jenny said when her mother was in bed, propped up on a couple of pillows. "You need to see a doctor."

Her mother closed her eyes for a moment. The skin around her eyes was dark.

"You don't want to stay here, do you?" asked Jenny.

Her mother looked at Piyali.

"Don't look at her." Jenny had an urge to stamp her foot. She tried to keep her voice calm. "You need to be in a hospital."

Her mother moved her head. It was neither a nod nor a shake.

"She really needs to rest," said Piyali. "She'll be much better in the morning."

Her mother looked gratefully at Piyali. "Just need sleep."

By the time Jenny's father came back with a tray of supper, she was asleep.

Jenny told Piyali and her father she wanted an early night too, ignoring her father's protestations that she hadn't had any supper.

As she made her way along the path in the direction of her room, the mountains were blackening and the water was silver. The waves on the shore were as gentle as breath. A couple of yellow lights were shining far across the waters of Loch Nevis. Jenny wished she could be inside one of those houses on the other side of the broad bay.

Her mother was resting; that was best. Jenny wouldn't go to her room just yet. She'd find the lane and go to the village to find out about boats. If there wasn't a ferry, she'd pay someone to take them across. Lots of people must have boats. She had her credit and debit cards and she could go to a cash machine in Mallaig. She would go and fetch her mother early, before anyone else was up.

She wasn't going to ask her mother what she wanted anymore; she was going to tell her what was happening.

"Hiya," said a male voice behind her, catching up with her even though she was walking quickly.

Bugger. It was Cameron. What a coincidence. They evidently weren't going to leave her alone for long. Even the sound of his footsteps was annoying. Well, he could walk with her all the way to Inverie if he wanted. Or she would get him to show her where the telephone was. He seemed a little more helpful than her father. Then she could ring Dominic. Talk about something that had nothing to do with her family. Would he be sitting round-backed with concentration inside the electromagnetic field of his computer, or was he out in the field itself, on the tundra, scraping away snow, chipping at pre-Cambrian rock with his hammer, the shaft worn to the shape of his grip?

"Off for a night stroll?" Cameron said when he was alongside her.

"Could you take me to the phone?"

"Sure." He barely hesitated. He really was playing the good cop.

She asked him where the telephone was and he told her it was in a separate building by the entrance to Ben Gallachie. "Landlines don't emit EMFs apparently, so why not have it in the main building?" Jenny said.

"It's too invasive. We focus here on face-to-face communication, on four-dimensional relationships. The phone is useful, don't get me wrong, but we want to choose when we use it, not the other way around."

Jenny wasn't going to admit she wasn't a fan of the telephone either.

"We're doing really exciting work with EMFs, your dad probably told you." Cameron was a talker like her father. That didn't mean she had to listen. "We reorder and repolarize the charged particles. You should visit our workshop tomorrow. One day polarizers will be everywhere. We make them here. We're selling quite a few. We've got the minis and the portables. You'll have seen your dad's, no doubt. That bag he was carrying. We're working on making them really portable. We set them up each night when we're travelling."

He was leading her along another of the paths. Soft yellow night lights had come on at ground level, as few as necessary to light the way without thinning the darkness.

"Hey, can we make one detour? You have to see this."

"No, I want to go straight to the phone."

"It's not even a detour. Here, look." Cameron stopped where there was a gap in the bushes. "Ta da! This is our Earthship."

It was the building she'd seen when she'd arrived that looked like a large greenhouse partly buried by a landslide. It was built into a grassy slope, one storey high, and mostly made of glass at the front. It made her think about how the Inuit built homes from ice and snow.

"Shall we pop in? Your mum helped build it."

"No." She didn't care what she said to him.

She briefly looked, though. She could see banana plants, yuccas, fig trees and other flora she didn't recognize, and wicker chairs and sofas and large cushions and rugs on the wooden floor, all lit by lamplight. A contrived coziness that was difficult not to like. She couldn't see anyone inside.

"There's a wall made of cans and a wall made of bottles," Cameron said, catching her up when she started walking again. "Your mum helped make those. Not load-bearing walls. Dividers. Sure you don't want to look?"

"I'm sure."

"You're very direct, aren't you? Don't get me wrong. I like it. Most people on the outside aren't like that."

"The only reason I'm here is to get my mother," Jenny said.

"We're taking good care of her."

"I can see that you think you are. But she needs to be in hospital."

"Hospitals are great for treating bodies, but not so good at the spiritual side of things."

It was what her father had said to her. Now they were walking in silence. Jenny knew it wouldn't last long.

"I trained as an architect," Cameron said. "I found out about Earthships when I was backpacking in the States and ever since then, I wanted to build one. And we did. We can build anything we like here, anything sustainable. We've got our own hydroelectric power scheme. It's better than any career I could have had."

Jenny could see where this was leading.

"You're in academia, right? You could help Viparanda finish writing all the teachings," Cameron told her. "You could study under him and then you could teach. We need teachers."

It was almost amusing, listening to him try to find a Gallachist niche for her. She could see how disillusioned young people like him found their way here. A trained architect, just out of college, full of ideas and idealistic urges. Then there was a recession. He probably couldn't get a job, certainly not one with purpose or where you could have all this freedom. No money worries, food and board provided. Living with people who valued your skills and encouraged you to use them. Creating beautiful buildings that would never be stained by traffic fumes or graffiti, or urinated against or pulled down to make way for a road or a supermarket.

Yes, she could see how someone would come here, thinking it was the beginning, not realizing it was the end.

Cameron took a breath. He was going to try another tack. "I was a wreck when I came. I had a job at an architect's in Glasgow, which I knew would lead to something if I hung in there. Nice girlfriend, fun. You know? It wasn't enough."

You don't say.

"I felt empty," Cameron said. He steered her towards a left fork in the path. "I started drinking too much, partying too much. Started taking ecstasy, then crack. Lost the girlfriend. Looked for another one, or several."

You could do what you liked to your body in your teens and twenties. Jenny knew of plenty of people at university who lived that way and got away with it. Clear skin, slim bodies. Young bodies drawn in pencil, not yet in ink.

"What about you?" said Cameron to her silence. "Have you had your lost years?"

"I'm not here for therapy," Jenny said. "I'm here for my mother."

"What I've learnt is that everyone's shut inside a secret cage of pain. It's not a question of who's in one, it's a question of how to get out. That's what was such a relief about coming here. Realizing it wasn't only me."

Jenny could see the gates at last, tall, black and closed. Quite possibly locked. There was a small, stone building to the left, lit by an outside light. Surely that was where the telephone was.

"For a lot of people, me included, it's relationships that screw things up. What about you, Jenny? Do you have a guy at the moment? I'm sure you do. I hope he's treating you well."

She stopped to face him. She could see from his expression he thought he'd got through to her at last. He smiled, willing her to confess that Dominic treated her badly, when it was Christopher and the beach that had flashed in her mind just now. Christopher doing up his belt.

"I just want you to have what I have, Jenny. What all of us here have."

Jenny pointed at the little building by the gates. "Is that where the phone is?"

Jenny picked up the receiver and dialled the number of the research centre. She'd give Cameron some money to cover the long-distance call. She would owe the Gallachists nothing. The ringing sounded as small and far away as it was, across an ocean of water and ice. She looked through the window. Cameron had left her and gone outside, hopefully well out of earshot. Was the line bugged? Was she being paranoid?

"Hi there." A woman's voice.

"Kay?" Tears came into Jenny's eyes.

"Jen! How's it going? How's your mom?"

Jenny breathed. "Definitely stronger. On the mend, but it's going to take a while."

"That's awesome," Kay said. "I bet she was real happy to see you."

Best to keep it simple. "Yes, she was. How are you? How's your work going?"

"Oh, you know. Building up trust takes time."

"You're doing such important work, Kay. Really helping people."

"That's sweet of you. Look, Dom's not at the centre right now. Sorry. I could double-check, but I'm pretty sure he's not —"

"No, it's okay. Just tell him I called, could you?"

"Sure. Oh, he'll be so sorry. You guys. I'm real happy for you. He's got a grin on his face the whole time. I reckon he sleeps with that smile on his face."

Perhaps it was just as well that Dominic hadn't been there. She wouldn't have been able to have a proper conversation anyway, not with Cameron lurking outside in the shadows, making sure she didn't breach the Gallachist peace. Never mind wanting to become an architect; he should have become a police officer. He obviously already liked wearing a uniform.

Cameron came up to her as she left the building. Jenny looked at the closed gates and the dark lane beyond. She knew if she walked to Inverie now, Cameron would insist on coming with her. It was getting late; there were no street lights; she didn't know the terrain. She didn't even know if there was a pub where she could ask about boats. It was too late to knock on people's doors. She suddenly didn't have the energy to argue with Cameron, demand he let her go alone. And if he followed her, he'd report back on her search for a boat. Best to wait until the morning. Get her mother up early and take her in the wheelchair to the village.

Twenty-eight

JENNY COULDN'T SLEEP. There was no noise to keep her awake. No traffic, no drunken neds or students in the street below. No snow-mobiles roaring past. Jenny couldn't even hear the waves on the shore because she had her window closed, because if the window was open she definitely couldn't sleep. She'd tried. She was too worried that someone would climb into the room. To do what, she didn't know. She was being irrational. She hadn't got undressed; she was lying in bed fully clothed.

Did she think a Gallachist would come in and erase her mind while she slept? She got up and stood for a while in darkness at the window, looking at the gleam of light on the sea now that the moon had risen. A few more hours and she could go to her mother's room and get her away from here. If anyone did anything to stop her mother leaving, then Jenny would go to Mallaig and fetch the police.

She went over to her jacket draped over her rucksack and took out the chocolate. It didn't make sense with it full of caffeine, but she knew from experience if she ate enough of it, it helped her sleep. The sugar overload shut her body down: the Valium effect. She sat on the bed and ate it quickly, hardly tasting it. When it was all gone, she shoved the wrapper in a rucksack pocket and got back into bed.

Eyes closed, she tried to imagine she was in her bed at the research centre. What if Maddie was right and it was just her accent that Dominic liked? What if he was already forgetting about her? Or had he decided she was too much trouble, far more craziness than he wanted or needed.

Night thoughts. You couldn't trust them. She knew that. Night thoughts were badly written essays. No argument, no data analysis, no counter-argument. Certainly no conclusion.

She got up again and fetched her Iqaluit stone. She went back to bed and lay with it on her stomach, her hands clasped over it. Her parents had made their decision eight years ago. This was where they had chosen to be. Jenny could leave right now if she wanted, climb over the gates if they were locked, walk to the village and wait for the dawn. Leave her mother to the Gallachists, let her lie on the bed she had made, sit in the Earthship she had built.

She could feel the chocolate lodged in her esophagus as if her throat were a backed-up lavatory. She'd tried to move forward, not backward. She'd eased herself into the river, rather than letting herself be pulled back and forth by waves on a shore. She'd made her home, her life in Edinburgh. She'd never been back to visit Willowbrae or even Peebles. Perhaps if she'd taken the Free Minds advice and kept in touch with her parents, she'd know who they were now; she'd know what her mother was thinking, if there was still hope. She might even know how to get through to her father.

No. Her father had become a different person. Probably even before they'd stood in the halls of residence carpark. It was too late. Jenny had been too late when it came to Jean too. It was nearly two years after she left Willowbrae before she wrote to Jean. She'd been training herself to stop thinking about her parents and what had happened but that was no excuse. She'd heard nothing for several weeks until, at last, Jean's husband Alan had written back with a cheap ballpoint pen on lined paper to tell her that Jean was dead. Her cancer had come back. It had spread to her bones, her liver and finally her brain.

Jenny got out of bed and rushed to the bathroom. Chocolate slopped into the toilet bowl, a dollop splashing water up onto her cheek. She knelt on the floor of the bathroom waiting. Nothing more came, even though her stomach didn't feel empty. She breathed through her nose and resisted the temptation to tickle her throat with her fingers to induce more retching. She rinsed out her mouth with water and cleaned her teeth.

She checked her watch. Half past two in the morning.

She could take her mother away from this place right now.

She put her wash bag in her rucksack, fastened the straps and lifted it onto the bed so she could turn and hoist it onto her shoulders. Leaving her room, she followed the path through the woods to her mother's room. The buttery ground lights were still on, making it easy to find her way. At her mother's wooden door, she paused.

What if the gates were locked?

The night air was cold. They couldn't hide in the bushes until someone came along and opened the gates. They could be there for hours. And even if the gates were open, there wouldn't be any shelter while they waited for the first ferry to arrive — or until they could knock on someone's door and ask to use a phone to find a boat company to come and fetch them.

Her mother was better off where she was for now. She needed rest.

Jenny could go now, on her own, to check the gates. Then creep into her mother's room and wait for the dawn.

Jenny felt calmer as her body moved. She went the same way Cameron had taken her, walking on grass as much as possible to muffle her footsteps. There didn't seem to be anybody else about. Did they really not have any kind of security watch except Cameron's unsubtle attempts to keep an eye on her? These people were so naïve. They had no idea how much hostility there was against them out in the real world.

Here were the gates. She crossed the gravel as quietly as she could. A security light flashed on. She stopped, listening. No one calling out. No footsteps. She kept moving until she reached the gates.

There was a bolt. No padlock. She drew the bolt back and pulled one of the tall gates towards her. It opened smoothly, quietly.

Now she could go back to her mother. As soon as it was light, she'd wake her mother and take her away from this place.

When she reached her mother's room, Jenny twisted the doorknob gently and went in. Her mother, lying on her back, stirred. Jenny stood still. Her mother didn't appear to wake up.

Jenny eased her rucksack off as quietly as she could. As it thudded softly to the floor, a figure rose up from the other side of her mother's bed. Jenny gasped and the figure gasped too. It was Piyali. She'd been lying on the floor.

They faced each other through the grey light until Piyali giggled and slapped her hand to her mouth. She came over to Jenny's side of the bed.

"Great minds think alike," whispered Jenny, for something to say. "Has she been okay?"

"She's been sleeping well. I didn't want her to be on her own. There's a mat you can use. I brought it here. You stay and I'll go back to my room."

When Piyali had gone, Jenny laid the thin yoga mat down next to her rucksack. Piyali apparently hadn't been using a pillow or a sheet or blanket. Jenny rolled up a sweater for a pillow and used her jacket as a makeshift sheet. Not that she expected to sleep. She lay listening to her mother's breathing, trying to relax to the rhythm of it.

Jenny woke when she heard her mother groan. She quickly got up from the floor to check her. She looked all right. Her eyes were closed and she was breathing. Perhaps it had been a yawn.

It was light. Time to go. She'd fallen asleep after all. Jenny checked her watch. Damn. Nearly six o'clock. She shouldn't have gone to sleep. They should have left by now.

She didn't know how long it would be before anyone else would appear. No doubt Gallachists were early risers. As she looked around the room to see what they needed to take, her mother reached out her hand, lowering it in a slow pat. Jenny sat on the bed.

"Hard floor?" Her mother smiled, her mouth drooping a little on her right side.

So her mother knew she'd been there after all.

"It was surprisingly comfortable." Jenny smiled too. "Did you sleep okay?"

Her mother's head movement was ambiguous. She seemed to realize it and groaned.

"Do you want some breakfast?" Jenny said.

Her mother wrinkled her nose. "Too early."

A nervousness skittered inside Jenny's chest. This was it. She was taking her mother out of here now. She opened the cupboard and drawers and knelt down to look under the bed for a bag to pack her mother's things. She found the leather handbag and checked that her mother's purse and driving licence were inside. There was no sign of a larger bag.

"I don't need. Things." Was her mother in a hurry too?

"Toothbrush and underwear at least." Jenny took a couple of what looked like folded dresses out of the chest of drawers, along with her mother's copper-red shawl. "Then we'll get you dressed."

Her mother looked confused.

"I'm taking you back to hospital. Get you checked," Jenny told her. "In Inverness, they thought you were going to a private hospital, not here. Not to a drafty pyramid balanced over a stream. I don't even know how your people managed it, how they got you discharged. I'm going to speak to your doctor at Inverness about that."

Her mother looked as if she had gone all the way upstairs and forgotten what she went up for. "I left hospital."

"Yes, but you need to go back." Her mother's understanding seemed to flicker like a failing fluorescent light.

The door opened and Jenny quickly turned. It was her father, carrying a tray with porridge, toast, tea and apple juice. "Good morning," he said cheerfully.

"Do you always deliver breakfast at this hour?" Jenny said.

"The morning's the best part of the day." Which wasn't an answer at all.

Jenny carried on looking for anything useful to pack. A kurta or two and some trousers. A hairbrush. She piled them up on the bed.

"What's going on?" her father said.

"Holiday." Was her mother joking or had she got the word wrong?

"I'm taking her to get checked by a doctor." She didn't want to say she was taking her mother to a hospital; she didn't want to be that specific.

"We've been through this. There's no need." Jenny knew that light tone, how her father pretended to pick up a subject as if there was no weight to it. "She's doing well here," he said. "All the medical profession will do is pump her full of drugs."

"Drugs have their uses," Jenny said.

Her mother frowned. "The loo," she said. She didn't want to use the wheelchair, so Jenny put her arm around her and helped her to the bathroom. She helped raise up her nightdress and lowered her slowly onto the seat. They looked at each other as they heard voices in the bedroom.

Her mother's pee gushed into the toilet bowl as if she hadn't been for days. She giggled.

"Niagara Falls," Jenny said.

Jenny tore off some toilet paper and looked away as her mother wiped.

Piyali was in her mother's room when they returned.

"Let's get her dressed," Jenny said quietly when Piyali came over to help ease Jenny's mother back down onto the bed.

"You're not leaving. You know that, don't you?" Jenny's father said to her mother. He sounded cross, the cheery lightness had clouded over.

Jenny's mother seemed surprised by the comment. "Yes," she said.

"We're helping her get dressed now," Jenny said to her father. "Don't look."

Her father laughed.

"I'm serious. You're not married anymore, remember?"

"Oh, for heaven's sake." He went to the window, though, and stood with his back to them, looking out.

Piyali and Jenny worked together to help Jenny's mother get dressed.

Piyali was more at ease here than she had been at the hospital, Jenny noticed. More practical. Jenny was suddenly glad her mother had had Piyali by her side all these years.

Still facing the window, her father said, "Your mother never fully made the transition. I don't want to speak for you, Moksha, but I think you're having difficulties with your articulation. When I say transition, Jenny, I mean the transition to the Gallachist. The transition to equalization."

Jenny wanted to stick his head down the loo and flush out his brain. If he could hear the rubbish he was talking.

"No. I was fair. The girls." Her mother's speech was a little less jerky this morning, Jenny was sure of it.

Her father sighed. "You weren't honest." He turned around. It didn't matter; her mother was clothed. They were settling her back on the bed now. "The money she gave you and your sisters, Jenny, it belongs to Ben. She shouldn't have given it to you. You can't enter Gallachism in a state of dishonesty. You should give us the money back, Jenny. It's not even the money, per se. It's the failure of transference."

So taking away Willowbrae wasn't enough. Now he wanted to take her flat away as well.

"*You* agreed." Her mother's voice was clear. "It was a —" She struggled to remember the word. "Promise. No." They waited for her to think of it. "Tithe!" she said triumphantly.

Jenny's father sat down in the armchair. He seemed to be enjoying sparring with her. "The opposite, I think. A tithe is giving ten percent of your income to the cause. Not to your daughters."

"The cause was us," Jenny said. She might as well join in.

"Yes," her mother said.

"And I don't recall agreeing," her father said. "I think you're conveniently misremembering. You're good at that."

Piyali placed the breakfast tray on Jenny's mother's lap, then arranged her hands in a palms-together prayer position, her thumbs resting against her sternum. "Let's fetch a mediator —"

Jenny's father interrupted her. "When we found out, Jenny, your mother was given a choice of two directions. Leave or stay and make amends. She chose to make amends but in, what, almost eight years of clock-time, she's never fulfilled that obligation. She evidently went back to that point in clock-time, whether consciously or not, and selected that other direction. She left."

"And there was the small detail of her being ill," Jenny said. "You haven't factored that into your so-called directions." She went into the bathroom to collect her mother's toothbrush and a pot of what was probably face cream. There was no makeup anywhere.

"This is your chance, Moksha," Jenny's father said from the armchair, his legs crossed, "your chance to equalize and make amends."

"And what does making amends entail exactly?" Jenny asked to keep him talking while she packed. She carefully took a pillow from behind her mother's back and slid off its pillow case. That would do as a bag. Her father didn't seem to be registering what she was doing.

"The gist of it is that you carry out certain actions, do things for your group to compensate for the interference you brought into that group. You work with each member and agree on something that will help compensate. It's very simple."

Piyali tried again. "Should we not fetch —"

"I can handle it," Jenny's father snapped. "You see?" He stood up, glowering at Jenny's mother. "This is what you do. You create all this turbulence. You've made things difficult for me ever since we came. Last week, I was in Kerala with Viparanda, and the next thing I know I'm leaving him in the lurch and having to come all the way back because you've disappeared and you hadn't detached from me properly. And you, Piyali, I can't believe you let her lead you along."

Jenny undid her rucksack and squashed the pillow case containing her mother's belongings inside.

"I don't know what you think you're doing," her father said.

"People who have had one stroke often have another." Jenny tried to sound composed and matter-of-fact. "My mother should be under the care of a doctor, not sitting in a pyramid over a stream."

Her father sighed. "You've been indoctrinated by the conventional medical system," he said, attempting patience. "Of course that system works to a point. It stitches up cuts, mends broken legs, it can even replace worn-out organs. But injuries are never localized. When your body suffers a trauma, that trauma affects every single cell in your body. It stains every particle of the energy that binds your physicality. You can't just sew up the cut. That doesn't remove the trauma. If anything, it adds to it."

Jenny's mother was leaning back on her pillows, her eyes half-closed. Piyali was kneeling on the floor by the bed holding Jenny's mother's hand.

"Despite her failure to equalize, Moksha's had a lot of training," Jenny's father continued. "She's very responsive to our procedures. She's healing rapidly."

Jenny wanted her mother to say something. "She's not strong enough for all this."

"Your mother is the strongest woman I know." It was her father's old voice. Just for a second.

"Not anymore she isn't," Jenny said. "Look what you've done to her."

Her father put his hands on his hips. He seemed to be working out the best strategy. "Look, you're very sensitive, Jenny. Your colours are strong, which means your perception levels are high. That's unusual in a non-Gallachist. You want to help your mother, I know that. And you are. Your presence here is helping her a lot."

"Yes, I'm sure all these arguments are really helping." The anger came now. She tried to breathe in air from outside, from the cold loch, the solid ridges and gullies, the coarse firs. "What are you afraid of? Why don't you want her to see a doctor?"

"She's had enough drugs pumped into her system," her father said. "If she stays here, she's guaranteed to get better. If she goes back, there's no knowing what will happen. Have you actually asked her if she wants to go? Of course you haven't, because you know you won't like the answer."

Jenny's mother looked blank. She opened her mouth and closed it again.

"For God's sake," Jenny said. "Look at her. She's not in a position to make a decision about what to have for breakfast, let alone her treatment."

"Now that," her father said, "is a deeply counter-elucidating remark."

Jenny heaved her rucksack onto the bed so it would be easier to put it on. "Piyali?"

Piyali looked up, startled.

"Help me get her into her wheelchair."

Piyali, still kneeling, turned to Jenny's father.

"No, don't look at him!" Jenny shouted. "Do what *you* want to do."

Piyali winced and stood up. Jenny heard her father tut.

Jenny grabbed the wheelchair and shoved the seat flat. She took her mother's breakfast tray away and eased her around so she was sitting with her legs on the floor. Jenny was watching every change in her mother's expression, every movement of her body. Her mother was not resisting; she wanted to come with her.

"You're putting your mother's life in danger," Jenny's father said. "Not just her body but her spiritual state."

Jenny ignored him and, with Piyali's help, lifted her mother into the wheelchair. Piyali fetched Jenny's mother's coat and put it on her. Jenny had forgotten about that.

"If you go with them, Moksha," her father said as Jenny hoisted her rucksack onto her shoulders, "you know what it's going to take for you to come back here, don't you? It probably won't be possible in this lifetime."

Jenny's mother looked as if words were floating around inside her head and she had no way of catching them.

Jenny started pushing the wheelchair towards the door.

Her father moved to block the way. "She's not leaving."

Piyali gasped.

"Get out of the way," Jenny told him.

"No."

Jenny came around from behind the wheelchair and stood in front of him. "Get out of the way," she repeated.

She moved forward and her father raised both his hands as if he were going to push her back.

"Don't you dare." Jenny spoke as calmly as she could. "If you don't let us out, I'm going to climb through that window instead and get the police. And then I'll talk to the media. I know that's the only reason you waited for me at the hospital, to make sure I didn't cause any trouble. I'm not stupid."

Her father shook his head as if what she was saying was ridiculous and not worth a response.

"Get out of the way. It's that or the police."

He didn't move.

"It's your choice," Jenny said. "You know I mean it."

He hesitated then stepped aside. Jenny moved between him and the door. "Piyali," she said. "Take my mother out, please."

Jenny waited until Piyali and her mother were outside before she followed.

When she was outside on the path and holding the handles of the wheelchair again, she turned. Her father was standing in the doorway watching them.

"Doesn't one small part of you want to come with us?" He was caught off-guard by the question, she could tell. "No, of course not. Being a Gallachist is far more important than being with your family. Well, we're off your hands now. We're leaving and you're not going to do anything else to stop us. If you still know me at all, you'll know I mean what I say. Police. Media."

She pushed the wheelchair forward. The sea was glittering through the trees. She briefly closed her eyes and felt the sun warm her eyelids as she walked. She wasn't going to look back.

Even though it was still early, she could see a few people walking along the paths in different directions. No one was rushing. Everyone looked tranquil, as if they had no desire to be anywhere else or even knew that anywhere else existed.

Three figures were coming towards her and her mother. Women. Only one of them wearing sage.

Maddie and Sophie.

No. How could it be?

She heard her mother inhale.

Jenny wheeled her mother towards them. It was really them. Sophie looked just the same, as if nothing ever flustered her. Slender in her jeans, her fair hair smooth and neat. Maddie all in black, gazing around as she walked, perplexed.

Jenny looked behind her. Piyali was standing on the path, watching. Her father was still in the doorway.

"They just turned up," the woman in sage called to Jenny's father. She was small and birdlike and had a Yorkshire accent. "I thought I should bring them to you. They've come all the way from London! Isn't that nice? They'd heard Moksha was feeling poorly and wanted to see her and wish her well."

"I bet they did." Jenny's father was coming up behind Jenny now. "Thanks, Sumana, you can leave them with me."

Jenny noticed her sisters didn't say goodbye to Sumana, or thank you. This place had made them rude too, just as it had her. She gripped the wheelchair. She wanted to hug her sisters but she wasn't going to let go.

"How on earth did you get here?" she asked them.

"Good question," Sophie said. "The train journey lasted about three decades and finally delivered us to Mallaig in the middle of the night. I hadn't realized electricity hadn't reached here yet. We had to grope our way to the nearest hotel in darkness and hope they'd left the back door open. I won't even mention the boat ride."

Their father was standing near Jenny now. "Don't come any closer," she told him.

Sophie grimaced. "Looks like we've come at the right time."

Maddie bent down to talk to their mother, soft-voiced. Jenny couldn't hear what she was saying.

Their mother reached out her hand towards Sophie and Sophie took it.

"So this is where you've been hiding." Sophie let go of her mother's hand and folded her arms.

"Thank. You," their mother said.

"What for?"

Their mother didn't answer, only kept gazing at Sophie. Jenny tried not to do anything to break this fragile moment. It was the first time Sophie and her mother had made eye or skin contact for twelve years. What did that do to you, to touch the body that had formed inside your own after so long?

A rasping sound came out of Jenny's mouth. She pressed her lips together to stop more noise coming out. She couldn't feel the ground. She couldn't tell where her feet were. All she could feel was Maddie grabbing her shoulders.

"We're here," Maddie whispered.

"Okay," Sophie said decisively. "There'll be a boat going back across in, what . . ." she unfolded her arms to look at her watch, "forty-eight minutes, so I think we can make that one."

"You really think," said their father, "I'd trust you to look after your mother? Or anyone, in fact."

"Oh." Sophie pretended to take a moment to understand. "We're still talking about that, are we? I forgot I'm a murderer."

Their mother didn't look anywhere near as angry as their father; she was still smiling at Sophie. Had the stroke annihilated the anger, or had it dissipated before that?

"Coming here," their father said, "I had to confront the likelihood that your behaviour towards Grandfather was deliberate, yes. I wish you'd taken responsibility, acknowledged the enormity of what you'd done. I took responsibility. I've worked on that. I've elucidated that interference. If you stay here for a while, you can do that too. I really think you should, Sophie. Only you know the truth. This is your chance to make amends. Return yourself whole to the world."

"Leave her alone," Jenny told her father. "It was years ago."

"I can't trust her with Moksha unless she makes amends."

"I don't know who *Moksha* is," Sophie said, "but if you're talking about our mother, we didn't actually come here for her. We came for Jenny. Having lost both our parents to this loony bin, we didn't fancy losing our sister as well. Having said that," Sophie added, turning to their mother, "I'm sure there's room in the boat for one more."

Their mother smiled, then seemed to think of something. She twisted in the wheelchair. Jenny followed her gaze and saw Piyali standing on the path a few feet away, pale and bewildered.

"Piyali," Jenny said quietly as she went up to her. "Don't you want to say goodbye to my mother?"

Piyali seemed to come out of a trance. "Thank you." She rushed to the wheelchair.

Jenny knew it was futile, but she would make one last attempt. She would deal with this differently from that day in the carpark at the halls of residence. Inside her head, she found a picture of her father sitting at the easel at Willowbrae, a paintbrush in his hand, yellow paint smudged on his knuckles. She looked at him now and sent him the image, a mental email.

His eyes moved past hers to the sea.

She went over to Maddie and Sophie, keeping her father in her peripheral vision in case he went too near their mother.

"It's like *Little House on the Prairie* meets *Star Trek*," Maddie was saying.

They all watched Piyali. She was bending over, hugging their mother.

"That's Piyali," Jenny said. "The one who was at the hospital."

"She's found herself a new daughter by the looks of things," Sophie said.

"What do you think?" Jenny said.

Sophie shrugged.

"Think about what?" Maddie said.

"Could do, I suppose," Sophie said.

"Could do what?" said Maddie.

Jenny went back over to her mother and tapped Piyali gently on the shoulder. Piyali stood up. Her face was red and blotchy. "You can come with us if you want."

Jenny's mother grasped Piyali's hand. "Yes."

Piyali smiled.

Jenny saw Sophie looking at her watch.

"Is there anything you want to grab from your room?" Jenny asked Piyali.

Piyali shook her head then slapped her hand to her mouth. "Your money," she said to Jenny. "They have it."

"It doesn't matter in the scheme of things."

"Piyali," Jenny's father said, listening. "I want you to realize the consequences of your actions if you leave again. Transferring back to elucidation is likely to prove impossible for you for many lifetimes."

It was the same threat he'd given Jenny's mother.

Piyali didn't look at him. She turned to Jenny. "Please. Just a minute." She ran back towards Jenny's mother's room.

Jenny put her hands on the wheelchair. She didn't trust what her father might do without either her or Piyali close by.

Piyali came back out of the room. She was putting something in her pocket.

"Let's go then," Jenny said loudly to everyone.

When Piyali was back at the wheelchair, she said softly, "Just keep walking."

"Bloody hell," said Maddie, finally understanding that Piyali was coming with them. "Does anyone else need rescuing?"

Twenty-nine

NONE OF THEM LOOKED back as they walked through the Ben Gallachie grounds, not even Piyali. Nor did they speak for a while, as if what had just happened needed to work its way through them like a fish bone. Jenny was certainly too tense to talk; she kept looking around to make sure no one was approaching them.

"This isn't the most wheelchair-friendly place, is it?" Sophie said eventually. Jenny was grateful for the ordinariness of the comment. "The boat, the gravelly paths. Even I've noticed that," Sophie added.

"Can I push?" Piyali asked Jenny. "You've got to carry your bag."

"My rucksack," clarified Jenny, as if she were teaching Piyali English. "Thanks, that would be great." Her shoulders were starting to feel as if they were full of pins.

There were people inside the dining hall eating breakfast as they passed.

"So *all* the women have short hair." Maddie said. "The clothes certainly look comfortable. Sage is the new black, apparently."

Jenny glanced at Piyali to see how she was reacting to her sisters' humour.

"You okay?" she whispered.

Piyali nodded. "They're being sarcastic, aren't they?"

"It's all they know," Jenny said.

"I like sarcasm," said Piyali. "It's funny."

"I believe that's the point."

The entrance to Ben Gallachie was coming up. Jenny unbolted the gates, watched each of them go through as intently as a shepherd, and closed the gates behind them.

It was easier for Piyali to push the wheelchair once they were off the track and on the paved road that led to the village of Inverie. There was no pavement so they walked in the lane, taking up the width of the road. Jenny was glad it was still early. There shouldn't be too many people about. Just as she was thinking this, an elderly lady came out her front door. There were swathes of daffodils in her garden and what may have been azaleas, although Jenny wasn't very good at cultivated flowers. The lilac tree was in bloom — Jenny could smell it too — and she could see a scrunch of papery love-in-a-mist by the gate.

Jenny called good morning to the lady and she nodded back in reply, straight-mouthed and unsmiling. The villagers would be used to seeing the Gallachists with their strange clothes and their short hair. They must have been a peculiar sight: one Gallachist in a wheelchair, one too young to know any better, a backpacker and two stylish young women who looked as if they'd be more at home on Kensington High Street with their fashionable little black backpacks over their slim shoulders.

"Is there really a boat soon?" Jenny said.

"No idea," Sophie said. "It was a glitch in our precision planning. We paid a burly fisherman to bring us over at the crack of dawn. He didn't want to hang around to take us back again, strangely enough."

"I don't think boats exactly come every five minutes like the Tube," Jenny said.

"I'm sure we'll be able to ask someone," said Sophie, "and, unlike the rest of you technophobes, I have what's called a mobile phone on me."

"If you can get a signal." Maddie veered over to Piyali. "I'll push for a bit."

Piyali smiled and stepped aside from the wheelchair.

"There's also something called a public telephone," Sophie said.

"And plan C is knocking on someone's door. I'm sure anyone would be only too happy to help once they know we've got two escapees with us. See? I've thought of everything."

"I'm really grateful," Jenny said, more seriously. "I couldn't believe it when I saw you."

"You nearly fainted," Maddie said.

"Can you blame me? I never thought I'd ever see either of you in Scotland again. I'm surprised you remembered where it was."

Their mother hadn't said anything since they'd wheeled her through the gates. Her new, lopsided smile was in place, though; she was enjoying the banter. They carried on past the little white stone cottages with low slate roofs. The buildings looked as much part of the landscape as the bright broadleaves behind them and the dark evergreens farther away. The water was only a short distance from the houses, across the narrow lane, a strip of grass and the narrow beach.

They reached a small pier and a sign that said there was a ferry. Jenny shrugged off her rucksack and Maddie stopped pushing the wheelchair. Piyali went over and put the brakes on.

"Next ferry in just over an hour," Jenny said, reading the sign.

"Hallelujah," Sophie said.

"Shame the pub's not open yet," Maddie said.

Sophie shuddered. "Christ, can you imagine living in a place this small? You'd end up related to everyone else."

Jenny could imagine it. Living where you had to get on a boat to go anywhere else or walk over a mountain range, living there with Dominic.

There was a bench by the pier. Sophie and Maddie sat down on it heavily, as if they'd been walking all day, and then shifted to make room for Jenny in the middle. Piyali crouched beside their mother in her wheelchair. Jenny could hear her asking if she was warm enough.

"You don't think he'll follow us, do you?" Maddie took out a cigarette and lit it.

Jenny got up off the bench to get away from the smoke. She found a rock to sit on.

"I mean," said Maddie to their mother, "surely he's not just going to let you go. You're married, after all."

"Ah," said Jenny from her rock. "Apparently, that's not the case anymore. It's a Gallachist thing, to do with being spiritually independent. Correct me if I'm wrong, Piyali. What it means is that our parents got divorced."

"Fuck. Is that true?" Sophie said to their mother.

Their mother hesitated. "It's hard to —"

"I'll bet," said Sophie.

"It's something called dissolution," explained Jenny to spare their mother. "The idea is you exist in this world completely independently and that ties like marriage limit you. Is that about right, Piyali?"

Piyali looked too scared to say anything.

Jenny wouldn't mention yet that you could dissolve your relationships with your children too. She wanted Sophie and Maddie to help her get their mother to a hospital. Sophie's small, neat face was closed. Jenny wanted to know what she was thinking. But then she always wanted to know what Sophie was thinking. Jenny looked across the inlet in the direction of Mallaig.

"I wondered about finding a doctor here, in Mallaig. But I think we should get farther away." Jenny turned to her mother. "We'll take you to Edinburgh, to the hospital there. Okay?"

Her mother was looking at the water as if she'd seen something sink into it and was waiting for it to resurface.

"Is that okay with you?" Jenny repeated.

"We'll just take her," Sophie said.

"How do we get there? By train?" Maddie said it as if she were hoping not.

"Car," Jenny said. "It will be more comfortable for —" She paused. She couldn't say *Mummy*. "Then we can stop whenever we want. Though I don't know if Mallaig does one-way car hires."

Sophie took her phone out of her pocket. "Voila. We have the technology." She flipped it open. "Bugger. No signal."

Jenny laughed. "I saw a phone box. Back there a bit." She stood up.

"I'll go," Sophie said. "Give me your change."

Jenny and Maddie took out their purses.

"So," said Sophie. "We need a car hire from Mallaig, one-way to

Edinburgh. A car big enough for five plus wheelchair. And your car-buncle." She nodded at Jenny's rucksack.

She left her own tiny backpack with them and walked back along the way they'd come, her hands in the pockets of her jeans.

It was strange not to be the only one working out what to do and how to do it.

Thirty

NO ONE WAS SICK on the ferry back to Mallaig. Jenny's mother and Piyali looked pale. Maddie and Sophie looked as if they couldn't work out how come they were in the same dream. At Mallaig, they got a taxi from the harbour to a garage where Sophie had booked a Ford Mondeo. Black, which pleased Maddie. Jenny and Sophie said they'd take turns driving them to Edinburgh. Maddie couldn't drive anyway; she'd never had lessons. That didn't mean she'd be happy sitting in the back seat, however, although she relented when Jenny pointed out their mother had suffered a stroke and might appreciate the leg room. Piyali, fortunately, said she was content to sit in the middle on the back seat for the whole one hundred and eighty-five-mile journey.

As Jenny drove, it was easy to believe that it was fascination with the landscape that was keeping them all quiet, especially Maddie and Sophie, who had arrived in darkness. She wanted them to love the gleaming lochs, the steep slopes and pinnacles, the white-painted houses barely sheltered by straggly stands of pine trees.

Entering Glen Coe, she glanced up at Aonach Eagach ridge. She'd walked it during her university days. Clambered it. It was arguably the narrowest ridge on the British mainland. You could die on it easily. People did. There had been one heart-dropping lurch, one swing when her daypack unbalanced her, the straps too loose.

Even there, when she should have been concentrating on each hand and foothold as the mountain tipped dizzyingly from her whichever position she was in, she remembered wishing she could bring her father here one day. Damn him. They could have been Munro baggers together, pushing pins into a map of Scotland up in the kitchen at Willowbrae. On your own, you tended to go back to the mountains you knew rather than explore new ones. She started fiddling with the radio to find a station. By the time they were out of Glen Coe and crossing Rannoch Moor, she'd given up. She adored the crumpled undulations of this watery moor; she didn't need any other entertainment.

Now and again as she drove, she glanced in the rear-view mirror. Maddie was looking out her window with a slight scowl, Piyali's clear blue eyes were fixed on the view through the windscreen straight ahead and Sophie was sitting back looking as if she were used to being chauffeured around every day. Their mother, each time Jenny looked, was asleep.

Somewhere past Loch Ba, Maddie came out of her reverie. Perhaps it was the sight of a single, small and windswept tree by the side of the road, the only tree they'd seen for miles.

"I had a phone call from loverboy, by the way," Maddie said, rather loudly.

Jenny thought Maddie was talking to Sophie.

"You know," said Maddie, even more loudly, "your Canadian boyfriend."

Jenny avoided looking in the rear-view mirror. "Dominic?"

"Do you have lots of Canadian boyfriends?" Maddie said. "Stop being so coy. He remembered you'd said I was an artist, so he tracked me down through the Damage website."

"Who's this?" said Sophie, paying attention now.

"Jenny's Canadian boyfriend."

"What's he like?" Sophie said it more to Maddie than Jenny.

"Gorgeous, if his voice is anything to go by. That accent. All silky. He's a real sweetie. He was worried Jenny was going to get kidnapped and brainwashed. You haven't told him much about us, have you, Jenny? Well. I did my bit. I filled in what I could in the Ross family saga."

Jenny groaned.

"He got me worried about you. Made me feel like a bad sister, letting you go off to that weird place with our mad father. I felt quite told off. In a nice way."

"So that's why you dragged me all the way to this *Wuthering Heights* film set," Sophie said. "*Wuthering Heights* meets *The Wicker Man*."

"He's okay, is he?" Jenny asked.

"Ah, I forgot to ask him how *he* was. It was all Jenny, Jenny, Jenny. I promised to tell you to ring him. He made me actually promise."

After some time driving in silence, Jenny slowed down, indicated right and turned into a viewpoint parking area. There were two coaches there, spilling out middle-aged tourists. Americans, Jenny reckoned, judging by the large stomachs and large cameras. The sky was cloudless, giving them a clear view of Loch Tulla and Ben Lui beyond.

"I need a leg stretch." Jenny switched off the engine and checked to see that her mother was all right. She couldn't see her chest moving and her eyes were shut. Jenny touched her mother's hand as lightly as she could. She stirred, not opening her eyes. She was just asleep. Jenny relaxed.

Jenny twisted to the back seat to wordlessly get Sophie and Maddie's attention. Sophie made eye contact while Maddie was apparently fascinated by the American tourists, as was Piyali by the looks of things.

"They're a different species. Scientifically proven," Maddie said. "They can only wear synthetic fibres."

Piyali giggled.

As Jenny got out of the car, she heard the tour guide saying something about the West Highland Way. Sophie got out of the car too. Maddie was still sitting inside, entertaining Piyali, so Sophie went back over to the car window and gave it a sharp rap. Maddie made an exasperated face and got out of the car. She joined Jenny and Sophie standing apart from the tourists and looking at broad blue mountains and a shining tape of river curling to Loch Tulla. They faced the view rather than each other.

"This is enough fresh air to keep me going for another millennium," Maddie said. They'd banned her from smoking in the car. Even so, she didn't light up now.

"I'm thinking about what happens next," Jenny said. "My flat is up three flights of stairs. There's no lift. She won't be able to get up there when she gets out of hospital, possibly not for a long while, not even after rehabilitation, if she has that." She took a breath. "If she has rehabilitation, which I think is pretty common, it could be for at least a few weeks. I don't want to move to another flat permanently, but I'll sublet my place and rent something else that's on a ground floor so she can stay there with me for as long as it takes for her to get better."

"What about Boffin Island?" Maddie said.

"I'll postpone my research to next year. There's lots I can be getting on with. Desktop research."

"That's a lot to give up," Sophie said.

"What about Dominic?" Maddie said.

"I don't have a choice. She's still our mother," said Jenny. "I mean, even if she ends up wanting to go back there when she's better."

"God, do you really think so?" Maddie said.

Jenny shrugged. "I can't work it out. I think she knows she needs medical care. Beyond that, I've no idea. She's in a daze. Look," she added, "there are a couple of things you should know." This would be easier now that she had a plan.

"Uh-oh," Maddie said.

Sophie pressed her lips together.

She told them their mother had got into trouble for giving each of them money from the Willowbrae sale. Sophie kicked a pebble onto the grass. Then she told them what her father had admitted about their parents having *dissolved* their relationship with their daughters as well as each other, though she doubted anything had been done legally, whether that was even possible.

"Fine by me." Sophie slipped her hands into her back pockets. "It's all so weird. I mean, you can't deny you had children, can you, or that you're genetically related to them? Christ, if she goes back there, then that's really it. I'll be happy to dissolve or whatever it's called. I'll send her the paperwork."

They walked back to the car, the wind buffeting Maddie's curls and flicking strands of Sophie's hair into her mouth. Sophie calmly hooked the hair away.

Piyali had got out of the car and was crouching beside their mother in the front seat, her back to the view. She was probably used to spectacular panoramas, growing up where she had.

"How old is she?" Sophie asked.

"Sixteen," said Jenny. "That's good, isn't it?"

"Yes. You can leave home without your parents' consent."

Sophie would know.

"She can stay with me," Jenny said, "for as long as our mother does, anyway." As she went around to the driver's seat, Sophie asked if she wanted a break from driving.

"Thanks, it's okay," Jenny said. "I know these roads and it can get a bit tricky after Stirling." And it would keep her thoughts away from Dominic. Her love for this Scottish landscape was a physical sensation; she was infatuated with the rough rocks, bristly grass and soft heather, the grey sky that was as heavy and solid as land. This was her home. How could she and Dominic carry on a relationship so far apart? Perhaps it just wasn't meant to be. Or perhaps he'd be in Nunavut next year too and they could pick up where they left off. She couldn't think about it, not now.

Thirty-one

THEY WENT STRAIGHT to Edinburgh Royal Infirmary. The five of them went inside, Jenny wheeling their mother to the counter to register her at the Accident and Emergency desk. It occurred to Jenny that the wheelchair belonged to Ben Gallachie. If it did, well, never mind.

"I'd help," said Sophie, hanging back, "but you do speak the language."

The receptionist had many questions. It was hard at first to think how long her mother had been away from hospital; Jenny had lost track of time. Two nights and three days, she said when she'd worked it out. Jenny wasn't able to say whether her mother had had another stroke since the one in Inverness or indeed whether she'd had one before she'd left Ben Gallachie. The receptionist's final question made Jenny roll her eyes, although she smiled too. The receptionist wanted to know if the young woman who Jenny had come in with, who was now seated in the waiting area, was Sophie Ross, the actor. She was a fan. She'd loved the television serial, *Dateline*, where Sophie played a reporter.

Her mother was smiling as Jenny wheeled her over to the others. "The receptionist recognized you," Jenny told Sophie.

"That's all we need," Maddie said. "We'll have the paparazzi here next. Hey, Piyali. Have you ever seen television? Sophie here is famous."

When the nurse came at last to collect their mother, she said only one of them could come with her while they settled her in. Jenny said she'd go and picked up the pillowcase of her mother's clothes she'd brought in from the car. She was about to follow the nurse when Piyali put her hand in her pocket and took out what she'd run back to collect at Ben Gallachie: the polarizer. She gave Jenny a questioning look and Jenny opened the pillowcase so Piyali could put it in. She should really do some research, but she didn't see the harm. The expression on Piyali's face made it clear how much it meant to her.

Jenny took a deep breath as the nurse wheeled their mother away and she followed. At last, their mother was back where she'd get proper treatment. Jenny was still checking her mother's face, her body language, making sure her mother was doing nothing against her will. Not that she was going to ask her mother directly if she was happy to be readmitted; she wasn't going to risk her mother saying no.

"This is a great flat." Maddie came into the kitchen part of the living room. "Lovely high ceilings, and you've done it all really nicely. I love the turquoise paint in the bathroom." She leant over the counter. "Got any biscuits?"

"Try those cupboards." Jenny pointed with her head as she was filling the kettle.

"Don't spoil your supper," said Sophie, playing Jean Brodie again. She took four mugs down from a shelf. "Our carry-out's arriving any minute."

"Oh, not for me. I want Piyali to try them. I don't think she's ever seen biscuits before."

"God, Maddie, she's not a toy," Sophie said.

"Bourbons. Brilliant." Maddie took the packet over to Piyali on the futon.

Jenny plugged in the fridge.

When she'd fed a biscuit to Piyali, Maddie picked up a sculpture of a muskox from the coffee table. She smoothed her fingers over the roughness of carved fur, the silkiness of the polished head and horns. "Gorgeous. Whose is it?"

She meant who was the sculptor, Jenny knew. "It's Inuit. Agatha Lyberth. Probably quite valuable, seeing as she's died now. It's soapstone. The horns are caribou antler. I got it in Greenland."

"When did you go to Greenland?" said Maddie sharply.

Jenny sighed. "In my second year."

"With her sugar daddy," Sophie said.

"He was only ten years older than me."

Maddie passed the sculpture to Piyali, who asked what it was. Jenny told her it was a muskox.

"Aren't they extinct?" Sophie said.

"No, that's the mammoth," said Jenny.

Maddie stood and picked up a wooden carving from the mantelpiece. "I love this." She turned it over to look at the base for the artist's initials. "Is this Inuit too?"

"Well, no," Jenny said, "though the theme is."

"It's got a wonderful presence," Maddie added. "Polar bear? It's so fluid. Who's it by?"

Jenny considered lying. Telling her sister that she'd found it in a second-hand shop. Sophie was looking at her oddly, as if she suspected. "I did it," Jenny admitted. "Ages ago." Maybe saying she didn't carve it recently would blunt the thorn. It wasn't a lie.

"Really." Maddie's voice flattened.

Jenny avoided looking at her. "I was just messing about. I was copying, really. It's a flying bear. They were said to be the shamans' spirit helpers. Usually in something like ivory, of course, not wood."

Maddie put it down without saying anything, nor did she hand it to Piyali. She sat back on the futon and picked up the muskox again, cupping it like a large mug of tea. Piyali got up and went over to the bear. She glanced at Jenny, as if she were trying to work her out.

"I knew you'd done it," said Sophie quietly in the kitchen where Jenny was starting a shopping list. "You were always drawing in Brighton. And I see you've still got your stones."

"Are you a Christian?" Piyali had taken the Bible off the bookshelf now and was flicking through it.

"No. I'm not anything," Jenny said. "Lots of people have Bibles even though they're not Christian."

"Why?" It was a good question.

"Well, it's so much part of our culture, I suppose. Lots of people used to be Christian, our ancestors, relatives." It wasn't a very good answer.

Maddie stood and took the Bible from Piyali. "This was Grandfather's," she said, surprised. "I didn't know you had this."

"Nor did I," Sophie said.

Jenny wrote down *fruit* and wished people would stop looking at her stuff. She'd asked her father if she could have it when they cleared out Grandfather's room together in Brighton; Maddie and Sophie hadn't helped with any of the sorting out.

"Do you know much about Christianity, Piyali?" Sophie asked.

"I learnt about all the most dominant world religions. It's amazing what people believe."

Jenny made sure she didn't laugh. She opened some cupboard doors to see what else they needed. They wouldn't be able to live for long on baked beans and tomato soup.

"What are these?" Piyali was treating her flat like a shop. Now she'd picked up a handful of little grey stones from the mantelpiece.

"My Greenland stones."

"They're so pretty," Piyali said. "And this one?" She picked up the stone that Jenny had collected from Birling Gap Beach when she was eleven. The one that was chalk and had a thumb hold. "Why does it have this other little stone in the dip?"

"Oh, I remember your stones," Maddie said. "You were so funny, carrying them about."

"The big one's from a beach in Sussex, the white one," Jenny told Piyali. "The pebble is from another beach. I just like how they fitted together. I pick up stones from all sorts of places." She tried to sound casual, as if her worry stones had no significance.

The doorbell rang. "Saved by the bell," Sophie said. "Do they bring it all the way up here?"

"Unfortunately not," said Jenny.

"We'll go." Maddie beckoned Piyali.

"You might want a fag while you're down there," Sophie called after her. "I have a feeling this flat is non-smoking."

"She'll probably get Piyali to have a puff too," Jenny said.

When the front door had closed, Jenny went over to the bookcase and picked up a wooden carving of a rounded, simplified, female figure holding three children in her lap, her knees and arms forming a basket for them. Jenny wedged the sculpture into the crook of her arm and picked up the carving beside it. Another female figure, this one without any children. There were other, smaller pieces, carved into the shapes of seals, bears, horses and sheep. She would come back for those.

"What are you doing?" Sophie said.

"You saw her face." Jenny carried them towards her bedroom.

"Put them back," Sophie called after her.

"It's not worth it," Jenny called back. "She gets so prickly. She's the artist, not me."

Sophie followed her into the bedroom. "That's her problem, not yours. They're gorgeous, Jenny. You should be proud of them. Give them to me." Sophie held out her arms. "Come on."

Jenny sighed theatrically and handed them over. Sophie took them back to the shelf. "That's better. Did you have lessons? Fine art wasn't part of your degree, was it? Or your PhD?"

Jenny felt her face heat and bent down to straighten out the rucks in the rug. "No, I was just trying it out. They're very stylized, which is another way of saying basic."

"No lessons?" Sophie clarified. "I mean, I don't know anything about art really, except from Maddie, and the gallery in Brighton I suppose, but they look bloody brilliant to me. Really skilled."

Jenny made a face and went into the kitchen to get out cutlery for the food that was hopefully coming up the stairs any minute.

"You can't hate them that much," Sophie pointed out. "You've put them on your shelf. Which is good. They should be seen."

Jenny took out four forks and four knives, glad to be able to look down at the drawer. "It's not that I like them, particularly, it's just that seeing them as I potter around the flat helps me see what needs to be done to them or whether they're finished."

"Spoken like a true artist."

Jenny gave Sophie a sarcastic smile and opened another drawer to look for napkins, even though she knew the carry-out would include some.

"You've got a true talent and it would be an absolute crime to waste it," Sophie told her, mimicking their mother. They looked at each other and laughed.

As Sophie lay in Jenny's bed breathing softly, Jenny tapped at her keyboard, seeing only by the light from the computer. She replied to an email from Karen, telling her briefly what was going on and suggesting they meet up in the next couple of days. She filled in her old friend Helen as well. She should have phoned them, really, but it was too late tonight and emailing, explaining her situation in writing, felt like practice for the next message she was going to write. The email that should have been a phone call. There were three messages from Dominic. Each of them saying in different ways that she shouldn't spend any more time than she had to at Ben Gallachie and to let him know immediately when she was safely away from *that place*.

She pressed reply to his most recent message and rested her fingers on the keys. It took several attempts.

Hi Dominic

It's been a crazy few days. My mother is now back in hospital where she should be, this time here in Edinburgh where we all are now, safe and sound. I'm sorry I haven't been in touch, it's been hard getting to a computer or phone. The thing is, I can't come back to Iqaluit this year. I've got to stay here to make sure my mother is okay and help her with her rehabilitation. I'm really hoping I can come back next year instead. I'm really struggling to put this into words.

I'm sorry.

Jenny

She read it four times and pressed "send."

"Were you emailing your Dominic?" said Sophie sleepily as Jenny got into bed beside her.

Jenny pulled her portion of the duvet up so it covered her chin. She was suddenly cold. "Sorry if I kept you awake. How's Michael? Still practising the piano twenty-three hours a day?"

"I expect so, but I no longer have the privilege of knowing. He's left me. Or did I leave him? I'm not sure. I'm back in London now anyway."

"Oh no. I'm sorry."

"It's okay. It's been in the cards for a while, almost as soon as I moved in, to be honest."

"So you're back in your flat?"

"Yes. It's nice, actually, to be in my own space again. And back in London. Bath is so twee. And I spent half my life on the train to London and I really, really hate sitting on trains."

"Sophie?" Jenny lay in the dark with her eyes open.

"Jenny?" echoed Sophie.

"Can I ask you something?"

"Maybe."

"Do you ever play the violin? You were so good," Jenny whispered. "Brilliant."

"You're just saying that because I was nice about your sculptures."

Jenny smiled in the dark. They were both so awkward when it came to complimenting each other. "I just wanted to know if you still had Grandfather's violin. If you ever play it. Or any violin."

She could hear Sophie breathing.

"You don't have to tell me if you don't want to," Jenny added.

"I didn't in Bath," Sophie whispered after a few moments. "Not when I was living with a child prodigy. It helps that I'm back in my own flat."

"You know what?" Jenny said suddenly, not knowing until that moment that she was going to say it. "I don't care what happened with Grandfather. It really, really doesn't matter anymore."

Jenny lay waiting for Sophie to say something cross and turn over so she was facing away. Yet the silence continued, covering them like an extra blanket, and somehow Jenny knew Sophie was glad she'd said it.

The telephone was ringing. Jenny opened her eyes. She had no idea what time it was; she hadn't plugged her clock radio back in yet and there wasn't enough light to see her watch.

Sophie groaned. "Bloody hell. Who's that?"

Jenny's stomach convulsed. It was the hospital, surely. Something had happened to their mother. She rushed to the phone in the hallway.

"Hello?" It came out as a whisper so she said it again.

"Jenny?" It was Dominic. She switched on the lamp beside the phone and sat down on a little wooden chair. It wasn't her reading chair — that had gone with Willowbrae — but she'd found one very similar.

"Are you okay?" His voice sounded as if were dissolving like a contrail.

"Yes, my mother's back in hospital now."

"But I mean you. Are you okay? What about your research?" She could hear the beginnings of the uncompromising tone she was becoming familiar with, the inflection that meant he was angry, that he cared. "What about your dad? Your sisters? Don't they have a responsibility in all this?"

Sophie was standing in the bedroom doorway. Jenny shook her head to convey that it wasn't to do with their mother. Sophie got the message and went back to bed. There was no sight or sound of Maddie or Piyali, who were sharing the futon in the living room.

"My father stayed at Ben Gallachie." Jenny tried to keep her voice low. "He tried to stop me bringing my mother back to hospital. He's not an option."

"Your sisters?"

"No. They're not —" She stopped and started again, more quietly. "Look, I haven't told you all the gory details, but there's a lot of history. Sophie doesn't get on with my mother. They're at loggerheads." Jenny lowered her voice even more. "And Maddie just isn't very practical. Anyway, they've got their careers."

"And you haven't?"

A flare shot up from her navel to her throat. "It's hard to explain. It's complicated. I have to help my mother. It's what I have to do."

"There has to be another way."

Jenny's forehead was hot and her bare feet were cold. Her eyes were burning. "I've been thinking the whole time."

"Can't we talk it through together?"

Jenny felt scolded, like a child. "I'm not used to having someone, you know, to talk things through with."

"Shit," Dominic said. "What time is it there?"

"I've no idea, but it's very dark."

"It's nine-fifteen here. Shit, sorry. It's two-fifteen a.m. I woke you up."

"It was worth it," Jenny told him, starting to smile, "even for a bollocking."

"I'm going to call you again tomorrow, okay? We're going to work this out."

They said goodbye and Jenny went back to bed. She lay there trying not to make plans on her own, trying to imagine making plans with someone else — with Dominic — for an entire lifetime.

She tried but she couldn't see any way around it; she had to defer her research. Her head felt like a saucepan of popcorn. All the things she had to do kept exploding in her head: return the hire car, ring Aynslie, her supervisor, visit her mother in hospital, talk to a doctor about rehabilitation, start looking for ground-floor flats, write the advert to rent out her flat, see if she could start back at the Canadian Studies Centre soon, email Udloriak, the research centre manager, to ask him to ship back the things she'd left in her room in Iqaluit, or, no, Dominic could do that. Dominic. Surely he could see she had no alternative. She had to stay.

Thirty-two

THE MORNING LIGHT on the sandstone buildings was dappled and soft like water. Once she had got a few things done, Jenny would take Maddie, Sophie and Piyali for a walk up Arthur's Seat whether they wanted to come or not. They needed to see why Edinburgh was such a special city. Not even London had a mountain in the middle of it.

Coming home, it was good to be treading up the stone stairs with her hands full of shopping bags again. She'd forgotten how she enjoyed the pull at her hips as she took each step. When she wasn't carrying shopping, she would rush up the steps as quickly as she could; it was good training for hillwalking. She was going to get Karen up a hill this summer too. Maybe Tinto. That was a good one to start with.

Jenny plonked her keys and the shopping bags down on the kitchen counter. Sophie and Piyali were up and dressed and sitting on the futon, looking at art books from Jenny's bookcase. Sophie had Georges Braque and Piyali had Franz Marc.

Maddie came out of Jenny's room. "I was on your computer. You don't mind, do you?"

"Of course not."

"Everyone's very excited about the ILOVEYOU virus," Maddie said. "Perhaps that's what your Canadian is infected with."

"Very funny. Who wants toast? Jam? Honey? Marmite? Or we could have omelettes? I got eggs, cheese, mushrooms, tomatoes."

Sophie stood next to Maddie on the other side of the counter. "We want you to come and sit down."

"Isn't anyone hungry?"

"We'll do that in a minute," Sophie said. "Come and sit down."

Jenny did as she was told and sat in the armchair by the window.

"My flat's on the ground floor." Sophie seemed to be expecting a reaction from Jenny.

"I know," Jenny said. "I have been there, remember?"

"What I mean is," said Sophie, "we're going to get her transferred to Teddington and then I'll look after her with Piyali's help."

"And my help," Maddie said indignantly.

Jenny couldn't immediately understand what they meant. It was like trying to pedal when your bicycle chain has fallen off.

"You can go back to Boffin Island," Maddie said. "We don't want you to give that up."

"You can go back to your Canadian too," Sophie added.

Jenny frowned at Sophie. "Were you listening to that call?"

"Didn't need to." Sophie rolled her eyes.

Jenny felt as if her scalp were floating. She looked out the window at Arthur's Seat. Was it possible? Could this really be a way for her to go back? "Can you do that?" she asked, trying to be practical. "Just transfer someone from Scotland to England?"

"I don't remember seeing any border guards at Hadrian's Wall," Sophie said. "It might be at the point when she leaves hospital to start rehabilitation or physiotherapy or whatever that she comes south. We'll look into it. But the upshot is, you're not to worry about it. We'll sort it out. As long as you don't mind us staying in your flat for a bit."

Jenny shook her head to mean of course not. "But," she said to Sophie, "will you be able to do this? I mean, you haven't exactly seen eye to eye with our mother for the last twelve years. Have you thought this through?"

She shouldn't have said that.

Sophie's cheeks pinked. "I might not have your academic prowess, but I can think."

"I just meant," Jenny tried to backtrack, "that this is a big thing you're offering to do." She tried not to say anything else. She wanted to give Sophie the chance to change her mind if she wanted to.

"It all goes on inside your head, doesn't it, Jenny?" Sophie said. "You work it all out and then deliver your decision like, I don't know, a judge or something. You always think you know how everyone else feels about everything. Well, you don't."

Jenny held her palms up. "I'm sorry." This was why she loved studying silent, inanimate objects you could look at from all sides.

"I'm not saying I'll ever be best friends with her," Sophie added. "I mean, she's never exactly been the perfect mother."

"There are three of us," Maddie said. "Piyali will be hands-on, won't you?"

Piyali nodded. She was sitting quietly, listening.

"Are you okay about this?" Jenny said to her.

"I'll go wherever Moksha goes," Piyali said. "Margaret," she added.

Piyali in London. It would be like *Crocodile Dundee*.

"What if," said Jenny, cautiously, "our mother wants to go back to Ben Gallachie?"

"Then back she goes." Sophie hugged her knees. "I won't stop her. And I won't have anything more to do with her ever again. Good riddance."

There was silence again. To go back to Baffin Island now, after all. To be with Dominic. To carry on interviewing Kavavaow Ishulutak. To look for black and green deposits of cool soapstone when the snow melted and touch it. "Are you really sure?" Would her sisters really do this for their mother, for her?

"We wouldn't say it if we weren't," Sophie said.

Jenny took a deep breath. "Thank you. Thank you!" She rushed over to Sophie and kissed her on the cheek. Then she kissed Maddie. She even kissed Piyali.

"Okay, okay." Sophie wiped her cheek with the back of her wrist. "Let's not get carried away. I might change my mind and drive her all the way back across the wuthering moors and dump her back at that bloody harbour."

"It's three and a half months." Jenny couldn't stop grinning. She wanted to ring Dominic right now. He'd be asleep, wouldn't he? She was too agitated to be able to work out the time difference. "I'll be back at the end of August. Maybe she'll be a lot stronger by then and she can come and live with me here. I'll take my turn then."

"No need to think about all that now," Sophie said. "Let's just take it day by day."

Jenny put out cereal, milk and bowls while Sophie put some toast on and Maddie leant on the counter doing nothing. Noticing Piyali go to the bathroom, Jenny said, "You do realize she's going to need a lot of looking after, don't you? She doesn't have a clue. I mean, she doesn't even know how to use a map."

"*I* don't know how to use a map," Maddie said.

"Or money," Jenny said. "She doesn't have a clue about money."

"Can't really help you there, either." Maddie unscrewed the lid from the coffee jar and sniffed.

"She'll be fine," said Sophie. "We'll sort her out."

"There's a group in Glasgow called Free Minds," Jenny told them. "They help get people out of cults. I bet there are similar groups in London. Bound to be. They'd help you with Piyali. They probably have, I don't know, workshops or something."

"We'll be fine," Sophie said. "You're going to have to trust us, Professor Ross."

"I'm going to paint her." Maddie spooned coffee granules into a mug. "She's agreed."

After they returned from visiting their mother in hospital that afternoon, Jenny told her sisters she had a headache and was going for a bicycle ride to get some air. She cycled towards Portobello and the beach, listening to the different sounds her tires made. The road was a patchwork quilt of surfaces, pink, sandy, black, grey. She liked the black best as it was smoothest and quietest, although the grey was like toffee with nuts in it and made the most interesting rumbling noise.

She'd met her friend Karen in a café that morning. Pouring the last of the Earl Grey into Jenny's cup, Karen had suddenly said, "Blast from the past. Remember Christopher who was in the same degree year as us? Mid-Atlantic accent? I bumped into him on Lothian Road a couple of weeks ago."

Jenny concentrated on sipping her tea. He was still living in Edinburgh, Karen said. Had been all this time and wasn't it funny they'd never bumped into him before. He was working at a solicitor's, he'd told her. Breckenridge or something. Married with two sprogs. Already.

Karen didn't know about Christopher and what had happened on North Berwick beach. No one knew except Helen. Jenny and Karen hadn't been friends back then. She might tell Karen one day. Then again, she probably wouldn't.

She was almost at the sea now. The internet café she'd remembered being across the road from Portobello Beach was still there. When she'd locked up her bicycle, she went inside and ordered a hot chocolate and sat at a computer terminal. She opened a search engine and typed in *Breckenridge solicitor Christopher Williamson*. The most ordinary of names.

There was no photograph of him, for which she was grateful. His name was there, among a list of about a dozen names with no other details. She read the office address — it was in the Newington area of Edinburgh, a little too close for comfort, although nowhere in Edinburgh was that far away — and noted that Breckenridge and Murray, the firm's name, was an estate agent as well. Perhaps Christopher wasn't a solicitor at all; perhaps he was an estate agent and had been too embarrassed to admit that to Karen. That would be about right.

She tried different search engines. There was no information about him ever having been charged with anything. Perhaps, then, she hadn't been part of an emerging pattern, not that a lack of newspaper reports was any proof. She opened a new window for her email.

She'd already rung that morning to Dominic and told him about Sophie and Maddie's marvellous plan. She didn't have to go over any of that. She just needed to tell him now by email what it was hard to say out loud: that she'd never had a proper relationship, that she'd probably been the victim of an assault, and give him some, if not all, of the details. She was sorry she was emailing this and not saying it, she told him. It was hard to talk about. There was more she wanted to tell him about her family as well, something to do with Sophie in particular that could wait until she saw him. Yet more than anything, she wanted to know so much about him.

She sent the email and left the café without finishing her hot chocolate. As she crossed the road, she took the Christopher pebble out of her trouser pocket. She'd plucked it from the Birling Gap stone Piyali had picked up the evening before. She walked across the damp sand and went as near to the water as she could get. She considered it but decided she wasn't going to take off her boots to paddle; she wasn't going to remove any of her clothing. She stood with the tips of her boots where they might get wet if a bigger wave came and looked at the small dark pebble in the palm of her hand. That particular beach was down the firth and along the curving coast, out of sight.

It was a nice pebble. Round and smooth. It had done its job all these years. She lifted her arm, angled her elbow and flung it as far as she could into the water. She wasn't particularly good at throwing, but it didn't matter how far it went. The splash it made soon reabsorbed into the smooth sea.

Thirty-three

LOOKING THROUGH THE plane window, Jenny could see that the ocean was still iced over and the land was still covered in snow. There were no signs of melting. She had only been away for two weeks. She wasn't sure how that was possible. She was trusting her sisters, perhaps for the first time, to be truthful. She had leant over the hospital bed and kissed her mother goodbye.

Her mother had gripped Jenny's hand with cool fingers. "I'm glad you're going back. You must finish your work." Her body was still weak, but her speech was improving every day. "You know you're my cleverest daughter."

Jenny shook her head at her mother, glad that Maddie and Sophie were in the hospital café, out of earshot. "You haven't changed that much."

"There's a man?" Her mother's grin was still lopsided. Perhaps it always would be now. She must have been listening in the car.

"Hopefully." Jenny grinned back.

Jenny had no idea if her mother would return to Ben Gallachie. That was not a question to ask at a hospital bedside. Although it would be asked sooner or later.

Three thousand miles away in Nunavut, Jenny might be able to stand back from the canvas of her family as if she were looking at a pointillist painting, letting the individual dots merge into identifiable forms. Later, she might go closer and analyze how tiny painted dots gave the illusion of solidity.

Jenny leant back in her seat and sighed loudly without meaning to. A woman across the aisle looked at her and smiled. Jenny smiled back apologetically. Perhaps this family of hers was as fractured as a Cubist painting, rather than pointillist. Or perhaps it was as easy to understand as a Constable landscape.

As the plane descended, Iqaluit looked cluttered and disorganized, and Jenny had no urge to tidy it up. There was the Lego-yellow airport terminal. There was the ugly, red research centre. In her luggage, she had half a dozen Picnic chocolate bars for Dominic. She hadn't eaten any of them.

She felt in her jacket pocket. There were two pebbles there. The new one she had picked up on Portobello Beach when she threw the Christopher stone into the sea. And the old Portobello stone from the day she left Willowbrae and moved into the halls of residence. They were both small and white and smooth. She already wasn't sure which was which. She had plans for them; she would walk out on the chunks of ice that packed the inlet and throw them as far as she could into Frobisher Bay. Or she might keep them. She liked the light sound they made when she tapped them together.

The Iqaluit stone, which she had dug out of the snow just fifteen days ago, she had left in her flat. It was on the mantelpiece next to the other stones, ready for her return.

EPILOGUE

IT WAS POSSIBLE to take a book outside at midnight now and still be able to read it. All the snow had gone; Iqaluit looked scruffy and make-shift without it, as Jenny had known it would. The ice in Frobisher Bay hadn't melted yet, though. It would all be gone by the middle of July, the locals said.

It had been a month since her return to Baffin Island. Jenny was spending hours in Kavavaow's Ishulutak studio watching, asking many questions, being an art historian, getting on her with PhD. Kavavaow asked Jenny many questions too. Sometimes, she forgot to take notes or double-check that the voice recorder was on.

A week or so ago, Kavavaow had asked Jenny to tell him which rasp he should use. He was working on a soapstone sculpture of a sealift raised up and trapped by ice. Jenny hadn't yet seen one of the giant cargo ships that brought supplies to Nunavut each summer. Neverthe-less, the sculpture looked almost finished to her.

She was about to say she had no idea which rasp he should use. Then she realized she did. "The cabinet rasp," she said. "I think."

Kavavaow smiled and picked up the cabinet rasp. "Yes, getting close to sanding now."

Jenny had been spending time with Agatha Aglak too, the artist who worked in a hangar with a helicopter at one end, who she'd been trying to interview before she went back to Scotland. Agatha said she'd only let Jenny interview her if she could carry on working while they talked. She couldn't waste any time. "I'm not gonna hit forty. I got a lot to do."

Agatha was thirty-two. Her mother and grandmother had died of breast cancer.

Agatha wanted Jenny to work while they talked. She gave Jenny the task of melting wax in an oil drum on a two-burner camping stove. Jenny tried not to wonder where the helicopter fuel was stored or worry about health and safety regulations. Both wearing oven gloves, Jenny and Agatha lifted the barrel and poured liquid wax into a large tray. Jenny then quickly put a barren ground caribou antler into the tray and Agatha was ready with a scoop to coat it in as much wax as possible before the wax congealed.

Jenny loved picking up the antlers. They were heavier than a branch would be of the same size. She lifted an antler and she felt a network of neurons connecting her to lichen, hoof, fetus, gun.

Once the wax had hardened, the antlers — about fifteen pairs — would be fixed inside the structure Agatha was building at the back of the hangar that looked like a rib cage lying on its side, large enough to walk into. The ribs were sheets of plywood dipped in wax. Jenny realized she'd seen them being made when she'd first visited the hangar.

Jenny talked to her mother about Agatha each time she rang the rehabilitation centre in London. How she was helping the artist by lifting, holding, pouring.

It was easy telling her mother about Agatha Aglak. It was harder talking about what was happening with Kavavaow Ishulutak. So far, she'd told only Dominic that she'd found the courage to show Kavavaow the wooden carving she was working on, a rock ptarmigan, the official bird of Nunavut. Kavavaow had held it in both hands and smiled. The next time she visited, he picked out a block of dark green soapstone and told her to come and carve it whenever she liked.

Dominic kissed Jenny when she got back to the research centre and told him that.

Jenny wanted to tell her mother things. It was just that she didn't want to risk becoming her twelve-year-old self again, hearing her mother tell her she couldn't be an artist because she didn't have the talent.

It was when her mother commented during their next phone conversation how friendly everyone in Iqaluit seemed to be that she let herself blurt it out. "Kavavaow Ishulutak is so nice; he's given me a chunk of stone to have a go at." She said it as lightly as she could.

"Your beautiful sticks," her mother said. "I remember them."

So her mother had noticed the wood spirits in Jenny's bedroom at Willowbrae. Noticed and never mentioned them.

"You shouldn't have burnt them," her mother said.

Most evenings, after a communal supper with Kay and Ryan and whoever else was staying at the research centre, Jenny and Dominic would go for a walk, talking about their work that day. Jenny worried that surely she was breaking rules; she was supposed to observe artists, ask them questions, take notes and photographs, not put on gloves and help them, not spend her evenings picking beads of wax off her sleeves with her fingernails or brushing off stone dust.

When Dominic vented his frustrations with the bureaucracy he worked within, Jenny helped him stop thinking about it by asking him to explain geological terms to her: fluvial, periglacial, ablation, aeolian.

Jenny told Dominic she was trying to write a letter to her father. She showed him the drafts. She wanted to do things differently this time. Follow the advice of the Free Minds office she'd rejected before. It wasn't that she expected her father to leave Ben Gallachie; she only wanted to show him that it was possible to live a life outside Gallachism and be happy. She hadn't posted the letter yet, though. "I might just send a postcard," she joked.

One evening as they walked towards Geraldine Lake, Jenny said,

"Do you think I made the right decision? Was it selfish of me to come back here?" It was easier to talk about the decision after it had been made, now they were together. "I should have stayed to help with my mother."

"Your sisters are doing fine, by the sounds of it. You'll take your turn when you go back," Dominic reminded her.

Jenny was returning in August to continue her PhD, after she'd completed her research and after she and Dominic had visited his mother in Calgary. He had grandparents, aunts, uncles and cousins for her to meet too.

Yesterday, she had emailed him information about a geosciences position she'd seen advertised at the University of Edinburgh. In response, he had emailed her a photograph of a man in a kilt holding an umbrella, followed by another email with a link to a list of Edinburgh's ten most romantic restaurants.

Nothing had been said aloud yet, but an idea was forming like the ice crystals of cirrus clouds high in a blue sky.

ACKNOWLEDGEMENTS

I have served a long apprenticeship in writing my first novel, and I am deeply grateful to everyone who has mentored, taught and supported me as I wrote, rewrote, revised and rewrote once again. I can't remember a time when I didn't dream of writing a novel, and I thank the fabulous team at Ronsdale Press for making my dream come true and for making this book the best it can be.

Thank you to Patricia Robertson for her friendship and guidance and for leading the novel workshop out of which my dear writing group emerged. Thank you to Ellen Bielawski, Patti Flather and Lily Gontard for all their wisdom and advice over the years and for always believing in Jenny and her story. Thank you to my courageous comrades in the literary arts, Katherine Lawrence and Kristina Bresnen. And thank you to Zoe Wicomb, Vanessa Holt and Caroline Upcher for helping me all that time ago when I lived in Scotland to believe I was capable of writing and publishing a novel.

I am forever grateful to my parents, Patricia and John, for their love and for caring so terribly deeply about their five children, at great cost to their own spirits. I also thank Matthew, Rebecca, Lucy and Melissa for being my siblings and for showing me that there are pros and cons to being the youngest but, I have to admit, mostly pros.

The north is a mesmerizing, multifaceted place. Thank you to the Kwanlin Dün First Nation and Ta'an Kwäch'än Council for allowing me to live and write on their Traditional Territories in Yukon, a land I feel blessed to awaken upon every day. I also thank all the Inuit artists who helped inspire Jenny's discovery of the artistic landscape for this novel. I am grateful to the Nunavut Arts and Crafts Association, Inuit Art Foundation, Inuit Tapiriit Kanatami, Inuit Circumpolar Council and the Nunatta Sunakkutaangit Museum for all their help and for all they do to help Inuit art thrive.

I feel much gratitude for all the places in Britain that helped me bring this novel into being: the landscapes of the Scottish Borders and the Southern Uplands and the towns and cities of Peebles, Edinburgh, London and Brighton. Thank you to Communities Scotland, a Scottish government agency, for sending me to the Knoydart Peninsula, and thank you to the Government of Yukon for sending me to Iqaluit. These were work trips, not research trips, but the writing seeped in nevertheless. And thank you to the Scheiber family of Fiddlehead Farm for building a meditation hut over a creek.

As always and most of all, I thank my husband, Glenn Rudman, for his support through the vicissitudes of the writing life and for not minding about all the stones I bring into the house.

ABOUT THE AUTHOR

Joanna Lilley is the author of the short story collection, *The Birthday Books*, and the poetry collections *The Fleece Era* (nominated for the Fred Cogswell Award for Excellence in Poetry) and *If There Were Roads*. *Worry Stones* is her first novel. Joanna has a Bachelor of Arts (Honours) in the Study of Art and English Literature from the Cambridgeshire College of Arts and Technology, and an MLitt in Creative Writing from the Universities of Glasgow and Strathclyde. Born in the south of England, Joanna has always had a yearning to go north. She lived in Scotland with her husband for eight years before they emigrated to Canada to make their home north of the 60th parallel in Whitehorse, Yukon. Find Joanna online at www.joannalilley.com and on Twitter, @circumpolarjo.